Love Affair in B Minor

A Novel by

Sergei Miro

Order this book online at www.trafford.com
or email orders@trafford.com

Most Trafford titles are also available at major online book retailers.

Print information available on the last page.

ISBN: 978-1-4907-5173-3 (sc)
ISBN: 978-1-4907-5172-6 (hc)
ISBN: 978-1-4907-5174-0 (e)

Library of Congress Control Number: 2015900065

Edited by Courtney Luk
Book Cover by Erin Mauterer
Type Setting & Book Design by Courtney Luk

Trafford rev. 01/05/2015

North America & international
toll-free: 1 888 232 4444 (USA & Canada)
fax: 812 355 4082

Love Affair in B Minor

After his escape from Hungary during the Revolt, Verga Caszar seeks to find freedom as a nomad, eventually wandering through the halls of Akademischer Musikverein, a music school in Graz. His musical talent sends him to Vienna to compete in the Young Pianist International Talent Competition, where he experiences his first taste of true love and true vengeance. Verga must decide what he wants more: his dream of becoming a famous pianist or the well-being of his lover. But what happens when he isn't given the opportunity to choose? Verga finds himself in another desperate escape plan reminiscent of his fleeing from his home country, this time heading to America, the melting pot of freedom and democracy.

ABOUT THE AUTHOR Sergei Miro, a China native, immigrated to Israel in 1953 and moved to the United States in 1964. He is a member of the American Institute of Architects, and has had his own practice for 40 years in New York City. He resides in New Jersey with his wife, two sons and grandchildren. His autobiography is titled *Cycle of Destiny from the Land of Dragon to the Promised Land*. He has also written a historical fiction romance, titled *Treasure of Sanssouci Park*.

CONTENTS

Part 1

Part 2

Part 3

Part 1

ONE

"Fasten your seatbelts. We'll be landing in Ferihegy International Airport in thirty minutes."

The pilot's announcement wakened me from my sleep. I looked through the window, where passing land was visible. It was late afternoon, and the sun was sinking toward the west, casting a golden orange hue on full clouds.

An extended landing gear jolted the plane, and the engine's noise diminished. The plane made its final approach. I closed my eyes, leaning my head on the seat and thinking. I was excited to be back in Hungary. Just ten months prior, on October 23, 2006, people commemorated fifty years since the Hungarian uprising against the Soviet Union. President Bush gave a speech, saying, "The story of Hungarian democracy represents the triumph of liberty over tyranny." The revolt on that ordinary day was still vivid in my memory.

***

I was a student in Béla Bartók Secondary School in Budapest. In my notebook, I noted the date, October 23, 1956, and sat in front of the Steinway Studio practice piano. The afternoon sun filled the room with bright sun rays. One window was slightly open, letting cool October breeze into the room. Lifting the piano fallboard, I placed my fingers on the keyboard and started practicing scales. My fingers glided up and down black and white keys with increased tempo. I was waiting for my piano teacher, Professor Pál Kadosa. Suddenly, I heard a disturbance outside the studio, a rush of running steps, then loud shouts.

"Freedom! Freedom!"

I stopped playing, listening curiously. *What is that commotion?* When I heard loud noises pour from the open window, I knew it was coming from the street below. I rushed to the window to investigate. In the street, a noisy crowd was formed, shouting and waving Hungarian flags.

"Rise up, Magyars! Your homeland calls you! The time is now! It is now or never! We shall be free or be slaves! Rise up, Magyars!" the crowd bellowed.

A classmate of mine burst into the studio room, shouting, "Verga, let's go! Hurry up and join us!"

I grabbed my briefcase and coat and followed him to the street, joining the crowd. "Where are we going?"

"To Petőfi Square," my friend replied.

Thousands filled the plaza. Students, teachers, and office workers, arm in arm, shouted, "Freedom! Russians, go home!"

Traffic came to a halt. A rush of demonstrators moved down Stephen's *Nagykörut* (boulevard), toward the Danube River and *Margit Hid* (Margaret Bridge). From the side streets, a wave of people was coming from Buda, exchanging shouts with people on building balconies, waving flags and yelling, *"Vivat! Vivat!* [Long live freedom!]"

I was swept with the crowd in excitement of the demonstration.

***

The jolt of the plane wheels on the runway snapped me from my thoughts. The plane stopped, and we all disembarked. The customs officer stamped my passport: "Arrived 8.20.07 Budapest." I picked up my luggage, and we exited the arrival hall. A wave of signs flashed in front of me, limo drivers looking for their customers. I searched the crowd and found my driver. He held the sign "Mr. Caszar." As I exited the terminal, the driver asked in accented English, "Are you first time in Budapest?"

"No," I replied.

In the car, the driver asked, "Are you a guest at the hotel, Radisson Beke?"

"Yes, Radisson Hotel."

"Oh, welcome, my countryman. Are you here for business or holiday?"

"I'm here for a short visit as a tourist."

The drive to central Budapest was not long. Night fell when the limo stopped in front of the ornate past-century building on Terez Korut, 43. It housed the elegant Radisson Beke Hotel. The building had a famous façade featuring György Szondi's mosaic murals on the exterior walls.

Dressed in a red jacket, the front desk receptionist greeted me, "Welcome to Budapest, Mr. Caszar. Your beautiful suite is ready just as you have requested on the top of the seventh floor overlooking Kossuth Lajos tér. Enjoy your stay!" Then she handed me the room keys.

The suite was spacious, a large bedroom with a king-sized bed decorated with an ornate dark wood headboard. There was an adjoining marble bathroom. The sitting room had a table and a sofa with two comfortable antique armchairs. Two large windows faced the street. I could hear fireworks coming from the direction of Gellért Hill. I parted the curtains. Exploding fireworks lit the sky with a vivid, cascading display of colors. I reminded myself that it was the twentieth of August, Saint Stephen's Day, a holiday for the Hungarians. I stood, looking at the display from outside. I thought, *What a nice way to start my visit in Budapest.* I stood in silence and watched the finale of multiple exploding fireworks. Then it was over, and a silent night fell in the city.

I was hungry, and on the table were complimentary trays of fruits, chocolates, and Hungarian pastries and a bottle of wine. I was not tired and decided to admire the city lights. Shutting the light in the sitting room, I placed the armchair closer to the windows, propped my feet on the windowsill, and opened the bottle of Tokaji Aszú, a dessert wine. I poured the golden liquid into a glass. The full-bodied wine filled my nostrils with the smell of a bouquet of flowers. I tasted the sweet, rich "angel's drink" and sunk into the leather armchair. Relaxed and content, I sipped the wine and gazed at the lit parliament building in the distance. I remembered when I was sixteen years old.

***

In October '56, I marched shoulder to shoulder with a crowd toward the parliament building excited and shouting, "Freedom! Freedom!" The afternoon sun set a golden hue around Kossuth Lajos tér. A huge bright red five-point star dominated the parliament building. Someone shouted, "Turn off the lights of the red star!"

Others yelled, "Take the star down!"

More shouts came from the crowd. "Russians, go home! Freedom! Return Imre Nagy to power!"

All eyes turned toward the parliament building. There on the balcony were several speakers giving speeches. The crowd sang the national anthem written by Ferenc Kölcsey. Then a poem by Sándor Petőfi was read, and the crowd responded with shouts of "Freedom! Freedom!"

A woman standing next to me turned and smiled at me. She pinned a Hungarian flag in the shape of a bow (*kokarda*) of red, white, and green on my coat. I was swept with pride to be a Hungarian.

Night came, and with a heart full of emotions, I slowly moved through the crowd then started running through the side streets toward home.

Passing Vörösmarty tér, I stopped to look at the statue of the poet sitting and eying me. A quote from him was chiseled into the stone: "The Hungarian nation united. Your homeland, Hungary, serve unwaveringly." It struck me how appropriate the quote was for that day's event. Then I walked slowly toward my apartment building on Király Street.

Oh my god, what a day! It was exciting. I entered the apartment, asking, "Dad, are you home?"

Silence. No one answered. I rushed toward the radio and switched it on. It was the voice of Ernő Gerő, the first secretary of the Communist Central Committee. He spoke in a repulsive voice and made outrageous statements, accusing the demonstrators of being hostile to the Soviet Union and being anarchists. Ernő Gerő was a hard-line Communist, and his views created tension with the Hungarians since he deposed the popular reformer Nagy.

I switched to *Voice of America*. From the streets of Budapest, the reporter broadcasted, "The peaceful demonstrations in the streets turned violent after hearing the speech from Ernő Gerő on the radio. The crowd rushed toward the radio station trying to break its doors. The police responded with tear gas. The crowd then threw stones at the radio station windows. A man drove a truck into the building doors in an attempt to break them. Clashes with armed police broke out in other neighborhoods of the city. A reporter noticed another truck drive by with young people holding a large soaring Hungarian flag with a hole in the middle. The Communist seal was cut off. A reporter interviewed an anonymous eyewitness who said the statue of Stalin was toppled, and it was being destroyed by an angry crowd, who was smashing it with sledgehammers."

I was glued to the radio broadcast. It was reported live from the streets. I looked at the clock. It was after midnight, and my father was not home. I grew worried but switched off the radio and went to bed. Since I was unable to sleep, the day's events occupied my mind. *Oh my god, it's unbelievable how things happened so fast.* Soon enough, I fell asleep. I was awoken when I heard footsteps in my bedroom. It was my father. He came over and kissed my forehead. "Go to sleep. Everything will be all right."

***

I woke up looking at the watch. It was 2:00 a.m. I must have fallen asleep in front of the window, an empty bottle of wine standing on the windowsill. I stood up and went to the bedroom.

TWO

A phone rang. It was the hotel front desk. "Good morning. This is your wake-up call," a sweet woman's voice aroused me from my dreaming sleep.

I reached for my watch on the night table. It was 8:00 a.m. Eyes open, lying in bed, I listened to the rumbling noise coming from the adjacent sitting room. The sounds of heavy traffic came from the street below and through the window I cranked open last night. My mind drifted again to October 24, 1956.

***

At five that morning, I was awake in bed when I heard a vibration from outside. *Is it another earthquake?* I thought we just had one past spring. It rattled Budapest with a 5.6 on the Richter scale. Luckily, nothing was damaged in the apartment.

When the phone rang in the salon, my father picked it up. He spoke to someone for a few minutes then hung up. "What's up?" I asked, standing in the salon, looking at my father with sleepy eyes.

Father said, "The Russian T-34 tanks are moving into the city." I sensed fear creeping into my heart. Father sat on the sofa, deep in thought. Then he said, "I want you to pack a suitcase with your belongings. You are to leave Budapest today to Kőszeg."

"But I have school today," I protested.

"Forget school. We are in the beginning of a struggle for freedom. It is too dangerous for you to stay in Budapest. I want you safe."

"I'm sixteen, Dad. I want to be in the revolution too."

"My boy," Father said, "I've been through war before. It is not a picnic. People will die. The Russians will try to crush us with their tanks. I lost your mother to the Nazis, and I don't intend to lose you to the Soviets."

"What about you?"

"I need to do my duty. I did not resist the Nazis. Now is my calling. I will resist the Soviets. I do not want you to be a slave. I want you to be Hungarian and free. Hurry up. We will be leaving for the train station in an hour."

Reluctantly, I went to my room and packed my belongings, taking my music notes and placing them in the briefcase. The events of last night faded away, and gloom set in.

Later that cool morning, pedestrians walked to work. Tension filled the air. T-34 tanks moved slowly on the cobblestones with noisy tracks. Some shops were closed. People hurried to buy food and groceries. Everyone sensed that something would happen soon.

***

I stopped daydreaming and looked at my watch. It was 8:30 a.m. Clean shaven and dressed, I was anxious to go for a morning walk. The hotel was only two blocks from Nyugati Square, one of the major transportation stations in Budapest.

"Good morning," the doorman greeted me at the hotel door.

Teréz körút was one of the major thoroughfares that joined Nyugati Square and Szent István körút. The three streets led to Margaret Bridge over the Danube River. With city dwellers rushing to work, I tried to recollect my memory. The buildings were familiar to me, but everything looked so different—the cars, people, clothes, and building façades. Signs advertised different restaurants—Italian eateries, Chinese restaurants, McDonald's, and other ethnic foods—and shops full of merchandise, both foreign and domestic goods. I did not recognize the streets. They changed dramatically from the Spartan Communist days as I remembered Budapest.

I stopped at the coffee shop across the Nyugati railway terminal and ordered a cup of cappuccino. Sitting at a table, sipping the morning joe, I observed the rush of commuters going in and out of the station. For a moment, I imagined myself with my father in the crowd. That was fifty years ago.

***

The station that morning was mobbed with people. A Soviet T-34 tank stood at the corner of the street. Russian soldiers milled around next to Hungarian police officers. "Wait here," Father said and then was swallowed into the crowd.

After half an hour, he reappeared. "I used my official documents to buy tickets and avoid the long line."

I asked my father, "Where is everybody going?"

"They are all leaving Budapest to live in a safer place. People are scared."

"When will I see you?" I asked as we made our way to the train platform.

"I will call you and let you know. I spoke to your uncle Elek. He's expecting you." Then he handed me the tickets, embracing and kissing me. "I have to go. Have a safe trip. Call me when you arrive at Kőszeg." And then he left and disappeared into the crowd.

***

The empty cup of coffee brought me to reality. The railroad station's large clock showed 9:15:10 a.m. Since I needed to get back to meet the tour guide, I walked briskly to the Radisson Beke Hotel.

At breakfast, I thought that everything changed after fifty years. I changed too. Sipping a cup of coffee, I resurrected my memory from the past. How strange, I thought I saw myself with Father in a crowd at the railroad station. *Well*, I said to myself, *I always had a vivid imagination.* I snapped from my thoughts. It was time to meet my tour guide in the lobby.

A young man in his thirties greeted me at the lobby. "My name is Peter Kovacsi," he said, shaking hands with me. "I'm your travel guide."

"It's nice to meet you. Please sit down." I offered a cup of coffee.

"No thanks. I already had two."

We sat in the lobby's comfortable chairs. I said, "Peter, you speak perfect English. Tell me about yourself."

"Thank you. I'm a PhD candidate, and my interest is world history. I work part-time as a travel guide to support myself. What are you interested to see in Budapest?"

I replied, "I will be here for a week. What do you suggest I visit?"

"My recommendation is to start with seeing the Budapest top 10 sites. I suggest we start today with the parliament building and the Gellért Monument." He handed me a six-day itinerary.

"I see you included the opera house, the national museum, and the national gallery."

"Yes, of course. I see you, Mr. Caszar, are an artist. I included some private galleries for your visit."

I said, "I would like to visit the Béla Bartók School and take a walk around Király Street. I wonder if I'll recognize the apartment building I lived in as a child. And I would like to visit the Jewish neighborhood and tour the Moorish great synagogue."

"Of course," Peter said. "It is on my list. Today, we will start with our visit to the parliament building. Tonight, I made for you a reservation in one of the best-known restaurants in the Castle District, Fortuna Étterem. It occupies a cellar in a historic house. Is 8:00 okay?"

"Would you join me?"

"No thanks. I study and write my papers at night. You are very kind. Tell me tomorrow how you enjoyed the place. For Thursday, I have a ticket for you to a concert at the opera house. It's complimentary from my travel agency." Then he handed me an envelope. "This is your first-class train tickets to Kőszeg and your reservation for a hotel. There are only three hotels in town. There are many more on the Austrian side."

I said, "I want to stay in walking distance to the old city."

"Okay," Peter said, "I booked for you Hotel Írottkő. It's an old building. I hope you enjoy it."

"That's fine."

Peter stood up. "Let's start your tour. Do you prefer a car ride to the parliament building or a walk? It's only a short distance from here."

"I prefer to walk."

"Let's go. The limo will meet us at the parliament building."

THREE

*E*arly Saturday morning, I checked out of the hotel and was on my way to the Nyugati train station.

I boarded the ten o'clock train to Kőszeg via Szombathely, seated in the first-class cabin. It was fifty years ago when I took the train from Kőszeg, my birthplace, not realizing that I would be gone for so long. It is only one hundred kilometers from Budapest. The town is eight hundred years old and situated in the county of Vas. The town is called the Jewel Box of Hungary for its mountains, lush vineyards, and picturesque architecture.

I looked at the train window and noticed my image reflected in the glass. Based on black-and-white photos, I'm a split image of my mother. I don't remember her. I was only four years old when the Nazis and Gestapo swooped into Kőszeg. It was the last year of war in 1944. The town had a sizable Jewish population. One of them, my mother, Zsuszanna Vardy, was the town's piano teacher; and on that dreadful day of '44, she was picked up by the Hungarian gendarmes. She was buying morning bread at my grandfather's bakery. She was thrown into a concentration camp on the outskirts of Kőszeg. Father's family, who was Catholic, pleaded with the Hungarian and Nazi authority to have her released but to no avail. Then typhus broke in the camp, and she perished with the other five hundred inmates. Father never married again and worshipped her memory. I understood why he wanted to protect my well-being when the Soviets came. I was his only link to the memory of my mother.

After her death, Uncle Elek and my aunt, Najnal, raised me until the age of fourteen in the center of town on a zigzag street called Panjnins, opposite the town castle. It had been the ancestral hall of our Caszar family for five generations. Uncle Elek was a language teacher. He taught me two languages since childhood: English and German. I considered my uncle and aunt as another set of parents.

Then I moved back to live with my father in Budapest and enrolled in the school of music. I was a gifted piano player like my mother. I was accepted into the Béla Bartók School of Music.

My father was a senior electrical engineer and worked for the Hungarian Electric Utility Company, MVMT at OVIT, a subsidiary company providing a high-voltage transmission network, a well-paid government job that provided him with good benefits, a four-room apartment in a good neighborhood, free medical, free tuition for my school, a company car with all expenses paid, a discount for public transportation, and a one-month vacation at company resorts. Father resisted being a member of the Communist party, and as a result, he was not advanced beyond his current position. His political views were anti-Soviet, which he kept to himself. He was active in secrecy in *Pesti srácok* (Revolutionary Budapest Boys). He was a Hungarian patriot at heart.

An announcement was made over the train's intercom. The conductor announced, "Kőszeg, last stop. All passengers must disembark."

Upon arriving at the hotel, the receptionist said, "Welcome to the Jewel Box of Hungary, Mr. Caszar. Your suite is ready. Enjoy your stay."

"Do I have any messages?"

"One moment." The receptionist left the desk to the adjoining room. "Yes, Mr. Caszar. I have an envelope for you from Mr. Kodra and a message. He will meet you at the lobby tonight at 6:00 p.m."

"Thanks," I said, placing the envelope in my pocket.

The bell rang, and the bellhop picked up my suitcases and said, "Follow me."

In the room, I opened the envelope. There was a short note. It was from my second cousin, Demeter.

Dear Verga,

Welcome to Kőszeg! As I mentioned to you yesterday on the phone, I will meet you tonight for dinner. Eva will meet you at the hotel at 3:00 p.m. with the keys to the house on Panjnins Street. There are clean chairs and tables in the front room. I hope you will recognize the house.

Your cousin,
Demeter

Eva and Demeter were the only relatives living in Kőszeg. Demeter was a child of my uncle, and when Elek passed away in 1972, he left the ancestral home on Panjnins Street as an inheritance to Demeter and me.

I was anxious and excited to walk around the town. I met Eva in the lobby.

"How are your wife and daughter?" she asked.

"They are fine. They are in China. My wife is getting acupuncture treatments."

"Is everything all right?"

"Yes, it will help her with her vision."

As we walked toward Panjnins Street, I recognized the inner town. The building shops and signs were new, but the rest was like it was frozen in time. Eva said, "Within the five acres of the inner historic town, there are only 102 houses and ours one of them. Kőszeg had many fires. The houses are built of wood." She pointed toward Jurisich Square. "You see the town hall? The entry is now in the cellar, and the fourteen stairs now lead to the original floor level all because of change in elevations from layers of fire and debris."

We walked toward the Irottku Tower. Eva said, "This is the highest peak in town. In English, it is called the Tower of Written Stone. From the top, we can see the entire town of Kőszeg."

We reached the famous zigzagging street. My heart started pounding with excitement. I recognized the street and the houses. It used to be all residential. Now it was mixed with tourist shops and galleries occupying the front of the buildings.

I stood in front of my house, looking at it. Except for the first-floor window changes, the rest of the house was exactly as I had seen it fifty years ago. With a shaking hand, I opened the door. The rush of memory flooded my mind. "Oh my god," I said in a loud voice, looking at the front room. "Down there is the kitchen!" I pointed to Eva. "And upstairs, my bedroom."

Looking at the interior of the house, I said, "It's a small house. My memory played tricks on me. I envisioned a large one. You know, things seem bigger as a child."

We sat at the table next to each other, looking at the room in silence. In the corner was a large object covered with a white sheet. I stood up slowly and uncovered it. It was a bright piano. Tears flooded my eyes. "Oh my god," I said. "This is my mother's piano on which I learned to play." A doll, black colored, upright. I slowly lifted the lid. I was greeted with a faded golden-and-gray plaque that said "Maxim Frères, Paris and London," with images of Queen Victoria's and Prince Albert's profiles staring at me. Tears rolled down my cheeks. I touched the keys. The piano was out of tune. The English manufacturer of this upright made thousands. It was mass-produced, cheap and low priced, but it was the only piano my mother could afford at that time. I put the chair in front of the piano and closed my eyes, sitting in silence. I played Fredric Chopin's The Grand Polonaise in F-sharp Minor. Dull and gray like before a storm, I played with an ominous air. I followed notes measure by measure. It sounded like a strange harmony, out of tune. I abruptly stopped playing. I placed my two hands on my face, shaking and sobbing.

"I'm sorry," I said, "I just couldn't hold my emotions."

"Verga, let it all out. You'll feel better."

I composed my thoughts then said, "I remember the morning of November 4, 1956."

***

I woke up to the sound of the radio in the kitchen. Uncle was sitting at the kitchen table with a cup of tea and glasses on, listening to the radio broadcast from *Voice of America*. The latest news blared through the speaker. Uncle lowered the volume and said, "Jó reggelt [good morning]."

"Any good news?" I asked.

"No," Uncle said, "the Russians surrounded Budapest and, at dawn, launched an all out assault on the city."

"Are America and the West going to help us now?" I asked in a concerned voice.

My uncle looked at me with a serious face then answered, "I don't think they will. They are occupied with the Suez crisis in Egypt since October 29. The Suez Canal is more important to them than our uprising. I think they have written us off. We are at the mercy of the Soviets. Big Bear will crush us. We are surrounded by the Soviets on all sides, and Austria decided neutrality on this conflict. They are scared of the Soviets too. We are alone now."

"Did you hear from my father?" I asked.

"No, but I know he will call."

Then Uncle attempted to distract me from the current events. "Verga, I have here a list of items we need from the grocery store. Please dress up and get them. You have been glued to the radio for some time now. You need fresh air." Uncle gave me the list.

The sun was shining on that cool November day. Everything seemed to be normal on the streets of Kőszeg. Pedestrians rushed about their business, stores opened, traffic crowded the street, two Hungarian military trucks were parked in the neighborhood, soldiers milled around, and no more Russian tanks were visible on the streets. Back home with the groceries, I placed them on the kitchen counter.

"Your father called," my uncle said.

"How is he?" I asked.

"He's fine. He needs to stay in the city. There is a general strike by workers at the electric company, and his presence is needed."

"Did he say when he will be back?"

"He will let us know," my uncle replied. "Your father instructed you to go to the storage room and remove the two duffel bags with mountain climbing gear. Put on the side the belaying ropes, the colored ones, which he just purchased last year in Vienna; two harnesses; twelve quickdraws; four belay devices; the rapper racks; and belay gloves, the new ones from Austria. In the storage room, in the wooden box, take the cable zip trolley, which you used in the woods last summer, and put it in a separate bag." There was silence. Then he said, "Please sit and write it down."

I was surprised by my father's request. I said, "Are we going mountain climbing?" It was my father and my's hobby.

"No, I don't think so," Uncle said. "Your father did not say why he needs the gear, but do as he asks."

During the day, I listened to the radio station Free Europe. News broke from Budapest. Serious fights started between the Hungarian freedom fighters and the Soviets. Russian tanks lobbied shells on the city buildings. A reporter said that the national archive building was on fire and flames were spreading throughout the city. Some Russian tanks seemed to be burning on the streets. Bullets zigzagged throughout the streets, and pedestrians ran for cover. Many innocent people died. Streets were barricaded by mountains of cobblestones and overturned cars. Ambulance sirens were heard rushing through the streets. More Russian tanks and troops arrived by land and by air. I thought, *What happened in the past days? People filled their hearts with fate and freedom. It made them proud Hungarians united together. Now the dream is starting to crumble.* I still hoped the West would intervene.

Late that night, I heard a loud scream. It was a woman's voice, a spine-chilling, loud cry.

What's happening? Kőszeg is usually a peaceful town. Why is someone screaming in the street? I put a coat over my pajamas and went to investigate. It was a cold late November night. Neighbors' lights were switched on. As I ambled around the corner, I saw two men helping and lifting a distraught woman from the street and then disappeared with her at the next corner.

Oh my god, what's happening to us? I thought to myself. The last ten days were the most terrifying of my life. Back in bed, all quiet, I couldn't fall asleep. Eyes wide open, I was concerned. For the past two weeks, I was not able to reach my father by phone. The news from Budapest was horrible. Twenty thousand fresh graves were dug. The glorious revolution fell apart. The secret police was now rounding up men. People started disappearing without a trace. Kőszeg was flooded with refugees trying to cross west to Austria. Russian and Hungarian troops arrived in town. The countryside was reinforced by Hungarian border guards. An eyewitness said a T-54 tank was seen in the woods. Nightly shooting was heard from the border. I did not know what the next day would bring and was frustrated not knowing where my father was. *Why did he not call? Is he alive?* All these thoughts flooded my mind. I looked at the clock. It was after three in the morning. I tried to sleep.

In the morning, I asked my next-door neighbor, "What was with that woman last night?"

The neighbor pulled me into his house and closed the door. Standing in the vestibule, he said, "Verga, we need to be careful what we speak of in public. You understand why?"

I nodded yes.

"You just don't know who is listening in on your conversations these days. Terrible, terrible story we heard from that woman. She and her husband escaped from the horrors of Budapest in a truck, then took a train to Kőszeg, thinking to cross to Austria. At the border, they were turned away. They did not have the right documents. A strange man approached them and introduced himself as a local guide. For a small amount of cash, he would cross them over to Austria through No-Man's Land on the outskirts of town. They agreed. Last night, he took them into the woods five kilometers south of the town. The woman asked where they were going. He didn't answer but said to move quickly.

"After walking deep into the woods, he stopped and said, 'Go straight and you will pass a ditch. On the other side is No-Man's Land. Run into the woods. You will be free.' And then he left them alone.

"So they started walking in the direction pointed out by the guide. Then they heard noises. Uniformed shadows of men slowly appeared in the forest and came closer. One of the uniformed men shouted, 'Put your hands up!'

"'Don't shoot,' her husband cried.

"They were Hungarian border guards. They knew why they were in the woods. The husband begged them to let them go. For a few minutes, there was silence. Then the leader of the guards said, 'We are very sorry. We are Hungarian too. We can't allow anyone just like that to cross the border. We may be court-marshaled and executed for that.'

"Then the woman started to beg them to let them go. She said she's pregnant with a child and desperately needed to get to a doctor. The guards turned around and had a quiet conversation among themselves then agreed to let them go. They ran as they approached the ditch. They heard someone yell, 'Stop! Hands up!' It was in Russian and came from the woods. They hesitated, and then her husband said to run to No-Man's Land. They jumped into the ditch. Then the Russians started firing. She fell on the ground and looked at the ditch's edge and called her husband's name. He was dead.

"The Russians never went to the woods to investigate. The Hungarian border guards picked her up. They drove her to town then let her go and drove away. She was left on the street. She was hysterical. The men across the street took her away into their home. Horrible! What's happening with our country? How is your father?"

"He's fine. He should be coming soon." I was in shock to hear the woman's story. With a heavy heart, I left my neighbor's.

To my surprise, when I came home, my father was there dressed in Hungarian Electric Company blue overalls and jacket, not shaven with a month's beard on his face. I rushed into his arms. We hugged each other. "When did you arrive?" I asked.

"Oh, just ten minutes ago."

Uncle Elek stood, smiling. "How about breakfast?"

Father moved to the kitchen, removing his jacket. "Thanks, Elek. I need to wash myself. I haven't had a shower in a week."

"Coffee or tea?" Elek asked.

"Coffee, please."

I went to bring clean clothes and towels.

Sitting at the kitchen table, my father shaven and clean, wearing a white shirt, drank coffee. Uncle and I looked at him and waited to hear his story. Father put his cup down and said, "Things are bad; the revolution collapsed. Many of my friends died or were arrested. The *Államvédelmi Hatóság* [secret police] is looking for me too. I haven't been in my apartment for the last two weeks, hiding in my friends' homes every night in a different location. It's only some time when they will come for me here." He looked at me and said, "My boy, we must leave Hungary tonight."

Father's surprising words shook me. I froze in my chair. "Why?" I said. "This is our home."

"Listen to me," Father said. "I fought the Russians my way. I sabotaged electrical substations in various locations in Budapest. I successfully shut down the electrical power in the airport. Not one Russian was able to land for forty-eight hours. The secret police and the Russian KGB couldn't figure out who was responsible for the sabotage. They're after me and my colleagues. They will find us. It is only a matter of time. We have no time to waste."

"Father, they're shooting at people trying to escape. The border is reinforced and guarded by the Russians. There are tanks in the woods. It's hard to escape."

"I'm aware of the border conditions. I am prepared for this kind of situation. Last summer, I had a plan if we needed to escape. Now we will execute it tonight or I am doomed."

Father's word *doomed* shook me to my core. I felt my father's voice of urgency. My heart pounded hard.

My uncle had said nothing, just listened. Then he said, "Why are you guys wasting time? Start moving." He moved his hands in the air.

***

I stopped to look at the watch. It was after 5:00 p.m. I said to Eva, "Thank you for listening to my story."

She wiped her eyes with her handkerchief. She said, "Dear cousin, your story is our story. I feel your despair. Thank you for sharing your memories with me."

"We need to go back to the hotel. At seven, we're meeting Demeter for dinner."

FOUR

The receptionist in the lobby called to inform me that Demeter and Eva had arrived in the lobby.

"It's nice to see you, Demeter."

"Welcome to Kőszeg," he said.

"Thanks."

"Did you have a good look at our house?"

"Yes, and Eva gave me a tour of the city." I turned to Eva. "Shall we have a drink?"

"No thanks. I will have a drink at dinner."

"What about you, Demeter?"

"Yes, okay, let's go to the lounge."

I looked at Eva again. She said, "You guys talk business. I need to make a phone call and will join you later."

"Okay," I said, putting my hand on Demeter's shoulder. We headed to the bar area.

I ordered a bottle of Egri Bikavér red wine, the famous Hungarian red wine also known as bull's blood. The legend said that this famous wine dates back to the sixteenth century when Magyars defended the Eger Fortress against the invading Turks. After five weeks of siege, the castle commander ordered the defenders to drink local red wine. It gave them the fighting spirit. They drank until their beards dripped with wine. Then they charged into battle. The Turks saw them and became frightened. They evacuated. It is believed that their opponents had been drinking a bull's blood.

"For your help," I said, raising my glass.

"For yours," Demeter replied. Then he turned toward me and said, "So did you recognize the house?"

"Oh my god, nothing changed. It took me back to fifty years ago. Thanks for taking care of the house for so many years, Demeter."

"Thank you for providing funds for repairs all these years."

They conversed in English since Demeter and Eva spoke the language perfectly. Both of them were language teachers. Eva taught in a local high school. Demeter was a teacher of English and German in the Jurisich Miklós International School of Languages.

Demeter put the wine glass on the bar counter then said, "Verga, as I told you, we have a buyer for the property. They're offering the highest price so far. As you noticed, that street is now a popular destination for tourists. No one lives there anymore. It's all a commercial street now. Our property is one of the last that's still vacant and in the best condition. We can close the deal tomorrow. All the papers are ready at the lawyer's office. What do you say?"

I was silent for a minute. Then I said, "Demeter, I know you're in need of money and the sale of the house will be a great financial deal for you. Today, in visiting the house, I made that decision when I sat in front of the piano, touching the keyboard that my mother touched and sitting in front of the table that my father sat in last. You know, that table was the one I sat in with Father on that dreadful day. I changed my mind. I don't want to sell it."

Demeter's face turned serious, asking, "Why?"

I said, looking at Demeter sipping wine, "I have a proposition for you. I will buy your share. What do you say?"

Demeter was caught off guard. He was silent for a minute, and then he said, "At what price?"

"The current offer price."

"What about all the funds you've invested in the past for repairs and taxes?"

Smiling, I said, "All those past expenses paid are no more."

"You are very generous," Demeter said, his face lighting up.

"Do we have a deal?"

"Yes," Demeter said, shaking his head smiling.

"Make arrangements tomorrow with the lawyer so we can continue this deal," I said. "I have one request for you, Demeter. Find a good piano restorer. I want to recondition my mother's Maxim Frères upright. And on a second note, my daughter will be coming to town in two months to look at the property. I want to open an art gallery on the first floor, and I want you to be my agent to take care of the premises until then."

"It will be my pleasure," Demeter said. "A gallery on the street is a great idea," Demeter said. "Now let's go celebrate your arrival. I reserved a table in a Hungarian restaurant with gypsy music for tonight's dinner. They serve your favorite dish, beef chuck goulash in hot paprika sauce, just the way you like it."

Eva came and ordered white wine. "I see you finished talking business."

"Yes," I replied.

We stood up to leave when Demeter said, "Don't forget, tomorrow morning, be ready at nine. I'm taking you to our ancestral cemetery. I have a surprise in store for you."

"A surprise? What kind of surprise?"

"I'm not telling you," Demeter said as we exited the bar.

The restaurant was half full, mostly tourists like us. An ensemble of Roma musicians of strings, bass, and accordion played gypsy-style melodies. My dish of goulash was just right—peppery, the way I like it. I parted with Demeter and Eva at midnight.

I sat on the lounge chair, holding a glass of wine in my room, and remembered that evening in November of '56.

***

Father pulled out an official Hungarian Electric Company map of Kőszeg, including electrical transmission towers' locations and power lines. He spread it on the kitchen table. I got a close look at it. Uncle Elek put his eyeglasses on his face. Father stood bending over the map. Then he said, "This is my plan. Today, I drove to town in the official Electric Company truck, and I'm wearing the company uniform. I will do a reconnaissance visit around the tower marked T-204. You will notice it is close to the Austrian border. Tower numbers 205, 206, etc., are on the Austrian side of the border. Now only few officials in my company know that when the Soviets vacated Austria in 1955, the Austrian Utility Company requested the Hungarians to disconnect the usage of these towers because they straddled old Austrian and Hungarian borders. Last year, the Hungarian Electric Company constructed new transmission towers"—he pointed on the map—"straight all the way from Sopron to Kőszeg and to Szombathely. Now towers 204 and 205 have no electric power. They are dead, but the transmission lines are still intact. The Hungarian Electric Company and the Austrians are still negotiating the removal of the dead transmission lines. This is my plan. The distance between tower 204 and tower 205 is three hundred meters. The power line is sagging fifteen meters from the ground. Right at this point is No-Man's Land on the Austrian side. Now comes the hard part of the plan. Tonight, we climb on the tower. We hook up our cables on the zip trolley, which was designed to travel on power lines. We hook up our rapper racks and zip over the border. The trolley will stop and rest at the lowest point of the sagging power line. Then we'll propel down and disconnect ourselves from the line and escape into the woods, free on the Austrian side."

Crazy, audacious plan, I thought. I said, "Father, there are troops in the woods near the border. They will stop us from reaching tower 204."

"Not so fast," Father said. "I made fake paperwork for repairs to be done on tower 204. Both of us will dress in Hungarian Electric Company work uniforms. I will drive a company car. No one will stop us. Let's check the climbing gear." And with that, we went to the storage room.

That afternoon, Father came back from reconnaissance to tower 204. He was stopped by Hungarian troops by the border but was given permission to proceed. He told the Hungarian border guards that he will need parts for the repairs and will be back this afternoon.

We dressed in official uniforms. I packed a hiking bag with the most valuable possessions I had: a photo of my mother, music notebooks, and clothes. Uncle made two sandwiches and placed them in my bag. At 3:00 p.m., it was time to say good-bye and head on an unknown and dangerous mission of escaping to freedom. I hugged my uncle hard. He knew he might never see me again. Uncle Elek was a strong character, being able to control his emotions. He wished us a successful escape and knew both of us were experienced mountain climbers, and the power line tower was like scaling another rock.

We drove toward the south side of Kőszeg. In ten kilometers, we switched to a dirt road in the woods toward T-204 and the international border. In two kilometers, we came to a road block. Hungarian and Russian troops approached us. Father showed them his paperwork. The Russian guard looked at the back of the truck then waved us to drive off.

We parked the truck at the tower gate. A sign in red was posted: "Danger. Do not enter. High-voltage lines." A skeleton with crossbones symbol was depicted. Father quietly cut the lock. The plan was to climb the tower and attach the trolley zip carriage that was already there to the power line and have it ready then linger around the tower until nightfall.

We successfully attached the zip trolley carriage to the cable line. As we stood at the height of thirty meters on top of the tower, the view was so peaceful. Cool November air whipped my face. I was calm and controlled. My emotions disappeared. I was like a piano player carefully not missing any notes. I concentrated on my father's instructions.

Tower T-205 was visible on the other side of the forest and, near the meadow, No-Man's Land. It was quiet in the forest.

I helped Father test the zip trolley. We let it slide a few meters on the cable and settled for the night. Sitting in the car, Father said, "Let's rehearse the plan. I climb the tower and you follow me using the safety line as a guide to the top. Hook up, test the line, and test the zip trolley. You go first. Hook up to the zip trolley, test the line, ride the trolley, stop, unhook yourself, hook up the cable line, rappel down, and run to the forest."

I rehearsed the plan in my mind several times. "When will you join me?"

"Within a few minutes," he answered.

"What will we do next?"

"We will hike to the nearest village approximately five kilometers."

I sat in silence eating my sandwich. Father closed his eyes and rested his head on the car seat.

A little while later, I woke him up. "Dad, it's ten to seven."

He got out of the car, standing in front of the electric tower. It was a cold and windy night. "Perfect moonless night," Father said.

We hooked up the zip line harnesses. I placed the knapsack on my shoulder and put on gloves. "I'm ready."

"Follow me," Father said and started climbing the tower.

At the top, wind flapped the ropes around the tower. As he put on a dark blue jacket and black woolen hat, I looked at my father. He looked through binoculars, scanning No-Man's Land. "All clear," he said.

My heart raced. I was excited, not knowing what to expect on the other side, realizing I'm leaving my home unsure of when I would be back. A feeling of security filled my heart. I trusted my father.

A car light was visible passing on the other side of the border, illuminating the treetops, then all quiet.

"Ready?"

"Yes."

"Hook up." The click of the quickdraw assured that I was hooked. Father tested the line. "Remember to rappel as quickly as possible to the ground. Unhook and run fast into the woods."

I nodded. Holding the trolley in one hand and the tower structure in the other, Father tapped my shoulder. "Go."

I let go, riding the trolley like a roller coaster. It moved fast. A screeching noise echoed throughout the forest. It surprised me, and I became concerned. In seconds, I reached the low point of the sagging electric line and stopped. Swinging in the wind like a yo-yo, I unhooked myself from the trolley zip and readied to rappel down when a searchlight on the Austrian side lit the forest. The search beam blinded me for a second. I let go, sliding on the rope. The beam followed me for a second and then switched off. I reached the ground, lying low, and unhooked myself. Ready to run to the woods, I hesitated. I looked up the dangling rope from the trolley. Now it was being pulled back to the tower, T-204. It was reassuring. Father pulled the trolley back. Then I heard a car engine, and lights came from the Hungarian border. A searchlight switched on. The beam rested on T-204. I heard shouting in Russian. Then a shot rang out from the tower. I froze on the ground. I didn't know Father had a gun. He tried to shoot the searchlight. I looked at the zip trolley. It was still being pulled back and was halfway toward the tower. More shots, then a rush of machine guns came from the forest, hitting the electric tower with ricocheting sparks. I cried in a loud voice, "Pull the line! Pull the line!" The trolley moved closer and closer toward the tower then stopped. I held my breath. More shouts rang in the woods. Then the zip trolley slid and rolled back and stopped at the low point. The rope dangled, swinging in the wind.

I heard a voice in the forest in German. "*Schnell! Schnell!* [Fast! Fast!] Run, run into the woods!" I picked myself up and ran into the forest.

FIVE

The next day, after an early breakfast, Demeter picked me up at the hotel. He drove a short distance to the cemetery. Demeter was in a happy mood. He told me, "I have a surprise for you." I asked him, "What is the surprise?"

"You'll find out." The car slowed down on the country road then stopped. "We will take a shortcut through the woods."

Leaving the car on the road, we trekked down a narrow path until we were engulfed by shrubs of oak and pine trees. Then we came to an open field. Up the hill was the cemetery. A light breeze moved tree branches, exposing vivid strays of sunbeams. My heart beat in excitement. I had not seen my mother's grave since I lived in Budapest. Now I did not recognize the surroundings. Everything had changed. Trees had grown taller, and the cemetery had gotten larger. White gravestones and crosses shone bright in the morning sun. We walked between rows of crosses for a few meters. Not too far from the forest's edge, there it was: the Caszars' family burial ground of five generations. I stopped looking at the gravestones and crosses, turned toward Demeter, and said, "I don't see my mother's grave."

"Be patient, please. Sit on this bench."

I looked at Demeter, who walked between the monuments then stopped at the edge of the plot, standing like a theatrical musician on stage. He reached his hand to a tarp and, lifting it up, exposed a large bright black granite monument. For a moment, I was perplexed and confused. I stood up to read the chiseled name on the stone. "Oh my god," I let out a loud cry, rushing toward the grave. "Oh my god." I kneeled in front of the stone. There, chiseled deep into granite and highlighted with gold paint was my father's name, Kazmer Caszar, and my mother's name, Zsuszanna. It sparkled from the sun shining on the black stone. "You devil, Demeter, why did you not tell me that you found my father's body?"

"I wanted to surprise you."

"You definitely did. How did you find his burial place?"

"Please sit down. I will tell you. As you know, Elek tried to recover your father's body from the Hungarian border guards. They said they have nobody by the name, Kazmer. Uncle Elek continued to search for him but to no avail. On his deathbed, he made me swear to continue searching for his grave. In 1989, new government came to power, and the old regime of hard Communists was out. A year later, the Soviet troops left the country for good. I began a painstaking search. It took me a few trips to Budapest to comb through the secret police archives. After hours of looking through documents, I found a written report of the incident near tower 204 in Kőszeg. It mentioned one person escaped to Austria and one person was dead at the tower. There were no documents of the person's name. The body was given to a town gravedigger for burial in an unmarked grave."

I said, "Yes, Father packed all our documents in my backpack when I escaped."

"Well," Demeter said, "a lightbulb went off in my head. Remember Nador, the old man in the black dirty jacket, the town gravedigger?"

"Vaguely."

"He died just a few weeks after your escape. Nador had a son named Gabor. He's younger than us. Now he is the town surveyor. So I went to see him in city hall. I asked him if he knew any information about the location of your father's grave. He replied negative; but then he said his father was a simple man, uneducated, but kept a black notebook and meticulously recorded every grave he dug. He marked the location, date, and the name of the deceased. He asked me if I would like to look through it. I was elated. Within a few days, he gave me the notebook. The cover was torn, and the pages were stained with sweat. He must have kept it in his shirt pocket when digging graves. A large rubber band kept all the pages intact. Well, I zoomed to the pages from November 1956. There were five recorded entries in the notebook, and one of them was your father. He must have recognized him because he entered his full name, Kazmer Caszar, marked carefully with a penciled cross next to his name. He also clearly noted the location of the dig. By counting footsteps in two different directions, one from an oak tree nearby and the other the nearest gravestone, I found him.

"I knew you would be coming this year, so I kept it as a secret from you until today."

I stood up with tears on my face, hugging Demeter. "Demeter, I like the quote on the stone." I read it aloud. "There is no flag large enough to cover the shame of killing innocent people."

Demeter said, "In one of my English classes, I asked the students of mine to write their favorite quotes so we can discuss them in class. One of my students wrote it on the blackboard, and it stuck with me. The quote was written by Howard Zinn."

Examining the stone, I said, "Demeter, I respect your sensitivity. I know my mother was Jewish at birth but converted to Catholicism. I like the placement of the seven-branch menorah, symbolizing the seven levels of heaven, on top of the stone with a cross below it. It is very appropriate."

"We Caszars don't forget our ancestry. You know, Verga, how your father and Elek managed to get hold of your mother's body for burial?"

"Forgive me, I vaguely recall. Please tell me again."

"As you know, your mother was arrested and put into a concentration camp on the outskirts of Kőszeg; then typhoid broke out in the camp and 4,500 inmates perished. She was one of them. Uncle Elek told me that the family learned that the Nazi camp commander was planning to bury all the bodies in the field on the outskirts of town and the town doctor was to supervise the burial. Our family approached him and asked him to have Zsuzanna's body buried after cremation in a shallow marked grave. He was paid with her gold jewelry. He agreed. After a few months, one evening, Uncle Elek and your father dug her remains and buried her in our family plot unmarked. After the defeat of Germany, a stone was placed on the grave. Two months ago, I replaced it with this new black granite monument."

I said, "Thank you, Demeter," hugging him.

Then I pulled a piece of paper from my jacket. "May I read a prayer?"

Only when you drink from the river of silence shall you indeed sing.

And when you have reached the mountain top, then you shall begin to climb.

And when the earth shall claim your limbs, then shall you truly dance.

There was silence for a few minutes; then Demeter said, "That is a beautiful prayer." He rose to walk toward the other family plots, giving me a moment alone to think.

I sat on a bench, closed my eyes, and sunk into deep thoughts of mediation. I remembered the electrical tower where my father gave his life so I can live as a free man. Now T-204 was commemorated as a shrine in my mind. It was an altar where my father became holy. Like an ancient altar, it was opened to the sky, so his soul rose up toward the heavens, but his body now rested in place next to his beloved wife. I felt a connection with the spirits of my mother and father. It was sacred, unseen, and untouchable. They spoke to me. I lost time and place until the sound of footsteps stirred me from my deep meditation.

Demeter asked, "Are we ready to go back to town?"

In silence, we walked toward the car. During the ride back, I sat next to Demeter. "At what time are you leaving tomorrow?" he asked.

"I was planning to visit old acquaintances in Graz, but now I change my mind."

"Why's that?" he asked.

"At the cemetery, I was thinking of a quote. 'If the life paradox is that those of us who leave only monuments behind as a record of their existence vanish with time, then our bodies turn to ashes, our spirits free, but our written words live on.' I always wanted to write of my journey. Now I feel it is the right time to do it. I will stay in Kőszeg for the next two months and write my memoir."

"I think that's a splendid idea. Go ahead and write your story," Demeter said.

"Can you find me a quiet place to rent for two months?"

"No problem. I'm sorry you can't stay in our house. We are in the midst of major renovations."

"No problem. I'll stay in a hotel until you find a place. I also will need a typist."

"I have a student who is excellent in typing. Her English is very good."

"Great. Then it's all set."

SIX

The doorbell rang. It was Florka, one of Demeter's English students. I met her a week prior, and yesterday, we had started our writing sessions. She said, "Good afternoon, Mr. Caszar."

"Good afternoon, Florka. You can call me Verga."

She had a small body. Her brown hair was neatly tied behind a handkerchief, and large glasses rested on her pug nose. "It's a hot day," she said, wiping sweat from her forehead with her hand. She had ridden her bike to the hotel.

"Please, go to the washroom and freshen up," I said.

The bell rang again. It was room service. A young man brought a large basket of fruit and a large bottle of sparkling water with ice. Florka and I made ourselves comfortable, sitting at the table. I glanced at her. "Are you ready to start?"

"Yes," she said. She opened her Toshiba laptop, which I had lent her. She looked at me, smiling. She had large violet eyes like the color of iris.

"Yes, let's see." I looked through my notes. "Where did we stop yesterday?"

"You ran into the forest after hearing commotion at the tower."

"Okay, let's continue."

***

I was disoriented and in shock. I was led into an Austrian federal army patrol truck. Someone placed a blanket on me. Seated in the back

31

of the truck, I shivered and tried to comprehend what had just happened, not knowing if my father was dead or alive. I was confused and distressed. A flashlight was lit, momentarily blinding me. I instinctively placed my hands over my eyes. A uniformed soldier stood at the rear of the truck, pointing the flashlight at me. He asked in a stern voice, "Do you speak German?"

"Yes," I answered.

"What is your name?"

"Verga."

"How old are you?"

"Sixteen."

"Where are you coming from?"

"Kőszeg."

"Who was with you at the tower?"

"My father."

"Anyone else?"

"No. Is my father all right?" I asked in a concerned voice.

There was short silence; then the soldier said, "We do not know his condition. Why did you escape from Hungary?" I did not answer. He repeated the question again, but I remained silent. Then I banged my head and was flooded with emotions and started crying. The soldier got into the truck, sat next to me, placed his hand on my shoulder, and said, "It is okay, no more questions. Everything will be all right."

Then he barked orders, and the entire patrol group jumped into the truck. He spoke into a radio, "Delta, moving to base. We have one refugee on board. Out."

"Roger, proceed to drop out. Over and out."

The truck drove on the dirt road and into the woods.

The Hungarian Revolution in 1956 provided Austria with unexpected independence just one year before the country had regained its full independence from Allied occupation since the end of World War II. Austria fulfilled its desire to be a self-declared neutral nation. Despite the ideological differences with the Iron Curtain nations in 1956, Austria cleared all mines and removed the border fence between Austria and Hungary to ease the tension between east and west. They called it the Green Détente. On October 27, 1956, the people of Austria were overwhelmed by an unprecedented sense of solidarity from Hungarians for their genuine affirmation of demands for freedom and democracy. In

Austria, the International Red Cross pitched in to accept two hundred thousand Hungarian refugees who escaped from the failed Hungarian revolt. Austria struggled with an inexorable tide of refugees. Some integrated into the society, some joined relatives abroad, and others had no idea where to go.

The army truck drove to the nearest town of Oberwart. It was thirty-eight kilometers from Kőszeg and eighty-five kilometers from the second largest city in Austria, Graz. Oberwart had a sizable Hungarian ethnic population. The military truck stopped in front of the police station. I was led into the office.

A soldier said, "Good luck, young man," and left the room.

The door opened, and a police officer walked in, holding a folder in his hand. "Good evening," he said in perfect Hungarian. Sitting in front of the desk, facing me, he took a cigarette from his pocket. "Do you smoke?" he asked.

"No."

"Do you mind?"

"No, please," I said.

He introduced himself as Officer Konstantin. "What is your name?"

"Verga Caszar."

"Would you like something to drink? Water or tea?"

"Tea, please."

"How about a cheese sandwich?"

"Yes, please," I replied. With a hot tea and sandwich in my hand, my hunger subsided and I began to relax.

The officer took his hat and placed it on the table. He was in his forties with graying hair and kind green eyes. Puffing a cigarette, looking at me, he said, "The soldier told me of your unusual escape, quite daring I shall say. Sorry to say, we do not have information on your father's condition. Let's hope for the best. Now I need to ask you for some personal information. Then I will make an arrangement for you to stay the night in town. Tomorrow, you will be processed by the Red Cross. Do you have an ID on you?"

"Yes." I looked through my bag.

"Please empty the entire contents on the table. Whose photo is this?" he questioned, pointing to my one photograph.

"My mother."

"And where is your mother now?"

I was silent for a minute. "She's dead."

"I'm sorry to hear that," the officer said, extinguishing his cigarette in the ash. "When did she die?"

"In 1944 during World War II."

"Did your father remarry?"

"No."

"Why did you decide to leave Hungary?" I was silent again. I wasn't sure if I should tell the officer the truth. He sensed my hesitation and said, "You are now in Austria. Don't be afraid. You can speak your mind. I need to fill in your application so you can stay here in Austria legally."

"It wasn't safe to live in Hungary anymore. The revolution became dangerous."

The officer finished filling the application. "Do you have any relatives in Austria?"

"Not that I know," I said.

"Anywhere in the world?"

"No, I don't think so." I did not mention Uncle Elek. I was afraid of being turned over to the Hungarian border guards.

"No more questions for today." He looked at his watch. "I will be back in fifteen minutes."

I felt tired and wanted to sleep somewhere—anywhere. I placed my hands on my bag, rested my head, and dozed off. I was awoken gently by the police officer. Next to him was standing an elderly short woman dressed in a black coat and a black woolen hat. She smiled at me. "This is Ms. Valaria, Verga. You will be staying in her house for tonight, and tomorrow, she will take you to the Red Cross station. Is this okay?"

I said, "Thanks, good night."

I was exhausted. I wanted to just close my eyes.

Ms. Valaria was an ethnically Hungarian woman and a member of the local Calvinist parish in town. She was active in providing the arriving refugees with food, clothing, and shelter. She lived only a few blocks from the police station in the Hungarian district, Felszeg, the oldest part of town.

After I felt rested and was well fed, the next day, Ms. Valaria took me to the old parish church in town. It was adjacent to a kindergarten and the cultural center hall. It served the Austro-Hungarian community. It was the most important Magyar educational and religious center in the Burgenland district of Austria. The cultural center was a meeting place for the refugees, a temporary station for the Red Cross. That morning was cloudy and cold. I entered the main hall. It was full of refugees and noisy families sitting on cots and chairs, waiting to be transported to the refugee centers. I thanked Ms. Valaria for giving me a warm bed and food for the night. She kissed me on my forehead and wished me the best of luck. She said she's going to the church next door to pray for my well-being. "Perhaps," she asked, "would you like to join me in prayer?"

I declined.

I made myself comfortable in the corner of the hall, sitting and listening to the families' small talk. Children ran around, laughing and calling each other by name. Bundles, suitcases, and boxes were piled in one corner of the center. I was deep in thought. *What will happen to me? I have no one. I'm on my own. No word from my father.* I closed my eyes. Then I heard a voice behind me, and I turned around. Seated there was a young man of early twenties, blond, dressed in a brown jacket and rimmed glasses, smiling at me. He said, "My name is Odon. What's your name?"

"Verga."

"Nice to meet you, Verga. Where are you from?"

"Kőszeg."

"I'm from Budapest."

We started a friendly conversation. Odon was a talkative fellow. He asked a lot of questions and offered me a chocolate bar. He told me he was a university student and had fought in the streets of Budapest until the Russian tanks broke through the barricades. He had retreated back to the university grounds, but many of his classmates were missing. They had fled the country. His family was living in the small town of Pásztó when he learned that his favorite professor of journalism was shot when he was bringing groceries to his mother. It shook Odon to the core. In a few days, he decided to leave Hungary for Austria. He crossed No-Man's Land around Sempoly.

"What about you?" he said. "Tell me your story of why you're here."

I was comfortable with Odon. I told him my part of the journey to freedom.

"Incredible! Daredevil escape. Fantastic story," he said. "I hope your father is alive and well."

"I have not heard good news yet."

"Well, cheer up. Fill your lungs with the air of freedom. Did you say you were a piano student?"

"Yes."

"How good are you?"

"My teachers say I have a gift of music. I guess I'm like my mother. She was a piano teacher."

Odon pointed to the center of the stage. A long piano stood covered with a gray blanket. "Verga, go and play something for us. Cheer us up with music."

"No, I don't feel like playing now."

"Come on." Odon stood up. "We're all Hungarians here." He grabbed my hand and nudged me toward the piano.

I removed the cover from the piano, and to my surprise, in front of me was a black lacquered old Viennese piano. On the plaque was the name Gebrüder Stingl Klavier Fabriken Wien. The keyboards were of ivory, slightly yellowed. I touched the keys and played scales. Deep bass tones emanating from the piano satisfied my ears. The piano produced very full, robust, and sweet, delicate warm tones. I got the urge to play. I looked at Odon standing next to me. "What should I play?" I asked.

"What about Beethoven?"

"Yes, of course. Beethoven." I adjusted the piano bench. I played the Beethoven tune Bagatelle No. 25 in A Minor *Für Elise*. The piano music filled the hall with sweet notes for the next three minutes. Then I stopped. Applause rolled from the refugees. I bowed slightly.

"Play more," someone shouted.

"Play again," someone else said.

I was surprised by the response. Odon said, "You are very good. Play for them."

This time, I played Joseph Haydn's keyboard sonata in E-flat major, *Hob. XVI: 49*—allegro, a happy tune. More shouting and clapping erupted, encouraging me to play more. I took my notes from my bag. I chose music from Chopin and placed it on the piano. I played *Mazurkas* op. 56, then Nocturne, op. 55, no. 2, and finished with *Fantaisie* Impromptu op. 66. During the twenty minutes, I lost myself in piano playing. I poured all my feelings on the keyboard. Hush fell in the hall. Some eyes held tears as the refugees listened.

I glanced at my notes on the piano. A handwritten quote in black ink was written by my teacher. "Verga, put your soul into it. Play the way you feel!"

That morning, I felt like weeping, and I poured my despair on the Stingl keyboard. It responded with melancholic sounds made by vibrating strings.

SEVEN

The Red Cross facility in the southern Vienna suburbs was filled to capacity. Hungarian refugees flocked to Austria by the thousands and were placed around the country. It was late afternoon and snowy when I arrived on the Red Cross transport to Graz, a student city with six universities and a population close to a quarter million. It was a cultural city, home to the oldest institute of music education and performing arts in Austria.

I stood in line for an hour to be processed by the Red Cross in an old gymnasium building that served as a temporary refugee center. It was lunchtime, and I was served *tafelspitz* (boiled beef) with roasted potatoes and minced apples and a sauce of sour cream with horseradish. I was hungry and asked for seconds. Then I grabbed a cup of tea and punschkrapfen, also known as a punch doughnut, and went to my bed at the far corner of the gymnasium. The place was full of noisy people, kids running around, and babies crying. In my corner were gym lockers and the washroom. I took a warm shower and felt relaxed lying on my cot and dozed off. In the afternoon, I was called to be examined by medical doctors. I was given a clean bill of health.

Since I was considered a minor, I was ushered to see a child psychologist in the next cubicle. To my surprise, the psychologist was a friendly young man in his early thirties. He introduced himself as Dr. Bernard Fulop. As he reviewed my application, somehow, my name was familiar to him. He asked, "Where are you from, Verga?"

"From Kőszeg."

Dr. Fulop put the application on the side of the table, stood up, and went to the other side of the office to pick up his briefcase. He removed a folded newspaper, spreading it on the table, flipping through the pages, then folding them into halves, reading in silence. Looking at the doctor with interest, I thought, *What is he reading?* No words were exchanged. The doctor was engrossed in reading something in the newspaper. Then he looked at me. "Are you the young man who crossed No-Man's Land on a zip trolley?"

I was surprised to hear that question. "Yes."

The doctor put the newspaper down then said, "Do you know a man by the name of Odon?"

"Yes, I met him yesterday in Oberwat at the Red Cross facility."

"Did you tell him your escape story?"

"Yes, we talked in the center. He was one of the refugees too."

Dr. Fulop put his glasses on his face. "Did Odon identify himself as a reporter?"

"Reporter? No, he said he was a student."

"I see," the doctor said and folded the newspaper. He looked at me and said, "From now on, young man, while you're in this Red Cross center, if anyone approaches you and asks you about your escape, say you need to check with Dr. Bernard Fulop before revealing that information. Is that understood?"

I was surprised at the request. I said, "I don't understand. Why?"

The doctor leaned closer to me, looking into my eyes. "Because there are people who want to take advantage of you. This morning, the director of the facility was inundated with requests from radio, TV, and the press to have you interviewed. He replied that there is no such person in our facility. This fellow, Odon, is a reporter in disguise. This is not the first time that he snuck into our Red Cross facility, looking for a sensational story that he can sell to the press. Sometimes he makes up stories and skews the truth. You are an innocent, vulnerable young man, and I don't want you to be hurt from unwanted publicity. Is that a good answer?" He eyed me for a response.

I nodded. This was a didactic shock, a lesson to not trust strangers. "I guess I understand."

"Good, young man, now you can go. I will see you again late afternoon after I see the facility director." He stood up smiling and put his hand on my shoulder. "You can see me or ask for me any time."

"Thanks." Then I left the office.

Later that day, Dr. Fulop came looking for me. He said, "Please come to my office."

Sitting, facing me, the doctor said, "Verga, I have an unpleasant thing to tell you." He paused, searching for the right words. My heart sunk. I suspected this was about my father. The night before, I had a nightmare that my father got stuck on the electric tower, tangled with ropes, unable to free himself. Then the Russian soldiers started shooting at him. Like crucified Christ, he hung on the tower, dead. I had woken up in sweats.

The doctor said, "Your father did not make it to freedom. He was shot by the border guards. I'm terribly sorry for your loss." He held my hands.

My whole body shook, and I burst into tears. Last night's bad dream became reality. *What will become of me now? All alone in a strange country with no family, no one to lean on. How will I survive?* Tears ran down my cheeks.

"It is okay to cry. I'm sorry for your loss," the doctor repeated as he embraced me. I held him tight. I had no one else to grieve with, and I felt safe with him.

"Verga, I have gotten permission from the director to take you out from this facility. My sister has a large apartment in town, and for a few days, I want you to stay with her. This place is not suitable for you to be alone." I was silent. Then he said, "Would this be agreeable with you?"

I nodded, wiping my tears.

"Good. Tonight, I will take you there. You will love her place. She plays the piano. Now go pick up your bag and come back here when you're ready."

"Thanks for your help, Doctor," I said.

"No problem. Everything will be all right," the doctor said, hugging my shoulder.

I felt a little relieved that someone was looking after my well-being. With a heavy heart, I walked toward my sleeping corner.

"Are you ready?" asked Dr. Fulop.

"Yes," I said, picking up my belongings.

We drove in Dr. Fulop's Volkswagen to his sister's home. The door opened, and a woman in her thirties greeted us. "Come in, young man." The doctor and I entered the apartment. "I heard so much about you," she said. "Please come to the salon."

It was an old apartment in excellent condition, smartly furnished with a French empire-style sofa and side chairs. Large oil paintings of landscapes depicting stormy winter landscapes and waterfalls hung on the wall. In the salon was a grand Bösendorfer, the aristocrat of piano, that caught my eyes.

"My name is Sari." The woman extended her arm smiling, and I shook her warm hand. She wore a smart A-line black dress with white pearls on her neck, had jet-black hair to her shoulders, and stood tall in short-heeled shoes. Her pretty face reflected radiance, and she had kind, clear blue eyes. She noticed me glancing at the piano. She said, "This old grand piano model 290 has been in our family for many years." She brushed the piano with her hand affectionately. "My brother had no desire to learn to play, but I love this piano and learned when I was a child. I understand you're a music student and play well."

I said, "I want to be a concert pianist. I have not played a Bösendorfer piano, but I've been told it has a magical sound. Besides the eighty-eight keys, it has an additional nine bass notes and hidden keys."

"Indeed it has. The piano is made of solid spruce, which adds to the coloration of the sound. However, it does not have the same pianissimo as a Steinway."

Dr. Fulop excused himself. He had another appointment in town. "I will see you tomorrow, Verga. Good night." He left me alone with Sari.

"Sit down and tell me about yourself."

We talked late into the night. I felt welcomed with my new friend. For a short moment, I had forgotten the pain of my father's death. The Fulops were third-generation ethnical Hungarians in Austria. Their ancestors settled in Graz and opened a bakery.

Sari was engaged to a university professor. They were planning to be married in July of next year. She was a lawyer, working for the federal government.

Her home contained six rooms, and I was given a bedroom of my own. I was left alone in the apartment during the day and took the opportunity to practice my music. I fell in love with the piano. It had an easy touch and silvery tone. Playing the piano helped me heal my pain and gave me confidence to look for a brighter future. In the evening, Dr. Fulop joined us for dinner. The doctor had evening sessions with me to help me cope with the loss of my father. Then we watched the black-and-white television. It was just last year that ORF Radio Wien introduced

TV broadcasts in Austria. We watched the evening news program, *Zeit im Bild* (*The Times in Pictures*). I was fascinated by the images coming from the tube and was glued to the TV.

It was December 1956. The news from Hungary was grim. Their revolution collapsed, and Austria was struggling with the flood of refugees. There were riots in the Red Cross camps in Vienna. The conditions in the camps came to a breaking point. The Suez crisis dominated the headlines. Nikita Khrushchev was cornered saying to the West, "We will bury you. Of course, we will not bury you with a shovel. Your own working class will bury you." Elvis Presley released his first album, *Heartbreak Hotel*. It was the first time I heard the tunes of rock and roll on the airwaves. Sony introduced its first transistor radio for sale.

For the next two weeks, I became part of the family. I was thankful to the Fulops for giving me a temporary home. Then an international crisis surfaced. The People's Republic of Hungary asked for extraditions of those who committed domestic terrorism in the Hungarian Revolt. My father's name came up on the list. The Fulops were outraged with the false accusations. Sari, as a lawyer, prepared affidavit, dismissing the erroneous allegations. She called it a "stupid Communist sham," a plot to cover up their debauchery of crushing the people's revolt. She submitted an official request for asylum in Austria on my behalf.

One snowy December evening before Christmas, Sari had a guest in her apartment: her former music teacher, Victor Premengen. He listened to me play Franz Liszt's Etude op. 144, no. 2 *La Leggierezza*. Victor sat in the chair in the salon. He turned to Sari and said, "The kid has a gift and a God-given talent for piano playing. His hands were relaxed, and they are unusually large. The finger movement on the keyboard was like sparks of energy, a true sign of becoming a virtuoso. I think we have here a genius in the making. I must find him a good teacher to guide him." He paused then said, "I know one person who should hear Verga play, Dr. Bernard Richter of the Akademischer Musikverein."

EIGHT

The Akademischer Musikverein in Graz was located at Schloss Dientzenhofer Palace. It was home to the Fisher Dientzenhofer family since 1745. Fisher came from a wealthy family in Bohemia. In 1713, he inherited a large track of land along the Mur River in Graz. He was a well-educated man. In 1740, he was invited to teach law and economic science in the University of Graz. Fisher was a devoted Catholic, and in 1745, he decided to build a baroque-style palace for himself. After the Vienna Conference of 1815 and the defeat of Napoleon, a spirit of modern ideas blossomed in Europe. In 1845, the grandson of Fisher, Johan von Dientzenhofer, inspired by the Napoleonic Reforms, transformed the plush palace into Akademischer Musikverein for the advancement of education in music in Graz, a training ground for piano, violin, and cello students. From 1945 to 1952, Austria was an Allied-occupation zone under Soviet control, and Schloss Dientzenhofer seized to function as a school of music. It became the headquarters of the Soviet military occupation command post.

Dr. Bernard Richter convinced the Soviets to return the schloss to its original use as a school of music, and in 1952, the Russians vacated the premises. Since then, Dr. Richter was in charge of the magnificent baroque palace, which constituted a two-story pavilion and a small chapel. In 1880, an addition was made to double the capacity of the music studios in the rear of the schloss. During the same period, two one-story service buildings were built for dormitories and housing for the academy teaching staff. The building faced the magnificent garden along the Mur River. The entire complex was situated in the Rosenggreneg Forest. On the weekends, the schloss was open to the public for a few hours for visiting the academy museum and for hearing music recitals performed by the students.

Dr. Bernard Richter was a complicated man, talented instrumentalist, music critic, and conductor, which had taken a second role in his music career. Teaching was his calling, and he was also the principal director of the music school. He had a stern face and acidic tongue and was bald, intelligent, autocratic, and a diminutive sort of Freudian man. He was a creature of habit, arriving to work at precisely 11:00 a.m. every Monday. He left his *burö* (office) and started his weekly walk toward the academy conference room for his teachers' staff meeting. As he passed the practice studios along the corridor, he deliberately stopped at the front of various doors, listening to the students practice their instruments. Dr. Richter had exceptional hearing. He was able to detect a defective piano or missed notes while students played, which he immediately made a mental note to discuss with the students' teachers. The teaching staff was always taken off guard by his accurate comments and assessments of the students' musical progress. He was highly respected by the teachers.

I was engrossed in the slow movement of Franz Liszt's Sonata in B Minor S. 178, concentrating on the notes. Professor Constantina Wordzinka stood next to the piano, following the score, flipping the note pages on the music stand, her hands moving like a conductor. "Andante. Andante," she said, lowering her handing in notation. Then toward the recapitulation, she raised her voice, "More pianissimo," banging her pencil on the music stand. Then I finished the beautiful recapitulation and coda. "Well done," she said. "You can do better. We need to practice from the measure 331 to 459 another few times until we get it right." She looked at her watch. It was 11:15. "Oh, I'm late," she said. She closed the music notes and made a notation of today's play in her journal. She noted the date: May 5, 1960.

I was sitting on the piano bench when she said, "Take a break. I have to go to my weekly meeting. I will see you in the studio after 2:00." She pulled a small mirror from her bag, looking at her face. Then she proceeded to put red lipstick on her lips, fix her hair, and look at herself one more time. She tilted her mirror slightly, noticing my image. I was dressed in a white shirt and black trousers with a sweater on my shoulders. She glanced at me. Then she quickly placed the mirror into the bag and left in a hurry.

I glanced at the watch on the piano. It was eleven thirty. I remembered that when I was a senior, occasionally Dr. Richter would ask me to join him on his walk to his staff meeting. He would ask me if I detected missed or off notes. Then he made me take notes as I listened to his commentary. As we passed the last studio corridor, he would dismiss me like a Persian soldier—one hand behind his back, the other holding his soft leather lancer briefcase under his arm—and proceed with a fast pace toward the conference room.

I continued practicing, contemplating how to improve my weak points. I replayed Franz Liszt's piece again and then relaxed with some scales. After an hour, Professor Wordzinka burst into the studio. Her face flushed with excitement. "Verga, I have good news."

"What?"

She pulled a chair and faced me, holding my hands. "Let me tell you what just took place in the conference room. As always, at our meetings, Dr. Richter presided at the head of the table. I sat next to him on the left. On the right sat Rudolph, taking notes in his red leather-bound notebook. Dr. Richter sat in silence, looking at us, smiling. Then he congratulated me. He said you were selected to represent us in Vienna in the piano competition for young talent!"

My heart jolted. I sprung from my seat and hugged her. Tears flowed from her eyes. "Wow, what great news! Why are you crying?"

"I am overwhelmed with joy."

I sat down looking at her. She wiped her tears with a handkerchief, smiled, and said, "Let me continue. Applause erupted at the conference table, all eyes on me. The announcement took me by surprise. I was in tears. Congratulations were said on both sides of the table. Dr. Richter stood, looking proudly at me.

"I said, 'This was really wonderful news. As you all know, I took Verga under my wing as a teacher almost four years ago. When Dr. Richter and I saw Verga the first time and heard him play, we knew we had a talent in our hands. Thanks to Dr. Richter finding Verga a financial sponsor, the von Glucks, I was able to devote my time to guide him and give him uninterrupted devotion to achieve this success. Thank you for all your support.'

"Dr. Richter was proud of my dedication to you and said it is an honor for our academy to achieve this. He turned to me and invited me to have lunch with him to discuss the details."

"What fantastic news," I said.

"Verga, what do you think of my suggestion? You graduate from the master's program next week. I want to invite you to stay in my house in Vienna to practice for the competition. What do you say?"

I was overwhelmed. "Thanks, it will be great."

"I will be leaving after the graduation ceremony. Get your belongings thereafter, and when you're ready, give me a call. Okay, no slacking, let's finish today's practice."

NINE

*I*t was a sunny day in July of 1960 and my last day of classes. That morning, I headed for my meeting with the music academy director.

Knocking on the door to his office, I heard Dr. Richter's voice. "Please, come in." He was seated at his desk with a pile of paper sitting on the tabletop. Lifting his head, he said. "Please sit down, Verga," waving his hand toward the leather armchair on the other side of the room. He continued writing. I sat in silence, looking at him. He put his pen down, removed his spectacles, stood up, and joined me on the other armchair. As always, he was dandy in appearance, wearing a gray suit, white shirt, and a yellow polka-dot bowtie. "Coffee, tea, or water?"

"No thanks."

He poured water into his glass. Wiping his forehead, he said, "Verga, I wanted to have a talk with you before you leave for Vienna. Is it on a 2:00 p.m. bus?"

"Yes."

"I am elated with your progress, and congratulations for your completion of your master's classes. I followed your progress for the past four years. What can I say? You have a God-given talent for music. You were born to play piano."

"Thank you, Dr. Richter."

"I'm thankful for Professor Wordzinka for having her home available to you to practice."

"Yes, I am thankful too. I was pleasantly surprised."

"Have you decided what repertoire you will perform at the competition?"

"Yes." I took a piece of paper from my shirt pocket and handed it to him.

Dr. Richter put on his glasses, reading aloud.

> First Play: Schubert Drei Klavierstücke, D.946, second
> piece of the three piano pieces of no. 2, E-flat major
> Time Duration of Play: 10 minutes, 19 seconds
> Pause: 10 seconds
> Second Play: Rachmaninoff, part of Third Concerto
> Time Duration of Play: 10 minutes, 3 seconds
> Total Play Time: 20 minutes, 32 seconds

"Very interesting," said Dr. Richter. "If my memory serves me right, did the American pianist Mr. Cliburn play Rachmaninoff's Third Concerto at Moscow Tchaikovsky's competition in 1958?"

"Yes, and he brought the house on their feet. I listened to it on the live broadcast. He was fantastic." I edged to the front of the chair. "I want that success too. I can play Rachmaninoff well. He is one of my favorite composers. Dr. Richter, you should have heard the audience shouting, 'First prize, first prize!'"

"I'm glad you're so excited. Bravo, Verga." Then he placed his hands like a prayer on his lips, looking at me in silence. "Be careful not to be overconfident. How shall I say, don't be too cocky. You're having three respectful opponents, good piano players. Did you discuss your repertoire with Professor Wordzinka?"

"Not yet. I will when I see her."

"I will be in Vienna in two weeks to cast a lot on your behalf in order to determine the order of the contestants' presentations. At the same time, I will need to file with the judges your repertoire, so make your final decision. I've also prepared a brief biographical résumé on your behalf for press release. Please review it." He handed me two sheets.

"Thank you."

Dr. Richter stood up and went to his desk, picking up an envelope. "This is a list of appointments I arranged for you in Vienna for possible jobs. You know, the Graz symphony for young performers is offering you a soloist piano position. My recommendation is not to accept it at this time. You are meant to play with the best."

"Thanks," I said.

"Now on a different subject, your sponsors, the von Gluck family, are presenting you with a grant of 20,000 schillings to allow you to launch your professional career." He handed me an envelope. "Spend it wisely. All other expenses for the competition, we will take care of it for you." I was surprised. I never expected such generosity from my roommate's family. Hans, a cello student, and I were close friends for the past four years, but to sponsor me was huge.

"If you win the first prize, remember, Verga, the winner is to represent Austria in late August in Milan, Italy, in the Young Pianist International Talent Competition. The first prize is 50,000 schillings, and with that comes a lucrative recording contract. It will open doors to the best orchestra houses in the world. So, young man"—he stood up shaking my hand—"good luck. Work hard. There is no time to waste, and I will see you in Vienna in two weeks to check your progress."

I thanked him for all he had done for me and left the office in good spirits.

I said good-bye to all my academy friends and especially to my roommate, Hans von Gluck. I thanked him and his family for their devotional financial support.

Hans replied, "I plan to be in the audience to listen to you play. Don't disappoint me."

"Hans, I promise I will not let you down. I promise to be at my best." I took one of my clay sculptures, my own interpretation of *The Kiss* by Rodin. I said, "Hans, give this to your sister. It is a present from me to remember our good times together."

I was happy yet sad to leave the academy. With two suitcases, which were all my worldly possessions on this earth, I boarded the bus to Vienna. On the bus, I sat deep in the seat, relaxed. The bus was half filled with passengers. I closed my eyes thinking of my time at the music school. It flashed in front of me like a slow-motion movie.

I was sixteen years old in a strange country—scared, insecure, without family. Then I met Professor Wordzinka. She was like a rescue angel dispatched from heaven. She came into my life and ignited in me a Promethean flame, a passion for music and art.

Opening my eyes, I looked through the window, thinking how lucky I was to have Professor Wordzinka as a teacher. She instructed me with the same techniques as the pianist Glen Gould. Professor Wordzinka was influenced by the Chilean-born Antonio Alberto Garcia Guerrero, who happened to be Glen's teacher.

I remembered when Professor Wordzinka made me watch the black-and-white documentary movie of Glen Gould playing the piano again and again, saying "That's the way to play piano." The first time I watched the movie of Glen playing Bach and Beethoven was in 1958 in the Soviet Union. It was like a magical machine striking beautiful notes. From that moment, I wanted to play piano like Glen Gould. I lowered my piano stool and learned to strike the keyboard from above. I struggled with this technique. It felt unnatural to me, but I was determined to master it. After months of practice, I did.

Professor Wordzinka had allowed me to experiment. My playing became of greater clarity and erudition, especially in contrapuntal passages. The students called me "the Hungarian Gould." Dr. Richter was not amused. He was a classist by heart. He argued with my teacher for allowing me to experiment. He believed in traditional piano techniques. In due time, I won him over with my distinctive personal approach to piano playing. Professor Wordzinka, like Franz Liszt, believed when playing music, the student must not create carbon copies of the composer's intent but be inspired to play with his or her artistic individuality.

However, she forbade me from playing jazz and rock and roll. She said it would corrupt me, but Hans loved that music. He secretly smuggled records into our room. We listened to them, sharing earphones with each other, and I developed a love for jazz. I was also forbidden from playing contact sports. "You could injure your hand," she said. Secretly, I learned how to ride a bicycle. I think she knew but ignored it.

On holidays, I was a frequent guest of the Gluck family. They lived on a large estate on the outskirts of Graz. There, I found out how rich people lived; and secretly, I wanted to live like them. His parents were fond of me. Hans's mother had said that I was a good influence on her son. I played piano, entertaining guests. Sometimes Hans joined me with the cello and his mother on the violin in a chamber ensemble. Hans's sister, Ingrid, occasionally sang. She had a sweet nightingale voice. Ingrid was infatuated with me. She was only fifteen years old, young and pretty.

We developed a close friendship. I was grateful to the Gluck family for their support.

Now I was twenty years old and was prepared for the music world. I devoted all my energy to playing piano. I did not know much of how other people lived, unprepared for life outside the academy. I became a good pianist but was naïve about amore. I had no relations with the opposite sex.

Eventually, the monotonous movement of the bus rocked me to sleep. I was awakened by a sudden stop-and-go movement. There was traffic on the streets of Vienna. I took my black notebook, searching for Professor Wordzinka's address. She lived on Rubayer Lane in the Agergud neighborhood. I remembered visiting her once. There was a large hospital not too far from her residence on a quiet residential street near the Danube Canal. I recalled the time when we walked around the neighborhood. She pointed at the number 19 on Bergasse, an apartment building. She said, "This is a famous address. Here lived and worked the famous father of psychoanalysis, Sigmund Freud. My father-in-law, Joseph Heilbronner, who was a renowned surgeon, knew Freud on a personal basis. He had bought a house on Rubayer Lane because it was close to the imperial hospital." I remember the unusual façade of Professor Wordzinka's house. It had an impressive front with an elaborate large round stained glass window adorned with art nouveau detailing. She told me that Dr. Joseph loved Jugendstil architecture and befriended Otto Wagner, a Viennese architect, and had him renovate his residence.

I stood in front of the house, ringing the doorbell. Maria, the Polish housekeeper, opened the door and, recognizing me, said, "Please come in, Verga."

At the top of the stairs stood Professor Wordzinka. For a minute, I did not recognize her in a V-neck floral shirt, blue trousers, a large white belt buckle over her waist, and barefoot. She held a cup in her hand. "Come in, Verga." I was struck by her appearance. I had never seen her in such modern, casual attire. In the academy, she was always dressed in black and white. "Why are you standing there? Please come in." I picked up my suitcases and entered the house. "Welcome to my home. How was the bus ride?"

"Oh, thanks, without any hitch. How are you?" I put my suitcases down.

"Very good. Are you hungry? Of course you are. Maria will make you something to eat."

I was given a bedroom on the second level. Professor Wordzinka's bedroom and study were on the third. The library, salon, and kitchen were on the first. There was a ground level for the storage and laundry room. I changed my clothes and came down to the salon. In the corner was a black lacquered 1930s grand Steinway piano model O. I circled it, admiring the piano like a pilot checking an airplane before takeoff. I touched the lid and put the drop up, looking into the soundboard, touching and examining the felt hammers that looked new. I pulled out the piano stool and lowered it, opening the fallboard. I lightly pressed on the three piano pedals satisfied. Looking through the music sheets on top of the piano, I decided to play Brahms's Piano Quartet no. 1, op. 25.

A few minutes into my playing, Professor Wordzinka walked into the salon. I stopped playing and stood up.

She said, "Sit down. No need to stand up. Relax."

"I was checking the clarity of the piano. It sounds great. I like its lyrical quality."

"Wonderful," she said. "You have a lot of practice ahead of you." She pulled over a chair and sat next to me. I smelled sweet herbal perfume, thinking she never used it at the academy. If she did, it was a mild cologne.

Turning toward her, I said, "Professor Wordzinka, thank you for your invitation to stay and practice in your home."

"Verga, from now on, call me Constantina. We're no longer teacher and student. Let us become informal with each other. It is my pleasure to have you in my house. After all, I invested four years of my time teaching and guiding you. I would like to see the fruits of my labor come to life. I want to see you win first prize."

"I will not disappoint you."

"Please finish playing Brahms. I like the music." She stood up and sat on the leather armchair, crossed her legs, closed her eyes, and listened to my piano playing in silence.

I finished Brahms, paused, and then started playing Chopin's Nocturne in D-flat Major, op. 27, no. 2 while keeping my eyes on Constantina. Her eyes never opened during my performance, both ears listening to me play. I was engrossed in the music when I heard Maria's voice. "Frau Constantina, dinner is ready."

"Thanks, Maria. This will be all for tonight. *Możesz iść do domu wcześnie dzisiaj* [You can go home early today]," she said in Polish.

"*Dziękuje dobranoc* [Thank you. Good night]."

"Good night, Maria."

Constantina and I sat at the table. She served me a plate of rind goulash, an original Hungarian dish now part of an Austrian culinary table. "It's hot," I said. "I love the spiced beef with paprika."

"I'm glad you like it." She gave me a side dish of salad. I noticed my goulash was void of traditional dumplings. "Verga, I'm putting you on a high-energy diet with wholesome food. You need strength for the next few weeks. No sugar stuff. Please chew slowly, and be aware of what you eat." She poured water with mint into my glass. "Did you decide on your repertoire?"

"Yes." I took the list from my shirt pocket and handed it to her. "My choice of music will be Schubert and Rachmaninoff." I ate in silence, looking at her reaction.

"Verga, I like Schubert. I'm not sure why you chose Rachmaninoff."

"Rachmaninoff has a technical difficulty in playing, and Mr. Cliburn chose it for the Tchaikovsky competition in Moscow."

"Verga, it is too tacky. You are Hungarian. You are to play in front of an Austrian-Hungarian audience, not in Moscow in front of Russians. I think it is more appropriate to select a piece from Franz Liszt, a Hungarian composer. It fits your temperament. What do you think of *La Campanella*? You play it so well."

I was silent. She was right. "Let me sleep on it," I said.

She changed the subject. "Let's go for a walk. It is a beautiful night, and we can talk."

As we walked along the Danube Canal, we discussed my practice schedule for the coming week. She said, "I'm repeating myself, but I'll say it again. You are gifted to be born with large hands and long fingers, but your playing still lacks maturity. You have a tendency to interpret the composers with your own coloration. Be careful. In a competition, you need to stick to the score. Impress the judges with your technical abilities and charm. It will work for you. Focus on the score. Combine it with an anecdote, a metaphor, and wit." We stopped walking. "Let's go back."

"I have something on my mind. May I speak openly?"

"Of course, speak your mind. You always do."

"You know me like an open book. I know very little about you. I never dared to ask you as a student."

"What would you like to know?"

"About your childhood, your life, desires. I know you were born in Poland. When did you come to Austria? Things like that."

There was silence from her. She stopped walking. "Verga, let's put on our sweaters. It's getting chilly." We walked a few steps. She said, "Let's sit here."

We sat in silence, looking at the barge slowly passing in the canal and joggers going by our bench. It was dusk now. I glanced at her face, thinking how beautiful she truly was. She stared into the distance. Then she said, "I was born in Lodz, Poland, to a very pious Catholic family. As a child, I was taken to play violin. I played in church services. I excelled in music at the age of eighteen and entered an academy of music in Krakow, studying cello and piano. You know, Verga, my professor of music was Krzysztof Penderecki. I also studied history, philosophy, and art in Jagellonian University, in Krakow. During that time, I developed a severe bleeding in my uterus and had to be hospitalized. I had a large tumor in my ovaries. The recommendation was to have surgery, but the best surgeons were in Vienna, Austria. My father was a successful businessperson; he sold and repaired textile spinning and weaving machines in Lodz and was well-to-do. He took me to Vienna. My tumor was successfully removed. It was not cancerous. My bleeding stopped, and I recovered, but I can't bear children." She was silent, a tear running down her cheek, leaving a wet trail on her face. "I developed a phobia. I was afraid of having relationships with men. I became a recluse and shied away from any relationship with the opposite sex. I poured all my energy into my studies. I graduated from the University of Vienna and enrolled into the master's program in music and eastern philosophy. I was twenty-four at the time when I met my future husband, Dr. Mayer, a psychologist. He was a visiting professor and gave lectures on human sexuality. I was impressed with his knowledge on the subject, and I enrolled in all his lectures. One day after class, I approached him and asked him if he could take me as one of his patients. He agreed. After a year of sessions, he cured me of my phobia. He liberated me, and I never looked back again. He made me who I am today. I fell in love with the man and moved to live with him. Then we got married in 1936; but it was a long time ago, nearly seventeen years have passed, since my husband, Mayer, was taken away from me." She stopped talking momentarily. Then she said, "You know, Verga, nature has given us two sovereign masters, pain and pleasure, and we humans need to avoid pain and search for pleasure. Now you know me better." She smiled. Then she changed the subject. "Tomorrow is Saturday, your day off. On Monday, you will start practice. Tomorrow, I have an appointment in the morning, and Maria has a day off too."

I said, "May I take you out to a restaurant to thank you for your hospitality?"

"Oh, Verga, that is very sweet of you. Tomorrow, I wanted to take you out to Frauenhuber Café."

"Let me invite you," I said.

"Well, let's decide tomorrow."

As we walked, I asked, "What happened to your husband, Mayer, may I ask?"

She was silent for a long time then said, "I will tell you some other time." She got hold of my hand. "Let's go home."

TEN

Constantina started her day with daily yoga exercise on the second level, adjacent to my bedroom. When she passed the bathroom, she glanced past the door, which was ajar. My nude body was visible as I wiped myself, facing the mirror. In the mirror, I noticed her glance, pause, and walk away. I realized I forgot to close the door. Embarrassed, I thought about how careless I was and what I should say to her, and I locked the door.

I was in the kitchen drinking coffee when she walked in. "Good morning," I said.

"Good morning." Not a word of embarrassment. She poured herself a cup of coffee. "What are your plans for today?"

"I will play piano for an hour. Then I decided to take a walk to get familiar with the neighborhood."

"Good idea."

"I noticed you have a lot of books. May I browse through them?"

"Of course, Verga. The shelves are stuffed with many books: medicine, music, history books and art catalogs. You may find something of interest to you."

She left the house for an appointment in town and would be back in the afternoon. I liked her choice of clothes for the day: beige pants, white shirt, hair neatly covered with a colorful, silk handkerchief tied behind her neck. Like a beautiful model, she vanished into the street.

It was a cloudy day, threatening rain. The sun parked between clouds. I walked along Freyung Strasse, the elegant part of the city with a formal medieval complex of three beautiful baroque palaces, Hildebrandt and Kinsky. As I walked, I admired the sculpture of Neptune on top of the stock exchange building façade. I turned and strolled onto Renngasse to Freyung Square. They were connected by a shopping arcade. The morning crowd was in the square going about their business. I stopped at Café Central, once a place for writers and free thinkers. It was still one of the splendid coffeehouses in Vienna. With a cup of Einspänner coffee (large coffee with whipped cream on top) and the newspaper, I was content.

Back home, I took off my shoes and walked to the library. The shelves were bending from the loads of books of all kinds of subjects, like human sexuality, a topic I knew nothing about. I decided to browse through them. I came to the title *Hinduism and Sensual Pleasure*. I opened the first page of the first chapter "Kama Sutra." I decided to flip through the pages, making myself comfortable, reading in an old leather brown chair. I was engrossed in the Eastern art of lovemaking. It was all new to me.

I did not hear Constantina enter the house. She stood and leaned on the doorframe of the library. "What are you reading, Verga?" Her voice startled me.

Looking at her, I said, "Oh, you scared me." She smiled. I felt awkward and put the book face down, covering the title with my large hands. "A book on human sexuality."

She walked into the library and fanned an arc. "Oh, there are many books about that. Mayer wrote several books on this subject. May I recommend one of them to you?" She pulled a book from the shelf and gave it to me. I put it next to me on the round table, exposing the title of the book in my lap.

"Oh, kama sutra." She picked up the book, flipping through the pages. "The Buddhist teaching of the Eastern approach to sexuality. A good book. It is a guide to sex, ethics, morality, and how to achieve karma. Unfortunately, in our Western society, we view this book as pure pornography, not understanding the Buddhist view on sexuality, which teaches us to follow the middle path and to avoid extremes."

I changed the subject. "I'm impressed with the Oriental art books in the house. This painting—is it original?" I pointed to the framed artwork between the books on the shelf.

"Yes, a wood-cut print."

"Who is the artist?'

"Hokusai. He is known for his three volume books of Shunga Japanese erotica published in 1814. My husband, Mayer, was fond of him and kept this painting. He was against collecting artwork, though. He believed that collecting for oneself was an act of elitism. He believed that the artwork belonged in a public space for everyone."

"I don't understand what the artist is trying to convey in the painting."

Constantina stood in front of the painting, looking at it, and said, "The art title of this painting is *The Dream of the Fisherman's Wife.* It's an image of the Japan's Edo period, a contemporary story of the Princess Tamatory, who was pursued by sea creatures, including octopuses, and died while searching for family pearls. This is Hokusai's interpretation of that story, depicting a young ama diver sexually entwined with a pair of octopuses." She paused, pointing her finger. "That large octopus has his arms around the ama, performing cunnilingus."

I swallowed hard shifting my legs, feeling awkward. She had never mentioned oral sex in our conversations.

She continued, "Yes, I left the painting on the wall as a token of remembrance of the past." She then changed the subject. "I went shopping today. Would you like to see what I bought?" She put the two shopping boxes on the side table.

"Yes, please show me."

Uncovering the boxes, she pulled out a green dress with white polka-dot fabric, modeling it against her figure. Grinning, she asked, "What do you think?"

"Outstanding dress. The green matches your eyes. I like it very much." Then I noticed her new hairdo. It was very much a la Jackie O.

"Thanks. It is the latest fashion from London. Look at these boots." She placed a pair of white ankle boots on the box.

"Beautiful."

"I decided to take you to the Belvedere Gallery and Gardens tomorrow. I shall wear this dress."

"Great. I always wanted to visit there."

She put the dress back into the box. I said, "My invitation to take you to the Frauenhuber Café is standing. Please say yes."

Our eyes met. It was a long gaze in silence. She had a slight smile on her face. "Thanks, Verga. We have a date tonight."

Joy overwhelmed me. "Great," I said. It was the first time I invited someone to go out with me.

I heard her say, "I'm going to my room. I'll see you later." She picked up her shopping boxes and left the room.

I stood up and went to the salon. I had an urge to play the piano. Placing Mozart music sheets on the piano, I played Sonata no. 8, K310, one of only three minor key sonatas in Mozart's repertoire. I played it with real drama, then slow movements, and struck the keys with dark pathos echoing in the room. I finished playing and looked at the keys for a long moment, then stood up, and went to my room.

For tonight, I put on my blue blazer, black pants, and a white shirt. Constantina wore a wine-colored dress and a sweater over her shoulders.

I flagged a taxi. "Himmelpfortgasse no. 6," she said to the driver.

"Frauenhuber Café?" he asked.

"Yes."

The driver dropped us off on the opposite side of the street. As we walked toward the café house, she said, "This place has a history of its own. It is a really old establishment acquired by Franz Jahn, who was a Hungarian like you. Jahn was a cook in Schonbrunn for Maria Theresa, the empress in 1773. The emperor, Joseph III, gave him a position in Augarten. There was a saying in Vienna, 'No one can make coffee like Jahn in Augarten.'"

We reached the coffeehouse and entered. We were greeted, "Gna diger frau" by the maitre d'. "How are you, Frau Heilbronner?" He bowed slightly then faced me. "Gna diger herr." He looked at Constantina again. "The usual table?"

"Please, room number 3, Frank," she said.

"Please follow me."

The coffeehouse was arranged into small living rooms, each full of customers. Room number three had a parquet floor and small carpets. The walls were decorated with Rococo and Bedemeir landscapes and paintings of coquettish ladies and gentlemen making music. We sat at a table facing each other. "What a lovely place," I said.

She removed her sweater, exposing her broad shoulders from the low-cut dress, a single string of pinkish pearls decorating her long neck. I said, "I noticed the waiters recognized you as we walked in."

She smiled. "Yes, I have been coming here as a regular for many years." Listening to Mozart's music playing in the background, she said, "Did you know Mozart performed here on March 4, 1791?"

"No, I did not know."

Our waiter appeared, interrupting her and handing us the menu. Glancing at it, she said, "*Gemischter Salat* [mixed vegetable salad]."

"What would you like to drink?" asked the waiter.

"Just water, please."

"And for you, sir?"

"I will have the same."

Frank came to the table with a silver tray and three small glasses. "For your health, madam. Some schnapps? On the house," he said. "For you, Frau Heilbronner, black currant juice. For us gentlemen, grape-flavored stern [milky-colored alcoholic drink]." We raised our glasses. "To your health," Frank said.

We emptied the glasses. The drink warmed my heart. "That was very nice of you, Frank," she said.

"Thank you."

Then she introduced me to him, saying, "This is the talented young pianist that I was telling you about."

"My pleasure." He shook my hand and said, "Frau Heilbronner bragged of your talent. I wish you all the success."

"Thanks," I said, and with that, he left us alone.

Looking at each other, we smiled. She said, "Verga, did you decide what to play for the competition?"

"Yes, it will be Schubert and Franz Liszt."

"Excellent choice. As of Monday, you will start a rigid schedule of practice. You must win this competition. It will make me really proud." She placed her hands on her chest. "You will have to practice eight hours a day. I know it's hard, but the reward is great. You must make some sacrifices for your future." She placed her hand over mine on the table. Her hand was gentle and warm. A strange sensation like a jolt of electricity pulsed through my body.

I looked into her eyes and said, "For all you have done for me, I will work hard to win first prize." I said it in such confidence it surprised me.

She squeezed my hand lightly in response. I wanted to hold her hand longer. Then the waiter came with our food. Eating slowly, I watched the fork touch her lips—how sensual she looked. For dessert, she allowed some sugar today. We ordered a large piece of sachertorte. She said to the waiter, "And two coffees please."

She took the last piece on her fork. "This is for you."

I opened my mouth. She slowly lifted the fork and placed it between my lips, smiling and looking at me, her eyes a clear forest green. I tasted the sweetness of that last morsel. It was like a kiss. Relaxed with Mozart playing in the coffeehouse and sipping coffee from porcelain cups, we sat in silence in our own thoughts.

Then I asked, "I know that you and Dr. Richter have known each other for a long time. When did you meet?"

"Oh, it was many years ago. For two years, he was a patient of my late husband."

"Was he sick?"

"Not physically but mentally. He had a nervous breakdown. He had difficulty handling his emotions." She was silent trying to find the right words. Then she looked at me seriously. "What I will tell you now is not to be revealed to others. Promise me, Verga."

"Yes, my lips are sealed."

She took a sip of coffee. "In 1938, Germany annexed Austria. At the same time, Hitler's terror regime began tightening its grip on every area of Austrian society. The Nazis did not tolerate gypsies, Jews, and homosexuals. Arrests and persecutions of them followed. Dr. Richter lived a 'carefree' life."

I interrupted her. "I don't understand. What do you mean carefree?"

"How can I say this politely? He is attracted to members of the same sex."

"You mean *schwul*, homosexual?"

"That word is too clinical. I would use the French word *gai* or *gay*."

She paused looking at my reaction. I was not surprised. "There were rumors in the academy that Dr. Richter was gay, but I wasn't sure. I thought that you were secret lovers."

"No, Verga, we're just very good friends."

"I'm sorry to interrupt you. Please continue."

"Dr. Richter, being a closet homosexual, it weighed heavy on him. He did not know how to deal with it in public. My late husband befriended him, and they had a common interest in music and art. In 1939, the lives of the Jews became intolerable in Austria. I begged my husband to leave Austria. He had family in Switzerland and in London, but he refused. He said his family had lived in Austria for generations. Mayer's ancestors had served the Austrian imperial crown in the medical profession. His father had been a renowned surgeon and had served in World War I with honors and had received accommodations. No one would touch us. Well, how wrong he was." She took another sip of coffee. Her face saddened.

"In 1940, one evening, the bell rang at our house. The Gestapo was at the door. They came for my husband to arrest him. That evening became my nightmare. He argued with the Gestapo. He put on his father's military jacket with all the decorations and medals. The Gestapo laughed at him. They dragged him from the house. I tried to hold them back. They pushed me around. They tore his jacket and threw it on the ground like a discarded rag. He was beaten and pushed into a car and driven away. Horrible, horrible!" She put her hands on her face. Tears rolled down her cheek. "It was the last time I saw him. I was hysterical. I called Dr. Richter. His uncle was a high official in the SS, and I asked for help. Dr. Richter came over and calmed me down. He promised to ask for help from his uncle. A few days later, he came back. His uncle was not happy. He said he was angry with him because of his association with the Jews. Then he informed me that Mayer was shipped to Auschwitz. His uncle advised that for my safety, I must live in Vienna. Dr. Richter offered me a way out, a teaching position in the academy of music in Graz. He was just recently appointed academy director. He forged my documents as an unmarried woman. We made a pact. He will protect me, and I will become his official companion in all academy functions."

I said, "I thought you were lovers, and so did many of the students in the academy."

"No, Verga, it suited both of us. We survived the onslaught of World War II and the Nazi regime. You know, Verga, Rudolph, the academy administrator, is Dr. Richter's companion of twenty years."

"I never suspected it." The revelation shook me. I felt naïve for not noticing. I saw pain in her eyes. "I'm sorry to hear this horrible story. I can feel your grief."

She finished the coffee and said, "Life must go on. Are we ready to go home?"

We left the coffeehouse and hailed a taxi.

ELEVEN

*O*n Sunday, I looked forward to the day's planned visit to the gardens of Belvedere and its gallery. That morning, I got out of bed and took a shower then walked toward the meditation room. I peeked inside, and to my surprise, Constantina was there on her last yoga stretch. I was unsure if I should enter, for I didn't want to disturb her. Standing by the doorframe, barefoot, in shorts and a T-shirt, my hair still dripping with water from the shower, I admired her flexibility, thinking to myself, *It's remarkable how strong she is at the age of forty-four.* She noticed me. "Guten morgen."

"Guten morgen."

"Come in, Verga. I'm finished." We sat facing each other and assumed the lotus position.

I asked, "What time will we be leaving for the Belvedere?"

"At nine thirty. The gallery opens at ten." She set an alarm for forty-five minutes. "Let's begin."

We closed our eyes, and I sunk into dynamic tranquility, and serenity set in.

Later, as I sat in the kitchen with a cup of coffee in my hand, Constantina appeared by the door dressed in her new clothes, white big-framed sunglasses, and short white gloves. Her hair was backcombed into a bouffant, white handkerchief draped over and tied behind. For a moment, she took my breath away. I put the cup of coffee down, spilling some of it on the table. She looked like she just walked out of the pages of *Vogue* magazine. "Are we ready?" Her voice woke me from my thoughts.

"Yes, let's go."

We hopped into a taxi. "Belvedere," she said.

"Belvedere Gardens?" the driver asked.

"Yes."

"Gna diger frau."

We stopped in front of the Belvedere summer palace. Looking at the complex, I heard her voice. "The palace was commissioned by Prince Eugene of Savoy. The prince bought the land in 1697 and expanded the land until 1721. In 1775, he built the palace and the Belvedere Castle as his summer residence. In 1806, Emperor Joseph II transformed the summer palace into a picture gallery and opened it to the public. In 1890, the art collection was transformed into Kunsthistorisches Museum in town, and the castle became a residence of the arch duke, Franz Ferdinand. As you know, he was assassinated in Serbia. After World War I, the Republic of Austria set up the Austrian gallery in Belvedere, offering an exquisite overview of Austrian art from the Middle Ages to the present. Would you like to see works by Renoir, Monet, Sehieler, Kokoschka, and Klimt?"

"Yes, especially Gustav Klimt's paintings."

We toured the gallery, and I spent most of the time in Gustav Klimt's section, especially *The Kiss*, making notes in my notebook. I lost time admiring his work. Constantina nudged me. "Hungry?"

"No," I said.

"I'm hungry."

"Okay, let's have a coffee."

We shared a sandwich and a pastry in the cafeteria, resting our legs.

She looked at her watch and said, "We're running out of time, Verga. Let's see the gardens."

I was reluctant to leave the gallery, but I followed her outdoors. The bright summer light greeted us, blinding our vision. Standing under the palace portico, I tried to adjust my vision. In front of us was an outstanding view of the garden creation in French style. Past shrubs and flowerbeds, we could see the lower cascade basin spew water. I admired the upper Belvedere garden and the bouquet of trees arranged in geometrical patterns, a beautiful scene. The garden perspective ended with a single-story castle of Prince Eugene's most significant eighteenth-century baroque palace.

I stood next to Constantina and admired her appearance. She looked like a celebrity who walked out of the Cannes Film Festival. "Let's walk," she said.

As I strolled beside her in silence toward the upper cascade, water flowed over five shallow steps into a pool below. I broke the silence and said, "I was mesmerized by Gustav Klimt's paintings. They're so full of love. I can't rid *The Kiss* from my mind. I like the *Beethoven Frieze* too. I felt Beethoven's Ninth Symphony radiating from the artwork, and I felt compassion and ambition moving the knight in shining armor to fight for humanity's yearning for happiness. I also liked Schiller's quote from '*Ode an die Freude*' ['Ode to Joy']: 'Joy, fair spark of divinity, here's a kiss for all the world.'"

She listened to me speak as we walked but said nothing. We reached the statue of the Sphinxes and stopped to look at it, a bizarre composition of a lion's body with a woman's head with round pronounced breasts. I tried to understand the meaning of it. I heard Constantina's voice. "This imposing sculpture represents the nature of female strength and human intelligence." Then she said smiling, "Verga, did you notice the face of the body is a woman?"

"How interesting."

We climbed the garden steps, reaching the lower cascade gardens. She turned around and said, "Let's sit. My legs are killing me. I shouldn't have worn my new shoes today."

We sat on the nearest bench under the protection of trees from the scorching sun. She removed her shoes to the sound of relief. Facing me, she said, "Tell me, what you liked about *The Kiss*? You spent most of your time looking at it and taking notes."

I was thinking, glancing at the garden void. "I like Klimt's composition of the two-dimensional ornamentation of the characters and the effect of it on the canvas, its material, and its visual charm. It drew my eye to the two lovers' seductive beauty as they embraced. It's an unusual, erotic vision of pure delight." I paused for a moment then continued with my impression. "The lovers are standing on a precipice with a flowering meadow at their feet. They are completely absorbed in one another while the golden paint surrounds them in a kind of golden halo, so religious, with no reference to time or place." I paused again, collecting my thoughts. "I was wondering why the man's face is obscured while the woman's face shows bliss and delight from the kiss. So pure, so clean, so perfect, so erotic—it startled me."

She hesitated. "I've seen this painting many times, and each time, I notice something new. I agree with you. *The Kiss* is so pure and clean, but you must ask yourself what is pure and clean. Today, I looked at *The Kiss* in a different perspective. Is the painting pure and clean? I asked myself what I meant by that, Verga, and considered the lovers' attitude. For example, think about when lovers kiss and their open mouths join, tongues in each other's mouth. You may think it's wonderful, and indeed it is. On the other hand, consider this: a stranger kisses you and sticks her tongue in your mouth. It will be disgusting. Kissing is an example of both exaggerated qualities, the most wonderful, sexy act. You will consider one act as clean and the other disgusting and dirty. You know, Verga, when I looked at Rodin's sculpture, I think that behind those sealed lips, we humans protect one of the most personal spaces of the body. We part our lips to draw in breath of inspiration or to speak intimate feelings into a beloved's ear, finally surrendering the private self through one's lips to the lips of another in a kiss.

I was taken aback by her observation. She always looked at the world philosophically, but I had never heard her discuss such intimate ideas. I felt a strange excitement listening to her explanation. "Your vision of *The Kiss* is quite remarkable," I said.

She touched my hand. "I'm in pain. Let's head back home. These shoes are killing me. I can hardly walk."

She ambled barefoot to Eugene Strasse where we hailed a taxi. In the taxi, I was thinking. She was clear in her interpretation of *The Kiss*. Philosophers can tell you about works of art in an aspect you had not imagined.

TWELVE

*I*t was late afternoon when we reached the house. She took a seat on the vestibule stair. "My feet are swollen," she said, struggling to remove her new boots.

I leaned over and said, "Let me help you." Bracing her leg between mine, I removed her boot slowly then the other one.

"Thanks," she said. "What a relief. I shouldn't have worn these boots for the first time at the museum."

I still held her leg and instinctively massaged her bare foot. Her legs were warm and delicate. "Oh, that is so good," she said. I proceeded to massage the other leg. "Thanks, Verga. That is very nice of you."

"You're welcome. Thank you for a great day. I've always wanted to visit a museum and see the great paintings."

"I knew you wanted to see those Belvedere paintings. It made me happy to see you enjoy them and the garden. Next time, I would like to take you to the museum quarters to visit the museum of nineteenth- and twentieth-century art." And with that, she stood up. "Let's take a rest." She leaned over and kissed my cheek, then left to her bedroom, leaving a trail of her herbal perfume on my face.

Lying on my bed, I tried to close my eyes, but they were wide open staring at the ceiling, my mind drifting to today's visit and the Klimt *Kiss.* I remembered years past. I had attended art classes as a student in Graz. I had befriended a young female art student, a real flower child. Now I tried to remember what her name was. *Oh yes, Annaliese, a strange creature.* One day, she grabbed me in the school corridor and kissed me on my lips. Then she pushed me against the wall, passionately kissing me, and then walked away. I still remembered her wet, warm lips. One day, she stopped coming to class. I wondered what had happened to that girl. Then my eyelids felt heavy, and I fell asleep.

I woke up looking at the clock. It was seven in the evening. I jumped from bed, washed my face, and put on a clean shirt. Quiet in the house, I walked to the salon and stood in front of the large window facing the Danube Canal. Darkness set on the city. On the canal, a long boat with its pilot lights on glided in silence. My eyes followed the boat. Then it vanished from the edge of the window. My mind was still occupied with today's events: the garden and the woods of Belvedere. I thought of how much I enjoyed the conversation with Constantina. I heard the music of Antonin Dvorak. It crept louder and louder in my head. It was the composition "Silent Woods" op. 68 for piano.

I pulled the chair in front of the Steinway, searching through piles of sheet music on top of the piano. I knew the score by memory, but like a child in need of his security blanket, I looked for the Dvorak music sheets. After I placed the notes on the piano, my hands were poised on the keyboard ready to play when Constantina walked into the room wearing a red flowery Japanese kimono, barefoot. She walked toward me, a smile on her face. "How was your rest?"

"I'm like a new person," I said. "How was yours?"

"I feel energized." She wiggled her toes. "And my legs are rested too."

She glanced at the sheet of music on the piano. "'Silent Woods'? How come?"

"Yes, I'm inspired by the Belvedere Gardens."

"That's great," she said. Then she walked toward the cello stand and pulled a chair next to me. My eyes followed her. Sitting next to me, she tuned the strings. We sat silently for a few seconds, looking at each other. "Let's start."

She pulled on the strings, her eyes gently closed, body swaying back and forth. Her delicate hands fingered the cello strings, up and down. She opened her eyes, focusing on the moving bow, rocking gently like a branch on a tree swaying in the breeze. *She looks so sensual when she plays the cello*, I thought. She reminded me of a painting I saw, a portrait of Suggia Guchemina, a Portuguese cellist. Constantina had her grace and style when playing. I complemented the sounds of her cello with the piano. I closed my eyes, my mind drifting with the resonance of music, hands gliding on the keyboard, our hands pouring the most beautiful sound into the salon. It was like a storm surge of energy being released and unruffled under bright, clear sky. It was magical. We were united as one. I imagined we were two birds flying in the wind through the woods of Belvedere, soaring high then diving low, chasing each other through the woods but not catching each other. We stopped playing. I opened my eyes. She looked at me in silence. A strange feeling crept into me with unknown physical excitement. We smiled at each other. Then she stood up and rested her cello on the stand, then sat in the salon leather armchair, sinking deep into the seat, her face bursting with happiness. I noticed her hair was tucked neat and high with two red Oriental combs. She resembled a geisha.

Hand resting on the armchair, cross-legged, she sat looking at me. "We make the perfect music when we accompany each other. Playing with you is always delightful."

I said, "This is the Dvorak composition needed to be played by two of us."

She smiled. "You know, Verga, Dvorak's music is so different than that of his friend, Brahms's. He is more like Beethoven, romantic like the two of us."

I said, "Talking about romantic composers, for me, Alexander Scriabin comes to mind. This is what I mean." I placed my hand on the keyboard and started to play Scriabin's Piano Sonata no. 4, op. 30. I played the first movement, "Andante," with romantic feelings and a delicate touch, shifting through harmonic play. My fingers touched the piano keys in a mysterious interpretation of Scriabin's notes—mystifying and sensual. Constantina closed her eyes, absorbing the sound echoing from the salon walls. I finished the first movement then paused. On the second movement, "Prestissimo Volando," my hands exploded on the keyboard with youthful virility and a lively, buoyant melody full of life. Then I followed with lyrical sounds coming from the Steinway strings. I repeated the powerful first movement again then went into the end, a recapitulation coda. I ended the sonata with virtuosic playing, my fingers flourishing, gliding over black-and-white keys. Then silence.

She stood up, excited. "Bravo!" she cried, clapping her hands. She approached me and said, "Verga, that play was wonderful, mysterious, lyrical, harmonic. I detected a change in your play today. Your interpretation of Scriabin's music touched me. Bravo!" She reached for me and kissed my cheek.

I held a satisfactory smile and said, "I'm inspired today." I looked at her, how beautiful she was in her red kimono.

As she moved, I sensed her perfume omitting from her hidden body. The image of Klimt's *Kiss* crept into my mind again. I gazed at her beautiful eyes—green, the color of a forest—mysterious. She left a smile on her red wet lips.

I interrupted the silence. "Let's play together again. How about Franz Liszt's Nocturne in E Major for four hands?" In the academy, we occasionally played this music to relax ourselves and release the tension of the day.

I started playing and she joined me in a sonnet no. 104. My eyes closed, sensing her warm body next to me, the image of *Kiss* still on my mind. Lovers embraced. It excited my senses. My hand glided in an unusual way over the keyboard in a perfect union, pouring music from the belly of the Steinway. It was magical. We sat in silence, taking a deep breath of satisfaction. The music still vibrated in my ears. I looked at her. Her cheeks were radiant as if she was scorched by the hot sun. I leaned over her and kissed her lips. It was just a gentle kiss. Her eyes widened. She did not resist my sudden impulse.

Shameful, I lowered my head, looking at the piano keys. I said, "I apologize for my unwanted behavior. I shouldn't have done it."

She was silent for a moment, looking at me. "Nothing to apologize for. Your kiss was a spontaneous expression of your feelings toward me."

"You're not angry at me?" I asked, a relieved tone in my voice.

"Why should I be angry?"

Our eyes met in a deep penetrating gaze, not saying a word. I leaned toward her, my blood surged, and our eyes locked on one another. Lips touched. She closed her eyes. We kissed long. I placed my hand around her waist. I felt her hands over my shoulder, her mouth wet, slightly open. We kissed passionately. Then she stood up, holding my hand. She had a pensive expression, her face blushed, and she gazed at me, face lit with desire. We turned to face each other, gazing deeper and deeper. We were like brewing clouds before a storm. I breathed with excitement. We plunged into each other's arms in a lovers' embrace, mouths open and tongues touching. I felt a rush in my body, sensing her rapid breathing in my mouth. I kissed her neck, then her shoulders. She let out a sound of joy. She found my hand and placed it on her breast, fingers touching. I felt her hard nipple through the kimono and a burning desire in my stomach as my hand glided under her Oriental robe, exploring her bare skin. She let out a low moan, a strange hum. I felt like my pants would explode with my hard one pressing against my underwear. She opened her eyes, looking at me in a haze. Her hand held mine. She looked at me and whispered, "I want all of you."

I trembled, my words stuck in my mind, *Love me. Love me as I love you.*

In silence, she led me upstairs to her bedroom. We entered her private boudoir. It was the first time I was in her inner sanctum. We stood in front of an elaborate art nouveau—decorated bed and white sheets and pillows contrasting the dark wood and golden bed frame. I helped her remove the kimono with trembling hands. Slowly, it was like lifting a curtain from a precious jewel: her body. She took off her balconette bra, exposing her breasts. They were small, round, and firm. She had a ballerina chest, small nipples protruding like dark berries framed in a small circle of pink. When she stood in front of me, her wide sheer low-cut panties revealed she was trimmed into a heart like a ridged marble statue, a figure of a mature woman—broad shoulders, small waist, perfect round thighs, and long legs. Since she had been practicing yoga for many years, her body had no trace of her age. I swallowed hard, my body shaking with anticipation of lovemaking. I kissed her body and breasts. She embraced me tight. Then in a raspy voice, she said, "I will be right back."

I released my grip as she glided toward the bathroom. Standing anxiously next to the bed half undressed, I removed the rest of my clothes except for my underwear. Looking at the bed, I noticed a large painting over the headboard. It was *An Allegory of Venus and Cupid* by the painter Bronzino. It depicted Venus and Cupid engaging in an amorous kiss. Cupid's mother is slipping the tip of her tongue between her son's lips, portraying sly, incestuous carnality. With my eyes on Venus's image, for a moment, her face dissolved into Constantina's. I was mesmerized by the painting when I heard her coming from the bathroom. It was like she had walked from the canvas.

The door half shut spewed a stream of light onto the floor. She stopped at the dresser, switched on the record player, and lit incense. The fragrance evoked the presence of the divine and the flowering gardens of paradise. The sound of waves crashing on the sandy shore poured in a low volume from the speaker. She came to me, removing the white towel from her. I removed my boxer briefs, revealing my youthful frame. We embraced and kissed again, our hands exploring each other's bodies, her legs slightly spread, and my fingers on her Venus gate. I felt slick oil and smelled the scent of her herbal perfume omitting from her lower body. I touched her between her legs. As my fingers explored her, she responded with a sound of pleasure. Then she whispered in my ear, "Please be gentle."

We lay in bed, my hand gliding between her legs. She moved to my touch. Her breath was ecstatic. The low sound of wind and seagulls sounded in the room from the record. She used this nature recording sound during our meditation sessions. It was magical. My heart melted away with lust. I lay in her embrace, gazing at her green dreamy eyes. There was something primal in her look tonight. My hard one pressed against her stomach. I was intoxicated. We were skin to skin. I wanted to unite us in an ancient rhythmical dance, a duet of passion, but I was unsure. It was my first time making love to a woman, and she sensed my hesitation. Her hand got hold of my swollen length, guiding it slowly between her legs. I felt her hands on my buttocks, gently pushing me, inviting me in. Slowly and gently, I felt her lubrication as I entered her. She was tight. She held me, sliding me all the way. As she let out a rush of expelled air, her body relaxed. I rested in her temple. My whole body tingled with waves of pleasure. We were one. Not moving, I felt her tightness melt away. She held me close. We were bound to each other like an oyster to his shell. It was paradise. Our mouths gasped for air as we kissed passionately. Then she whispered into my ear, "Follow me," her hands on my back, legs elevated. She glided me into her. Then I rocked up and down, my head on her shoulder, kissing her sweet-scented neck. I pushed deeper and deeper. With each thrust, she responded with a pleasurable cry. It was music in the making, like piano note swells, push—pull, our bodies were notes of nightingale exploding into crescendo.

I breathed hard and approached my limits. Still following her, I whispered into her ear, "I can't hold anymore." I climaxed with a sudden thunderous force and a loud cry. I felt my body's energy release. Fission was added, fusing our cells into one.

"Don't stop. Follow me," she said with a low, hushed voice. I felt her hands bracing my hips, enfolding me in her cocoon. We thrust into each other until I was exhausted. I slowed down. Then we stopped. We lay out of breath in each other's arms, savoring the moment. Her eyes were wide open abandonment in a warm bliss. She kissed me. Looking at her, I said in a low voice, "I couldn't control myself. I was too excited. It was my first. I will be better next time."

"Shhh." She put her fingers on my lips. Then she kissed me. "You are wonderful. I loved our lovemaking. I never felt this way in a long time. You are loving and gentle." She put me at ease. I lay on her chest listening to her heartbeat, her hands on my back caressing me.

I said, "I have never felt this kind of pleasurable sensation, and I want to give the same to you."

"Darling, you know me and my philosophy on life."

"I know. You follow Eastern philosophy."

"We in the west have a notion that perfect sex is to climax with an orgasm. If not, it's bad sex and a failure. You, darling, reached your orgasm today, and your sensation is now over. It's as if some part of your body is itching; you scratch it, and the sensation is over. I did not reach a climax today, but look at me." She lifted my head holding it with her two hands. Our eyes focused on each other. "I am still excited," she said. "I still feel you in my body. I still feel the pleasure. My entire body still feels the sensation. It will be with me for hours. So reaching a climax is not the ultimate enlightenment. It's not to say that not having a sexual climax is good, but when it comes, it is bliss."

I leaned and kissed her warm red lips. Then I moved out of her, lying next to her on the pillow. I said, "I have a confession. I have always had a crush on you. There were many nights I lay in bed fantasizing about making love to you."

"I felt your feelings toward me. Women can sense it. When you play the piano, when we talk to each other, when we meditate together."

I said, "You were so conservative in looks. Your demeanor was unapproachable. Look, but do not touch. And here we are in each other's arms. You're a different person. We talk about sex. I thought you were practicing celibacy. How wrong was I. Behind those black-and-white clothes in school, I have now discovered a different person, an uninhibited, loving, sensual woman locked in a beautiful body."

"Yes, darling, that's me—a conservative, strict teacher. I had to be. I follow Buddhist ethics and teachings. I know what is right and what is wrong. And wrong would be having intimate relations between teacher and student, but you are not a student anymore. You are twenty-one years old and untouched. It's exciting for me to relieve your youth. I didn't plan this lovemaking with you. It just happened. In fact, I haven't slept with a man in a long time." She paused in silence then said, "I will confess to you. I was attracted to you too. From your good looks to your youthful vigor, your musical talent, and your intellect." She kissed me. "You know, I have desires too. I will confess to you. This morning, I was passing your bathroom, and the door was ajar. I noticed your nude body in the mirror. I stopped for a moment. My heart raced. I felt longing for a man's touch, a feeling that was dormant in me for a while like frost. Tonight, you melted it away, and now I ask myself if I'm still attractive. You know, Verga, for me, time is passing fast. I'm twenty years older. I want to be noticed. I want to be loved. And I want to give love too." She smiled. "I sound like a teacher again."

"I don't mind. I love listening to you talk."

"It's getting late. Let's rest. Darling, shut off the bathroom light." I embraced her warm skin against mine. I wrapped my legs around her body, moving closer to her. I sensed her warm pulse. In the darkness, we looked at each other and smiled. "Good night, my dear." She kissed my lips.

THIRTEEN

I dreamt she was naked in my arms. I felt her. My eyes opened. It was not a dream. I was lying next to her. She was asleep, though, her bare flesh warm against mine. As I looked at the clock, it was six in the morning. Sunrays poured through the open folds of the curtains, spreading into the dark room. I reached and kissed her neck, shoulders, and back. She moved. My desire reignited, and I fully awakened. She looked at me with clear eyes, smiled, and then embraced me. She was still sleepy but alert. "Good morning, darling," she said in a low voice.

"Good morning," I said, kissing her inviting wet lips then her berry-pink nipples, sliding my tongue over her firm stomach.

Her hands rolled me over her body. Our mouths joined in a passionate kiss—a hungry deep kiss, tongue to tongue. I felt that she wanted me. Then suddenly, she slipped from the embrace, stood up, and said, "I will be right back," gliding naked toward the bathroom.

I was surprised by her sudden move. I lay back awaiting her return. She appeared at the door of the bathroom, light shining on her body. She shut the light then came to bed. Her black hair now tacked high on her head was decorated with two large red Oriental combs. I imagined us positioned together like the combs in the top of her beautiful black hair. Lying next to me, she asked, "How did you sleep?" while her fingers ran deep into my long hair.

"I had such a restful sleep," I replied. "What about you?"

"I slept and dreamt that I was in paradise." She glanced at the clock on the night table. "Six thirty? It's early. Maria is shopping today, and I expect her at ten."

I was half listening to her, engrossed in kissing her neck, my hard one fully awakened, pressing against her body. She said, "The mattress is too soft, and last night, I almost sunk into it."

She jumped out of bed, and I followed her to the wooden parquet floor, unsure of what she meant by that. She wrapped herself with the bedsheet and walked toward the windows, adjusting the curtains. The morning sun shone full blast into the room. "It will be a beautiful day today," she said. "Help me with the blanket."

I grabbed the blanket, placing it on the floor. Light shined on the spread blanket, inviting us to its warmth. I lay on my back, looking at her, and she placed a pillow under my buttocks. I was intrigued by her move. I lay there with excitement. *What's next?* I asked myself. She crouched over me with her legs spread apart, squatting, her Venus wide open. I lay there. I was her slave. Her hand got a hold of my erected penis, slowly gliding it to her open gate, not letting me enter. She leaned over, and we kissed deeply. Her tongue played with mine. Her mouth was sweet with a hint of menthol and a mixture of herbs. My desire exploded with anticipation. She lowered her body slowly, sliding over my erection. I felt her differently than last night. Today, it was void of tightness. I was rippled with pleasure. It reminded me of the feeling when I play Schumann's arabesque on the piano. My fingers made their way to her breast, loving her. Her eyes closed. She was on cloud nine. We moved, starting slow, thrusting deep into each other, in and out. Now my mind exploded, hearing a piano melody, "Fantaisie sur un air Russe," and a resplendent calm overtook me. I lost time and place. She took a deep breath then lowered her body. I felt her full weight on my legs. Her tempo was slow and then fast. She moved for a long time like a spirited finale. She rushed with an explosive twist, in and out like a conductor rushing to the end. Her face contorted with pleasure, body shaking with spasms. She let out a strange sound. I looked at her face. I was concerned. I whispered, "Are you all right? Am I hurting you?"

Her eyes opened momentarily, gazing at me with deep dark-colored eyes like a forest in a storm. "No, don't stop." Then her eyes shut again.

I felt my limits now, and I rushed to the mountaintop with a rapture of pleasure. I let out a cry. As I held her waist tight, we moved together steadily and then stopped, gasping for air like fish in a water tank. She collapsed on my chest, exhausted. We lay in silence for a while, listening to our hearts beating in unison. In a raspy voice, I heard her say, "That was the bliss of karma. I have not felt like that in a long time."

Excited, I said, "I reached the top too. I hope I was not too rough on you." I still felt her warmth.

"You were wonderful, gentle, and passionate." Her lips kissed my chest, her hand gliding over my body, resting on my now-subsided erection. She whispered, "You are circumcised."

I was surprised by her statement. "Yes," I said. "Father told me that when I was ten days old, my mother took me to the town's rabbi to be circumcised. It was my mother's decision. It caught my father off guard. After all, my mother was Jewish and had converted to Christianity. Her answer was 'Jesus was a Jew and was circumcised too.' What do you call that in Hebrew? I forget."

"Brith milla," she said.

I looked at her in a surprised way. "How come you know this?"

"Mayer was a Jew. Although he never practiced the religion, once he said to me, no one asked his permission to be circumcised. It was his parents' decision. You know, Verga, I wanted to know more about the chosen people, so I read every book on the Jewish subject in our library. I learned some Hebrew words. I remember my husband saying the quackery of penis pruning, the degradation of the flesh, for the greater glory of God, as God especially loves Jews for it. Isn't it ridiculous?" She turned around and faced me smiling. "You know, darling, in ancient Greece, the aesthetics of defining the body as beautiful is not to alter any part of it artificially. I say leave this aesthetics debate to philosophers." She winked then said, "Your mother, darling, wanted to preserve her Jewish heritage in you."

I replied, "I know almost nothing about the Jewish people or their customs. What did you learn from books?"

Her face grew serious. There was silence for a long moment. Then she said, "Moses did not write the Torah, and even the scriptures are not the word of God. I quote the Jewish writer and philosopher Lion Feuchtwanger: 'What is written is changed and becomes the death of spoken word. It is a mask and a distortion what wood is to the living tree. Only the mouth to the wise does it rise up and live.' I learned that when reading the Torah, one must give due value to every letter and word.

For example, did you know Shema, the centerpiece of the morning and evening Jewish prayer, has 248 words corresponding to the 248 limbs in our body?"

"How interesting," I said. I thought that she was a wise teacher. She always explained to me music and art and gave mundane things such grave details. She always opened my mind. "I am an unbeliever."

"Verga, you were born as a Jew, so carry your heritage with dignity. Remember, all faiths are good, so long as they lead to good behavior. It is not shameful to be a Jew. Now they have a state of their own, Israel." Then she changed the subject. "Let's meditate."

She stood up and extended her hand toward me, lifting me from the floor. She wrapped herself in the blanket and then opened the windows, fresh air pouring in. As she placed the blanket near the window, her naked body was illuminated by early morning sunrays. I admired her silhouette. We assumed the lotus position facing each other, two naked bodies like Adam and Eve looking at each other without any guilt. Holding my hands, she placed them into her palms, eyes closed, and we sank into deep meditation. My mind cleared of our amour as I welcomed the peaceful void.

It was hard to practice piano for hours, starting at eight in the morning with an hour break for lunch then resuming for four hours of practice in the afternoon. In the evening, we took a walk along the Danube Canal then ate a light dinner. It became routine. Constantina did not have a television in the house. In the evenings, I read and listened to records. We conversed, reflecting on my day's practice and taking notes on my performance. She insisted that I have a good eight-hour sleep every night. We abstained from lovemaking. She said, "Leave the lovemaking for the weekend. It will distract you and suck your good energy." But it was hard for me to control my desire. Our past lovemaking was on my mind. I tasted the forbidden fruit of paradise, and I was hungry for more; however, I refrained from showing any amour during the day. I behaved like a student with his teacher in school in front of Maria, the housekeeper. In the evenings when Maria was out of the house, my affection toward Constantina came out. My behavior changed. I became a romantic again, but she was a gatekeeper and controlled our desires. She was loving, intimate, and allowed it up to a point. She had a strong character, and I complained to a deaf ear. She insisted on practice, practice, practice.

"Your playing is getting better," she said, but by Thursday, I was tired, and my play lacked passion. She said, "Your play is muted and lacks coloration and enthusiasm, too mechanical. What happened?"

"I'm hurting all over my body."

"That is no excuse. You've done it before many times."

"My mind is adrift. I need a break."

"It's hard on me too, but I don't complain. You need to keep going. The competition is next week. You must be ready like a good athlete. You have to be in the best shape to win."

"I will win. I promise. I will do my best. I'm a good player. It's all in my mind. I need rest to clear my head."

She stood up and took my hand into hers. "Darling," she said, "I understand. I'm pushing you too hard. You're right. Come to the bathroom. I'll fill the tub with hot water. Soak your body and rest. It is almost 6:00. You have played enough for today."

Naked, a towel behind my neck, I rested my body in the warm water. With herbal vapor in my nostrils, my mind at ease, I closed my eyes and sank into peaceful rest. I lost track of time. Tartini's trumpet concerto was playing in the bedroom. I sensed Constantina's footsteps in the bathroom and opened my eyes. "I need soaking too," she said. She touched the water. "It's cold," and proceeded to pour more hot water into the tub. Standing naked, she opened the bottle of herbal oil, pouring it into the water. The smell of exquisite flowers filled the air. She entered the tub. "Move a little. Make room for me." As she sat opposite me, our legs between each other's, I got hold of her hand.

"Let's make love," I said.

She smiled. "We promised each other not until the weekend."

"I can't control my desire." My legs touched and fondled between her legs.

Enjoying my touch, she closed her eyes and relaxed into the water, saying nothing. I closed my eyes and felt her leg between mine, caressing my awakened hard one. We lay like that until our bodies sapped all the warmth from the water. "The water has gotten cold," I said, standing up, my hand extended toward her.

She came out of the tub with water dripping, running over her body. She placed a towel over me, and we kissed. Without a word, we stepped into the bedroom. I took her lubricating oil and rubbed it into her warm gate. Silently, we plunged into uncontrolled, passionate lovemaking on the floor. It was wild, a kind of rough sex. When it was all over, we lay out of breath on the floor, looking at the blankness of the ceiling, smiling, satisfied like kids just finishing a delicious, sweet dessert. It was a sweet lovemaking.

The next day, I was full of enthusiasm. My piano playing was flawless with a new fervor. "Verga, this is your best play this week."

"Thanks to you." She smiled.

On Saturday, I had a tailor fitting in town. I ordered a formal jacket and pants for my upcoming performance. My wardrobe until today consisted of a few shirts, a few black trousers, one black blazer, and one pair of jeans, which I just bought for myself with the money that was given to me. I had been a full-time student. In these past four years, all my modest needs had been provided by the academy. I had earned pocket money at school working as a helper to a gardener, and on Sundays, I had been a tour guide at the academy. Now I realized I needed to find employment. At the tailor shop, I chose an unconventional jacket, black and gray with a paisley pattern, the latest style from London. Constantina said, "It looks great on you. I hope Dr. Richter will not object. It's a unique look."

I said, "I don't care. I had enough of the black-and-white uniform that I was wearing for years." It was the sixties, and color was everywhere, and I wanted to be different.

In the afternoon, we arrived in a taxi at the Imperial Academy of Music and Performing Arts in the heart of Vienna. I needed to select a piano for the competition and my performance for the following Saturday. The stage manager greeted us and gave us a tour backstage in the concert hall—a lovely, classic old institution. On the stage were two Steinway pianos waiting for me to try. One was manufactured in New York, the other one from the workshop in Hamburg. All Steinway pianos are handcrafted with very little automation. Each piano had a distinctive character of its own. Otto, the piano tuner, greeted me on stage. "I can tune the pianos to match the one in Professor Heilbronner's salon," he said.

Sitting in front of the Hamburg Steinway, I played Mozart's "Rondo Alla Turca." Then I played the same melody on the New York Steinway. "I'm not sure if I'm satisfied with the sound of either one," I said. I tried the Hamburg Steinway again then the New Yorker, saying, "I think I like the New York Steinway better. It has a classical tone." I asked Otto to adjust it and tighten up the strings on the minor chords. Then I tried it again. "It still sounds deep, not quite clear, and, in the end, an echo too."

Otto adjusted the strings like an auto mechanic under the hood. Satisfied, he said, "Try now."

I played scales on it back and forth. "Now it sounds brilliant! Not too round, and the echo is gone. Great! I choose this piano." I pulled out the piano bench, which was adjustable to my height. I played for ten minutes Alexander Scriaban's *Fantaisie* op. 28.

Clapping from a few audience members followed the end of my play. I bowed slightly toward them. Constantina walked onto the stage smiling. "You sounded great! Clear, consistent, brilliant, and the acoustics in the hull are fabulous."

"Thanks." Looking at the audience, I asked, "Who are those people?"

"Oh, just the academy staff of the general manager's office."

"And who is that man in the front row in the blue jacket taking notes?"

"Oh, that's Emile von Fuch, Mimi Schmidt's piano instructor and music manager. She's one of your competitors." I thought his looks were not imperious. "Mimi is scheduled to be here in an hour to play," said Constantina. "She prefers to play on her own piano. It was delivered here yesterday."

"It's good to be rich."

We stepped from the stage. A man with a striped shirt and brown jacket came rushing toward us. "Excuse me," he said. "May I introduce myself?"

Looking at him, he looked familiar. He introduced himself. "Odon."

I interrupted him. "I know you, Odon. We met years ago in the Red Cross shelter."

"That's right. I want to apologize for my unethical behavior at that time."

"I forgive you, Odon. That was a long time ago." I introduced him to Constantina.

Odon said, "I work for the *Wien [Vienna] Evening Gazette.* Verga, I want to make up for my unprofessional journalistic behavior. Can we sit in the lobby? I would like to explain."

Once in the lobby, Odon said, "Verga, with your permission, I want to write a story in the *Evening Gazette.* I've followed your piano talent. I heard you've played in a few recitals. You are a great pianist. Your selection as a finalist in this prestigious competition is a real achievement for any pianist, but hardly anyone knows your name in Austria except for a few in the music circle. In comparison, one of your competitors, Mimi Schmidt, her name is well-known. She is a graduate of this academy. She comes from an illustrious family. She's talented at the piano, and her looks resemble Romy Schneider, a popular Austrian actress who played Sissi. You are at a disadvantage. You are not a native born but Hungarian like me. As a Hungarian, I want to put you, so to speak, on the map, make you a household name. That publicity will be good for you, and I can write it. Let me interview you and Professor Heilbronner and take a few photos. I will make you famous overnight." He was looking at me and then Constantina. She was dumbfounded. He knew how to be charming and spoke eloquently.

She said, "Mr. Odon, please give me your business card, and I will contact you."

"Great." He handed his credentials. Then we parted.

Riding in a taxi toward home, sitting in silence, I was thinking about what Odon said: "I will make you famous."

"Darling," she said, interrupting my thoughts, "let's stop here and walk home so we can talk."

"Great idea," I said.

Walking at a slow pace, she said, "I need to check this Odon for his credentials. The newspaper he claims to work for is an evening daily, has a good reputation, and is popular with readers. It will be good publicity for you. Oh, by the way, I did not tell you that you will be interviewed by the ORF TV station with the other competitors for a special broadcast on the evening news for the 8:00 p.m. special to be aired Tuesday."

"How come I find this out today?"

"Forgive me. I did not want to distract you from your practice."

We walked in silence; then she spoke again, "Verga, Mimi is your main competitor. The others are good piano players, but Mimi is the real talent like you. If you don't know, remember she has her faults. She is arrogant, spoiled, immature, younger than you are, and known to be short-tempered. She is a freak when it comes to public performances. In the past, she had walked away from a performance. Her excuse, the audience was not to her liking. It's unfortunate that the competition committee selected her academy for the performance. It's her alma mater. Dr. Richter tried to change the location without success. Anyway, you're lucky. Your cast lot came. You play second in the competition. Dr. Richter said it will spook Mimi."

I was riveted by Constantina's account of my main competitor, Mimi. "I saw Mimi in her second round of competition. She's a truly beautiful creature and talented pianist. I will have to work harder. Maybe Odon can help me too."

We reached the house. The rays of the end of the day were sprinkled on the Danube Canal like sparks of gold. I turned toward her and said, "It's the weekend."

"Indeed," she said, smiling.

She took hold of my hand. We rushed into the house.

FOURTEEN

The phone had not stopped ringing from reporters requesting interviews with me for music magazines, recording companies, BBC Radio, and GDR TV station. Odon was right. The aftermath of the airing ORF TV broadcast featuring all the piano contestants and publishing my story in the *Wien Evening Gazette* gave me my fifteen minutes of fame, to which I was not accustomed.

Constantina was not amused. The constant barrage of phone calls disturbed the daily routine. She asked Dr. Richter for help. He appointed Rudolph to be my public relations advisor. He made his office during the day in Constantina's library. From then on, all requests for interviews had to pass through him. He was my official gatekeeper.

"Hans is on the line," Rudolph said.

I picked up the phone. "Hello, Hans, it is nice to hear your voice. How are you?"

"I'm fine. How are you doing? Congratulations! You made the 8:00 news. I watched it. You look great. We are all very proud of you, and my family sends their regards."

"Thanks, Hans. I miss you, my friend."

"How is your practice coming along? The big event is this Saturday. Are you nervous?"

"I'm practicing every day. You know Professor Wordzinka would make me practice and practice."

"I know. She's a tough teacher. She won't let you stop until blood is coming out of your fingers. I pity you."

I paused. "I have no complaints. I'm not a student anymore. It's different now."

"Well, I know you. You are very disciplined, not like me. I want you to know that my family is coming to cheer you on. Father arranged first-row tickets for all of us."

"Hans, your family's being there will make a big difference in my play. Thank you for your support and friendship. How is Ingrid?"

"She's fine. She loves your sculpture of *The Kiss* and placed it on her study table. She's eager to see you. We'll all be staying in our apartment in Vienna for the next week."

"That's great. I apologize for not calling you. I'm busy with my preparation for the big event. It's an once-in-a-lifetime opportunity for me. I sent a thank-you note to your parents for all they have done for me."

"Verga, my parents love you. It isn't a big deal for my father. Oh, by the way, I had a serious talk with him regarding my future. I decided to join his business to get experience in sales. He is sending me to America. He has offices on Wall Street and in Boston."

"That's great, but what about your career in music?"

"Verga, you know I love the cello, but I don't have the drive and passion for it the way you have for the piano. I want to experience other things in life—business, overseas, and women. You know what I mean?"

"Yes, I understand you. I still think you're a good cello player."

"Thanks, Verga. Don't work too hard. After you win, as I predict, we shall celebrate it in town. I'll take you to places to meet some girls. We'll have fun. You need to relax, my friend."

"Thanks."

"I took too much of your time. I'll let you go and see you on Saturday."

Once I hung up, the phone rang again. "Professor Heilbronner, it's for you," said Rudolph.

She was on the phone for a long hour.

That evening, Constantina and I took our daily walk along the Danube Canal. It was the only time we could be together in private. She said, "Verga, I got a call from my sister-in-law, Ruth. She and her husband, Richard, are coming for a week. They decided to make a stop in Vienna while they're on their way to the Dolomites. I wrote to her about you, and they decided to attend your performance. They're coming tomorrow for dinner. Isn't that exciting? I haven't seen them in five years."

"How nice. I'm delighted to meet someone from your family. How old are Ruth and Richard?"

"She's seventy-two if I'm not mistaken. And Richard is the same age, I think."

"Where are they from?"

"London."

"Did you ever visit them?"

"Yes, eight years ago. Now Richard is retired. He worked for the Ministry of Finance as an economist. Really lovely couple. Unfortunately, the only son they had passed away in World War II. He was a pilot."

We walked in silence. I hugged her. She leaned her head against my shoulder. "Verga, tomorrow, you are to practice Ravel's piano concerto in G major. The winner of the competition is to play with the conservatory's piano orchestra the next day at the presentation gala. I believe it will be you." She hugged me tight.

A rush of hot blood flowed in my veins and ignited my heart with energy. I reflected on the past few days. They were the most stressful in my life. Rudolph and Constantina ran my daily schedule, and I felt like a robot. I meditated twice a day to calm my nerves. I could not sleep and lost appetite and weight. I constantly thought of the competition. The only sane person in the house was Constantina. Like an experienced captain on a ship, she guided me through the days. She sat with me during all my meditations, stayed next to me during all my practices, and made sure I ate right and rested my hands. Now that Rudolph was around the house, I was careful not to let out our secret. It drove me crazy. By nighttime, I was exhausted.

On Friday evening, a day before the big event, I met Ruth and Richard—a nice couple, very polite, very English. "Where are you staying?" I asked Richard.

"At the Hotel Josefshof in the museum and town hall quarters."

"I love Josefstadt. Many good restaurants, popular theaters, and museums. Don't miss the Kunsthistorisches Museum," I said.

"Indeed, we have been there during our last visit. This time, we would like to see the Natural History Museum."

"That's a great idea. I'm honored to have you at my competition."

"Young man, when Constantina wrote about you being selected as a finalist, we decided to make a slight detour. We are very fond of

Constantina and wanted to share this special occasion with her. Young man, I wish you the best of luck."

"Thanks."

At precisely 7:00 p.m., Dr. Richter came to the house. Maria served schnapps in the salon. We all got comfortable sitting around the Steinway piano, conversing with each other. Constantina said to me, "Verga, please dress up in formal attire. We are ready to listen to your rehearsal."

I went to my room, dressed up, and came to the salon. All eyes were on me. Constantina was dressed in a black miniskirt and purple shirt. She wore pearls on her long neck. Her face, radiant, was full of encouragement. Rudolph commented, "I like your jacket."

Dr. Richter glanced at my paisley blue-gray nouveau jacket but said nothing.

"Indeed," said Richard. "Splendid."

I bowed slightly then sat in front of the piano. This would be my last rehearsal before my final presentation tomorrow. Sitting and looking at the piano fallboard for a few seconds, I turned and glanced at Constantina. She gave me a slight smile of encouragement. I played Franz Schubert's *Impromptus*, D. 899 (op. 90) no.1 in C Minor, no. 2 in E-flat Major, and no. 3 in G-flat Major. Like a poet, I delivered a stormy, romantic melody from the Steinway strings. My play recalled one of those harmonicas of which romantic Vienna held the monopoly, which the music masters Anton Bruckner, Beethoven, Joseph Haydn, and others so ingeniously constructed. I finished no. 3 with a slow deliberate play with tranquil air and a silvery, veiled tone. The entire play was constructed with my attentive listeners in mind. My inspiration of Schubert's *Impromptus* was like joining water and crystal, brilliant and clear. Notes vibrated in the salon as I finished. I lifted my fingers from the keyboard and paused for ten seconds. Then I played "The Grand Paganini Études" with such passion, ringing the imaginative hand bell with my fingers, striking the keyboard like a diamond cutter, splitting the sound into a thousand facets. The Steinway strings vibrated in a latent fire of Franz Liszt's notes of *La Campanella*. I stopped playing. The sound of the piano still vibrated in the salon. Silence.

Then the room erupted with applause. "Bravo!" They all stood up clapping. My eyes were on Constantina, her eyes watery with excitement. I bowed low.

"Brilliant performance," Dr. Richter said. "That is the way to play a piano. Bravo, Verga!" He turned to Constantina. "My dear, you are a masterful teacher. From a rough stone, you made a brilliant gem. I am proud of you both."

"Thanks," Constantina said, smiling. "You're all welcome to the dining room. Let's celebrate." Then she turned to me. "Verga, please change your clothes. You need them to be crisp and clean for tomorrow."

As we sat at the table, Maria served her Polish delicacy, pierogi with meat and cabbage, Dr. Richter's favorite. He placed his hand on Constantina's. "Dear, you are such a lucky lady having a talented cook like Maria. I don't know how you manage to keep your figure."

"Indeed," Richard said.

"I don't eat like that every day. Today is a special occasion, and Maria prepared dishes that you all like."

"Wine anyone?" Rudolph poured Riesling from the Wachau district, full-bodied Smaragd style.

Dr. Richter raised his glass, looking at me. He stood up. "For your success, Verga." Then he turned to Constantina. "To my best teacher."

We all emptied our glasses.

Maria served stuffed cabbage with meat in tomato sauce then mushroom soup. For the main dish, a platter from the ocean—fish with roasted potatoes, mushrooms, and eggs served with herbs. Rudolph opened another bottle of wine that Richard and Ruth brought, Austria's most popular, Gruner Veltliner 1958 vintage Kabinett.

Dr. Richter turned to me. "Are you ready to perform like today?"

"Yes."

Ruth interrupted me. "I don't know how you piano players can perform so confidently in public. I would be nervous. My knees would shake."

"I agree." Richard looked at me.

I answered, "I'm slightly nervous and have butterflies in my stomach. It's normal for me before any performance."

Dr. Richter poured apricot schnapps. Tasting it, he turned to Constantina. "Where did you get this delicious stern?"

"It's the same one I always serve you. I got it from Frauenhuber Café."

"Oh yes, I forgot. It's delicious."

Dinner resumed for a while as we became acquainted with one another. Soon, Dr. Richter tapped his fork on the crystal glass. "Please,

I'm sorry to interrupt you. I would like to remind everyone of tomorrow's schedule. We need to be at the Imperial Academy two hours before the performance. Verga, you are to play second, after Anton Wolf. Then Mimi Schmidt follows, and last is Siegfried Reger." He wiped his forehead with a handkerchief then continued, "I listened to the piano plays of Anton and Siegfried. They are promising piano players but are no match for you. Your main competitor is Mimi Schmidt. She is a powerful pianist."

Rudolph interrupted. "The music critics have already concluded that she will be the winner. All bets are on her. They wrote glowing articles." He pulled newspaper clippings from his red notebook.

Dr. Richter said, "Let's not listen to the critics. I've learned that in my long career in this business. They criticized Mahler's symphonies, which had enthusiastic public reception, but the critics did not understand it. One critic wrote, 'Mahler lacked talent even more spectacularly that he lacked genius.'"

Rudolph closed his notebook, and Dr. Richter pulled a sheet of paper from his jacket. "Let me talk about the judges of the competition." He adjusted his spectacles. "Sabrina Anna Sussmayr, national teacher of the year in 1959, piano critic, author of *Execess Music of Modernism*, and professor at Erasmus Conservatory." He lifted his head, saying, "Very respected music teacher and promoter of the new way of teaching piano. Sergey Ivanov, a respected Russian conductor of Lennin Grad Conservatory. I met him only once. Sensitive, thoughtful character. That's all that I know of him. Johann Nepomok Heselt, conductor of Vienna Imperial Conservatory, classicist, famously abrasive but very generous with his time." He turned to me, saying, "Verga, you have to impress this judge more than others. He has very keen hearing. He will pick up the minutest mistake on the keyboard. Professor Carl Eisler, gifted concert pianist, teacher, altered the history of the modern keyboard, Bohemian in look. He has a reputation of a kind of sage among the young audience. He will be the most receptive to your piano playing." He folded the list and put it back into his pocket and removed his spectacles.

I was attentively listening to him. He turned to me and said, "Verga, I quote Johannes Brahms: 'Playing music without craftsmanship and inspiration is a mere reed shaking in the wind.' Do not try to impress the judges. Be yourself. Make your play exciting. Keep it alive. Play with inspiration, and you will win."

Richard and Rudolph tapped on their crystal wine glasses. "Well said."

Constantina said, turning to Rudolph, "This past week has been one of my most hectic experiences. I want to thank you, Rudolph, for keeping the media at bay."

I stood up with a glass of wine in my hand. "Thank you, all, for your encouragement and support. I thank especially my beloved teacher. If I win tomorrow, it will be because of you." I turned and looked at Constantina. She grinned, bearing some of her white teeth. I took her hand and kissed it, looking into her eyes. I leaned and kissed Constantina on her cheeks and whispered in her ear, "Darling, I love you." She slightly pressed my hand.

Constantina said, "You gentlemen can go to the balcony. I know some of you would like to have a smoke. We women will clear the dishes."

It was a beautiful, warm July night. Rudolph offered cigars. Richard took one, but I shook my head.

Rudolph and Dr. Richter lit theirs in his silver holder, puffing smoke. He asked Richard, "Where will you be staying in Italy?"

"We're planning on taking a few excursions in the Dolomites then settle for three weeks at Malcesine by the shores of Lago Di Garda and the foot of Monte Baldo."

"Beautiful area. I love the Veneto Plain," Dr. Richter said.

Richard turned toward me. "I invited Constantina and you to stay with us. We rented a small house. There is plenty of room for all of us."

I was surprised by the invitation. "Thanks, Richard. I don't know what my schedule will be for next week. I have interviews with orchestra conductors. If I cannot join you, I will take a rain check."

"Splendid," said Richard, puffing his cigar, glancing at the Danube Canal.

Constantina served coffee and apple strudels. We conversed for half an hour; then Dr. Richter stood up and said, "It's getting late, almost 8:00 p.m., and tomorrow is a busy day. Shall we say good night?"

Maria and the guests left. I sat in the salon thinking of tomorrow's competition. Constantina's voice awakened me from my thoughts. "Verga, please help me with the dishes."

She handed me the china, and I placed them in a dining room dressoir as she said, "Verga, your playing today was exquisite. The hard practice has paid off."

"Thanks. I had a pleasant evening. I enjoyed talking to everyone. Dr. Richter was in a good mood today."

"He told me he's very optimistic for your performance."

I turned around and pulled Constantina to my body. She had a plate in her hand. I took it and set it on the table. Hugging her and looking into her eyes, I said, "It's all because of you."

Her green eyes sparkled, and she smiled. Then I uttered the words, "I love you."

Her eyes opened wide. Before she answered, I kissed her red lips then her neck. She embraced me. The smell of her fragrance awakened my desire. I whispered in her ear, "I like your new perfume. It smells like sugar and cloves."

In a low voice, she said, "This is Arpége. I'm glad you like it."

My hand glided over her body as I kissed her neck. "I love your new skirt."

Our mouths joined in a long wet kiss. She sensed my desire and whispered, "Let's go upstairs."

"Let's make love here."

Her face showed surprise for a moment. Then she whispered, "Darling, shut the light."

We embraced again in the dark dining room. A faint light came from the window. The reflection of the half moon on the dressoir's glass doors illuminated Constantina's face. *She's so beautiful,* I thought. *She resembles Klimt's painting of Judith.*

Lust overtook me. Holding her buttocks over her skirt, I lifted her off the floor. Surprised by my move, she wrapped her legs around me. Then, gently, I placed her on the table. "Oh, you're so strong," she whispered in an amused voice.

"You're not heavy."

We kissed, mouths open, tongues caressing each other. "Help me with this shirt."

I unbuttoned her purple shirt and let it fall to the floor, exposing her delicate but firm small breasts protruding from her brassiere, kissing them. Her hands rested on my back, her head slightly tilted back, enjoying my caresses. I removed her brassiere and moved my tongue over her nipples. She let out a sound of joy. Our mouths joined in a passionate kiss. She shifted her hands to remove her skirt. She wrapped her legs around my thighs, sitting on the table naked except for her black panties.

With sturdy hands, she unbuttoned my shirt, exposing my chest, kissing my neck then upper torso. Her lips were like a hot iron scorching my bare chest. I let out a sound of pleasure. My shirt dropped to the floor. Her hands glided over to my trousers and unbuckled my belt. They followed my top. She removed my briefs, running her hand over my love throb. I trembled from her touch and gently laid her body on the table. Her legs up, I removed her nylon stockings then her black underwear. She placed her legs on my shoulders. The image of Hokusai's painting of the ama diver surfaced in my mind. I kissed Constantina's thighs then her Venus, my tongue caressing her open gates. Her pleasured low moans echoed in the room. My tongue moved up to her flat belly, resting on her breast. My fingers caressed her wet Venus possessively, sweeping over her sensitive, aroused rosebud. She let out a cry of delight and let her legs down from my shoulders and placed them on the edge of the table, hands flattened, gripping each end of the tableside. Legs apart, she lifted her head momentarily, looking at me eyes wide open, anticipating what was to come. Her mouth opened, breathing with excitement. Then she tossed her head back, lying on the white table cloth, spreading her legs into the akimo yoga position, hands on her legs. My fingers gently parted her flesh. My tongue followed suit. Her moans were wild and joyous. With legs relaxed, she lifted her head, gazing at me, her black hair unraveled on her shoulders. Hands gripped mine. She whispered, "I want you closer." As she pulled me over, I felt her warm skin. Our fingers entwined, I came close to her Venus gates. I let my heart unlock her gate, not rushing, aware of her tightness, entering gently. As Constantina lifted her head again in anticipation of pain, my hands embraced her shoulders as our mouths joined. "Be gentle," she whispered in my ear.

"You tell me when to stop." I pressed down slowly then stopped. She let out a rush of air awaiting tightness, but there was none. Pushing deeper and deeper, I reached her temple. While I gazed at her face—her mouth open, lips wet, eyes closed, belly tight—she relaxed. Her hands gripped mine then fingers loosened. We were joined as one. I closed my eyes, standing and embracing her. I took a deep breath. My skin tingled with pleasure. Slowly, I moved in and out of her Venus. She joined me, thrusting firmly into me. I felt her fingers digging into my arms.

She whispered again, "I want you closer." I thrust harder. She let herself uninhibitedly move in and out with faster movements, taking me in deeper. Then her belly began to tense. Her hands on my back, her fingers dug into my flesh. I felt pain. Then she quivered. Her orgasm built so quickly, jolting her entire body. She let out a cry. Then she exploded with a loud moan, her head tossing sideways. I leaned over her body. She put her legs around my waist, wrapping me tight as her mouth searched for mine. I felt her tongue. My hard one tingled with spasms. I reached my limit and stopped moving. I lifted her from the table, still united, holding her. I walked her to the nearest chair. Her body embraced me tightly. She whispered in my ear, "Don't stop."

We sat down, and she kissed me passionately, gasping for air. She placed her spread legs against the wall and tilted her body back, her black hair unraveled, chaotic, like grapevines, as she held my neck tight for support. Closed eyed, she moved around me, sliding in and out, pushing her legs from the wall, thrusting hard. She climaxed again with a loud cry, letting her legs down on the floor, riding my hard one up and down. I reached my climax, crying and moaning with pleasure. We moved, pushed, and twisted into each other until we were out of breath and exhausted. Sitting in the chair in each other's arms, she broke the silence. "My god, this was karma I haven't had in a long time," she said in a muffled voice, kissing my neck.

"You came so fast."

"I did. I was surprised at myself," she said, her face gleaming with satisfaction. She bit my ear gently.

I felt a spark of pleasure tingling my head. "You climaxed so many times today, darling."

"We women can when lovemaking is just right, and today, I was in the right state of mind."

I was still aroused and hard inside her. She felt me. "You're not tired?"

"No, what time is it anyway?"

She looked at her watch. "10:00. Let's take a shower and go to bed. We have a busy day tomorrow."

She stood up, sliding from my penis. I put her back on my lap—kissing her breast, looking into her eyes—and said, "I love you."

She kissed me. "Verga, darling, how sweet are your words, but love is only words. You don't have to say it. I feel your love. Do you feel mine?"

"Yes, I do."

"It's late, and you need your rest. I love you too."

FIFTEEN

Dressed in jeans, my formal wear in a bag, I went to the salon. Constantina and Rudolph were waiting for me. "Are you ready for the big event?" he asked.

"Yes, I'm ready."

Constantina was dressed in a formal black dress and a short white jacket. Today, she had a classy hairdo, mimicking Sophia Loren's slick Vidal Sassoon hairstyle, a string of pearls on her neck. She glanced at her watch. "In five minutes, the taxi should be coming," she said in a clam voice, examining my hair. Then with her fingertips, she loosened up my stiff, conservative hairstyle. "Now you look better." She winked. "Do you have all your clothes in the bag?"

"Yes."

"The new bowtie and handkerchief?"

"Yes, thanks."

The sound of a horn was heard from outside. Rudolph glanced through the window. "The taxi's here. Let's go."

Dressed in a black formal tuxedo, Rudolph followed us to the front door. "You forgot your purse and gloves!" I yelled, grabbing them.

"Thanks, Verga. My mind is somewhere else today," she said.

"To where?" the driver asked.

"Vienna Imperial Conservatory," Rudolph answered, sitting next to the driver.

In the backseat, Constantina asked, "Are you nervous?"

"A little."

She took my hand in hers. "You will do fine. Take a deep breath."

"I did."

"Take another one."

At the conservatory, Rudolph slipped into a crowd to admire the stage. An usher dressed in a tuxedo greeted Constantina and me. "Good evening, Frau Heilbronner, Herr Caszar. Please follow me. I will take you to your room."

We walked down the stairs to the lower level. "Please." The usher opened the door.

The room was small with two couches, two chairs, a dresser with a large makeup mirror, and a counter with a small sink. I hung my clothes on the stand and took a seat on the couch. The room was brightly lit and carpeted. Walls were painted pale yellow. A vase with red roses sat on the dresser. Constantina took off her jacket and placed it on the chair, examining her face in the mirror. "I'm going upstairs to meet the master of ceremony. I will be back," said Constantina. She glanced at the large clock on the wall: twelve thirty-five. "Oh, in half an hour, we're expected upstairs for the pre-competition reception to meet the judges, contestants, and a few special guests. Then at 2:00, the competition starts, so while I'm out, please dress up."

There was a knock on the door. "Please come in," I said, buttoning my shirt.

It was Rudolph. He held a water pitcher and a box of candy. "Compliments of the stage manager," he said, opening the box. "Mozartkugel. Do you want one?"

He handed the box to me. "No, I can't eat anything today."

"Okay, have some water." He poured some into a glass.

"Thanks, Rudolph."

I was nervous and started pacing around the room, humming the piano score in my head and, at the same time, trying to relax my arms, shaking them lightly. Rudolph sat on the sofa, took a notebook, and wrote something. I glanced at the clock. It was almost 1:00 p.m. *Where's Constantina?* I was restless. The door opened; and Constantina entered the room, took her purse, then said, "Let's go to the reception."

Just then, Dr. Richter walked into the room dressed in a black tuxedo. "Gutentag [Good evening]," he said.

"Gutentag," I answered. "We were just ready to go upstairs to the reception."

Dr. Richter turned to me. "How are you holding up, Verga?"

"Just fine."

"Before we go to the reception, I want you to put on a smiling face. I don't want you to show any hint of nervousness. Drink water, no alcohol. I will introduce you to the judges. Shake their hands firmly, but not hard. Be polite. Shake hands with all the contestants and wish them good luck. Try to start a conversation with Mimi. Be charming. Be yourself. Take a deep breath. Exhale slowly. Good, let's go upstairs."

The reception was held in the academy's formal tearoom, a baroque-style interior decorated with mirrors, three large crystal chandeliers hanging from the coffered ceiling, and a parquet floor. Paintings of famous composers and conductors hung on the walls. Five large windows reflected the day's light into the room. The sound of a string quartet playing Haydn's String Quartet no. 63 in B-Flat Major, op. 76, no. 4, "Sunrise," echoed in the room. The room was full of people dressed in black and white. Some ladies dressed in bright red or dark blue.

A waiter came by with a tray. "Champagne or wine?" he asked.

"No thanks, just water please."

With a glass in my hand, I followed Dr. Richter, a grin on my face. We circulated among the guests. Constantina followed behind me. As we approached a short woman in her midforties with brown hair, a round face, and alert eyes, Dr. Richter said, "Professor Sussmayr, let me introduce Verga Caszar, our contestant."

I bowed politely, smiling at the judge. "It is nice to get your acquaintance," I said. I shook her hand.

"Nice to meet you, young man," she said, pushing up her glasses higher on her sharp nose. "I heard good things from Professor Heilbronner about you."

I realized Constantina knew her in person. *She never mentioned it to me,* I thought. Constantina said, "How are you, Anna?" They struck up a conversation.

I bowed slightly and said, "It was nice meeting you."

She answered, "Good luck, Herr Caszar."

"Thanks."

Dr. Richter navigated through the crowd. He wanted me to meet all the judges. We managed to do it despite the short time we had. I was most impressed with the judge, Professor Carl Eisler; he was the friendliest. He was tall and slim and had blue eyes and long gray locks of hair down to his shoulders. He knew everything about my piano-playing abilities, which surprised me.

"Please introduce yourself to Mimi Schmidt," Dr. Richter said, "She is standing next to the window."

I glanced in her direction and recognized her. She wore a sleeveless black dress and a silvery scarf on her shoulder—a beautiful creature, I noted. She did look like Romy Schneider. I approached her. She was conversing with a woman, so I waited for the right moment then said, "Frau Schmidt, I'd like to introduce myself, Verga Caszar." Then I extended my hand toward her.

She looked at me as if asking, "Who are you?" and turned around and continued talking to the woman.

I lowered my hand and said, "It was nice meeting you, Frau Schmidt." I bowed like a gentleman and turned around and walked away, glancing at Dr. Richter, who had observed the entire scene.

"She will not shake my hand. What's wrong with her?"

"Don't be upset. She did it deliberately to throw you off balance. You did the right thing. I think you spooked her."

"Pompous, strange individual."

I met the rest of the contestants, Anton and Siegfried. Siegfried was a pleasant young man of sixteen. He reminded me of myself at that age. Anton, only fifteen, a serious fellow, twitched nervously as he spoke to me. I heard him play before and thought he was a promising pianist.

Constantina found me in the crowd. She said, "Darling, let's go to the room."

"I'm enjoying the reception."

"We need to meditate before the performance."

Reluctantly, I retired to the dressing room. Sitting on the couch, Constantina sat opposite me on a chair. "Close your eyes. Let's meditate for fifteen minutes."

I closed my eyes, but I could not meditate. My head was rushing with so many thoughts. I was edgy. I opened my eyes, looking at Constantina's face. She was calm. *She must not notice me*, I thought to myself. I moved my legs nervously. She opened her eyes, looking at me. I said, "I can't meditate. I just can't focus on my breathing. I'm too restless."

She took my hand into hers. "Look into my eyes. What do you see?"

"Green. Forest."

"Is the forest calm?"

"Yes, it looks so peaceful."

"Verga, you are in the forest, peaceful. Relax. Relax." She said, "Close your eyes. You are now walking in the forest all calm."

I imagined I was in the woods. I focused on my breathing, and the distraction disappeared. I lost track of time, spiritual contentment overtaking me.

"Wake up, Verga." I heard her voice. She clapped her hands.

"What happened? Did I fall asleep?"

"How do you feel now?"

I inhaled deep. "I feel so refreshed and relaxed, like I slept for hours." I stood up, hugging Constantina. "I feel like I found new energy, connected and calm." I looked at Constantina for answers.

She held my hand and said, "Verga, I hypnotized you to have you relax."

I was silent, looking at her with a blank face and an open mouth. "You did? I didn't know you could do that."

"Sorry, Verga. I did not tell you because I rarely practice the technique. Mayer taught me, but I don't remember when I last used it. You were so willing, so I did it. Forgive me for not asking for your permission."

I leaned over and kissed her lips. "Thanks. My nervousness is gone. I'm a new man." I stretched my hands.

"It's time to soak your hands."

I sat at the makeup counter. She wrapped a hot towel around my hands. My fingers relaxed. She looked at the clock. "Time is my enemy," she said. "It's already 1:45 p.m. I need to go to the concert hall. Verga, soak your hands with the hot towel for another fifteen minutes." She fixed her hair, looking in the mirror, and put on lipstick. Then she turned to me. "How do you feel?"

"Great! I'm like a stallion ready to jump the starting gate."

"Good, I have to go. The competition will start in ten minutes. Rudolph will escort you backstage in twenty minutes." She threw a kiss in the air and left the room.

I thought about how lucky I was to have Constantina in my life, when the door opened. It was Rudolph. "The program will start in five minutes." He switched on the speaker on the wall, adjusting the volume. The sound of the audience's roar could be heard. The master of ceremony came on. "Welcome to the Imperial Academy of Music, the oldest institution in Austria dedicated to the promotion of the arts and music. Today, we are sponsoring the fifth Young Pianist Competition, and the winner will represent Austria next month in Milan, Italy, in Europe's Young Pianist Competition. Let me introduce our first performer, Anton Wolf, the youngest of our contestants. He will perform the works of Beethoven and Mozart, starting with Beethoven's Piano Sonata no. 32 in C Minor, op. 111 and finishing with Mozart's 'Rondo Alla Turca.'"

The hall interrupted with loud applause. I wiped my hands and put the towel on the counter and sat on the couch, listening to Anton's performance. He began to play with powerful opening chords. I said, "Good start," but then within the next fifteen minutes, the play lacked rendition, missing the necessary sparks. In the end, the play lacked the essential nobility. I glanced at the clock on the wall. It was twenty minutes to my turn, and Rudolph said, "Verga, we need to go backstage. You're next."

I stood up, adjusting my dark blue bowtie and matching handkerchief, looking into the glass of the mirror. "Ready."

We reached backstage when Anton bowed and accepted a bouquet of roses from a well-dressed woman. Then he came backstage. His music teacher hugged him enthusiastically. I looked at the audience. There were so many faces. It was dark. Somewhere there was Constantina. I felt her presence. The stage hand rolled my Steinway onto the stage and placed my piano bench down. A hush fell in the hall.

The master of ceremony walked on stage. "Let me introduce our next contestant, Verga Caszar, graduate of the master's program at the Academy of Music, Graz. First, he'll play Schubert's *Impromptus*, D. 899 (op. 90), no. 1, no. 2, and no. 3 in G-flat Major and will finish with Franz Liszt's *La Campanella*, 'The Grand Paganini Études.'"

The stage manager tapped me on the shoulder. "Please, go."

I entered the stage. Lights blinded me. I stood in front of the Steinway, bowing to the audience's applause, took a deep breath, adjusted the piano seat, sat quietly for a few seconds, lifted my hands high, and then played Franz Schubert's piano pieces, which were composed in 1827 when Schubert was thirty years old, a year before his death. It's considered to be among the era's most important example of nineteenth-century Romantic works. I played the piece with a warm touch, humming the melody in my head, eyes closed. I played Franz Schubert's Impromptu op. 90, D 899. My hands played the first two themes without a companion. My fingers glided slowly into A-flat major and introduced a new melody. I closed my eyes, concentrating on the offbeat version of the first theme. Then my fingers played in G major, gradually switching to C major, and ending the play's tension with gentle tranquility.

I paused.

Lifting my hands, I played the second theme in E-flat major, fingers gliding over the keyboard with a lively, chromatic melody. In the middle section, I played dark but still lyrical sounds and ended the section with fingers oscillating like vibrating wings of cicadas. Fingers glided to the end with E flat, then a coda in modified B minor, alternating my fingers with the key of E-flat minor.

I paused.

I played no. 3 in G-flat major. Schubert's outstanding melodic piece was like Felix Mendelssohn's songs without words, a spacious and languid melody. My fingers moved on the keyboard with exquisite, somewhat shadowy play. Then in a relaxed flow of the keyboard, I felt Constantina's overhanging presence. It transported me to last night's amour in the dark room, only moonlight guiding our bodies. My fingers on the keyboard exploded with delicate, romantic notes in G major and 4/4 meter timing. The last note vibrated in the concert hall, and it was over. I opened my eyes. It was like I had just been awakened. I knew I had played the first part well.

Embedded with new energy in my fingertips, I plunged into Franz Liszt's *La Campanella*. I played a brisk allegro, my right hand jumping between intervals, hand high above the keyboard, emphasizing the jumps stretching for two whole octaves, timing myself with sixteen notes. I moved fast, avoiding tension within my hand muscles. The piece had technical difficulties and pitfalls, but I managed to navigate through them with ease. The Steinway strings vibrated harmonic rings of the imaginary hand bell. There was no time to think or reflect on anything. I needed full concentration for this fast étude, playing in precise sixteen intervals twice at thirty-second measures. Sweat collected on my forehead when I finished and stood up. There was a loud applause of "Bravo! Bravo!" and the audience stood up shouting.

I glanced at the first row. There, I recognized the Gluck family. Hans was clapping hard and showing the famous Churchill's V with his fingers. My eyes searched for Constantina. I found her next to Dr. Richter standing and applauding. She was grinning. Ingrid, Hans's sister, appeared on stage with a large bouquet of roses, proudly kissing me and giving me a French hug. Then she placed the roses into my lap. "You were fantastic," she said. "The best bell ring I have ever heard on the piano."

"Thanks, Ingrid." I bowed to the audience then walked backstage. I felt like I was walking on clouds.

"Bravo!" Hands clapped backstage.

Rudolph greeted me, shaking my hand. "What a great performance. It melted my heart. Schubert's play was so romantic I wanted to cry. A jaw-dropping performance."

"Thanks." I was dazzled from the reaction I heard.

I heard Rudolph say, "Do you want to stay backstage and listen to Mimi's performance?"

"Let's go to the room downstairs."

We left backstage as the stage hands rolled Mimi's piano to the center of the stage. I plopped myself on the sofa, elated. I had done my best.

The master of ceremony introduced Mimi Schmidt to the audience. "A graduate with honor from the Imperial Academy, second-place winner of the Mozart Competition in Salzburg, winner of the Austrian Young Piano Performer, Mimi Schmidt."

The audience burst with applause. Someone yelled, "Mimi first place!"

The master of ceremony presented her play. "Her first play will be the Hungarian Rhapsody no. 12 in C-sharp Minor by Franz Liszt. Second will be Nocturne in G Minor, op. 37, no. 1 by Chopin."

We heard a loud ovation from the speaker. Rudolph said, "She's definitely popular with the audience."

I remarked, "It's her home turf after all."

So far, she received the most enthusiastic welcome. I almost considered my defeat in silence.

Mimi hit the keyboard with Liszt's virtuoso piece. Ten minutes into the play, she skipped a note. For a minute, it startled me. *No, I heard it wrong*, I said to myself. Then her play lacked a sense of lyricism and sounded choppy. I could hear the Steinway strings resounding dispassionate and apathetic notes. I sat on the edge of the sofa. I couldn't believe what I was hearing. *Is it my imagine playing tricks on me?*

Then silence. I heard a noise of footsteps, and a hush passed in the hall. I stood up, looking at Rudolph. He was standing next to the speaker, turning the volume high. I asked, "Did we lose the sound?"

"No," Rudolph said. "Something is happening on stage."

Then the voice of the master of ceremony was heard loud and clear. "We apologize for the interruption. Mimi Schmidt has fallen ill and will not be able to finish her presentation." Spectators mumbled.

I was stunned. "What does this mean?"

Rudolph said in a calm voice, "She is out. I call it stage fright."

"She made a technical mistake. I heard her strike the wrong note."

"Her loss, your win."

I did not reply.

Siegfried played his repertoire next. It sounded like jumbled music in my head. I was deep in my thoughts. *Why am I not happy that Mimi's out of the competition? After all, she was disrespectful, chauvinistic, and aloof. But I feel sorry for her. Pianists sometimes have a bad day. We all make mistakes. We're not perfect. If it was me, how would I have reacted?*

I remembered Constantina's voice in my head. "If you hit the wrong note, keep playing. Do not stop. Finish your play with gusto and enthusiasm."

Why did she stop?

The door to the room opened, and a noisy crowd rushed in. I did not realize the competition was over. "Bravo, Verga!" screamed Hans, rushing to greet me.

I noticed the entire Gluck family was in my room, along with Dr. Richter, Maria and her husband, and well-wishers. Odon stood at the door. Reporters flashed cameras, blinding my eyes. Flowers were thrust into my lap. I was stunned by the clamor. Rudolph, at the door, pushed reporters away. I recognized Dr. Fulop and his sister, Sari, walking through the doorway. I rushed toward the mob. "Rudolph, please let them in. And let Odon, the reporter, in too."

I hugged Sari. "Congratulations," she said.

"I didn't know you were in the audience."

"We saw the TV special on Tuesday and recognized you."

"How can we miss this special occasion?" Dr. Fulop said.

"I'm honored to have you here. Please meet my dear friends." I introduced them to the Glucks.

Then I searched for Constantina. She was standing in the corner, crying with joy.

"Did I win?" I asked Dr. Richter.

"We don't know yet. The announcement will be made in half an hour."

"How was my performance?"

"Excellent. It moved the audience. Everyone's talking about it."

I walked toward Constantina. Holding her two hands in mine, looking into her eyes, I asked, "How did I do?"

"Darling, your two hands played as one. I can't describe my ineffable joy. I wept throughout the entire performance. When you played Schubert, I felt your touch in every strike of the keyboard—brilliant, romantic, vibrant, and splendid. It was a dream. Wow, today, you manifested yourself as a piano virtuoso, a true artist." She kissed me on both cheeks.

After a long hour of anticipation, the bell rang. Everyone shuffled back to the concert hall, waiting for the master of ceremony to come on stage.

"With great pleasure, I am pleased to announce the judges' decision of today's winners of the Young Talent Competition." He opened the envelope. "Third prize, Anton Wolf, please come up."

Anton stepped on the stage to the rush of applause, a bouquet of flowers pressed to his hands.

"Second prize, Siegfried Reger, please come to the stage." Again, there was a loud applause.

I stood backstage, my knees trembling, my heart jumping from my chest. I had no time to think. My name was called by the master of ceremony.

"Verga Caszar, first prize!"

"Bravo! Bravo!" was heard in the hall. Thunderous applause interrupted. I walked to the stage, bowed deep several times, was handed a bouquet of roses, and remained in shock.

Later that evening, I asked Dr. Richter, "What happened to Mimi?"

"She made a slight mistake and should have continued playing, but she is a perfectionist, self-critical. I heard one critic describe her as a gifted, spoiled brat. It was only Mimi's self-awareness, self-critical performance that wasn't to her liking. She walked off the stage. She stunned the audience."

The next day, Sunday, I woke up early not to disturb Constantina in her deep sleep. In the kitchen, I made myself a cup of coffee. The sun was just rising, and I opened the window. Fresh morning air filled the room.

I thought today would be a beautiful summer day. Drinking coffee and going over my Maurice Ravel's Piano Concerto score, I tapped my fingers on the table to the music in my head. I was jolted by Constantina's touch on my shoulder. She hugged me, kissing my neck.

"You scared me," I said.

"I did? I'm sorry."

"How are you feeling?"

"Wonderful."

I turned around and kissed her lips. "I can't get over how lucky I am to have won first prize last night."

"It's not luck. You played with your soul. You played to win."

"Thanks."

"You have a busy day today. At ten thirty, you are scheduled to practice Ravel's concerto with the academy orchestra; and tonight, we're having a gala presentation of the awards, then dinner with the Glucks to celebrate your win."

"I still think this is a dream."

"No, it's not a dream, sweetheart. Let's meditate. At ten, a car is coming to pick you up. The Glucks are providing you with a chauffeur car for today."

"I don't know how to repay them for their support."

"The Glucks' financial group is sponsoring tonight's ceremony too," she said.

"Are you coming to my rehearsal?"

"No, Verga, I need to take care of myself. Look at my hair. Look at my fingernails. I messed them up last night I was so nervous."

I was surprised by her reaction. "You are solid as a rock. No wind or storm moves you."

"Well, I'm human as you are. Let's go and meditate."

At the Imperial Academy, I was greeted by the conductor, Leonard Dittesdorf. "Congratulations, Herr Caszar, for last night's spectacular performance."

"Thanks."

"Are you ready to meet the orchestra players?"

"Yes, please."

I was dressed in jeans and a blue shirt and walked on the stage. I was greeted by enthusiastic loud applause. I bowed politely, shook hands with the first violinist, and sat at the piano, looking at the conductor.

He lifted his hand. I played Ravel's Concerto in G Major. I rehearsed it twice, repeating some portions of the piece several times, and listened to the conductor's instructions. By 1:00, I left the academy, satisfied with the rehearsal, and headed to Constantina's.

That night, as I glanced at my watch, it was 8:00. I stood backstage in formal wear. Constantina had changed my bowtie to black. I walked to the stage. The hall was full, and booming applause echoed. The conductor introduced me to the audience. I sat at the piano bench, waiting for his signal as his hand rose in the air. Looking at the orchestra then at me, he lowered his hand. I played the joyous first movement. Steinway strings reverberated in a unique blend of Basque and Spanish sounds and Ravel's jazz notes. Fingers glided on the keyboard. I stopped playing, listening to the orchestra. They played a short-lived tune reminiscent of the blues then melodic, rich sounds like George Gershwin's *Rhapsody in Blue*. I joined the orchestra with a quick chorale passage from the piano with mystical interpretations and then rested, listening to the orchestra. Then I repeated a quick interpretation of blues from the first play.

In the second movement, I played an elaborate restatement and then progressed, playing an energized coda that ended with a bawdy scale from the orchestra's brass. For a moment, there was silence. Then the hall interrupted with "Bravo!" The audience stood up, clapping. I searched the first row. Constantina was enthusiastically applauding.

The conductor accompanied me backstage while the audience was still on their feet. He turned toward me and said, "Herr Caszar, great performance. Are you ready for an encore?"

I nodded. We walked back on the stage, and I sat back at the piano. The orchestra and I repeated the third movement of Ravel's piece. The applause did not stop. Some were yelling, "More! More!"

The conductor glanced at me. I said, "I can play Chopin's Waltz in D-flat Major, op. 64," a short solid piece also known as the "Minute Waltz," a popular one-minute play. I finished it with gusto and theatrical performance then stood up.

The audience loved my encore. "Bravo! Bravo!"

Elated, I walked backstage. "Great performance, Verga." I was greeted by Dr. Richter and Constantina.

Back on stage, I was awarded a diploma and a prize of 50,000 schillings. I would be representing Austria next month in Milano, Italy, at the Young Pianist Competition.

After the short gala reception in the tearoom, Rudolph allowed reporters to interview me. "How long have you been playing?" a reporter asked.

"All my life, since I was four years old."

"I understand you are from Hungary. Do you consider yourself Hungarian or Austrian?"

"Austrian-Hungarian."

"How does it feel to win first prize?"

"It is a great honor," I said. "I would like to take this opportunity to thank all the people who have supported me: Dr. Fulop and his sister, Sari; Dr. Richter; my beloved teacher, Wordzinka Heilbronner; the Gluck family; the Austrian Red Cross, who gave me a home; and so many other people who believed in me and gave me their support."

The reporters asked more questions. Then Rudolph closed the press conference, promising to have another press day in the future. Exhausted and overjoyed, I left the stage.

The Glucks invited selected guests to a private dinner at Hotel Sacher Restaurant. It was a showcase for Imperial Vienna. We sat in the Anna Sacher dining room, which was decorated with rich green walls and dark wood paneling. Lobmeyr crystal chandeliers hung from the ceiling, and walls were decorated with paintings by Anton Faistauer.

I sat at a table with the Glucks. Clara, Hans's mother, turned toward me. "Verga, I understand you're staying with Professor Heilbronner. I spoke to Louis, and we're inviting you and the professor this coming weekend to our country estate in Bad Vösalu. I want you to stay there until you leave for Italy. The house would be all yours for the rest of the three weeks. You can practice there. We have a Steinway concerto piano. It's in perfect condition. What do you say?"

I did not know what to say. "Your family is so generous to me. How can I ever repay?"

"Oh, stop. Who's talking about repaying? You're considered part of our family. Quiet walks in the woods will rejuvenate you. You can concentrate on your repertoire for the next competition. We have a housekeeper there. She will take care of all your needs. Our chauffeur is available if you need to go somewhere, and the railroad station is only thirty minutes by bicycle. The city environment is not conducive for you."

"I thank you for your offer," I said. "I need to check with Professor Heilbronner for my practice schedule."

"Verga, I already did. She said it's a great idea."

I was taken aback. "She did?" After a pause, I said, "Thanks for your invitation."

"Let's celebrate!" She lifted her champagne glass. I clicked hers.

I said, *"Fur inre gesundheit* [For your health], madam."

Part 2

ONE

Sitting on the balcony, I glanced at the neat row of grapevines and gentle hills in front of me. It was a halcyon morning with the mist obscuring the nearby woods. The Glucks' estate was in the midst of vineyards in Bad Vöslau Village in lower Austria Thermenregion, thirty kilometers from Vienna. The country estate was built in the 1800s with all modern amenities. The last renovation was made in 1959. They added four additional guestrooms, and the house now had six bedrooms. I was given a room on the first floor next to Hans's. The other guestrooms were on the second floor.

I inhaled clean air. The aroma of ripe grapes was in the breeze. My eyes followed a flock of birds fluttering over the vineyards chasing each other, nibbling on sweet fruit. Then a hawk appeared, hovering with interest. My eyes lingered on the hawk. Then he dove from the sky like a falling stone only to be interrupted by ravens, knocking him from his dive and chasing him into the woods. I thought of how wonderful nature is. I was glad to be spending the next three weeks in the vineyards. Footsteps interrupted my thoughts. It was Constantina dressed in white pants and a floral shirt, a fresh smile on her face.

"Guten morgen [Good morning]."

"Guten morgen."

"What are you doing so early this morning?" She sat next to me on the wooden bench, a cup of hot tea in between her hands.

"I'm enjoying this country view."

"Yes, how wondrous nature is with rhythmic cycles of life. It's right in front of us. Seasons and time, life events, moments of conception, birth and death, and life goes on." She glanced into the distance, sipping the hot liquid.

"True," I said, changing the subject. "I didn't know the Glucks were in the wine business."

"Yes, they own several vineyards in this area. I was told this estate has been in the family since the 1800s. They also own and operate the popular *heuriger* [wine taverns] in Vienna."

"I know. Hans invited me to one. I didn't realize how popular the taverns are with tourists, a real money maker."

"They are a wealthy family and very generous with their money," she said.

"How can one be rich like the Glucks? I want to know the secret."

"It takes time to build a business and be successful."

"If I had their money, it would make me very happy."

She put her cup on the floor, looking at me. "Making money will not necessarily bring happiness. Darling, stop thinking how to get more money. Instead, focus on your life, how you are getting happiness out of what you have already. Being rich is okay, so long as you share your wealth with the less fortunate, giving to the needy and charity. That will make you happy."

Looking at Constantina, I thought, *I love this woman especially when she speaks her mind*. After a pause of silence, I said, "I got my happiness. I have you in my life."

"How sweet." She held my hands. "Remember, money cannot buy you love."

"At what time will you be leaving for Vienna?"

She looked at her watch. "At nine o'clock, in three hours. Why?"

"I will miss you."

"I will miss you too. Three weeks is a short time."

"Not for me. It will be like an eternity."

"Time is what you want to make of it. Spend your time wisely here. Meditate. Ponder about life. Take walks in the woods and vineyards. Connect with nature. Being alone is good for you. Connect with yourself. Practice piano. Paint. You haven't done art for some time. And you have other talents. Explore them all. The Glucks have a beautiful tennis court. Learn to play tennis. Ask Hans to recommend you an instructor. And I'm looking forward to spending time with Ruth and Richard. You know, she's not a youngster anymore, and I have not had a holiday in a long time."

"Please write me and call me when you will be back in town."

"I will, darling. Let's go inside. I think they're serving breakfast. I smell fresh bread."

That evening, I had a conversation with Hans. We sat on the balcony, enjoying the evening cool breeze. "Verga, do you want more wine?"

"Please, the red one." With a glass of wine in hand, I asked, "Hans, can you recommend me a tennis instructor?"

"I didn't know you wanted to play tennis. I will make a call to Sabrina. She's a great teacher and lives in Baden, the next town over."

"Thanks."

"You're welcome. In a month, my father wants me to travel to Hungary. Do you have any relatives there?"

"This is good news. I was born in Kőszeg and lived in Budapest. To what town are you going?"

"My father wants me to visit Edgar Region in Egervin Cooperatives. Then in a few months, he's sending me to America to promote our wines—the Zweigelts, Cabs, and St. Laurents—all estate-bottled, full-bodied, dry reds. In the past years, we made extraneous efforts to make wines internationally competitive."

"I love your wine, especially this Portugiesers."

Hans turned toward me. "Verga, take some of my business cards. More wine?"

"Yes, please." I looked at his card. "I'm impressed. Vice president of sales. I'm so happy for you." I put the glass on the railing.

"Verga, can I do anything for you while I'm in Hungary?"

"Oh yes, Hungary. You know, Hans, I'm ashamed to tell you that three years ago, I received a letter from my uncle Elek. He searched for me through the Red Cross. I did not answer it. I was afraid it may implicate him to me in some way. It has been on my conscience all these years. Can you do me a favor? Kőszeg is only a short ride from Budapest. I will give you an envelope with a letter and some money. I want to reestablish contact. Check for me if it's safe to do it, and please, tell my uncle everything you know about my life."

"It will be my pleasure," Hans said.

Three weeks passed like a flash. I had received four postcards from Constantina. She was having a great time with her sister-in-law. I had learned to play tennis and had practiced daily. I had painted dozens of watercolors of landscapes and still life. I had spent hours playing piano until late evenings. Rudolph had called me every day. He had arranged a passport for me. I had received several proposals from record companies, but Dr. Richter had advised me not to act on it until I came back from Italy. He had said, "Your situation will be better after the competition, even if you don't win first place. You can negotiate a better deal with the record companies then."

Hans had called. "Are you learning to play tennis?"

"Yes, my swing and serve improved. Sabrina is a very good instructor. Thanks for the recommendation."

"You're welcome. Verga, we're all coming to the house this weekend."

"Great, I miss you all."

That night, I had also received a call from Constantina. "Verga, I'm back in Vienna. I spoke to Clara, and she invited me to join her this weekend at the country estate."

"I can't wait to see you," I said.

"I miss you. How is your piano practice coming along?"

"Great. I'm like a new person. The country air reenergized me. I also painted a dozen pictures."

"I can't wait to see them."

"How is your trip?"

"Great. Ruth and I enjoyed each other's company, and Richard was a real gentleman. You have to see the Dolomites. What a magnificent place."

"I love mountains, especially climbing them. In a week, I'm going to Milano for the big event. Are you to accompany me?"

There was silence. "Verga, I'm not sure yet. Let's discuss it when I see you this weekend. Love you."

We hung up. This would be the last weekend in the country. Next week, I would be departing to Italy.

The house was lively with people again. After dinner, I sat in the large salon and played the music of Chopin and Anton Weber. Then we retired early. I kissed Constantina good night. We made plans for an early morning walk in the nearest forest. I lay in bed, eyes open, wishing Constantina was in my embrace.

I woke up early and went to the balcony. It was a cloudy day. *It may rain*, I thought. We should leave early while the weather was good. I went to the second floor and gently knocked on Constantina's bedroom. She opened the door and was already fully dressed in hiking shoes, a handkerchief on her head, a white long-sleeve shirt, and green pants. "I will be right down," she said.

I took my raincoat, filled a flask with water, and packed it in my backpack. I waited for her on the balcony.

The air was warm, and the slight breeze blew through the woods. We walked briskly on the dark trail. "How far do you want to hike?" I asked. I held her hand.

"Let's walk for an hour and find a place to meditate."

"I know a perfect spot: a small pond in a clearing."

"Is it the pond and yellow flowers that you painted?"

"Yes."

"Oh, it's a beautiful composition."

We continued walking. "Did you decide to join me in Milan?"

"Verga, I was thinking. Dr. Richter and Rudolph are to accompany you. I think I'll stay in Vienna. I will be a nuisance. I may distract you."

"You will be of no distraction to me. I was hoping you'd come. We can have a great time together. I was thinking, after the competition, we could take some tours, see an opera in La Scala, and visit Verona, perhaps Venice."

"It's very tempting, darling. Let me sleep on it."

"I've had other thoughts in my head for the last week." I swallowed hard and said, "I'm madly in love with you, my love. Can we stop having a secret relationship and let it out in the open? I want you in my life."

She was not surprised hearing my words but said nothing for a long time. We stopped walking. Looking into my eyes, she finally said, "Verga, darling, please don't get me wrong." She kissed me. "Darling, the last weeks were the most exciting in my life. First, my prayers were answered; you won the competition, and you are at a crossroad. Your future looks bright." She put her head on my shoulder. "You know, darling, you've awakened a dormant flame in me and ignited it into a fire, the flame of human desire, of being wanted and loved. I'm intoxicated by your love for me, but in reality, I'm twenty years older." Lifting her head, looking at me, her hand on my cheek, she said, "For me, the sun will be setting soon. Your life has just begun. It's so exciting that I can relive my youth with you, but, darling, we live in a conservative and prudish society. If our relationship is revealed, your future will be undone. Rumors will fly. True or not, you will become an outcast. There are jealous people out there who want you to fail. They will say Professor Heilbronner broke the teacher's rules. She had an inappropriate relation with a student. All doors will be shut in front of you. A scandal is a scandal. It will destroy you. As for me, darling, it will not make any difference. I lived my life seeing the worst in people. For your sake, let's leave things as they are."

We continued walking. I felt pain listening to her words. It made me think of how unfair our society was. It felt like we were on a fast-moving train and someone pulled the emergency brake, stopping us from reaching our destination. I felt disheartened. I said, "This is why you think our relationship had no chance from the start."

"Oh, Verga, I'm surprised at what you say. This is childish. I didn't say we have no chance. I very much want you in my life. You know me. I crave independence in mind and body. I did not give up on our relationship, but I don't want you to resent me later because you gave up on your music career for love. Possession and lust is not what we should strive for. Let's appreciate each other. I believe we can have a relationship based on both love and freedom. Let's not rush into something that we don't know how it will turn out." She kissed me and said in a low voice, "Enough talking. I want to see your special spot. Please take me there."

We passed squirrels collecting acorns. It was quiet on the trail. I said, "Let's take a shortcut through the woods toward the pond."

Constantina followed me through the shrubs. Leaves held morning dew and wet our shirts as we brushed against them. We arrived at the open meadow, and beyond was a small pond. The sun momentarily broke through dark clouds and gave a golden glow on a few small boulders around the pond. A light wind rippled the water with a silvery tone. A field of yellow was spread like a carpet in front of us.

"Wow, how beautiful is this," she said.

"Right here," I said, drawing the view. I pointed my finger to the scenery. The reflection of pine trees on the water gave it a dark, mysterious look. I turned to her, holding hands. We kissed. "I missed you, darling," I said, kissing her all over her face.

"I missed you too."

Then it grew dark, and we heard a rumbling noise of thunder in the distance. "We should head back," she said. "It may rain soon."

"I like to watch the rain in the woods. And the summer rain is a quick pour. Then sun breaks through the clouds. Let's go there, under the big tree on the edge of the pond."

As we walked toward the tree, a drop of rain hit my face. Then more. We started to run. I placed my raincoat on Constantina's head and sat on the grass and pine needles, watching the raindrops agitating the pond like boiling water in a cooking pot.

"So peaceful," she said. "How beautiful nature can be. Verga, look at these drops of water called rain. It's nothing but the process of water droplets falling from the sky. It's a beautiful ever-changing phenomenon, and it's happening now in front of our eyes. Darling, and we are part of nature too."

I pressed myself into her. We kissed, my hands gliding under her shirt, caressing her breast. She touched my hand, looking at me, an excited expression on her face. "Verga, let's be part of nature. I want to feel the rain and walk on grass barefoot. Let's take off our clothes." She stood up and undressed, removing her handkerchief, letting her hair down. Seeing her nakedness aroused me.

I removed my clothes. Naked and holding hands, we ran toward the sunflower field. Dragging her wet feet, Constantina ran away from me between flowers now bending low from the weight of water. I ran after her, creating a splash from my bare feet. Drops of water tingled my skin. I caught up with her in the middle of the field. She laughed and danced with her hands up like a child under a sprinkler. I joined her in a rain dance. Then I pulled her body to mine. I felt her warm skin against me. We kissed passionately. She said, "Let's sit down."

I sat on the wet grass, surrounded by yellow sunflowers. I looked at her luscious body as she let my hands down and walked to the field, collecting yellow and white wildflowers. Sitting opposite me, holding a large bouquet against her breasts, she put them down then instinctively began to weave them into a wreath, wildflowers as crowns. Then she placed one on my head, imitating nature's majestic wildflowers from the carpeted meadow with my hair. I set the other living crown atop hers. We kissed, holding hands. I made a ring with a flower's stem. Gazing into her eyes, I placed the ring on her finger. She placed her ring on my finger. Wearing the flower chaplets, we momentarily embodied a bride and groom, king and queen of nature; we sat in silence. Our eyes focused on each other. Light rain dripped on our heads and faces. She took my right hand and placed it over her heart then placed her right hand over my heart. We remained silent, connected spiritually. Our hearts beat as one.

Lightning lit the sky, shaking us to the core. Enormous thunder jolted us temporarily disorienting and dazing us. Electricity was in the air, tingling our bare skin. Our hearts pounded. We were thunderstruck. Without a word, I stood up and lifted Constantina from the grass. We ran toward the protection of the tree just in time as the sky opened up and a deluge of water hit the ground. The sky became dark, and lightning illuminated our naked bodies with a bluish hue. I sat on pine needles, leaning against the tree trunk. Constantina sat with her back on my legs, resting against me. I placed the raincoat like a blanket over our bodies. With her head on my shoulder, I felt her breath warm in my ear, looking at the rainfall. I kissed her neck. She smelled so fresh. My hands caressed her breast and nipples and slid over her warm flesh then her belly and rested on her Venus gate. She raised her legs and spread them wide, my fingers caressing her inner depths. She let out a sound of pleasure. She turned her face, and we kissed, our tongues meeting. Her hands moved to my erection. We sat in that position for a while. Then she stood up, eyeing me. She slowly sat on my legs. Holding my hard one, she gently placed it in her Venus and slid down slowly. Then we were one. I covered her back with the raincoat. We kissed open mouthed, slow, passionate, not moving, just enjoying each other. I felt her warmth, an old tightness melting away.

I held her buttocks gently, lifting and guiding her, thrusting into her. Looking into my eyes, she took my hand and placed it on her breast. "Feel my heart," she said. "It's pounding fast."

"Feel mine."

"Let's not rush." With dreamy eyes, she said, "Take a deep breath and exhale." I felt her inner body caress my penis. "Don't rush. Breathe slowly," she said. We moved, thrusting and breathing, sliding and breathing. My entire body tingled with pleasurable spasms.

Rain dripped on our bare skin, sliding down Constantina's back. "Darling, you're all wet," I said. She opened her eyes for a second, not responding. She lost herself in our uncontrollable passion, rocking firmly but in slow motion. Her eyes closed, breathing hard. I got so excited looking at her I reached my limits quickly. "I can't hold it anymore," I cried. I was swept with tides of pleasure.

"Slow down," she cried. Then she came behind me with love's climax. Her lower torso thrust, moving, shuttering again and again, her face buried in my shoulder. Oblivious to the rain now pouring on her skin, she moved again, slow but firm. Then her entire body jolted in spasms. She let out a low cry, kissing my open mouth, gasping for air. I held her tight. Thunder struck nearby. We instinctively embraced for protection. We stopped moving and sat in silence, catching our breaths, our hearts pounding. Suddenly, the rain stopped, and light wind kicked in, chilling our bodies. I covered her with the raincoat. She spoke in a tender voice with tearing eyes, "I love you."

I whispered, "Good god, I love you too. Let's dress up before we catch a cold."

The sky opened up, and the sun burst between the clouds. I used my undershirt as a towel to wipe her body. I helped her dress. Our heads wet, I said, "We are crazy." We laughed then walked on the trail toward the house. I said, "No one will suspect that we had wild sex in nature."

She said, "Let it be our secret." She paused then said, "Darling, sex in nature is not wild. I call it cosmic sexuality."

"How true. I call it mutual attraction and good karma." I thought that water is the prime symbol for fertility especially when it rains, and rain it did. "Oh my god, I completely forgot to tell you. I composed a piece. I dedicated it to you, my love. I called it 'Wondrous Moments.'"

We stopped walking. I searched my pockets and pulled out a damp piece of paper, unfolded it, and gave it to Constantina. Looking at the score, she said, "How romantic and mysterious! I like it. It reminds me of Mahler's Second Movement Symphony No. 5, which ends in a conclusive mystery." She folded the paper and gave it back. Smiling, she said, "I like the authentic cadence. How sweet! It's touching." She embraced me with a kiss.

"I will play this for you tonight in Vienna."

TWO

The piano music of Chopin, "Raindrop" Prelude op. 28, no. 15 in D-flat major sounded in the salon. I was engrossed in my play, imagining I was dancing in the rain in the field of sunflowers with Constantina. I played a romantic theme, fingers on the piano keys, lost in pouring my emotions on the Steinway strings. A hand touched me, embracing my back. Delicate fingers slid between the folds of my shirt, touching my chest, resting on my heart. I felt her warm face against my cheek. The aroma of Chanel No. 5 filled my nostrils. For a moment, I was lost. *Am I reliving our encounter in the woods? It's so real.* I turned around. It was Constantina. "Please finish your play," she whispered in my ear.

I continued playing, gliding on the keyboard, my fingers hitting notes like drops of rain. When I finished, she said, "Verga, that was so romantic. You captured our moment in nature. I couldn't resist holding you in my arms." I kissed her. "Darling," she said, "it is almost 6:30, and we have a dinner appointment at 7:30. Go dress up. We have to leave in half an hour."

Reluctantly, I went upstairs.

"Frauenhuber Café," she said to the taxi driver.

We walked toward our regular table in room number three. Dr. Richter and Rudolph greeted us. "*Guten abend* [Good evening]."

"*Guten abend.* Please sit down," Constantina said, dressed in a purple conservative dress. She put her purse on the table and sat against the wall. "Have you been waiting long?" she asked, removing white gloves.

"No, we just came in ten minutes ago." Looking at me, Dr. Richter said, "Verga, how are you?"

"I'm fine, thanks."

"May I?" Dr. Richter lit a cigarette and said, "Verga, are you all packed and ready for tomorrow?"

"Yes, Professor Heilbronner was kind enough to give me a small suitcase."

"Excellent. We will pick you up tomorrow at 10:00. Our flight to Milan is at 12:30 p.m."

The waiter came with the menu. "Anything to drink?" he asked.

"Rudolph, please order a bottle of wine," I suggested.

"Red or white?"

Constantina answered, "White, please."

Rudolph looked at the wine list. "*Chorherren Klosterneuburg* [chardonnay], please."

Dr. Richter continued talking with a cigarette between his fingers. "Let's go over the itinerary." Rudolph handed him his red leather memo book. Dr. Richter put his spectacles on his face. "Our flight is on Pan Am. They are one of the sponsors of the piano competition. We will be picked up at Milan Airport by a driver for a short ride to the city center. Our accommodations at the Grand Hotel et de Milan on Via Manzoni were arranged by the Gluck Financial Group. In the evening, we are having a get together gala at Palazzo Reale. It's only a short walk from the hotel. Verga, did you pack formal wear?"

"Yes, in a separate garment bag."

He pulled out a program sheet. "As of last week, there are twenty-four pianists competing. The competition is divided into four groups. You are in group B."

"Who is in group B?" I asked.

Just then, the waiter came with the bottle of wine and placed it into a silver bucket of ice. He uncorked the bottle and filled Rudolph's crystal goblet. Rudolph smelled, then sipped the wine, and nodded in approval.

Constantina lifted her glass. "Salute! Wow, delicious. Fresh and flowery aroma. Good selection, Rudolph."

"Thanks."

I sipped wine and listened to Dr. Richter, who said, "Let me continue. We arrive on Thursday. On Friday, the competition will start with elimination. Groups B and D. On Saturday, groups A and

C. Sunday is an off day, but a list of semifinalists will be posted that morning. I'm confident you will make the semifinals." He looked at me. "On Monday and Tuesday, the semifinalists will compete, and the result will be posted on Wednesday morning. Wednesday and Thursday will be off days. The finalists will compete Friday. On Saturday morning, a list of first-, second-, and third-place winners will be announced. On Saturday evening, there will be a gala and presentation of diplomas and prizes."

I repeated my question. "Who is on the list for group B?"

Dr. Richter flipped through the pages, looking at the red memo book. "Group B. Your competitors are Vincent Duparc from France, Newvryk Wieniawski from Poland, and Anton Kodaly from Hungary." Dr. Richter glanced at me and continued to read from his list. "Mangnus Sinding from Finland, Robert Henselt from West Germany, and you. You play last in the group."

"Hungarian? How interesting. I wonder who he is."

"I read his background. He studied in the Liszt Academy of Music in Budapest. On Wednesday, we are all invited to a tour of the city sponsored by the Milan Commerce and Business Community. In the evening, we are all invited to see *Tosca* at the Conservatorio di Musica.

"The conservatory provides a practice studio for each of the competitors; however, I arranged for a practice piano in the Austrian Consulate if you need. Let's review the competition repertoire. Verga, you chose to play in the elimination round Chopin's *Études* op. 10 and op. 25. In the semifinal round, you chose to play Schumann's *Fantaisie* in C Major op. 17 and Franz Schubert's Impromptu D. 899 (op. 90). And if you make the finals, your recital choice is Chopin's Prelude op. 28, no. 15 in D-flat Major and Ballad no. 1 in G Minor op. 23, one of the most complex and challenging pieces in piano repertoire. I think choosing Chopin is a smart move. There are four judges from Poland on the jury, and Chopin's music should resonate with the judges, especially the difficult coda."

Constantina interrupted, "Let's order the food. It's getting late."

The next morning, Constantina and I meditated. As we finished, she turned around toward me. "Don't forget to meditate every day. Don't eat heavy foods before the performance. Stay away from alcohol. Drink lots of water."

I was sitting on the floor, holding her hand. "I will miss you," I said.

"I will miss you too," she replied then stood up. "Verga, I want you to have this pendant." She took a black velvet box from the table and sat next to me. "It was my husband's. When the Gestapo pushed him and dragged him to the car, it was torn from his neck. I found it on the sidewalk. I want you to have it." She opened the box and placed the pendant around my neck.

I held the gold cylindrical tube, examining it. "What kind of jewelry is this?" I asked.

"The Jewish people call it a mezuzah, and the inside is Shema, prayer on parchment."

"I like the gold figurine design."

"I'm glad you like it. Mayer told me it was in his family for a long time."

"I'm honored to have it. Thank you."

"It has meaning for me. I lost my love and found another, and you should have it. It will remind you of me."

"Thanks, I will keep it next to my heart." I kissed her.

The door opened. It was Maria. "Good morning."

"Good morning, Maria. You are early today," I said.

"I want to wish you bon voyage and good luck. Please, breakfast is ready."

Dressed in black pants, white shirt, a tie, and jacket, I placed the suitcase on the floor in the vestibule. "The car should be here in ten minutes," Constantina said. "Let's go to the salon."

She was dressed in blue pants and a green-and-yellow polka-dotted silk shirt. Maria came from the kitchen with a paper bag. "I made apple pierogies for your trip."

"Thanks, Maria. I'll put them in my bag."

"Sit on the sofa," Constantina said. "It's a tradition I learned from the Russians. Before embarking on a long trip, we sit in silence for a minute, reflecting on the journey and wish for safe travel."

I sat on the sofa in silence, looking at Maria. She prayed and crossed her chest. She was a devoted Catholic. Constantina held my hand, eyes blank. I focused on the black Steinway, thinking of the many hours I spent with this instrument; it almost became part of me. I had poured my melancholy, happiness, joy, and dreams on the black-and-white keys. For some reason, I felt like I was saying good-bye. Then I was snapped from my thoughts.

"The car is here," Maria said.

The doorbell rang. It was Rudolph. "Good morning. Are you ready, Verga?" he said in his baritone voice that echoed throughout the house.

I turned toward Constantina. "I'm so sorry, darling, you're not coming with me."

"You'll do fine." Tears fell from her eyes.

"Why are you crying? I'll be back in two weeks."

"I am overjoyed at your successes."

I took my handkerchief and wiped her tears. She let a smile on her lush red lips. I wanted to kiss them but restrained myself. We hugged, her smell intoxicating me. I whispered in her ear, "I love you, darling."

"Me too," she said in a hushed voice. "Good luck, Verga."

Maria said good-bye. I hugged her. "I wish you a safe trip and to win first prize." She crossed herself again, holding her hands in a prayer.

Rudolph helped me with my suitcase. I walked to the black Mercedes, where the chauffeur held the door open. Dr. Richter waved to Constantina from the sidewalk. As the car drove, I glanced through the rear window. Constantina and Maria waved their hands. The image of them got smaller and smaller then vanished. Only Constantina's perfume on my cheek left her presence.

THREE

It was my first time on a plane. I found it a little scary although exciting. We landed in Milan Linate Airport. At 4:00 p.m., we arrived at the Grand Hotel et de Milan, also known as Milanese House of Giuseppe Verdi, where the composer wrote his famous operas, *Otello* and *Falstaff,* only minutes away from the doors of Teatro alla Scala and a short walk to Conservatorio di Musica Giuseppe Verdi, where the piano competition was to take place.

Near the hotel were Piazza del Duomo and Palazzo Reale, where we were invited to tonight's reception. At the front desk, the cheerful receptionist informed me that Maria Callas was staying at the hotel, and I hoped to see her in the lobby. My luxurious room was on the third floor overlooking Via Alessandro Manzoni.

That evening, dressed in formal wear, I met Dr. Richter and Rudolph in the lobby. We walked briskly toward Palazzo Reale. The air was warm. As we crossed the street, small cars and scooters zipped along busy Via Manzoni. Stores and cafés opened, full of cheerful, loud Italians dressed in the latest fashions. I admittedly fell in love with the pulse of the city. Passing Piazza Fontana, I saw a sculpture of a maiden holding a large pool of water overhead and spewing a stream into the lower pool below. Next to it was a magnificent cathedral, the Duomo, lit and shining white against its speared façade. It took my breath away.

Dr. Richter said, "Verga, take the opportunity to visit the Duomo and climb to the roof terraces. The view of the city from the roof is simply unforgettable."

Right behind the Duomo on Via dell'Arcivescovado was Palazzo Reale, a large imposing building with a neoclassical façade dated 1778 when Giuseppe Piermarini made it into a residence for Archduke Ferdinand of Austria.

A large banner hung on the building that read, "Welcome, International Young Pianist Competition, August 18–28, 1960."

We were greeted at the entrance by security men dressed in black suits. "Your names please?" They checked a list. "Welcome, please pick up your name tags." One pointed to a desk.

The elaborate Palazzo Hall was full of noisy attendants. Groups of people conversed with one another. Waiters in white jackets offered wine and soft drinks. I circulated through the crowd, looking at name tags and countries of origin: Poland, France, Bulgaria, Norway, and Switzerland. I had never experienced being at such an international gathering of musicians. My eyes searched for Anton Kodaly from Hungary, but I couldn't find him in the crowd. I wanted to hear from him about the lives of Hungarians after the failed revolt.

Accidentally, I bumped into a woman in a black gown. "Sorry," I said. She turned around. We looked at each other's name tags. "I'm sorry to disturb you."

"It is quite all right," she smiled, holding a glass of wine. "Verga Caszar? Austria? That sounds Hungarian."

"Yes, I was born in Hungary."

She extended her hand. "Clara Smith from Great Britain. You speak perfect English."

"Thanks."

Then she introduced me to the tall blonde she was talking to. "This is Natasha Kabayeva from Russia."

"It is my pleasure," I said.

Natasha spoke rudimentary English but smiled at me.

"Are you both in the competition?" I asked.

"Yes," Clara said, "and I presume you are too."

I nodded. Just then, an announcement was made. "Please proceed to the next room."

"I wish you good luck, ladies." Then we parted.

I searched for Dr. Richter and Rudolph when I remembered my seat assignment: row F 12. I ambled into the next room, sitting between a

Swede and a Bulgarian, listening to the master of ceremony. "Would the contestants please stand up?"

We stood, and applause echoed in the hall. Then he read all the pianists' names. We waved when our names were called. I finally saw Anton, a young man my age seated two rows in front of me. The master of ceremony introduced the judges, and then there were more speeches by competition sponsors.

Afterward, we were all invited to the next hall for a self-service banquet. I was impressed with the culinary spread. Milan is a powerhouse of industry, finance, and fashion; and Milan, more than any other Italian city, has embraced international cuisine. It was the first time I tasted risotto laced with butter and parmesan; asparagus topped with eggs and grated with local cheese; casseroles with meat, grains, and vegetables; more cheeses; and cold cuts. I remembered Constantina's advice. *Don't eat too much before the competition.* I stopped eating and turned away from eye-popping, tempting desserts.

I searched for Anton in the crowd and found him conversing with a man and a woman both dressed in black. I approached him, took a deep breath, then said in Hungarian, "May I introduce myself?"

He was surprised, turned around, and looked at my name tag, holding a plate of food. "Verga Caszar? Oh yes, I've heard of you," he said, extending his hand. He introduced me to the couple standing next to him. "Erno and Zsofia."

"It is a pleasure to meet you," I said.

They looked at me with interest. "Where are you staying?" Erno asked.

"At Hotel Milan."

"Very nice hotel," Zsofia said, drinking wine, examining me with piercing eyes.

I felt uncomfortable talking to Anton in front of the couple. He said, "Would you care for a cup of espresso?" He pointed to the nearby espresso counter.

"Yes, let's have a coffee."

We walked toward the coffee bar. As I was waiting for the waiter to make me an espresso, Anton, standing next to me, whispered in a low voice, "Verga, be careful of what you say to me. Erno and Zsofia are my handlers and agents of the *Államvédelmi Hatóság* [Hungarian Secret Police]."

I almost dropped my cup of coffee. I thought of how naïve I was, not realizing that Anton was watched by secret agents to make sure he would not defect to the West. I deliberately switched the conversation to music in a loud voice. I said, "Do you have an opinion on György Kurtág and his interpretation of Bartok's piano works?"

Anton's eyes lit up. Sipping coffee, he said, "You know, Verga, György is a great teacher. He just came from Paris after spending a year there. Now he is teaching piano at the Liszt Academy where I graduated. He is a wonderful, inspiring teacher."

Erno and Zsofia were not standing that far from us, listening to our conversation. Anton spoke loudly so they could hear us. Dr. Richter and Rudolph interrupted our discussion. "Verga, let's head back to your hotel. Tomorrow will be a busy day."

I shook Anton's hand. "*Sok szerecsét* [Good luck]. You are in group B like me."

"I know. I will see you tomorrow. *Jóéjt* [Good night]."

I turned toward Erno and Zsofia and nodded. "Jóéjt."

"Who is that couple?" Dr. Richter asked.

"Oh, just part of the Hungarian competition." As we walked toward the hotel, I thought that something bothered me about Erno and Zsofia, especially Zsofia. It was something about her dark eyes. She looked menacing, but I couldn't quite place it. *Oh well,* I said to myself, *you have a rich imagination.*

The next morning, the phone rang. "Mr. Caszar, this is your six o'clock wakeup call."

I opened the window and looked at the street below. It was deserted. The sun had just risen from the east. I stretched into a yoga meditation position. The cool morning breeze entered through the window. Dressed, I glanced at Via Manzoni again. Workers were cleaning the sidewalk. Some pedestrians rushed down the street with light traffic on the road. *Today will be another nice day,* I said to myself and decided to take a quick walk to explore the neighborhood before breakfast.

"Buongiorno," said the doorman.

"Good morning."

He opened the door for me. Walking briskly toward Piazza della Scala and stopping at Teatro alla Scala, I ambled under the arched masonry portico. The doors were locked. I thought of the many famous musicians, singers, and composers who had passed through these doors.

My heart pounded with excitement. I touched the door handles, thinking two thousand people had passed through these doors to listen and see opera or dance. I recalled my history lessons. The theater was originally known as the New Royal-Ducal Theatre alla Scala in 1778. Antonio Salieri's *Europa Riconosciuta* was performed. *What a coincidence. It's the same month.* Toscanini, Giuseppe Verdi, Giacomo Puccini, Soprano Renata te Baldi, and Maria Callas sang on the stage of alla Scala. For a moment, I had a foolish thought. *Maybe one day, I will perform here too.*

I continued walking toward the Galleria Vittorio Emanuele II. "Wow," I exclaimed, looking at the soaring space in front of me. I walked toward the middle of the octagonal room. My head tilted up, gazing at the glass skylight five stories high, thinking of it as a musical composition of marble, stone, glass, and iron, a symphony of architecture. Glancing at my watch, I saw that it was eight thirty. I needed to go back to meet Dr. Richter. Reluctantly, I walked to the hotel.

At 4:00 p.m., I was scheduled to play in front of the judges. I walked through the corridors of the conservatory toward Sala Puccini, which was normally used for chamber music performances; but for the next two days, it was reserved for the piano competition. Students rushed toward their studios as I strolled down corridors, my eyes admiring the portraits on the wall of past and present musicians, singers, and composers. I paused to look at Verdi's portrait, thinking this genius of opera was ironically refused admission to this institution and now it bears his name. I read the bronze plaque on the wall that stated that the Milan Conservatory was founded by Viciroy Eugene de Beauharnais in 1808, and now it was the largest institute of music education in Italy.

I continued walking and stopped in front of the library. I was told that it contained over 35,000 books and 460,000 pieces of written music, scores, and manuscripts—works of Mozart, Rossini, Donizetti, Bellini, Verdi, and others. I entered the library and sat at a long table, admiring the two-story space with balconies, books neatly stored behind caged doors, and students and researchers immersed in reading and writing. My eyes looked at the round windows on the second level, spewing the light of the day into the room. My watch showed 3:15 p.m. *I still have time*, I said to myself, thinking somewhere on these shelves were notes and scores of Frederick Chopin's *Études*, op. 10 and op. 25, which I was scheduled to perform in one hour. In front of me were young students the same age as Chopin when he composed his first étude: youthful, passionate, and charming. Regarding Chopin's *Études*, Franz Liszt said, "At times, his pieces are joyous, and at times, they're depressing like souls in torment who find no prayer of mercy needed for their salvation."

I took a deep breath, stood up, and continued walking toward Puccini's Hall, which was filled with noisy students. On the stage, which was decorated with red and white flower pots, was a lone Steinway piano. Students conversed in low voices. The first row was empty, reserved for judges. I ambled toward Dr. Richter who was waving to me. "Where have you been?" He looked nervous.

"In the library," I whispered.

"Why? You are scheduled to play in twenty minutes."

"I'm ready," I answered in a calm voice.

He proceeded to adjust my tie and straighten my shirt. "Sit here. Let's go over some of my observations of the players today." He looked through his notebook filled with notations, flipping some pages. "Neuryk Wieniawski from Poland. He played the *Études* this morning. It was beautiful. He missed some notes, but he played with such intelligence and good manners I will give him a pass. Your competitor in this group will be, I shall say, is the fellow you spoke with last night, Anton Kodaly of Hungary. He chose to perform Beethoven's Waldstein Sonata op. 53." Dr. Richter glanced at his comments. "He plays like how Liszt would perform an excellent interpretation of Beethoven, fast and crisp. I gave him a pass. Verga, I predict he will be one of the finalists in your group."

Now it was my turn to play Chopin. It was quiet. I sat in front of the piano, looking at the judges. The head judge stood up, announcing my play, "Verga Caszar has selected to play Chopin's *Études*, op. 10 and op. 25. Maximum playtime, thirty minutes. Please proceed when you are ready."

I took a deep breath, looking at the keyboard. Then I played the first piece with arpeggios, focusing on stretching my long fingers on my right hand and activating the piano hammers. My hands moved fast in hypnotic charm like stripping bark from a tree, skeletonizing Chopin's notes. I concentrated on the technical difficulty of the pieces, playing uninterrupted right-handed arpeggios then swift position changes. I overcame my first difficulty. My wandering fingers caressed the keyboard with magical chords in dizzying speed then slow dreamy movements. I was exhausted after playing seven Chopin *Études* and had six to go. Silence. I played op. 25 no. 1's right-handed melody with a supportive bass line accompanied with broken chords, both hands playing a haunting melody. I finished with Étude no. 6 in G-sharp Minor, harvesting all my emotions into my play. I finished playing with a beautiful harmony and visible grace. Silence. The Puccini Hall erupted in loud applause. My shirt was soaked with perspiration. I wiped my forehead with my handkerchief, my hands slightly shaking from strenuous finger stretching. I stood up and bowed deeply twice then stepped from the stage.

Dr. Richter smiled, embracing me enthusiastically. "Truly great play," he said. "Op. 25 no. 6 was very interesting. Some departure from the printed score. Otherwise, another fantastic play. Verga, you made me proud."

"Thanks." Exhausted but elated, we walked toward the exit. As I passed the last row, I noticed Zsofia in a black dress and a black hat, like a black widow. She set her penetrating eyes on me, a slight inscrutable smile adorning her large red lips. A chill passed through my spine.

Sunday was a day off. It was quiet on the street below. Lying in bed, I was still excited from last night's opera performance of *Tosca* in the Conservatorio di Musica. I thought of act 2. Tosca, in despair, agrees to submit to Scarpia in return for Cavaradossi's freedom. Scarpia tells his deputy, Spoletta, to arrange a mock execution, telling him, "As we did with Count Palmieri [fire with real bullets]." Following Spoletta's departure, Tosca sings her additional conditions, asking Scarpia to provide a safe convent for herself and her lover. As Scarpia triumphantly embraces her, she quietly takes a knife from the table and stabs him, crying, "This is Tosca's kiss." Scarpia falls dead.

That was a great performance by the students, I thought.

Looking at the clock, it was 8:15 a.m. At 10:00, a list of names would be posted for those who advance to the semifinal stage of the competition. *Will my name be on that list?* I promised Constantina I would call her at eleven to let her know.

In the lobby, Dr. Richter and Rudolph waited for me to have breakfast. "Good morning, Verga. How did you sleep?"

"Very well, thanks."

The waiter appeared. "What would you like for breakfast?"

"Just orange juice and coffee."

"Yes, right away, sir."

"You're not hungry today?" Rudolph asked while looking at the menu.

"No, I have no appetite this morning. My stomach is sour." I glanced at the clock. Nine twenty.

I glanced at Dr. Richter, who was calm, drinking coffee, showing no nervousness. He asked, "Verga, how did you like *Tosca* last night at the conservatory?"

"A great performance by the students. I've always liked *Tosca*, especially act 2, 'Tosca's Kiss.'"

"What are you planning to do today?"

"First, I'm anxious to see if I made the semifinals. It's been on my mind all morning."

"I'm confident you made the list." Dr. Richter lit a cigarette. "I will make a call in fifteen minutes. I know the judge's secretary, Antonio. He promised to let me know."

"That would be great," I said. "If I made the list, I would like to call Professor Heilbronner. And in the evening, I will go to the movies down the street to see *A Breath of Scandal* with Sofia Lauren. I heard of her, but I never had a chance to see her on the big screen."

Rudolph, eating his frittata with spinach and ham, said, "Have some of this focaccia bread. It is delicious." He offered it to me.

"Thanks."

"Would you like to join us? We're going to visit Pinacoteca di Brera, the art gallery."

"Thanks, I was planning to see Leonardo DaVinci's *Last Supper* in the refectory of Santa Maria delle Grazie and then walk around Castello Sforzesco and Via Dante."

"Good choice," Dr. Richter said, wiping his lips and looking at his watch. "Excuse me, I will make the call."

Fidgeting nervously, I waited and played with the fork on the table. Rudolph said, "Calm down, Verga," as he took the fork from my hand.

I stood up and went to the lobby. Dr. Richter was talking on the house phone, making notations on a piece of paper. I sat down in a nearby chair and eyed him. Dr. Richter came over with a serious expression then smiled. "I told you you would make the semifinals!"

I let out a heavy breath from my lungs. It was like a stone was lifted from my chest. My whole body relaxed. "That's great!" I banged my fist on the arm of the sofa. "Who is on the list?" I asked.

"The Polish pianist, Anton Kodaly, and you from group B. Within groups A, C, and D, is a total of eight semifinalists."

I rushed to my room to call Constantina. "I made the semifinals!" I screamed into the phone.

"Verga, I didn't doubt it. I miss you, love."

"I miss you too. I wish you were here. It's so different than Vienna, so alive, so refreshing, a relaxed atmosphere. And the Italians are so friendly."

"I know. I just came back from Italy."

"So much to see. We took a tour of the city. I love Milan. We were given a tour of Teatro alla Scala. I saw *Tosca* last night. I wish you were here."

"That sounds lovely. When are you scheduled to play the semifinals?"

"On Tuesday at 2:00 p.m. Tomorrow, I will take time to practice my repertoire."

"You will do fine. Concentrate on Weber's variations on 'Gypsy Song' and repeat your performance of Franz's impromptu and you will make the finals. I will let you go. Relax. Meditate. Do not eat heavy food. Drink lots of water. Love you."

After going to the theater, I returned to my room at 10:15 p.m. I switched the TV to channel 2. On the screen was a comedy in English with Italian subtitles. It was the first time I watched Jerry Lewis, an American comedian, on TV. He made me laugh. For the past few days, I hadn't bothered to watch the tube since I was concentrating on the piano repertoire. Then the phone rang. "Yes?"

"This is Fabiana, the front desk receptionist. You are invited to the lounge for a drink."

"Who is inviting me?" I looked at the clock: 10:15.

There was a silence on the wire. Then the voice of the desk receptionist came on. "A woman admirer of yours," she said.

"Are you sure this invitation is for me?"

"Yes, Mr. Caszar."

"Okay, I'll be there in fifteen minutes."

Who could this be? I thought. I did not know any woman here. I was curious to find out.

The hotel lounge was filled with people elegantly dressed, smoking and speaking loudly. A jazz band played a slow tune. Some ladies and gentlemen danced on the round dance floor. I went to the bar and ordered a glass of Campari and soda, wondering who the mystery woman could be. A waiter tapped my shoulder. "Yes?"

"Sorry, sir, you are invited to the table." He pointed to the far side of the dance floor.

I looked. It was the blonde, Zsofia, Anton's handler. I thought, *Why me? What does she want?*

"*Jó estét* [Good evening]," I spoke in Hungarian.

"*Jó estét*, Mr. Caszar."

"Thank you for your invitation."

"Please, sit down." She pointed to a chair next to her. She looked different today, fashionably dressed in a sexy red sleeveless dress, blond hair down to her shoulders, lips red. She smirked, dark eyes friendly. "Congratulations, I watched you play. You are a very talented pianist."

"Thanks."

"How do you like Milan?"

"I love the city. How about you?"

"I love Italy. For me, it's not the first time. Cigarette?"

"No," I said. "I don't smoke."

"May I?"

"Please."

She took a cigarette and slowly put it between her lush crimson lips. I took the lighter from her hand and lit it. She placed her two hands around mine, looking at me then lit her cigarette. She gently closed the lighter, smiling. "You're wondering why I asked for you."

"To be polite," I answered. "The pleasure is mine."

She blew the smoke sideways. "You know, Mr. Caszar—"

"Please, call me Verga."

"You know, Verga, listening to your play, you have a Hungarian soul. I could feel it. Only Hungarians can play like a virtuoso, like Liszt and George Cziffra, our treasured pianists. Would you like another drink?"

"How about you?" I waved to a waiter. "Please, what do you drink?"

"Vodka martini with an olive," she said.

"I will have Campari and soda."

"Very well." The waiter nodded and left.

"Thank you for your compliment. How is Anton doing? I haven't seen him in the conservatory," I said.

"He's fine. He's practicing for the second round of the competition. Let's talk about you. As I was saying, the situation in the People's

Republic of Hungary is changing. The standard of living is constantly rising. People are happy. Musicians and artists have great opportunities. The people of Hungary admire them. They are considered our stars. The state pays for all their expenses. They can travel abroad, no pressure, not like in the West, not like in the capitalist West, where it's 'dog eat dog.' Musicians and artists struggle and are manipulated by money-hungry managers and recording companies."

I thought, *Where is this conversation headed?*

"Verga, your country is calling you. You belong in Hungary. The state gave you your early education. It's time for you to give back and receive generosity from the people of Hungary. Your home is calling you."

The waiter came with the drinks. "Your room please?" He gave me the check.

"No, no," she said. "It's on me." She paid and tipped the waiter.

"Thanks for the drinks," I said.

"For Hungary." She lifted her glass.

I said, "For music, art, and freedom. Is that why you invited me? You should probably know I escaped from tyranny to freedom, and you ask me to go back to a state that killed my father? How could I?"

Her demeanor changed. Her friendly eyes changed to piercing and ominous. "Your father was a subatoire and ungrateful for what the people of Hungary gave to him." She took a sip of the martini. Then her look softened. She put on a jovial face. "But we Hungarian people are the forgiving type. Your father is forgiven for his deeds. You are welcomed back with open arms. Your talents will be well rewarded. In Austria, you will always be considered a foreigner." She smiled and put her hand on my leg. "Think about what I said. How about dancing?" she said in a seductive voice.

I looked at her, thinking, *A devil in a beautiful woman's body.* "I'm sorry, I don't dance." I stood up. "Thank you for the drinks. I have a busy day tomorrow."

"I'm disappointed," she said in a hostile voice, biting the olive with her white teeth.

"Thank you for your offer, but I am not interested to go back to Hungary."

She held the toothpick between her hands. Her demeanor turned sour, showing deep creases hidden behind a heavily powdered, petulant, irritable façade. "Too bad," she said, snapping the toothpick in two. Eyes turned mean, squinting.

"Thank you again for the drinks. Good night." I left the lounge in a hurry.

FOUR

ack at the hotel, I opened the door to my room. On the floor was a large brown envelope. Lifting it up, I saw "To Verga Caszar" written in black ink over the front. The envelope had a printed address, "Conservatorio di Musica." *It must be my play schedule*, I thought to myself. I placed it on the table and took a shower. I dried off and walked to the bedroom, a towel wrapped around my body.

Glancing at the envelope, I tore it open. I pulled out the contents: four eight-by-ten photos. Flipping through them, I froze. My heart stopped beating, my hands shaking. The pictures dropped to the floor. My legs wobbled. I sat on a chair motionless, horrified, looking at the arrangement of photos on the floor. *How is it possible? Who took these?* A thousand thoughts ran through my head. After the initial bombshell, I picked up the pictures. I spread them on the table, looking at the grainy black-and-white photos of Constantina and me dancing naked in the rain, Constantina and me kissing naked under the tree, Constantina on my lap in a grip of love. The last photo was of Constantina and me embracing, walking on the trail, our faces clearly depicted. I was stunned. *What is this all about? Blackmail? Extortion? How much will the extortionist ask for? How is it possible? Only a few people knew we were planning a walk in the woods. Hans, why would he do this? Anyone else?* My mind went blank. I took the envelope and looked inside. There was a typed note. With shaking hands, I read it,

Mr. Caszar, you are to be on the Duomo roof terrace today at 5:30 p.m. Come alone. No tricks. You are being watched.

I read the note several times and then dropped the message on the floor. The photos and message were vindictive like a jab to my face shaking me to the core. *Who is this from?* I wondered. I decided to call Hans but got his secretary instead.

"He is in a conference," she said. I left my hotel and room number so he could call me back.

It was after 3:00 p.m. as I nervously paced around my room. *Why hasn't he called?* I asked, agonized. The phone finally rang around the next hour I rushed to pick it up. It was Dr. Richter.

"How was your practice today?"

"Very well," I said in a deadened voice.

"Is everything okay?"

"Yes, yes, I'm just tired today."

"Do you want to join us for dinner tonight?"

"No thanks. I decided to rest today and go over my score."

"Good, we will see you for breakfast tomorrow."

"I'll be on time." I hung up, standing in the window, looking at the street. Pedestrians and traffic moved along, normal day events.

The phone rang. It was the hotel telephone operator. "Mr. Caszar, Mr. Gluck called, but your phone was busy. Would you like to place a call back to Vienna?"

"Yes, please," I said in an anxious voice.

"One moment."

My heart pounded as the phone line hummed. "Mr. Caszar, Mr. Gluck is on the line."

"Yes, put him through." Once the line transferred, I said, "Hans!"

"Hey, Verga, how have you been?"

"Not so good."

"What's the matter? Is the competition too much pressure?"

"No, I'm in the semifinals."

"I heard the news. That's great! What's on your mind?"

"Hans, I don't know how to begin."

"Try me. I'm listening."

"Hans, how long have we known each other?"

"At least four years. Why?"

"I need your advice. Can you keep a secret?"

"Of course, you know me."

"I'm in trouble."

"What kind of trouble?"

"I think I'm being blackmailed."

"Blackmailed? A straight guy like you blackmailed? What did you do?" I was silent. "Verga, are you there?"

"Yes, I am."

"Who is blackmailing you?"

"I don't know."

"Start from the beginning. Be clear."

"I came to my room and found an envelope with despicable photos, how shall I say, me in compromising positions, and I'm to meet the sender at 5:30 p.m. today."

"Okay, what's in the photos?"

"You know compromising, scandalous photos."

"Are you, shall I say, with a man?"

"No, Hans, you know me. This is me and a woman."

"A woman? Who?" I was silent. "Verga, if you don't tell me who, how can I help you?"

I didn't know what to say. "Hans, the woman is Professor Wordzinka."

There was a pause on the line. "Professor Wordzinka? Verga, for some reason, I suspected something between the two of you last time I saw you in our country estate. I noticed the way you spoke and looked at each other. Anyhow, that's not my business. What's in the photos? Tell me in detail."

"Last time we were in your country estate, we went for a walk in the woods. You know, how shall I say, something happened."

"You made love to her?"

I did not answer for a minute. "Yes, Hans, we made love."

"If I remember, it rained that day."

"Yes, it did rain."

"Oh, Verga, why in all places, would you make up in the open like that?"

"Hans, it happened. I can't figure out who is responsible for these photos. How did someone manage to get these? I'm scared. Someone is watching me."

He was quiet then said, "Make a list of the people you come in contact with who knew you would be in the country estate that weekend. Then eliminate the ones you think should be eliminated. List all your friends and enemies."

"Hans, I don't have enemies."

"Yes, you do. List them as enemy X. Does Professor Wordzinka know about this?"

"No, I did not call her."

"Good, keep this a secret. Meet with the extortionist. See what he wants, then call me tonight on the private line. Do you have the number?"

"Yes, it's on your business card."

"Okay, be cool. Go meet the blackmailer. If it's money, I can probably help. Do not promise anything. Be careful."

"Thanks, Hans."

"Okay, I'll let you go. Verga, you are a person of good taste and lover of beauty, I have to say, choosing a cultured woman like Professor Wordzinka."

At 5:00 p.m., I left the hotel toward Duomo's terraced roof, which was littered with many tourists taking photos and enjoying the aerial view of the city. I walked slowly, looking for the possible blackmailer within the crowd. This one with dark glasses, no. This one with the dark hat, no. Possibly this woman with the camera. After a while, I relinquished my search, my eyes wandering, looking over the roof of the galleria. Then I heard a man's voice talking to me in Hungarian. "Don't look at me. Walk slowly." I had heard that voice before. When? Where? I tried to place it.

"Erno," I said. He did not answer.

We walked slowly on the terrace between the tourists. I asked, "What do you want?"

"Mr. Caszar, if you make the finals in the competition, we want you to quit."

"And if I don't?"

"Simply putting it, we will publish these photos."

"I can go to the police. This is blackmail."

"The police will laugh at you."

"Austrians will not publish such photos."

"Here in Italy and England, they will. It will destroy your reputation, Mr. Caszar."

I swallowed hard and stopped walking by the railing, turning around, looking directly at his face. Erno wore black glasses. I said, "How much do you want?"

He let out a laugh. "You guys in the west always thinking about money. This has nothing to do with money. It has to do with the Hungarian Republic's prestige. No money can buy prestige or honor of the state."

"Is this all about your guy, Anton, making the finals, and I am in his way? How come you're so confident that Anton will make the finals?"

"We know he will make it, including all the socialist republic pianists, because we are culturally superior to the west. Did you see the list of judges?"

"How did you get these photos?"

"We have our methods. We've watched you since you won the first prize in Vienna. We keep files. Besides, the photos are taken in the woods, a public space."

"You're bluffing."

"We never bluff, Mr. Caszar."

"Is this your revenge for me saying no to Zsofia last night?"

"Mr. Caszar, you were very clear last night. Our motto is 'He who is not with us is against us.' So if you are to make the finals, quit before it is too late. We have more of those photos, and we intend to publish them all. Think hard about what I said." Then he walked away, leaving me standing on the terrace.

The confrontation was hard for me to understand. I spit on the floor. *To hell with the bullying state. They are bluffing and pressuring me, scaring me.* I rushed back to the hotel. I needed to think of possible photographers responsible for this blackmail. I made a short list and placed it on the mirror with two Band-Aid strips then started elimination of names. Two were left on the list: enemy X and Odon. *Odon? He did screw me over once before at the Red Cross center. I did tell him that I would be staying in the Glucks' estate for three weeks. Is it possible that he is responsible for this? Enemy X? Who can that be? Mimi Schmidt? Her manager, Emile von Fuch? Odon helped me write a fabulous article in the* Wein Evening Gazette. *Why would he take these photos? It doesn't make any sense. Is it for money? Is it possible that he sold these photos to the secret police? No, it doesn't make any sense. It must be enemy X, but who?* I came to a dead end.

I called Hans. No one answered. I placed a call to Constantina. The phone was busy, and for the next three hours, I wasn't able to reach either one of them. At 10:45 p.m., I rang Hans again. He picked up the phone. "Verga, is that you?" His voice was sad.

"Are you okay?" I said.

"Verga, I have bad news?"

"What is it?"

"I got a call from Maria. She was frantic. She wanted me to come right away. I took a taxi and rushed to Professor Wordzinka's home. Maria was in a panic, crying. I asked what happened. She told me she was in the laundry room downstairs ironing when she heard the doorbell ring. Professor Wordzinka answered it. Ten minutes thereafter, she heard the professor screaming. She grabbed a fireplace shovel and rushed upstairs just as Professor Wordzinka began struggling against a man. Maria surprised him. He pushed the professor, and she fell on the marble stair banging her head. The intruder escaped through the front door. Maria called the ambulance and the police. The professor asked Maria to call me. In Professor Wordzinka's lap, Maria found a crumbled envelope. She did not give it to the police; she gave it to me." My hands were shaking and I stopped breathing. Cold sweat ran down my face. My tongue froze in my mouth. "Verga, are you listening to me?"

I made an effort to answer, "Yes."

"Terrible, terrible. The police came and took fingerprints. Maria never told them about the envelope. They were the same photos you received today. I have them in my vault."

"This is all my fault. My lust got Constantina in trouble. It's all my fault." I trembled and mumbled, "How stupid I am."

"Verga, don't blame yourself. We need to deal with this with cool heads."

"I'm quitting the competition," I said.

"Stop it, stop it. I don't want to hear you're quitting. Don't show weakness. Be strong. Win your righteous place in the competition. Show this bastard that you are not afraid. Do it for Constantina and for me."

"Hans, I think I want to go back to Vienna. I must see her in the hospital."

"Don't do it. Stay where you are. I will check on her tomorrow."

"Hans, she needs me. I must leave tomorrow."

"No, Verga. If you quit, I will not support you. She's in the hospital under good care. Let her recover. She will not approve of your quitting. She never quit as a teacher. And before I forget, what does the extortionist want?" I was distraught. My mind was somewhere else, drifting toward horrible thoughts. "Verga, answer me. What do they want from you?"

"Hans, these agents from the Hungarian Secret Police want me to quit the competition."

He was silent then he said, "I think they're bluffing. I think they manufactured this on their own to boost their reputation. Ignore them, but be careful. God forbid they can hurt you. Lock the door. Don't open it for strangers. Stay with a crowd. Don't venture outside by yourself. I will try to arrange a private guard for you tomorrow. Okay, stay cool. I will talk to you tomorrow."

That evening, I slept very little, tossing and staring at the dark ceiling, jumping at the slightest noises from the hallway. My thoughts occupied me all night. *Should I continue with the competition or not?* Agitated, my mind drifted from Constantina's well-being to the threats of Erno and Zsophia. Finally, in the wee hours of morning, I fell asleep.

I woke up to the phone ringing. "Yes?" I answered.

It was Dr. Richter. "Verga, are you awake?"

"Yes."

"I need to see you."

"All right. I will take a shower. You can come in half an hour."

When Dr. Richter and Rudolph arrived, they sat on the armchairs facing me. Dr. Richter looked upset. Rudolph was quiet, glancing at me seriously.

"Verga, sorry to barge in like this so early." Dr. Richter paused then said, "Can I light a cigarette?" He opened the window and said, "Verga, I have bad news."

"Is it about Constantina?"

"Yes." He looked surprised.

"Hans called me last night. Terrible. I haven't slept all night." My voice strained, my body tensed, and my face showed irritability.

"I got a call from Clara this morning, telling me that Professor Heilbronner was assaulted during an attempt of robbery in her house. Horrible. What's happening in our beloved Vienna? We used to have our doors unlocked. Terrible. I'm waiting for Clara's call to let me know how she's doing." He distinguished his cigarette and closed the window. "Verga, I'm concerned about your performance today. Should I try to rearrange the schedule?"

I was silent for a minute, thinking of Hans's words, "Don't quit." It echoed in my head. "No, no. I will be fine. I have a small request. Can Rudolph stay with me? I don't want to be alone today."

"Of course," Rudolph said. "Should I order breakfast?"

"Please," I answered, buttoning my shirt with quivering fingers.

Hans called that morning. "Verga, how are you doing?"

"I'm upset and jittery. Otherwise, I'm all right. Rudolph is staying with me in the room. How is Constantina?"

"I spoke to the head nurse. No change since yesterday. She's sedated. They're planning to take X-rays of her head sometime today. Listen, Verga. I arranged for a private guard for you. His name is Luigi Paisiello. I also want you to change your room to the first floor. It will be a conjoining room with Luigi. He speaks good English. Listen to him and you will be all right. I still think the Hungarians are bluffing, trying to scare you. I wish you all the best. Make the finals. I will call you tonight."

"Thanks for everything, Hans."

The semifinals were held in the main auditorium of the conservatory. Standing backstage, I waited for my name to be called. Rudolph stood next to me, straightened my jacket, and adjusted my tie.

"You'll be fine. Play Schubert the way you played in Vienna, and you will make the finals. Take a deep breath. Exhale. Good."

My name was called on stage. Sitting on the piano chair, harnessing all my emotions and strength, I closed my eyes. Silence. All was quiet in the hall. I played *Fantaisie* in C Major op. 17, Schumann's piano tribute to Beethoven. My hands glided over the keyboard in passionate kaleidoscopic notes, thinking of beloved Constantina and my predicament. I dedicated today's performance to her. While playing, Friedrich von Schiller's poetic lines resonated in my head: "Through all the sounds of Earth's mingled dreams, lies one quiet note for the secret listener."

Oh, my secret love, can you hear me? Can you hear my notes coming from the Steinway? I played the tranquil melody as Schumann intended. He quoted Beethoven's words when he composed this piece: "Take then, these songs, my love."

During my second piece, "Triumphal March," my fingers played with constant symmetrical rhythms, gliding gracefully over the keyboard. Then my hands played exuberantly, leaping over the keys, sounding joyful notes. I remembered Constantina saying, "Verga, when you play this piece, it makes me hot and cold all over."

For the third piece, "Wreath of Stars," my hands glided with calm slow movements like nature manifested itself into a vast musical landscape, suggesting serenity, peace, and my despair. I ended with silence, eyes tearing.

The last play of my repertoire was Franz Schubert's impromptu. I performed it with the same technical ability as I last played it in Vienna, playing dark but still lyrical sounds, fingers oscillating like hummingbird wings. I finished the piece with exquisite melody, somewhat shadowy, emotional music with the last note vibrating throughout the concert hall. Drained, I bowed to the applause and briskly walked backstage right into Rudolph's arms, who hugged me.

"Verga, you played with such emotional intensity today. I broke into tears. It was deep and sensitive. You drew me into Schumann's mysterious, romantic, and enigmatic world."

"Thanks. Can you accompany me to my room?" I mumbled.

That afternoon, I met Luigi, a robust tall middle-aged man. He had a saddle nose and large hands. I moved to my new room at the first level above the lobby. Luigi said, "From now on, do not take the elevator. We will take the open stairs."

Our suites were connected by a door. "Do not lock it," he said. "From now on, you exit and enter through my room. Keep your door locked at all times."

That evening, Hans called. "How was your performance today?"

"Dr. Richter is very optimistic," I answered then anxiously asked, "How's Constantina?"

"No change, Verga. She's still in a deep sleep and has not awakened. She's heavily sedated. Do you feel better having Luigi watching you?"

"Yes, thanks. He acts like an experienced bodyguard."

"Our organization used his agency before. They are very professional."

"What should I say about Luigi and my room change to Dr. Richter?"

"Don't bother. I will call to let him know."

"Good. I will talk to you tomorrow."

That Wednesday evening, I was exhausted. I went to sleep early and woke up the next day refreshed. It was 6:00. I took a shower, then sat, and mediated for thirty minutes. I turned on the TV. The dominating news was the war in the Congo. In Europe, there was tension between east and west over the division of Berlin. In the Americas, Castro's Cuba introduced agrarian reforms and dispossessed large landowners. I shut the tube. A newspaper was shoved under my bedroom door. I opened the adjoining door and peeked in Luigi's room. The bed was empty, blanket and pillows on the floor. I closed the door, thinking, *He must be taking a shower.* I decided to go over my repertoire of Liszt's and Chopin's music in case I made the finals. Engrossed in reading the piano score, I tapped my fingers on the table. The morning sun brightly lit my room. I opened my window and heard clamor from the street.

The phone buzzed. It was Rudolph. "Good morning, Verga. Are you ready for breakfast? We are in the dining room."

"Don't wait for me. Please start. I will be there soon."

I knocked on Luigi's door. No answer. I opened it slightly. "Luigi, are you there?" Glancing in the room, I thought, *How strange. The bed is empty. The pillows and blanket are still on the floor.* Entering, I wondered if he had gone out. The door to the bathroom was ajar, displaying darkness inside. Curious, I switched the light on. The counter was clear except for a shaving kit, and towels were thrown on the floor. As I bent to pick them up, my eyes wandered to the shower curtain. It moved gently. *Someone is behind the curtain!* I froze then left the bathroom in a hurry, rushed to my room, locked the adjoining door, and braced a chair against the doorknob. Now I was in a panic. *Should I call hotel security?* Then it occurred to me. *That door was unlocked that whole time. If someone wanted to harm me, then he had all that time to do it. It must be my imagination.* I decided to look again in Luigi's room.

Entering the bathroom, I threw a towel on the shower curtain. *Oh my god!* I noticed someone's bare foot. Horrified, I stepped back. Then slowly, I approached the shower again. In one hand, I held an empty glass water bottle. The other slightly withdrew the curtain. On the shower floor was Luigi, legs and hands bound with rope. His mouth was shut with white surgical tape. His eyes were open wide. His cheek was bruised and bleeding. I rushed to remove the tape from his mouth. He spoke to me in Italian like a machine gun.

"Calm down, Luigi, what happened? Tell me in English."

He was still cursing in Italian when I loosened the ropes. He stood up. The shower curtain tore from the ceiling. "Fucking bastards! I will kill them!" He banged his fist on the door.

"Luigi, calm down. Sit down. Have water." He sat in the room, drinking from the bottle, emptying it. "Tell me what happened. Should I call the police?"

"No, no. No polizia." He waved his hands then touched his bruised face.

I went to the bathroom and fetched a wet towel. He placed it on his facial wound. "What happened, Luigi?"

"Fucking bastards! This morning, I was thrown from bed. The fucking woman hit me in the face then sat on me. I fought her, but she was strong. Then a man pinned me down. She placed her leg with her shoe on my face, and then they tied me down and dragged me to the shower and shoved me inside."

"Did you see their faces?" I asked.

"No, it was dark. They wore all black. Black hats, black gloves."

"How do you know it was a woman?"

Luigi stood up and went to the bathroom, still talking to me, examining his face in the mirror. "Fucking bastard! I could smell her perfume."

At this point, I knew it was the one woman here who would want to commit such a nefarious act: Zsophia. "What did they want?" I asked, standing at the door.

He looked in the mirror and said nothing, then turned around, standing in his underwear and T-shirt, looking at the shower. Bending, he picked up an envelope, looked at it, and then handed it to me. Black letters were written across it. "To Verga Caszar."

Luigi searched for bandages in his shaving kit. I stared at the envelope. Something was inside. I retreated to the room. Standing in front of the window, my heart raced. With trembling hands, I tore open the envelope. Something fell on the carpet floor. I bent to pick it up. It was a chicken leg bone broken in half and a note signed with a drawing of a skull and crossbones. Stunned, I stared at the two pieces of bones in my hand and then dropped them on the floor, horrified. I knew what that meant. This was a warning. This time, it was for real. The bastards, Erno and Zsophia, threatened to break my hands. I sat on the chair, looking at the two pieces of bone on the floor, thinking, *Should I quit the piano competition?* My mind flooded with doubt. *Get out of here. You must leave this place. It's not safe. It's not worth losing your fingers or breaking bones to compete.* For some reason, my attitude changed. Calm settled in me. My head cleared, and my heart rate slowed. I picked up the bones and placed them in the envelope.

In the bathroom, Luigi spoke in Italian then repeated in English, "Caszar, what's in the envelope?"

Thinking quickly, I said, "This is a warning for me, Luigi, of a personal vendetta."

He came from the bathroom, his face taped with two Band-Aids. He said, "I need to call my office. They will send another replacement, Mr. Caszar."

"Okay, Luigi. Make sure he speaks German or English." I stood up and said, "Luigi, I'm going to my room. I will call room service."

I locked the door.

Soon, there was a knock. "Who is there?"

"Room service with breakfast, sir."

Standing behind the door, I opened it. A waiter in a white jacket pushing a handcart entered my room. I closed the door. Looking at the waiter, I asked, "What is your name?"

"Gatano, sir."

"Gatano, I would like you to do me a favor. Can I borrow your jacket and cart?" I handed him two hundred twenty-five schillings. "I will leave this jacket in the kitchen on the cart."

He stood there, surprised, thinking, and eyeing the money. He said, "Okay, sir." He took off his jacket and gave it to me.

I put it on. "You stay here for fifteen minutes; then you can go."

I took my briefcase and a jacket and placed it under the white sheet on the cart. I took a deep breath, hoping no one was waiting to harm me in the corridor. I opened the door, not glancing down either side of the hall. I walked toward the service elevator, facing the door. All clear—no one was in the corridor.

Once downstairs, I rolled the cart to the kitchen floor, took off the white jacket and threw it on the cart, took my briefcase and jacket from under the white sheet, and calmly walked toward the service kitchen door. No one paid attention to me. I walked outside to an alley. Two waiters in white jackets were standing, talking aloud, and smoking cigarettes. They looked at me with interest but said nothing. I walked on Via Allesandro Manzoni, blending with the pedestrians. At the corner of Via Senato, I hailed a taxi. "Stazione Centrale," I said to the driver.

FIVE

*A*t Stazione Centrale, I noticed a sign: "Currency exchange." I had 5,000 schillings on me. I changed 2,000 schillings to Italian liras and grabbed an espresso coffee at the stand, glancing around the train station. *Where should I go? Somewhere to be safe and hide for a few days?* An announcement was made on the station intercom. "Departure to Venice on platform 2 in ten minutes."

I finished my coffee and rushed to the ticket counter. "Venezia," I said, pointing my fingers. "Uno, per favore." Then I rushed to the second platform.

As I sat in an empty compartment, a party of two noisy couples entered and made themselves comfortable, talking to me in Italian. "Buongiorno."

I said, "Mi dispiace che ìo non parlano italiano [I don't speak Italian]." The train moved as I introduced myself. "My name is Verga."

"Verga, an Americano?"

"No, no. I'm from Austria."

"Oh, Austria." The couple continued talking to one another in Italian.

For a while, I forgot why I was on the train. Lucia, a robust woman in her forties, talked to me nonstop, asking questions, which I had no way to answer. My Italian was proficient in musical terms only. Half an hour into the trip, my new Italian friends opened their bags, pulling out food—boiled eggs, prosciutto crudo, pancetta, and salame napoletano. Mario took the knife and sliced pecorino cheese and ciabatta bread. The smell of cheese filled the train compartment. A cork was pulled from homemade wine, and an Italian feast commenced. Eating and talking noisily, we conversed with hand motions and drawing pictures on paper, trying to understand each other. After a while, we all dozed off. It was quiet, just the noise of train wheels rushing on the rail to Venice. I looked out the window at passing landscape, thinking, *By now, Dr. Richter read my note I left in the room, wondering where I am.* I took my briefcase, removed the envelope with the blackmailers' black-and-white photos, sifting through them as I thought, *I need to destroy this evidence.* I went to the bathroom, ripped the photos into small pieces, opened the window, and tossed them, watching them fly in the air on the Veneto plain. When I returned to my train compartment, my thoughts shifted to Constantina. *I need to make a phone call when I arrive in Venice. I will stay a day or two then take a train or bus to Vienna.* Looking at the couples in my compartment, now sleeping on each other's shoulders, Lucia and Mario holding hands, I imagined my arms around Constantina. I closed my eyes and fell asleep.

In the afternoon, I arrived at Stazione di Venezia Santa Lucia at the Grand Canal. I parted with my Italian friends. Noisily, they rushed out from the train. I stopped at the tourist information booth and asked for a *pensioni* (boarding house). The clerk gave me a map and marked a few pensionis with an *X*. I followed the crowd downstairs to the vaporetto landing and took the boat toward the San Marco. The day was sunny, perfect August weather. The boat was full of passengers; and I heard several languages: German, English, French, and Italian. Venice was a tourist destination, and I felt safe being among locals. I disembarked at San Tomà Landing, four stops from the train station. Walking the narrow streets toward Rio Terra di Mombouli with map in hand, I found the Pensioni Goldoni, a four-story yellow-colored façade.

I entered the lobby. A large stair faced me. Next to it was a counter. The first floor was dark. The only source of light came from three large windows at the rear. My eyes tried to adjust from the bright outdoors. A woman in her fifties dressed in a black-and-white-colored shirt approached the counter. "Buongiorno, sir."

I asked, "Do you speak English?"

"Yes, I do."

"Do you have a room to rent?"

"Yes. For how long?"

"Two nights."

"Where are you from?"

"Vienna, Austria."

"Are you here for business or holiday?" She opened her registration book.

"For holiday," I answered and gave her my passport.

"Verga Caszar," she said. "Are you Hungarian?"

"Yes," I said. "You speak very good English."

She introduced herself. "My name is Elizabeth. I'm from Great Britain. I speak a little German, French, and, of course, Italian." She smiled. "Mr. Caszar, your room is on the fourth floor." She handed me the keys. "This one is for your room, and this one is for the front door. You come and go as you please. Make sure you lock the front door. My husband, Giorgio, and I run this pensioni. No visitors are allowed in your room. We have a sitting room here up front. You can read or watch TV, and over there is a house phone. You pay me before making a phone call. Please no cooking in the room. We have tea and coffee here in the lobby in the morning. Coffee shops are across the street, and there are many good restaurants. I'm more than happy to recommend one. Have a pleasant stay with us."

"Thanks. Can I make a call?"

"Yes."

I placed the call to Hans on his private line. There was no answer, so I figured I would call him later. I walked up the stairs to my room. On the fourth floor, I met Giorgio as he was coming downstairs from the roof. "Buongiorno," I introduced myself.

"Nice to meet you. How long will you stay with us?"

"For a couple days."

"Good. Enjoy yourself."

"Can I go to the roof to look at the view?"

"Yes, but lock the door from inside."

"Thanks."

The room was sparse and clean with a small toilet and a shower. I opened the curtains. The windows faced Via Terra di Bomboli. I felt hungry and looked at the watch. It was almost 5:00 p.m.

I stopped at the restaurant across the street and ordered a house special, spaghetti alle vongole. Fresh clams in piquant sauce were homemade, and it calmed my stomach. After a glass of frullato, iced milk with fresh fruit, I was content.

I walked back to the pensioni. I called Hans again. The phone kept ringing for a while then he picked up. "Hello?"

"Hans, it's me, Verga."

"Verga, all you all right?" he inquired in a concerned voice. "Where are you calling from?"

"I'm in Venice."

"Venice? What the hell are you doing in Venice?"

"Hans, I had to leave Milan. I was threatened. I took the first available train from Milan, and it was to Venice."

"Verga," his voice changed, "sit down. I have bad news."

My heart stopped pounding. I sat down. There was silence on the other line. "Verga, Constantina did not make it."

It did not register in my mind. I said, "What do you mean, Hans?"

"I'm so sorry," he said. "Constantina died last night from a blood hemorrhage in her head."

It struck me like lightning. My vision blanked. The room turned like a carousel. I dropped the phone on the floor and stood up then collapsed on my knees. Tears streamed down my cheeks. Elizabeth screamed for Giorgio to come. He rushed from the backroom, lifting me from the floor and bracing me on a chair.

"Are you all right?"

I did not answer. Giorgio picked up the phone from the floor and said something and then hung up. Elizabeth brought a glass of water and gave it to me, but I felt like throwing up. They conversed loudly in Italian.

"Should we call a doctor?"

I wiped my eyes. "No, no. Can you help me to my room?" I said in a hushed dead voice. Giorgio guided me upstairs.

I wanted to die. My world came to an end. I felt no purpose to live anymore. At the toilet, I threw up. Feeling sick and shaking, I lay in bed, blaming myself for this tragedy. I was so lonely. I remembered this same feeling from when I found out my father was killed that evening at No-Man's Land. I felt my life was like an inflated balloon suddenly bursting to pieces, all air gone, vacant. Emptiness took over me. I don't remember how many hours I lay awake, staring at the blank dark ceiling. Then with heavy eyes, I fell asleep.

I dreamt of Constantina and me running, holding hands in a field of yellow sunflowers. Then out of the woods, Erno and Zsophia appeared dressed in black. Zsophia grabbed Constantina by her hair and dragged her to the pond while Erno held his hands over my throat. Zsophia screamed, "Verga, quit the piano competition or I will drown your love!"

It seemed so real. Constantina screamed, "Don't quit! Don't quit!"

Zsophia drowned her voice, trying to push her head into the water. I shouted, "I'm quitting. Don't hurt her!" I tried to fight Erno, but his grip was strong, choking me. I couldn't breathe. Then I saw Constantina's body floating on the water motionless, a lovely face in peace. Her hands were folded over her body. Her hair, unraveled, moving gently above ripples in the water.

I woke up sweaty and shaking. It was so real. I lay frozen. Within several moments, I stood up, went to the table, switched on the desk light, sat down, took the black-and-white photo of Constantina and me holding hands and walking on the path in the woods, and placed it on the desk. I took a piece of paper and a pen from the drawer. With trembling hands, I wrote:

Dear Hans,

Adieu, my friend. When one loves somebody, it is the most notable and divine passion of the soul. Everything is clear. Now my loved ones have died, and I can't stand being apart. There is no more strength in me left to live. The last week wore me numb. My pain is too great. I love Constantina, and now there is a void in my life. I have tasted her lips. I drank her love. Death to me is only relief. It is the end of my journey. Don't be sad. Farewell, my friend.

I left the note on the table, draped a jacket over my back, took the picture, folded it neatly, and put it in my pocket next to my heart. With Puccini's music from *Tosca* in my head, I climbed the stairs to the roof, unbolting the door. Morning air hit my face. I gazed toward east, the Marco Campanile visible in the distance. Sunrays tried to break through dark clouds. In the distance, church bells rang, calling worshippers for morning mass. I loitered at the edge of the low parapet, looking down at the canal below. A gondola approached, gliding slowly on still water. A gondolier in a traditional beribboned straw hat, striped vest, and black trousers serenaded "O Sole Mio." In my head, I heard the shepherd's boy singing *"Lode Suspin"* ("I Give You Sights") from *Tosca*. A couple sitting on upholstered cushions embraced in the gondola leisurely passing below me. The singing of the gondolier faded away around the corner, leaving only ripples. Staring into murky waters, I saw Constantina's face smiling. *Tosca's* act 3 music playing in my mind, I leaned over the parapet ready to leap. I uttered the words, "Farewell, love and life." My mezuzah chain hung from my neck in front of me, swinging back and forth. I paused, eyeing it. I heard a rush of steps behind me. Then strong hands pulled me from the roof's edge.

"What are you doing?" Giorgio shouted. "Santa Maria! Santa Maria! You're a crazy man! You can kill yourself!" He sat me against the stair bulkhead, bracing my body against the wall. "Are you all right?" he asked, looking at my face.

I did not answer. I felt sick to my stomach. I was shaking.

"You must be sick. Let me take you to your room." He helped me descend the stairs.

I lay in my bed in the dark depressed and sick to my stomach. I wished I had jumped. That afternoon, the door to my room opened. Elizabeth came into the room with a tray. She placed it on the table next to my bed. "Verga, how do you feel?" She came close, examining me, placing her hand on my forehead. "You're kind of warm," she said. "You look terrible." She proceeded to part the curtains and crank the window open. Morning sun and street noise flooded in. "Fresh air will do you good. You need to eat something. I made you an egg sandwich and hot tea. Giorgio called the doctor. He will be here soon to see you."

I murmured, "Thanks."

"Please sit on the bed." She placed me against the pillows.

I said in a hushed voice, "I am not hungry."

Elizabeth placed the tray on my lap. "You need to eat to give you some strength." She poured the hot tea in the cup. "I will be back to pick up the tray." Then she left.

As I stared at the sandwich and tea, the smell of eggs and bacon awakened my appetite. I took a bite of the sandwich, slowly chewing it. Salt melted in my mouth. I remember Constantina saying, *"Der mensch ist, was en isst* [Man is what he eats]. Nutriment is a characteristic of life, impairment, and suffering. One eats to preserve life, but suffering and pain are involved in the search for food. The greatest suffering is living, and that is a final liberation of suffering. We suffer at that only because we cling to life, to our bodies, to our personalities, to material possessions, but if we are not clinging to these things, then that is not suffering."

My mind drifted, asking myself, *Am I suffering, or is this grief and despair that drove me to want to take my own life?* I closed my eyes and saw Constantina standing next to me as I played Chopin's music. She said, "Verga, remember," she quoted Buddah. "One who seeks the light in suffering is not free from suffering." With these thoughts in my head, I must have fallen asleep.

I was awakened by Elizabeth's voice. "Verga, the doctor is here to examine you."

I opened my eyes. Giorgio, Elizabeth, and an elderly gentleman with a white beard were staring at me. "Verga, this is Dr. Isciaki Bergmann. He speaks German."

The doctor sat next to my bed. He held my hand and checked my pulse. "Where are you from, Mr. Caszar?" He spoke in German.

"I'm from Vienna," I answered in a low impassionate voice.

"What brings you here to Venezia, young man?" He opened my shirt, listening to my heart.

Giorgio and Elizabeth stood behind the doctor, looking at me concerned.

"I was competing in the piano competition in Milan."

"Ah, a pianist. My wife is a piano player. How did you do in the competition?"

I swallowed hard and said, "I made the semifinals."

"I see. You did not make the finals?"

I was quiet, not answering, then said, "I don't know. I left Milan before finding out."

"I see." He put his stethoscope in his black bag, pronouncing, "Your chest is clear. May I ask, are you in pain?"

"Yes."

"What kind of pain?"

"I am grieving the death of a loved one."

"I see. I'm very sorry to hear that. May I ask who?"

He still held my hand. "She was my teacher."

"I remember my professor at medical school. When he passed suddenly, I grieved too," he said. He took a prescription note and started writing. "Rest and drink plenty of fluids. I'm prescribing you medicine drops in water twice a day for one week. Then come to my office for a checkup. You will be fine." He gave the prescription to Giorgio. The doctor stood up, looking at me. He asked, "Are you Jewish?"

"No, why?"

"You are wearing a mezuzah, and I was curious."

"Oh, the pendant. It was given by my teacher." Then I said in a saddened voice, "My mother was Jewish."

"I see. Well, take the medicine as I said. Rest. Stay in bed. I want to see you well, young man. I love classical music, and I want to hear you play. I would like you to come to my clinic in a week's time." I nodded. "Good," he said and shook my hand.

"Thank you, Dr. Bergmann."

A few days later, when I began to feel less drained and more composed, I called Hans.

"Verga, what happened to you? We're all worried and looking for you."

"Hans, I was sick."

"How sick? You could have at least called me."

"Sorry, Hans. I was emotionally drained, and I wanted to be alone."

"What is your telephone number where you're staying?"

"Hans, I don't want to talk to anyone except you."

"Okay, where are you staying?"

"At Pensioni Goldoni on Rio Terra Mombouli."

"Are you well enough to come to Vienna?"

"I need more time to think about my future, and I think this is a good place for me."

"Okay, take your time. Dr. Richter is furious. You made the finals. I had to tell him that you quit the competition, but I didn't tell anyone of the blackmail or that you're in Venice."

"Thanks, Hans. Tell Dr. Richter to stop looking for me."

"Verga," he said in a sad voice, "Ruth, Constantina's sister-in-law, came from London. The funeral was yesterday. Horrible, horrible. The entire staff from the Graz Academy was there in shock. Everyone is asking for your whereabouts. What should I say?"

"Tell them that I need more time. I lost the bearing on my compass. I'm out of whack. At this time, I don't want to go back to Vienna. It's too painful for me. Tell Dr. Richter I'm sorry to have quit like that, but I had to do it. I had my reasons. But I left my money in a drawer at Constantina's home in my bedroom. Can you wire the money to me so I can pay for the pensioni?"

"Yes, I will do that in the next few days. Do you need more money?"

"No, I still have some. Thanks. I will call you in a few days."

Later that week, I stopped at Dr. Bergmann's medical clinic in the SS Giovanni & Paolo Hospital in the Castello District. He greeted me warmly, "How do you feel now, young man?"

"Much better, Doctor. I came to thank you for coming to see me when I was sick."

"You're welcome. You look better, and the color of your skin is good. Your eyes are now full of life too."

"Thanks, but I'm still a little depressed."

"Sit down, Verga." The doctor sat behind his desk. "Let me tell you medically why you feel like that. When one is in love, the brain activates similar to a drug addict. It's a classic symptom of love and similar to the initial effect from drugs, like opiates, cocaine, and heroine. In fact, there is some truth to the notion that people can become addicted to love. You just went through a neurochemical withdrawal due to the loss of your loved one, similar to a drug addict. You will get over it, but it takes time."

I nodded. I felt a little better after listening to the doctor's explanation of my depression. "Thanks, Doctor. May I ask you what I owe for this visit?"

He stood up, extending his hand. "Nothing," he said, "Stay healthy."

"Thank you, Doctor."

During the next day, I wandered outdoors. I wanted to be with people. I strolled through the streets of Venice, trying to forget my sorrows. One day, I passed Galleria d'Arte Moderna on Santa Croce, admiring the magnificent Baroque palace. I entered and meandered through the exhibit rooms. It featured works by artists, such as Bonnard, Matisse, Miro, Klee, and Kandinsky.

I stopped in front of Klimt's painting of Salomé. My knees weakened. My heart pounded. I gazed at Salomé's face as it faded into Constantina's face. Memories of Constantina flooded my thoughts. I sat for a long time, looking at her image. Tears rolled down my cheeks. Through the painting, she spoke to me, "Verga, clear your mind from attachment to things, let go, and release yourself from needing to have permanency in your suffering. End your obsession of blaming yourself for my death."

As I sat in silence, staring at the painting, her voice dissolved. I realized that the death of Constantina did not mean the end of life; it was merely the death of the body she inhabited, but her spirit still remained attached to a different body: mine. I felt her presence. Through me, she shall live and seek new life. I remembered the quote by Leonardo da Vinci I wrote in my notebook: "As a well-spent day brings happy sleep, so life well used brings happy death." The death of Constantina reminded me of the inevitable end awaiting me, and this moment was a blip on my journey in this world. That day, I reached tranquility. I let go of the attachment to death, pain, and suffering. I left the Galleria d'Arte Moderna as a man reborn.

SIX

The more I stayed in Venice, the more I liked it, a city frozen in time. Once a powerful commercial and naval force in the Mediterranean, it had transformed itself into a romantic tourist city. The Old Lady of the Lagoon was virtually the same as it had been six hundred years ago. Venice is a city in northern Italy, sitting in a group of 118 small islands separated by canals and linked by bridges.

I was curious to explore the City of Dreams, and dreams I had. For the next two weeks, I walked the streets, alleys, and bridges of Venice. It transported me to another period, a different world where time seemed to stand still. Waterways and canals were present at every corner of the city and bustling with caring, happy, loving people on handcrafted gondolas. They were like giant fallen leaves floating on the water, quietly rippling, carrying people from one adventure to the next. People dressed in colorful clothes, moseying down endless streets, searching for artisans' treasures, wandering from store to store. For me, every day was like paradise. Majestic sunrises illuminated churches and cathedrals designed by Palladio and other talented architects. Among the most enticing discoveries were in the backstreets of Venice: bacri, teeny neighborhood bars that served some of the city's tastiest food and wine. Around midday and sometime during late afternoons, I ducked into the nearest bacro for a drink and a bite, often meeting strangers and having fascinating conversations with them. At night, I sat in the small piazzas with a cup of espresso or cappuccino, admiring the clear, starry night. Then slowly I strolled back to the pensioni. On one of these nights, I arrived early to my newfound home.

"Good evening, Verga," Elizabeth greeted me in the lobby. "You're back early today."

"Yes, it's a little chilly tonight."

"Yes, tomorrow, it will rain. The mountains and the sea combined give Venice lots of rain, more than other parts of Italy. What are you planning to do for the rest of the night?"

"I don't know. Perhaps I will catch up on my reading."

"Oh, I forgot to tell you. Today, on the TV, they're broadcasting a special from London, the Royal Variety Performance for Queen Elizabeth II. Would you like to watch it with us?"

"You're very kind. Who will be on the program?"

She unfolded the newspaper, searching, then said, "Tonight's performance features Nat King Cole. I like his singing. There will be Samuel David Jr. and Liberace. I never saw him before, but the program is very interesting and entertaining."

I thought, *Why not?* "Yes, I'll join you. Thank you."

"Great, it starts in an hour. Please come to our apartment."
"Thanks."

I stopped at the coffee shop across the street and bought a box of amaretto biscuits. Elizabeth greeted me at the apartment.

"Thanks for the biscuits. Please sit down."

"Orange, lime liquor, or grappa?" Giorgio asked.

"Grappa, please."

"Good choice." He poured a small glass for me and himself. "Salute."
"Cheers."

"Elizabeth, darling, what are you drinking?"

She was in the kitchen, making espresso. We heard her voice. "Nothing for me, darling."

Giorgio sat on a chair opposite me. "I'm happy to see you in good spirits."

"Thanks. It's the people and the air in Venice," I replied.

"What are your plans for the future?"

"I don't know yet. I don't want to go back to Vienna for now. I find it too stiff. I like Venice, free spirited. For the time being, I'm staying here."

"You're welcome to stay with us as long as you like. You know, Verga, as a piano player, you can find employment. There's the Teatro La Fenice, an opera house, and you should go one evening to Santa Maria della Pietà. It was Vivaldi's own church, and it's still used for concerts, or visit the Scuola Grande di San Giovanni Evangelista and the Palazzo Prigioni Vecchie, a very interesting place to conduct recitals and concerts, a prison attached to the Doge's Palace."

"Thanks for your advice. I'll be sure to check them out."

Elizabeth came with the coffee tray. I sipped the homemade brew and said, "I have a question to ask you, Giorgio. That morning, two weeks ago, when you found me at the edge of the parapet, was it by chance that you came to the roof?"

Giorgio put his cup of coffee down, wiping his lips. Elizabeth eyed him, wondering what he would say. "Since you brought up the subject, Verga, you are lucky. You will have a long life. Dear Madonna gave you another chance." He crossed himself. "I don't know. That morning, I woke up early and decided to release my homing pigeons for their daily flight, so I went to the roof."

I was silent for a few minutes. Then I stood up and hugged Giorgio. "Thank you for saving my life."

He was surprised. "Don't thank me. Thank our city patron, Saint Mark," he replied, smiling. Elizabeth grinned too.

I sat down and asked, "If you don't mind, my second question. Your name of Pensioni Goldoni, is it because the Museo Goldoni is in the neighborhood?"

Giorgio sipped coffee then said, "Nope, it's no coincidence. Carlo Goldoni is my great-great-grandfather. He lived from 1707 to 1793. He owned several properties on this street, and this building was left to my family. You should go visit the museum. It's on San Polo 2794."

"How interesting," I said. "I will."

Elizabeth glanced at her watch. "Giorgio, please switch on the TV."

We watched the broadcast from London. Nat King Cole performed. Then Samuel Davis sang and danced. I watched the show with interest. Then a piano was brought onto the stage, and crystal chandeliers glimmered above. A candelabrum was lit on the white Steinway. A handsome man dressed in flashy clothes walked in. He sat in front of the piano, all smiles. He had a long cape of ostrich feathers trailing behind him. The camera zoomed in on his hands. Every finger was decorated with sparkling rings. He announced his play, "Concerto for the Birds." Then he played "Misty," "Five Foot Two," and a rendition of "Chopsticks." Then he played Chopin. I did not know whether to be serious or laugh at his piano performance. He was not a typical classical pianist. He was an entertainer. I watched his sloppy fingering on the keyboard, wrong tempo, and unorganized phrases while he played. But the audience loved him. I sat with an open mouth, perplexed. I admired his talent as an entertainer, but I was brought up with straight classical traditions. This was like fresh winds blowing on me. I was amazed at the Queen of England. She was in the audience, enjoying the spectacle. I thought, *I can do this too. I am a better piano player.* That evening, I decided I wanted to be an entertainer like Liberace.

The next day, I was on a mission. I scouted all of Venice's music shops, searching for Liberace's records. I was amazed to find that he produced nearly seventy discs. In stores, I found only ten recorded by Columbia Records. Besides this selection, I proceeded to rummage through piles of records in the store. I decided to explore piles of rock and roll, blues, and jazz. I also bought a portable record player, sat in my room, and listened to the popular tunes, making notes to myself. Placing a record of Jerry Lee Lewis on the player, I listened to his singing and piano playing in "Great Balls of Fire." I was swept with desire to get familiar with all popular tunes of the fifties and sixties. I purchased records from Elvis Presley, Jonny Cash, Jerry Lee Lewis, and Roy Orbison. Then from the blues collection, I picked up the records of BB King; Muddy Waters; and the solo guitar, electric guitar, electric bass, and drum combos of Chuck Berry and Howling Wolf.

The next day, I approached Elizabeth. "Can you tell me where I can find a practice piano?"

She thought for a second and then said, "You know, Verga, I'm acquainted with Mrs. Jenny Parks. She makes her home in Murano—a well-to-do lady. I met her at Saint Giorgio's Anglican Church. Her husband was a well-known glass artist. She invited me to a small party once, and she played beautiful classical music. Her husband passed six years ago, and now she lives by herself. Her children are grown up and living in England, and every year, she spends several months there. Do you want me to call her?"

"Please, I would like to meet her."

Elizabeth took her phonebook and called Lady Jenny Parks. Politely, I stepped aside to the sitting room. I heard Elizabeth conversing on the phone. She came to me and gave me a piece of paper. She said, "That lady,

Jenny, lives by Rio Briati and the Grand Canal di Murano. You'll find her pink façade building. At the lower level is a gallery. Take the vaporetto to Murano and get off at Faro Landing. She would like to meet you on Wednesday at 4:00 for tea."

"I am very much obliged to you."

"You're welcome, Verga."

On Wednesday, I bought a bouquet of flowers and took a vaporetto to Murano Island. I rang the bell of Lady Jenny's enormous house. A maid dressed in a black-and-white collared shirt opened the door. "Please, enter. Lady Jenny is expecting you," she said in English with an Italian accent.

I climbed the stairs. The building was dated to the medieval days. It sat on the canal side of the island. Columns supported the extended second floor, forming a portico on the first level. I was greeted by an aristocratic-looking elderly woman with white hair and dressed in the latest couture and a large artistic pendant: square, colored, Murano glass in a silver frame with dragonflies on it. She extended her delicate, well-manicured hand. A large elegant ring decorated her finger. "It's my pleasure to meet you, Mr. Caszar."

"Mrs. Parks, the pleasure is mine, and I thank you for seeing me." I handed her the sunflowers.

"Oh, they are so beautiful." She handed the flowers to the maid. "Please sit down. Tea?"

"Yes, please."

"How do you take it? With milk?"

"Please, one spoon of sugar and a touch of milk."

"Very well, that's the way I like it too."

She poured the tea. I looked around the room. White plaster walls were decorated with many paintings and glass objects. A large glass chandelier with colorful glass flowers and butterflies swayed gently from the breeze. Four large windows faced the Grand Canal.

"I understand you are a pianist. Please tell me about yourself."

I felt so comfortable with Lady Jenny. She was warm and friendly. I told her briefly about my experience regarding music and where I came from.

"How interesting," she said. "I always wanted to become a concert pianist. I studied music in a conservatory in London before the war. Then my husband opened a studio in Murano. We moved here permanently in the thirties. We fell in love with Venice, and it has been my home since then."

"I love Venice too. There's something magical about this place. It transformed me."

She pointed to the piano, a baby black Steinway. She said, "You can try it." I stared at the piano like a child looking at ice cream. I terribly wanted to play it. "Go ahead. Try it."

I sat at the piano, opened the fallboard, and touched the keys. The sound of the piano was swift to my ears. I played Chopin's Nocturne in E-flat, op. 9, no. 2, "Night Moods." I played for six minutes then stopped.

I turned around toward Lady Jenny. "I love the sound."

She grinned. "Young man, I like the way you play," she said. "Elizabeth from the pensioni has probably told you of my visit to London to see my children. I'm leaving next week. It's my pleasure to have you practice on my piano while I'm away. My maid, Giovanna, will be in charge of my home in the meantime. Make arrangements with her when you'd like to practice."

"I'm very much obliged to have your home and this lovely piano to practice. May I compensate for Giovanna's time?"

"Don't be silly." She waved her hand. "The pleasure is mine to help a piano virtuoso like yourself."

For the next month, three times a week, I took the vaporetto to the Island of Murano to practice on Lady Jenny's piano. Giovanna, with a sour face, greeted me at the door. I realized I was not welcomed. My presence interfered with her daily routine, and she seemed uneasy having me in the house.

However, on my second week of practicing, I played pop tunes. I noticed that Giovanna had warmed up to my presence and occasionally would come from adjoining rooms to listen to me play. One day, I was engrossed in playing blues while she mopped the stone floor in the salon. I didn't pay attention to her. My fingers were over the keyboard, pounding the C chord for two beats, the F chord for two beats, and repeating that for two bars. I practiced basic blues riffs I had learned from the records I had purchased.

For a moment, I lifted my eyes from the keyboard. I saw that Giovanna had stopped mopping the floor and was listening to my play then slowly started dancing, holding the mop in her hand. I stopped playing, looking at her. She let out a chuckle, slightly embarrassed. I pounded louder on the piano, shaking the house with vibrations and yelled, "Giovanna, continuare danzare! Don't stop."

She smiled and slowly glided on the floor. She was light on her feet, improvising one-step and two-step patterns. Her emotions overtook her as she danced, responding to the African blues rhythm sounding from Jenny's piano. I yelled, "Giovanna, you're a natural dancer! Keep going."

She let the mop fall from her hand, engaged in her dance. With simplistic expressions, she sashayed on the floor, moving her hips to my up tempo. I stopped playing in amazement, eyeing her. She was embarrassed for letting loose. I clapped my hands. "Bravo, Giovanna, you are a good dancer."

Her face was radiant. She picked up the mop and leaned against the wall, looking at me. "What kind of music is that?" she asked.

"Blues."

"Blues? What's that?"

I thought about what to say. I read a quote from the sheet of music. "Blues is when you ain't got no money to pay for rent, you can't pay for food, you dun sure got the blues." We both laughed.

"I love dancing. I wanted to be a dancer," she said. "Please play something else."

"Of course." I stood in front of the piano and played rock and roll. Giovanna kicked her slippers into the air. She danced—quick, quick, slow, slow steps—first on the ball of her foot then on her heel. Then lowering her figure without any tension, her body and legs flexible like a winding spring, she let go, dancing to the music. I was inspired. My hands banging loud on the keys, I played with youthful, rebellious energy, swinging my body, improvising, sliding my hands down the keyboard. Quickly, my right hand was flying at what seemed like a hundred miles per hour while my left hand was constantly in action playing nonstop riffs. By the end, we were chortling. She was the happiest I've ever seen her.

The next day at noon, I invited Giovanna to a local bacari for a glass of wine. We shared a cicchetti plate, Venice's answer to Milan's aperitivo and Spain's tapas. Over the second glass of wine, Giovanna opened up to me and told me of her life. "I was married, now divorced with two boys. Pasquale, my ex-husband, who was a very good bricklayer, left to Padua for mason restoration work and never came back. Finally, six years ago, we were divorced." Her eyes grew sad.

I ordered more wine. "I'm sorry to hear this. Who's watching the kids?" I asked.

After sipping the red liquid, she put the glass down. "Do you smoke?"

"No, I've never gotten into it."

"Do you mind?"

"No."

She put a cigarette between her lips. I lit a match, lighting the cigarette. The sudden blow momentarily lit her large almond-shaped eyes framed by thick black eyebrows. She touched her lips with her delicate, unmanicured fingers, removing a speck of tobacco from her unkempt lips and adjusting her jet black hair. Smiling, she said, "No one invites me to bacaris these days. Mille grazie for this lunch."

"Prego, Giovanna, the pleasure is mine."

I thought of how simple she looked, no glamour to her face, but hidden inside her body was a volcano, a passion for dance. I felt sorry for her, realizing her unmet dreams to be a dancer. Her life was no *La Dolce Vita*. She was not Anita Ekberg, and I was not Marcello, and this was not Frederico Fellini's movie. For her, it was a day-to-day grinding life. Giovanna jolted me from daydreaming. She said, "I lived here in Murano all my life. My father was a fisherman, and now he is very sick and bedridden. My mother is taking care of him and watches my kids while I work."

"How long have you been working for Lady Jenny?"

"Oh, I've been working here since I was seventeen, and she is very good to me."

"Giovanna, you are an amazing, talented dancer."

"Grazie. And you are a great piano player."

"Grazie a tutti."

"As a young girl, I wanted to be a dancer and took some lessons, but I did not have the opportunity." She looked at her watch. "Oh my god, it's already 3:00. I must go back and finish cleaning."

"Let's go back. I want to practice some more anyway."

Two more weeks passed, and it was time for me to say goodbye to Giovanna. She said, "I'm sorry to see you go. Will I see you again?"

"Giovanna, grazie for everything. I enjoy your company and dancing. You made a difference in my practice. I had fun. I'll stop here to thank Lady Jenny when she comes back." I hugged her. "Continue dancing and good luck to you."

We parted that late afternoon. It was the last time I saw Giovanna.

"Buongiorno," Elizabeth greeted me in the morning. "Verga, this is your invoice for the month." She handed me the envelope.

As I sat in my room, looking at the invoice, the blues set in. I only had money left for two weeks. I was broke. All my savings were gone. I needed to find a job and fast. A feeling of desperation filled my thoughts. On the table was the black-and-white photo of Constantina. I thought, *All my life, someone else was always taking care of me. Now I need to take care of myself. I can borrow money from Hans, but that wouldn't be right. What should I do now?* My hands fidgeted with my mezuzah nervously. I removed the pendant from my neck, staring at it. *It's gold. I can sell it. No, that would be wrong.*

It reminded me of Constantina saying, "Keep this as a reminder of me. It will keep you safe."

Keep me safe? What's inside this pendant anyway? I became curious. Looking at the necklace, I asked, *Is there any way to open it?* I examined the mezuzah. I noticed the bottom portion of the cylinder was made to slide down. I took out a pocketknife. Slowly, carefully, I pried the bottom cap. It did not move. I tried again more forcefully. Slowly, it slid down. A scroll with a waxed cord fell on the table. Gently, I cut the cord and unraveled the scroll. The sun coming from the window momentarily blinded me. A bright, glowing sparkle came from the unraveled parchment. *What is this?* I lifted the piece of glass. It radiated brilliant blue, yellow, and silver rays. *How is this possible? Are these diamonds?* There were three jewels on the table. I put them on the side, looking at the unraveled parchment. Strange letters were written. *It must be in Hebrew*, I said to myself. *Did Constantina know the mezuzah contained diamonds? Probably not or else she would have told me. Do all mezuzahs contain treasures? I need to find out. Who should I ask?*

Then I remembered Howard Schwartz, the Bacco Bar proprietor. He wore a mezuzah and a cross on his neck. He was a proprietor of Howard's Cantine del Vino near the Stazione Ferrovie. It was a place for the young and hip crowd. Howard had come to Europe in the fifties in search of a utopian-left way of life. He had traveled the Mediterranean countries, supporting himself by playing blues with his electric guitar, performing on streets and in bars. Eventually, his travel had landed him in Venice, where he met his soon-to-be wife, Sabrina, a local girl. Howard confessed to me once, saying, "Sabrina changed my life. She told me, 'If you want to have a family, you must find a way to pay bills.'" With financial help from his family in the USA, Howard had hung his guitar and had worked to convert an old dilapidated store near Plazzo Laba into one of the most successful bacaris. He tended the Bacco Bar and Sabrina took charge of the kitchen, creating the tastiest cicchetti plates and the freshest fish and vegetable sandwiches. Howard had kept an interest in music, playing in his bacari and others, while managing the restaurant.

I put the diamonds in an envelope and placed the parchment scroll back in the pendant of the mezuzah and went to see Howard.

Over a glass of red wine from Corvina grapes and a sardine sandwich, I asked Howard, "Tell me, what is written in this mezuzah?" I pointed to his neck.

He laughed and said, "Verga, this is to remind us Jewish people of our connection to God."

"But what is written on the parchment scroll?"

Howard was thinking. "If I remember my days studying Hebrew, the scroll contains the Shema, a handwritten biblical passage; and on the reverse side is the written symbol, God, Sha-Dai, which means guardian of the doors of Israel. It will keep you safe. Have another glass of wine." He poured more and got ready to leave the bar.

"Howard, don't go just yet. I have an important question to ask you."

"Ask, my friend."

"Do all mezuzahs contain treasures?"

"A spiritual treasure?"

"No, real treasures."

"What do you mean, Verga? Be clear."

I took the envelope from my pocket and showed Howard the brilliant stones. "I found this inside my mezuzah."

He was taken aback and said, "What do you mean you found these diamonds?"

"I opened the parchment, and these diamonds fell from inside."

Howard took the envelope, looking at the sparkling diamonds. "Wow, these look like good stones." He gave it back to me and said, "Whoever gave you this mezuzah gave you the diamonds."

"My dear Constantina gave it to me. It was her late husband's," I said.

"Lucky you," Howard said. Now he braced his two elbows on the bar, looking at me, his brown hair hanging on his shoulders. He said, "The Jews were prosecuted for centuries. It was not safe anywhere, so they kept gold coins and diamonds for easy transport so they could survive and start their lives again. Someone put these diamonds in this mezuzah for that purpose."

Now it made sense to me. I said to Howard, "I need your advice. I need to find a job as a piano player."

"Verga, I know you're a talented pianist. I suggest you start visiting popular bars and restaurants. Have a drink, schmooze a little with bartenders and musicians, and demonstrate your abilities. After they hear you play, you'll find a job. Unfortunately, my place is too small. I don't have a place for a piano."

"Thanks, Howard, for your advice."

"Good luck, Verga."

I thought that as of tomorrow, I would start visiting the bars Howard suggested, but first, I would need to have proper attire.

The next day, I stopped at a jewelry store near upscale boutiques on the narrow zigzagging Mercerie running north between Piazza San Marco and the Rialto Bridge. I priced my 1.25 CT-D internally flawless diamond. I got the best price from Gioielleria at Rialto Bridge. My round diamond would fetch me three million lire. For all three diamonds, I was offered fourteen million lire, but I only sold one diamond, and I felt rich. Passing San Bartolomé, I entered and lit a candle in memory of Constantina. Touching my mezuzah, I remembered her words, "This will keep you safe." I felt untouchable.

At a clothing boutique, I bought a white jacket, black pants, and a pink ruffled shirt. Then I stopped at a beauty salon.

"Can I help you?" a receptionist greeted me.

"Yes, I want to color my hair."

She looked at me, surprised, and put her cigarette down. "What color?"

"Streaks of blond."

"Very well. We are busy now." She looked at her appointment book. "How about 3:00 p.m.?"

"Okay."

"What is your name?"

"Verga."

She wrote down, "Shampoo, trim, and color."

I left the salon, determined to change my appearance to become a standout entertainer. I wanted to be like Liberace.

That evening, dressed in my white jacket; pink shirt; large round gold-toned, turquoise necklace and a large turquoise stacked ring; my hair long and brown with streaks of blond and large Lozza sunglasses with brown marbleized top frames, I walked from my room to the lobby. Elizabeth almost dropped dead on the floor when she saw me.

"Verga, is that you?"

"Yes, it's me." I stood up with my hands spread. "What do you say?"

"You look so glamorous like an actor or movie producer. Where are you going?"

"Nowhere. I just wanted to get your reaction."

"You definitely look like a star."

"Great, this will be my performance costume." I stood next to the receptionist desk, looking at a Harry's Bar postcard on the counter. "Elizabeth, have you been to Harry's Bar?"

"Yes, a few years ago, an American couple stayed in the pensioni. They invited me and Giorgio for a drink. Why?"

I put the postcard back on the desk. "I wanted to check it out. Maybe tonight. I passed the bar several times but never went. I understand it's a landmark."

"It's certainly very popular with tourists. Go and have a good time."

"Do I need a jacket to wear?"

"Yes," she paused, looking at me then said, "Why change? You're dressed perfectly for the occasion. Get comfortable with your new appearance. How shall I say, test the waters, and see how people react to you."

"Grazie, Elizabeth, for your encouragement."

And so, I went to Harry's Bar. The place was mobbed with noisy tourists speaking in English. From their accent, I realized they were Americans. I made my way toward the crowded bar. A well-groomed bartender wearing a white jacket and black bowtie was in command of an extensive selection of drinks. Glasses of various drinks sat on the large marble counter. The bar was crowded. I squeezed myself beside two male tourists. One of them wore a large silver Stetson Western jacket and plaid shirt. The other gentleman wore a checkered jacket, white shirt, and a tie. The gentleman with the plaid top had an unlit fat cigar in his mouth, chewing the end of it. He looked at me with interest.

I said, "Good evening, gentlemen."

"Howdy," he said, staring at my getup.

I introduced myself, "Verga Caszar."

"Richard Benzilio and my friend, Jerry DiPalma." They shook my hand.

"Americans?" I asked.

"Yes, Jerry is from Maryland, and I'm from Kansas. And you are?" Richard asked.

"I'm from Vienna, Austria."

"Vienna? Must be a beautiful place."

"Yes indeed. Are you guys are part of this large group?"

"Yes," Richard answered. "Today is our first day in Venice. We're part of a group of 440 from America. And you?"

"I arrived here from Milan, intended to stay for a few days. I fell in love with Venice, and I'm here now for almost three months."

"What do you drink?" Jerry asked.

"What are you drinking, guys?"

"The famous fizz. What did the bartender call it?" Jerry searched for the name.

Richard said, "The Bellini."

"Yes, the Bellini."

The bartender looked at me. "Bellini for me, please," I said.

"Yes, sir."

"What do you do, Mr. Caszar?" Richard asked, pointing to my attire.

"I'm a musician, a piano player."

"Ah, very nice." Both of them became more relaxed.

"And you, gentlemen, what do you do in America?"

"We're car dealers."

I was not sure what that meant. "Do you sell cars?"

"Yes, we own a dealership. Jerry sells General Motors cars, and I sell Fords. What kind of car do you drive?"

"I don't own a car and, in fact, don't have a driver's license."

"Too bad. We could give you a good deal." They started laughing.

"Are you guys on a tour?"

"Yes, my boy," Richard said. "We belong to an Italian Heritage Club. We already went to Rome, Florence, Milan, the Veneto Plain, and now in Venice. We'll be here for three days; then we sail on our ship to Naples for another three days and then back to New York."

"Can I order another drink for you, gentlemen?" I waved to the bartender. "Another three Bellinis, and can you recommend me a live jazz club?" I asked him.

"Yes, sir." The bartender took a pencil and wrote the name of a club at Piazza San Marco on a piece of paper.

"Cheers," I said once he handed us the drinks.

Richard said, "I heard you asking the bartender for a jazz club."

"Do you like jazz?" I asked.

"Yes," they both answered.

"So please join me."

A group of eleven of us walked to the jazz club. The place was crowded. A band of three—a bassist, a pianist, and an electric guitarist—were playing light jazz tunes on a small stage. Richard ordered three bottles of red wine, smoking his cigar and listening to the music. My newfound friends wanted to know everything about me, and I was interested to know about America. Jerry's wife, Patricia, asked, "Verga, is it true that Americans finance Harry's Bar?"

"There is some truth to it," I said, sipping wine. "The story goes like this. A rich boy from Boston by the name of Harry Pickering was a regular at Hotel Europa in Venice, and Giuseppe Cipriani was a bartender. Harry was a regular at the bar of the hotel, spending money on drinks. After a few months, he disappeared. When he came back, Cipriani asked him why he did not come anymore. Harry replied, 'My aunt cut my allowance. I don't have money anymore.' So Cipriani lent him ten thousand dollars. Harry disappeared again for a long time, and Cipriani abandoned all hope of seeing his friend and money again. One day, Harry showed up, all fine and dressed up. He said, 'Here you are. Thanks for the money, and for my gratitude, I'm giving you thirty thousand dollars. I want you to open a bar of your own and call it Harry's Bar.' The bar attracted international clientele. The guestbook has the signature of Arturo Toscanini, Charlie Chaplin, Ernest Hemingway, Georges Braque, and others. And now yours and my signature are in the book."

The jazz trio stopped playing and announced a short break. Richard went to the stage. He spoke to the musicians and tipped the pianist. At the table, he eyed me. "Verga, let's hear you play. Play something American for us." The request caught me by surprise. The only reason I came to the jazz club was to scout the scene. I didn't intend to play. My face showed reluctance. "It's okay. The piano is yours for the next fifteen minutes," Richard said.

"Are you sure it's okay with the band?"

Patricia said, "Please play something for us."

I glanced at the jazz trio at the bar having a drink. I stood up and went toward them, introducing myself and shaking their hands. Then I sat in front of the piano. *What should I play?* Lifting my hands, I played the jazz tune by Ralph Burns, "Bijou." People in the club applauded, and the guitarist joined me. We finished playing, and I thanked the guitarist. I took the microphone and said, "For my American friends"—I pointed to the table—"I will play Gershwin's *Rhapsody in Blue.*" My hands glided over the keyboard with ease. I had practiced it several times on Jenny's piano. Glancing at the audience, I knew I had made a good impression on them. I finished playing and stood up. A loud bravo erupted. "More, more!"

"Grazie, grazie." I turned the stage to the musicians.

As the Americans and I were leaving the club, the owner of the jazz club stopped me and praised my piano playing. He gave me his business card. "Call me if you're looking for a job," he said.

I parted with my American friends and walked toward Ponte de Rialto.

That evening, a piece of paper was taped to my room door. Unfolding it, I saw that the note was from Elizabeth. *Verga, please call Howard. He called you three times this evening.* I looked at the watch. It was after midnight. I would call him later.

The next morning, I went down to the lobby. "Buongiorno," Elizabeth greeted me. "You must have enjoyed yourself last night. I didn't see you come in."

"Yes, I met the friendliest people from America, and we had a great time."

"I'm glad to hear that, Verga. Don't forget to call Howard."

"Yes, I will."

I called him. "Hi, Howard."

"Verga, I tried to reach you last night."

"Is everything all right?"

"Yes, yes, no problems, Verga. I want you to come meet this man, Anthony. He's looking for a good pianist. Maybe it can be a job for you."

We arranged for the three of us to meet in Howard's bacari. I was introduced by Howard to Anthony, a well-groomed man, tall, in his late thirties. He had a blue blazer over his shoulder. One of his hands was in a plaster cast. "How are you, young man?" Anthony said. "What's your name?"

"Verga."

"What kind of name is that?"

"Hungarian."

"Ah, Hungarian. I understand you are a talented pianist."

"Yes, I've been told I'm very good."

"Do you sing too?"

"No."

"What kind of music can you play?"

"Classic, pop, blues, and rock and roll."

"That is some repertoire."

"Well, I'm mostly a classical pianist, but I can play almost anything."

Anthony took a sip of coffee from a paper cup. "I would like to hear you play."

"There's no piano here, but I can arrange for us to rent one."

"No need to, but I meant to say, do you have time to accompany me to my ship? I have a Grand Steinway piano there."

"A ship? What do you mean?"

"I'm sorry I'm not telling you the whole story. I'm a pianist on the *Cristoforo Colombo*, but two days ago, I slipped on the floor and broke my hand. Now I can't play piano, and the ship is leaving Venice for Naples in two days. I need to find a replacement pianist for the rest of the trip. If you're qualified for the job, will you be interested?"

"What do I have to play?"

"I sing, and you accompany me during show time. In between, you play light pops and classics at the piano bar and during dinnertime. The tips are very good. You can make a year's pay over the voyage of one month."

"Where does the ship sail to?"

"It makes its port of call in Genoa, but now it's on a special cruise, and it will sail from Venice to Naples then New York."

"What a coincidence," I said. "I met some of your passengers last night. A very lively group of Italian Americans."

"So are you interested?"

"I'm not sure. I was never on a ship before."

"Let's go to the *Cristoforo Colombo*, and I will give you a tour, and you can see our theater. It sits three hundred people. You will love the ship."

"One moment, Anthony."

Howard and I walked to the edge of the bar counter. I asked, "Do you know this man?"

"Not much. In fact, very little. I met him yesterday at the Bacco Bar. He told me he had just arrived and was looking for a place to have lunch and stumbled upon my place. He saw my collection of electric guitars hanging on the wall, so we started talking about music. And then he explained his search for a pianist. I mentioned you, and his face lit up."

"What do you think I should do?"

"Verga, the only advice I have for you is based on my own journey. I left America years ago in search of the answer to my question, 'What is most important to me in my life? Is it music or something else?' In my travel, I found love. Now I have a partner in my life, Sabrina. We, together, successfully run the Bacco Bar, and I'm a happy man. Go see America. I say, if you never try new opportunities that come your way and experience new challenges, you never know if you'll be successful, but if you try, you may surprise yourself. Choose your destiny, whichever feels right. It will be the best decision for you."

"Thanks, Howard. I appreciate your advice. I made up my mind."

I approached Anthony and said, "Let's go and see the ship."

Part 3

ONE

I boarded the SS *Cristoforo Colombo* cruise liner. It was my first time on a ship. First, I saw the ocean liner's recently renovated small theater located on the fourth level. Standing on the stage, Anthony proudly pointed to the sea of red velvet seats. "Isn't it beautiful, Verga? What do you say? Isn't it pure luxury?"

"It's very impressive to have a theater on board."

"Very few ocean liners have a theater. Of course, it's not the *Queen Mary*, but it's the best we Italians can offer. The ship was launched in 1953, and after the tragic collision of the SS *Andrea Doria* with the MS *Stockholm* in 1956, the SS *Cristoforo Colombo* became the pride of Italy." He paused, allowing me to absorb the information then said, "The shipyard in Genoa is planning the next flagship. It will be called the SS *Leonardo da Vinci*. The shipping travel industry is in the midst of changes since the introduction of Boeing 747."

We walked on the stage toward the piano. "Look at this jewel." Anthony pointed with his left hand to the white lacquered shining Steinway piano. "Isn't it a delight? Look at this piano. Unfortunately, I can't play now." He pointed to his plaster cast. "Go ahead. Play." He gestured to me with a broad smile on his face.

I walked next to the piano, gliding my palm over the sleek, smooth top. I pulled the bench, adjusted the height, opened the fallboard, gazed at the keyboard, and closed my eyes. *What should I play? How about Beethoven?* I played Piano Sonata no. 8 in C Minor, op. 13, *Pathétique*, and slowly with solemnity, *Allegro di Motto e con Brio*, the theme-marked grave. I played for sixteen minutes, ending with swift cadence. I commented, "Wow, this piano has a wonderful sound."

Anthony stood looking at me. "What a surprise! Where did you learn to play like this? You're wonderful."

"Thanks. I had a good teacher." My face grew sad for a moment. "Oh well. May I play something else?"

Anthony, still standing and eyeing me, braced his right hand with his left. He came toward the piano. "Let's try this song. You accompany me. Are you familiar with Mario Lanza?"

"No, but I have heard his name before."

Anthony removed his jacket and placed it on top of the piano. There were stacks of score sheets on the piano. He flipped through them and placed a piano-vocal-score on the music rack. I looked at the title of the song, "Because You're Mine."

I said, "Okay, let's start. Are you ready?" I lifted my left hand in the air. "One, two, three." I played as Anthony sang:

Because you're mine

The brightest star I see looks down

My love, and envies me

Because you're mine, because you're mine.

His beautiful tenor voice filled the air. "Bravo, Verga, that was a perfect accompany."

"Thank you, Anthony. Your tenor voice is wonderful. I like your falsetto too."

"Mille grazie. I study with a good opera vocal teacher. This was a perfect play," Anthony said with a satisfied voice. He looked through the music sheets, pulling one. "Let's try this Neapolitan song 'Santa Lucia.' Are you familiar with this?"

"Yes, this song I've heard before." I looked at the song's score and tried to play the first few notes. "Okay, I'm ready, Anthony." My hands were on the keyboard.

Anthony opened his mouth. He sang:

Sul mare Luccica L'astro d'Argento

Placida L'onda prosero il vento

Venite all'agie brarchetta mia...

Santa Luccica! Santa Luccica!

I relaxed my hands, looking at Anthony. He placed his hand on my shoulder. "You're a natural piano player. As far as I'm concerned, the job is yours. Let me talk to my boss, Jean-Philippe Roussel. He's the chief entertainment director on the ship."

He picked up the phone at the bar area and talked to his boss in French. He hung up the phone and sat at the table. "Verga, Jean-Philippe will meet us later. He authorized me to talk business with you. Let's go to the ship's café." We took the elevator to the fifth-level deck and walked to the bow of the ship.

"Anthony, where are all the passengers? I see only a few staff members."

"They use the ship as a hotel. During the day, they're on shore. The ship has 229 first-class suites, 222 state rooms, and 604 tourist-class cabins. On board are 440 American tourists. In two days, we're sailing to Naples, where we will board 600 additional passengers, and then sail to New York with short stops in France and Spain."

We reached Café Tuscano, an airy room with panoramic windows overseeing the Grand Canal. There was a small counter with an espresso bar. A waiter came over. "Buongiorno. What can I get you, signori?"

Anthony glanced at me.

"A double espresso. Grazie," I said.

"For me, Birra Peroni."

Anthony pulled out a piece of paper and started writing on it. "I'm writing your job description. You're going to be part of our entertainment group. We're four musicians, four dancers, a singer, and I am the master of ceremony and sing too. You'll play piano in the evenings starting at 4:00 p.m. You'll play light classical tunes for half an hour in the main foyer before dinner. It's up to you to choose your own score. Every Wednesday and Saturday, show time is at nine and ten at night. On other nights, you play at the Bistro Bar from ten to eleven. You will accompany Laura at the bar area. The rest of the time, you are free, except when we rehearse for a show."

"What is the pay?"

"Your pay for the three weeks will be $750 plus room and board, all meals included. We provide the wardrobe, but you bring your own shirts. What do you say?" He poured beer into his glass, looking at me for an answer.

I thought, *This is my opportunity for an entertainer position.* I answered, "I'm not sure if I want this job. I love Venice."

"Why are you not sure? The money and the tips are very good. You will see the world. New York is a great city. We'll be in port for a week, and you'll have a chance to see a piece of America." He paused. "What else can I offer you?"

I thought fast. "What are my accommodations on the ship?"

"We all share cabins, two people per cabin. It's a standard accommodation on the ship."

"Is it below deck with no windows?"

"Yes."

"I need a window. I will consider the job if you place me in a tourist cabin, single bed with a window."

"As of now, we're booked for 1,040 passengers. We do have fifteen tourist cabins available. I can't guarantee a cabin for you. It's not up to me. I need to speak to my boss."

"I want a guarantee for a tourist cabin and $1,000 for my pay."

Anthony spilled beer from his mouth, wiping his lips with his hand. "Mamma mia, you're a tough negotiator. Verga, please understand I do not set the pay on this ship. It's all set by management in Genoa and my boss. I can probably arrange a tourist accommodation for you. Do me a favor. Accept the job, and I will make it up to you on the return trip. My boss can pay you a maximum of $800 now."

I stood up. "Let me think. I will let you know tomorrow."

"Mamma mia, I need your commitment today, Verga. Please sit down."

"*Domani* [tomorrow]," I said ready to leave.

"Let me speak to Jean-Philippe." He went to the bar and spoke on the phone.

"My boss is offering you $850 if you give him an answer now. Please sit down."

"Can I have another cup of espresso?" Drinking slowly, I was thinking. I put the cup down. "Okay, Anthony. We have a deal."

Anthony grinned, wrapping my hand, shaking it.

"Please, Anthony, put this in writing and in English so I can understand."

"Okay, no problem. I need you on board the ship tomorrow. I need to rehearse with you."

"I will be on board tomorrow afternoon."

"Can I offer you a drink? Beer or wine?"

"No grazie, Anthony. I will see you domani."

TWO

bserving the ship's departure from its mooring, I stood on deck with eager passengers. Slowly, the ship made its way down the Grand Canal, passing Doges Palace, the Campanile of San Marco, Santa Maria della Salute—a baroque church—then slowly floating, passing Venice's custom house to Dogana da Mar. This eastern promontory of Dorsoduro provided a panorama of the island of San Giorgio Maggiore, an eastern section of Giudecca. Pointing to the open Adriatic Sea, the ship sailed south along the eastern shore of the Italian boot toward Naples.

I was excited thinking of my new adventure cruising on an ocean liner toward the New World: America. Last night, I sat down to write a letter to Dr. Richter, pouring my heart out and explaining why I made the decision to take some time off from pursuing a classical music career. I told him I wanted to reflect on my future and experience other venues in music. I wrote my reason for fleeing the piano competition in Milan; the dread of bodily harm from the Zshopia and Erno was real to me. Then the news of the passing of my beloved teacher, Constantina, broke my spirit, and I was lost in sorrow and collapsed into depression, contemplating ending my life. Now I have recovered. An opportunity arose for a new entertaining job on an ocean liner, and I took it following my instincts, hoping I had made the right decision. I heard America could offer me many opportunities as a solo piano performer, and I was taking the chance. I thanked him for his guidance and unconditional support over the years. I will cherish it for the rest of my life. I ended the letter asking him for his forgiveness for not completing the piano competition and asked him for his support of my decision.

After, I called Hans. Alice, his secretary, told me he was on a weeklong tour in the vineyards of Hungary. I left a message. I would call him from New York.

Elizabeth and Giorgio wished me good luck on the cruise, and I promised to write them of my new adventure.

As I stood on the deck, the wind blew in my face. I looked at the watch. It was 2:30 p.m. I needed to go to my cabin and look over my piano repertoire for that evening. I glanced at the outskirts of Venice, Lido-Pellestrina, for the last time, thinking how much I got to love this city. I promised myself to be back.

In the grand foyer, I was surprised to find an upright dark wood piano Salle Pleyel et Cie. It was Frederick Chopin's favorite, a flagship of instruments of French artistic savoir faire. Dressed in a white jacket and pink shirt, I played light classical tunes. The piano had rich, velvety tones that echoed in the open space. In the foyer, there were boisterous, elegantly dressed passengers enjoying cocktails and wine, talking in small groups.

I heard a cry. "What a surprise! What are you doing on the ship?" It was Richard Benzilio and his wife, Patricia, whom I met at Harry's Bar.

She rushed toward me. "Verga, what a surprise!" She kissed me on the cheek.

I smiled and said, "I decided to see America."

"That's a good decision. Verga, you must sit at our table for dinner."

"Thanks for the invitation. You will have to request it from the maitre d'."

Richard, standing next to the piano, called Jerry DiPalma. "Hey, Jerry, look who's here."

Jerry was shocked too. He approached the piano, extending his hand. "Verga, it's nice to see you again."

Patricia said, "He'll be entertaining us on the ship. What a coincidence."

"It will be my pleasure to play for you, my friends."

Then the dining room doors opened, and the crowd proceeded to the tables.

After dinner, I played jazz music at the Bistro Bar for a small crowd, and the bar closed early.

The next morning, I was called with the rest of the ship's crew. We assembled on deck, listening to the second officer in charge of emergency evacuation. He read us instructions in English and Italian. My name was called. "Verga, did I pronounce it correctly?" the officer said.

"Yes, sir." I raised my hand. I wore an orange lifejacket.

He looked at me. "Verga, you need to tighten up all the buckles on your lifejacket."

"Yes, sir."

He looked at his list. "This is your first time on the ship?"

"Yes."

"I will assign you to be responsible for bringing a handicap person to the evacuation stage. We have none on board now, but that may change when we board passengers in Naples. I will let you know."

"Yes, sir."

Ten minutes later, an emergency alarm sounded on the ship. It consisted of seven short and one long siren. All passengers appeared on deck with lifejackets. It was only a drill.

Two days thereafter, the ship passed Amalfi Coast. All passengers on deck clicked their cameras. We passed the charming town of Amalfi with its medieval architecture situated on steep hills wedged between high mountains and sloped toward the sea. The ship passed the town of Praiano, an ancient fishing village, then the Island of Capri, and then the ship sailed into the Gulf of Naples.

Cristoforo Colombo docked at Naples port. I was on deck, admiring the city view. Naples was right in front of me with its wide bay, and in the background were the active Vesuvius volcanoes still capable of unleashing its fury to destroy civilization. The dock was bustling with activity. Boxes of produce were lined up. Longshoremen loaded crates, shouting in Neapolitan-accented Italian. Tourists were ready to disembark toward buses on the dock.

I had an appointment with Jean-Philippe, my boss, in his office. I knocked on his door.

"Come in." He was busy at his desk wearing a white uniform with white, black, and gold lapel epaulettes. Three gold strips with white indicated his rank: director of entertainment and the ship's chief purser. He took off his glasses. "Sit down, Verga. I am pleased with your performance. Our guests gave you a high mark for your entertainment. As a new member of the crew, I have guidelines for you. You are part of the ship's staff and have all the privileges of a staff member. Our captain wants the staff to interact with the guests; however, the captain has unwritten rules. Any sexual misconduct is not allowed with the guests. If he finds you violating this rule, you will be dismissed. Otherwise, you can fraternize with the ship's guests, have a drink, dance, and be social. Is that clear?"

"Yes, sir."

"Good, welcome aboard." He shook my hand. "Tonight, we shall meet at the theater. You will meet the rest of the entertainment group and rehearse for the next two days. For now, our passengers are on organized tours. In three days, we board the rest of the passengers. I need your passport. I will arrange the necessary visas for you. In the meantime, you can disembark. Go see Naples."

"What shall I see?"

"Oh, let me write a list."

"I like art and museums."

"I'm including those. Start with a walk in the Spaccanapoli neighborhood. It's not too far from the port. Watch your wallet. Let me see your watch." I showed him my West Clark pocket watch. "Okay, you can wear it. Do you have a camera?"

"No, I don't."

"Okay, visit the Capodimonte Museum. See *The Flagellation of Christ* painting by the great master, Caravaggio. Keep in mind that Naples is not Venice or Milan. I personally don't like it. I'm a northerner, but tourists are fascinated with Naples. There is a saying in Italian, '*Napolie un paradise abitatio da diavoli*' [Naples is paradise inhabited by devils]. Seductive, secretive, dirty, dark, and romantic in appearance. Quite a description, huh?" He laughed. "You tell me your impression. Be careful. Don't get into trouble with the local boys. I need you on board." He looked at the list. "Yes, visit Piazza Bellini and the archeological museum. Ask to see the ancient erotica collection. It's hidden away. Pay the guard, and he will let you in. This is the most corrupt city in Italy. Money opens doors to many of Naples's secrets. Stay away from Naples's two-legged forbidden fruits." He winked and smirked. "You may catch a disease." He smiled. "And tomorrow, you have an appointment with the ship's doctor. You need a clean bill of health before we sail. Go ahead. Enjoy the city."

As I headed for the door, I heard Jean-Philippe say, "Try the local pizza. You'll love it. And watch when you cross the streets. The city is chaos, and they run supreme in Naples."

As soon as I passed the port gatehouse, a dash of boys and young men descended upon me—hawking watches, cigarettes, and jewelry—and offered me to meet the most beautiful girls, showing me pictures and yelling, "Meet my sister."

I brushed them aside, showing no interest. Some of them trailed me for a block then gave up as I crossed the street.

The smell of fish, baked bread, and car fumes mixed into the air. I strolled along Via Nuova Marina toward Via Duomo. The street was busy with small zigzagging Fiat cars and Vespas.

I stopped to admire the Duomo di Napoli, a baroque church. It was built over the Basilica di Santa Restituta. Having limited time, I decided to look at the highlights of the Duomo treasures, Cappella del Tesoro di San Gennaro, the patron saint of Naples surrounded by gold and silver reliquaries. Behind the altar were two vials of the saint's blood; Neapolitans carried it throughout the city in procession several times a year. I was told by tourists standing next to me that the preserved blood appears to liquefy during the procession. The people of Naples say if it fails to do so, some catastrophe will befall the city.

I thanked them for the information and exited the candlelit church. After crossing the street past San Giorgio Maggiore, I headed toward Via Foria and the Museo Archeologico Nazionale. There was a long line of tourists at the ticket office. After thirty minutes, I entered the museum and headed to the ground floor by the Roman sculptures. I wanted to see the famous replica of Farnese Hercules, a copy of a large sculpture by a Greek master, Lysippus. Then I went to the mezzanine level and admired the large mosaic of Alexander depicting the great victory of a Persian emperor Darius. There was a small crowd of English-speaking insistent tourists at the end of the mezzanine arguing with a guard dressed in a gray uniform. I approached them and asked, "What is this about?"

"We want to see the collection of the Pompeian erotica, and the guard is telling us it's closed for today. So disappointing."

I was ready to leave when the guard settled the argument with a small bribe. The door opened, and I snuck in with the English tourists to a room displaying Pompeii's Gabinetto Segreto of erotica. After a quick tour, I left the museum and walked right into the heart of the city with crowded narrow streets of the dirty, dingy neighborhood of Spaccanapoli, the Greek word for "Split Naples." It split the city into east and west, the best-preserved scene from the Greek and Roman world. It's densely populated with shops, teeny pizzerias, bars, and chaotic city planning. Coming from orderly Austria, I was shocked. Cars, bikes, Vespas, and pedestrians occupied small roads. Between five-story building facades with balconies, laundry hung over the streets, dripping water as I walked. I escaped into a small pizzeria nearby and ordered Birra Peroni and margherita pizza. I had never experienced such a delightful pizza: thin, bubbling with cheese. The smell of mozzarella was like perfume. It tasted delicious—the ripe tomatoes, garlic, and anchovies. The sweetness of the sauce and the salted fish melted in my mouth. It was like a kiss on my lips.

The clock struck with a chime: 6:00 p.m. I walked outside. The breeze from the sea kicked in. The approach of evening turned the horizon orange against blue sky. I headed back toward the bay, making my way through the narrow alleys of Spaccanapoli. The noise of the city subsided. Women's and merchants' voices were heard as they haggled at open stalls. Boys' laughter echoed between buildings as they played ball. Priests and nuns in black carried heavy bags of produce and shuffled to their churches and monasteries. I was in a hurry, descending the stone paved steps, leaving the Old World behind me, thinking of something I overheard on the ship, "See Naples and die." I was not ready to depart this place. I wanted to see more of Naples, but it would have to be some other time.

THREE

I woke early, changed into a T-shirt and gym shorts, and then ambled to the ship's main deck. *Cristoforo Colombo* hummed with activity. Today, we would start our voyage to New York, and every voyage was a ship's show time.

On the loading dock, longshoremen moved forklifts, packing provisions and supplies into the belly of the ship. Inventory workers and the ship's head chef stood on the dock, shouting orders and checking the palettes. Fruits, vegetables, fresh meat, seafood, dairy, and baking goods were checked for freshness before being loaded onto the ship. The maintenance crew hosed and washed the ship's deck and windows. As I moved to the front of the ship, I passed the boarding gate. Custom and immigration officers set up a desk next to the ramp. Passenger boarding was scheduled for 10:00.

As I walked on the deck, I reflected on last night when I met the entertainment group. Pepino, the stage manager, introduced me to the dancers—Bethany, Maurice, Gia, and Dino—and the musicians—Santino on electric guitar and saxophone, Toma from Romania on accordion and violin, Palo on guitar and bass, and Teo on drums. I shook hands with a black jazz singer, Laura, from America. It was my first time meeting an African American woman. We rehearsed for an hour, and I felt that I fit into the group well.

With these thoughts in mind, I reached the secluded spot away from the ship's activity and placed a towel on the floor. This would be a good spot for the day's meditation. My watch showed six fifteen. A light breeze blew from the calm Naples bay. It was still dawn, and Naples was waking from her sleep. The honking noise of scooters was heard from the adjacent street. Sitting on the towel, I heard the orchestra of church bells ringing in the distance calling worshippers for morning mass. I looked up and a noisy flock of doves flew overhead, flying over the bay then disappearing. I could smell fish and baked goods. I tried to meditate, closing my eyes, oblivious to the commotion around me, concentrating on my breathing. Calm set in. I let go of my unneeded thoughts and sank into deep spiritual containment. Suddenly, a spray of water sprung me to my feet. A cleaning crew was washing the deck nearby. I picked up my towel, looking at my watch: seven fifteen. The sun broke through the morning haze. Today would be another bright day. I walked back to my cabin.

At ten, the passengers started to arrive, and by 1:00 p.m., the ship was loaded with noisy, excited guests. For the past few days, English had been the predominant language on the ship. Now it was Italian. At 2:00, the ship's horn sounded. An announcement was made over the intercom, "It's time for all visitors to exit the ship."

A rush of passengers filled every empty spot on the ship's deck, hugging, kissing, and saying good-bye to their loved ones. At precisely 3:00, the boarding ramp was removed. A tugboat maneuvered the ship away. A steam whistle sounded, blasting. Passengers waved their last good-bye. *Cristoforo Colombo* slowly sailed to the open sea, west to the horizon and late afternoon sun.

I stayed on deck, glancing at the panorama of Naples bay as it receded into the ocean. I glanced at the clock: 3:30. I needed to get ready for my play at the grand foyer.

That evening, Pepino, a fellow staff member, slipped me a note. Tomorrow at 10:00, the ship will conduct another evacuation drill exercise. My assignment was to help a guest in cabin 303.

The next day at precisely 10:00, an announcement was made to all passengers that the drill would be conducted shortly. Fifteen minutes later, a general alarm sounded, seven short blasts followed by one long one. The captain on the loudspeaker announced, "All passengers proceed to the evacuation station identified on your evacuation maps."

Wearing my lifejacket and yellow reflective vest with the words Emergency Guide, I walked to cabin 303 and knocked on the door.

"Entrare."

I opened the door. A young redheaded woman in dark glasses stood waiting for me. She appeared to be in her mid-twenties, dressed elegantly with short white boots and holding a long white cane. It was my first time encountering a blind person.

"Passo Parrlare in Inglesse? [May I speak in English?]"

"Please," she answered.

I introduced myself. "My name is Verga Caszar. I am your personal emergency guide. Please allow me to guide you to the evacuation station." I stood, unsure of what to do next. Hold her hand? I said, "Please follow me."

"Thank you," she answered.

I walked slowly in the corridor in front of her. She followed me using her cane as a guide. We reached the stairs. "May I?" I held her hand as we ascended the stairs.

"Thank you," she said. "What is your name again?"

"Verga Caszar."

"Thank you, Mr. Caszar. My name is Kelly O'Reilly."

"Nice to meet you, Miss O'Reilly."

We reached the drill station number 15. The deck was full of guests listening to the station officer giving drill instructions in English and Italian. After ten minutes, the all-clear sounded, and the exercise was over.

"May I accompany you back to your cabin?" I asked.

"That would be nice of you." She held my hand.

We spoke as we strolled to her room. "What do you do on the ship, Mr. Caszar?"

"I'm an entertainer."

"Entertainer?"

"Yes, I play piano."

"A piano player? What do you play?"

"Pop, jazz, and classical."

"Where are you from, Mr. Caszar?"

"I'm from Hungary, but I live in Austria." I remembered we were instructed to say that we are all from Italy. I had already broken a rule.

"You speak good English."

"Thanks."

We reached the cabin. "Thank you, Mr. Caszar."

"Please, call me Verga."

"Okay." She extended her hand. "Please call me Kelly." We shook hands. "Where do you play piano on the ship?"

"In the foyer before dinner and at the Bistro Bar from ten to eleven."

"I shall come and listen to you play."

"Oh, it will be my pleasure, Miss O'Reilly."

Bistro Bar was full of guests drinking, talking, smoking, and dancing. Waiters in white jackets and bowties served drinks. I played on the piano accompanied by Laura singing swing and light jazz songs. It was my first night accompanying her. She sang "All of You" then "Just One of Those Things," Cole Porter songs. After an hour, she took a break. I switched to playing Chopin's romantic tunes. The guests responded with generous tips, which I shared with Laura. I was so busy I did not pay attention to the guests at the bar. Around midnight, the place emptied. I noticed Kelly sitting at the far end of the bar. I wondered how long she had been there. I stopped playing and closed the fallboard, finished for the night. I went to the counter, ordered a Campari and soda, and then ambled over to Kelly's table.

"Good evening, Miss O'Reilly."

Large black glasses adorned her face. "Good evening. Please sit down," she said.

"Can I offer you a drink?"

"No thanks. Two glasses of wine. That's all I can handle."

Sipping my drink, I admired her outfit. She wore a red dress with a red scarf neatly wrapped around her neck. Two silver round earrings shone beside her face. Red hair was neatly combed behind her ear. She resembled Anouk Aimee, the actress, who I saw in the movie *La Dolce Vita* from Federico Fellini.

"I enjoyed listening to your piano playing, especially the classical tunes. You're a very good pianist. I detected your classical upbringing."

"Thanks. Do you like classical?"

"Yes, I love opera."

"Me too. Which one is your favorite?"

"Giuseppe Verdi's *La Traviata*, Mozart's *Così Fan Tutte* and *Don Giovanni*, and Richard Wagner's *The Flying Dutchman*. Sorry, my list is long. How about you?" She smiled.

"My list is long too. My favorite is *Tosca*, *Otello*, *Fidelio*; Richard Wagner's *Tristan und Isolde* and *The Rings*; and Puccini's *Madama*

Butterfly. Shall I continue? My list is too long, and it's getting late. The bar closes at midnight."

"It's that late?" she asked.

"Yes, it's ten to midnight. May I walk you to your cabin?"

She stood up. "Thank you. I can find my way to my cabin." She was silent for a moment then said, "If you don't mind."

"It's my pleasure to accompany you. It's not too far from mine."

She placed her hand around my arm, and we walked toward her room.

When we arrived, I asked, "May I open your cabin?"

She gave me the key, and I opened the door. "Good night, I had a pleasant evening," she said.

"Me too. I hope we can talk again."

"I'd love to, Verga. Good night."

In the morning, *Cristoforo Colombo* approached the shores of France and docked at the port of Marseille. The ship would stay in port for one full day.

I was in the bathroom shaving when the phone rang. "This is Verga speaking."

"Good morning, Verga." It was Kelly.

"Good morning, Miss O'Reilly."

"Please call me Kelly. Verga, I have a favor to ask you."

"Please go ahead." I took a towel and wiped shaving cream from my face.

"I understand we will be spending a day in Marseille. Would you be interested in accompanying me for a few hours? Of course I will pay you for your time."

"Kelly, it will be my pleasure, and you won't have to pay for my time, but I need to check with my boss for permission to disembark." There was silence on the line. "I'm pretty sure he will allow me to go on shore for a few hours. Can I call you back and let you know?"

"Yes, I'm embarrassed to inconvenience you."

"No, no, no. I wanted to go on shore anyway to visit Musée Cantini to see the contemporary paintings of the twentieth century, but of course, I will take you anywhere you wish to go."

"Please don't change your plans. I'll go with you to the museum."

I paused thinking, *How can she? She's blind.*

She sensed my silence. "Verga, please understand blind people do go to museums. You can explain what you see or read aloud about the artists and their work. Then after, perhaps I can invite you to a restaurant for the famous local fish stew dish, bouillabaisse."

"I'm sorry for not being sensitive."

"Verga, your reaction is normal. Please treat me like any other person. I have a disability, but I overcome it. Otherwise, I'm normal in other ways as any other person."

"I apologize. I hope you're not angry with me."

"Please, Verga, I'm not angry with you." Her voice was cheerful and friendly.

"Let me call you back."

"Thank you, Verga."

I hung up and went to the bathroom, looking in the mirror and suddenly remembering the shaving cream on my face. I thought about visiting the museum with Kelly, a visually impaired person. *She could slow me down. How would I communicate with her? Would she be a drag?* I wanted to see so much in a short time. *On the other hand, she's intelligent, good-looking, and has a pleasant personality. I really don't know her.* We had only met yesterday, but she intrigued me. I was not sure why. I couldn't put a finger on it.

Jean-Philippe gave me a five-hour leave on shore. I needed to be back by late afternoon for a rehearsal for a gala opening tomorrow.

The day was sunny and exuberant. Kelly was dressed in a white short-sleeved dress with a V-cut front and a pretty straw hat with a flowery band on her coppery red hair that was wrapped in a ponytail. Large white-framed glasses rested on her delicate, freckled face. Her lips were lightly colored a natural pink. She wore lime green sandals with a low heel and closed in front.

We left the port and hailed a taxi. "Musée Cantini, s'il vous plaît," I said.

In the taxi, Kelly said, "Verga, today you're my guest."

"No, Kelly, I'll pay for the museum. It was I who wanted to go there."

She placed her hand on mine. "Verga, as I said, you are my guest. The discussion is closed."

We arrived in front of Musée Cantini. "Quel est le trajet? [How much is the ride?]" She took francs from her purse and gave it to me. "Please pay the taxi driver."

Her arm was around mine as we walked through the museum's inner court. "You speak French?" I asked.

"Yes, I'm versed in three Latin languages: French, Italian, and Spanish."

"How come?"

"I studied classical Greek and Latin. I have a doctorate degree in ancient Greek and Roman philosophy."

"That's quite an accomplishment!"

We entered the lobby and strolled toward the ticket desk. Kelly spoke in French with the receptionist. She asked several questions that I did not understand. Then she paid for the tickets. As she put the change into her purse, I said, "May I ask you how you know the difference between the bills?"

"Oh, quite simple. Let's stand aside, and I will show you." We walked away from the ticket desk. "Look, Verga. I fold the domination of money in a particular way." She showed me one franc—left fold. Then five francs—folded crossway. "See how simple the solution?" She pointed to her wallet. I looked. It was divided into five compartments.

"It's really convenient." I handed the wallet back to her.

"The problem, Verga, is when I get change back. I must depend on a sighted person to tell me the money domination that I need to fold." She smiled.

"I'm impressed."

"Verga, you're my guide. I'm going to rely on you." She hooked her arm under mine.

In the first gallery, Kelly said, "Please find a seat. Would you read me this brochure?"

I guided her to a bench. She took off her straw hat and gave me the museum brochure. "Verga, I cannot understand how well-known museums like this have no English translation for the plaques by the artwork. They're only in French."

I was stunned to hear it and was silent for a minute. "Kelly, is that what the receptionist told you? Perhaps we should not have bought the tickets."

"No, no, Verga. The museum has important works by famous artists like Pablo Picasso, Fernand Léger, Max Ernst, and many more."

"If I can't read about the paintings, how can you enjoy the museum? You shouldn't have bought the tickets."

"Verga, as I said, today you are my eyes." She paused. "You can tell me what you're looking at."

I was uncomfortable with the suggestion. "Kelly, I don't think I can do this. I'm not too good with words, especially interpreting paintings. Ask me about music but not art." Before I finished, she took hold of my hand and leaned close to my face. I smelled her sweet perfume and looked at her glasses. I imagined that she could see me.

"Just tell me what you see in your own words, okay? Simple words. Anything that comes to your mind. The color of the painting, the subject, your impression of the work. Nothing complicated. You can do it, but if you feel like just looking at the paintings and not saying anything, that's okay too."

My tension and fear disappeared. I felt relaxed. Her voice was kind and encouraging. "I will do my best."

"Good, now you can read this." She pointed to the brochure. "The receptionist said this is the only thing they have in English."

I unfolded the colorful brochure. 'Musée Cantini' was printed on top. "This edifice was built in 1694 for the company Car Negre, and in 1709, the building was sold to the future mayor of Marseille, Jean-Baptiste Jacque Guy Therese de Montgrand. Then it was sold again to Louis Joseph Chaudoin. In 1888, the building that housed the museum was acquired by Jules Cantini, who donated it to the city of Marseille. In 1916, it became a decorative art museum. In 1936, it opened its doors as a museum of contemporary art. Now it houses a collection of paintings from Fauvisme, cubisme, and surréalisme and works from 1939 to 1960." There was a long list of exhibitors' work. I gave the paper back to Kelly.

"Now that we know a little about the museum, let's see the exhibits," she said.

We passed several paintings, and I read the names of the artists and provided brief descriptions of the compositions to her. I said, "Kelly, I noticed that the artists George Braque and Pablo Picasso experimented with mixing sand with their paints."

We stopped at *Papier Collage* by Pablo Picasso. "This composition of paper and wire is interesting. It depicts a guitar. I remember reading in a Picasso catalog that he repeatedly used this motif of a guitar as a tribute to the visual perception of the female body."

"In what style is the collage instructed?"

"Cubism. Layers of cardboard contrast each other. The form of the guitar looks realistic."

We walked to the next room. It displayed the works of other cubist artists. Holding Kelly's hand, I said, "Let's stop here in front of this still-life painting. I'm not familiar with Ferdinand Léger. The painting is an oil paint combination of tubes, cubes, funnels, and discs, all in vertical position connected to each other, painted in red, yellow, white, and black, which forms the volume on the canvas."

"What did the artist have in mind?"

"I think some kind of mechanical machinery full of energy, parts of the forms grinding against each other."

"I see you like the cubist period."

"Yes, it's interesting to me how the artists form their composition and color. I like this paper collage by Juan Gris, oil and charcoal on paper and canvas."

"Are you familiar with him?"

"No, it's my first time seeing his work."

"Tell me more of what you see."

I leaned closer to examine the painting. "Juan created objects of everyday use—folded newspapers, a cup, and a bottle—all combined into different colors of paint and intertwined in abstract form."

The last room displayed a collection of surrealist paintings by Max Ernst, Andre Masson, Roberto Matta, and others. The museum was not large, and after an hour, Kelly said, "Let's sit down."

We sat on a wooden bench. "Verga, thank you for your explanations. What do you think of the cubism period?"

"The cubist artists tried to express what they saw in front of them, but intentionally drew what is inside of us. What I mean is the artists used any combination of means to evoke the object. For instance, I saw a painting of a bottle. Picasso employed more than a single line of curves for its neck. Cubism is a different kind of art form. Creative, not like art from what you see but what you paint, sort of like photography or reproduction."

"And what do you think of surrealism?" She turned to me.

"I love that period. The surrealist artist, like Max Ernst, interpreted the relationship between the conscious and unconscious mind. I liked all the paintings we saw today. They show the artists' imaginations and their own dreams. I hope I answered your questions."

There was a smile on her face. "Indeed, you were eloquent with your words. Verga, continue to explore your passion for art. Cultivation of the mind is as necessary as food for the body. I notice your observation of the art could not be done without your observation of nature around you. You are a passionate individual. I detected it when you played the piano. I'm thankful you took me to the museum. I had a great time."

"You're welcome, Kelly."

"Now, Verga, I would like to reciprocate and invite you to a restaurant. I hope you're hungry."

"Yes, thanks."

We left the museum courtyard, and I hailed a taxi. Kelly handed a piece of paper to the taxi driver. "La Crabe Bleu" was scribed on it. It was built on a craggy stone jutting out into the sea. She said, "It was highly recommended by the ship's concierge. He told me the chef, Laurent, cooks exclusively with local fishermen's catch of the day. His signature dish is a famous local seafood stew or soup, bouillabaisse and bourride. Marseille is known for its wide range of Mediterranean cuisines. A few years ago, I stayed in the city for a week with a friend. We explored the diverse restaurants. I was very impressed."

"You didn't tell me you've been to this city before."

"I'm sorry. It never came up in conversation."

The taxi stopped at the restaurant. I thought about how much I wanted to know more about Kelly. She seemed mysterious, a trait I realized that I loved.

The restaurant was quite full as we walked toward our table. I recognized many faces. I said to Kelly, "This place must be good. There are many passengers from our ship here."

"Yes, indeed. This chef has a very good reputation, so the concierge said."

We sat at the table next to a large window overlooking the sea. A waiter arrived and asked if we wanted something to drink. "Please order a bottle of wine," she said.

"*Garcon, puis-je, avoir le menu?* [Waiter, please, can I have a menu?]" He handed one to me, and I ordered a bottle of white wine.

We sipped the drinks when they arrived. "Kelly, please tell me, are you on holiday in Italy?"

"Not really. I was invited to give a talk at the University of Rome. You're probably surprised that the blind give speeches." She chuckled.

"I'm not surprised. Please continue. I'm very much interested to listen."

The sun shone on her copper hair giving it a reddish, golden glow. She had beautiful features, and I wondered what she looked like without glasses.

"As I was saying before, I specialized in ancient Greek and Roman philosophy. I wrote many papers on the Roman philosopher and great statesman Cicero. Are you familiar with him?"

"To tell you the truth, not at all."

"One of the most influential Roman statesmen, orator, essayist, and philosopher—a great figure in Western civilization. His eloquent speeches and writings are natural law and his government ideals influenced American founding fathers, especially the second president of the United States, John Adams."

"Please tell me more. This is interesting."

"I talk too much, Verga. Let's order some food."

I looked at the menu. "How about we start with *coquille Saint-Jacques a la nage et au beurre de corail* [scallops in the shell with bright orange coral] as the first course? We can share it."

"Sounds great, and for the entrée?"

I glanced over the choices. "The house specialty is Mediterranean *bouillabaisse* [fish soup]."

"Good choice."

Kelly had a conversation with the waiter in French. Then she turned to me and said, "The waiter told me that the Mediterranean fish has more flavor than most other ocean fish, and the chef uses only the freshest of today's catch in his soup."

"Sounds splendid."

Once the waiter brought over the appetizer, we partook in the delicious scallops and idle chitchat. I asked Kelly, "How long did you stay in Naples?"

"Just for two days. This is my second visit to the city. After my visit to Rome, I was invited by the Italian Antiquarian Bookseller Association, of which I am a member, to give a talk at the Biblioteca Girolamini in Naples on the subject of the 145 recently published volumes of *World Book Encyclopedia* in Braille."

"Did you contribute to it?"

"Yes. I wrote a small portion about ancient Greek and Roman philosophy. I also sat on the board of editors at the American Printing House. They specialize in publishing audio and Braille books."

"I'm impressed. That's wonderful."

Our bouillabaisse arrived. The aroma of the broth awakened my appetite. When we finished, Kelly said, "Verga, tell me about yourself."

"My story is long." I looked at my watch. "I apologize, but I need to get back to the ship. I have a rehearsal this afternoon. I promise to continue our conversation later."

"Okay, I'm looking forward to it."

We finished our lunch. I ordered a double espresso. Then we hopped into a taxi for a ride back to the *Cristoforo Colombo*. Once in the taxi, Kelly said, "Verga, I had a wonderful time today."

"Me too, and I thank you for inviting me to spend time with you."

The radio in the taxi played a song in English, "I Didn't Know What Time It Was" by Lorenz Hart and Richard Rodgers. My senses slowly came alive, listening to the lyrics singing from the radio.

And now I know I was naïve

I didn't know what time it was
Then I met you
Oh, what a lovely time it was

I felt like holding Kelly in my arms but was afraid. I turned toward Kelly. Hearing this song was such a coincidence. I wondered if she felt the same way. She turned to me, looking at me in silence behind her dark glasses. I felt her warm body next to me. We were like two candles lit in a dark room. Their two shadows came closer, reaching to each other, fingers wanting to touch but not. The speaker kept playing Hart and Rodger's song. Fingers finally found one another, touching then clasping together. We sat in silence, each other in our own thoughts. The song switched to a French melody.

FOUR

$\mathcal{S}$tage lights switched on. Dressed in a red jacket, black pants, and a white shirt with a black bowtie, Anthony sprung onto the stage holding a microphone in his hand, the other in a cast hidden inside his jacket. He sang "Mambo Italiano" by Rosemary Clooney: "A boy went back to Napoli because he missed the scenery... Hey, mambo Italiano, hey, mambo, mambo Italiano..."

He finished with the words, "E lo che se dice you get happy in the pizza when you mambo Italiano."

A loud applause echoed throughout the ship's theater.

"Good evening, ladies and gentlemen. *Buona sera, signore e signori.* We have a great show for you tonight. What do you call someone who can speak two languages?"

"Bilingual," the audience replied.

"What do you call someone who can speak three languages?"

"Trilingual."

"What do you call someone who can only speak one language? American!"

Laughter broke in the theater. To our American guests, he sang "We Don't Speak Americano."

> Comme te po
> Comme te po
> Comme te po capi chi te vo bene sit u le parle mmiezzo
> Americano

(How can I

How can I

How can I make you understand that I care about you if

you speak half American?)

Will we make love under the moon?

How can you ever think I love you?

Act, act like American!

He acts like American!

Dancers emerged on stage behind a sheet of reflective plastic, twisting in erotic, sensual movements, snaking, crawling, and then leaping into the air. Women wore light pink tights; men were dressed in black and wore Venetian masks. A spotlight shone on stage—new scene.

Different dancers glided onto the stage. Men in formal black attire and women in sheer chiffon dresses danced the Waltz. The assembly of musicians played Johann Strauss's "Vienna Waltz." Pepino was the lighting director and shone different colored lights on each couple.

Anthony appeared and introduced Laura. She sang popular hit songs of the fifties: "I'm Sorry," "Sixteen Reasons," "I Want to Be Wanted," "All My Love," and the Italian song "Arrivederci."

Then he introduced me. I played Frederick Chopin's romantic piano Nocturne, no. 2, op. 62 and Mozart's *Fantasia* in D Minor, K. 397 and finished with Mozart's *Eine Kleine Nachtmusik* (*A Little Serenade*). The crowd applauded.

Anthony appeared on stage singing famous Neapolitan songs in English and Italian: "O'Sole Mio," "Funiculi Funiculi," "Santa Lucia, "Maria Mari," and "Luna Rossa."

Then he closed the performance with a comedy bit. "Why are most Italian men named Tony? When they got on the boat to America, the immigration agent stamped 'To NY' on their foreheads." The audience rose with a chuckle. "The trouble with eating Italian food is that five or six days later, you're hungry again." They laughed louder, a successful performance. "Good night, *buonanotte.*"

After playing in two shows that night, I was exhausted. I had a drink with one of the musicians at the bar then retired to my cabin.

The next day, the ship arrived at the port of Costa del Sol, Málaga, a bustling city and the second largest port in Spain, home to beautiful beaches, gardens, and museums. It was also the city of the birth of Pablo Picasso. When we arrived, Málaga was still in the midst of renaissance.

The next day, the *Cristoforo Colombo* was to start crossing the Atlantic to New York. I was given a short leave in the meantime. Kelly and I made plans for the day. The weather was warm and sunny under a bright blue sky. I decided to skip the museums and guided tours for Kelly's sake. A taxi driver dropped us off at Playa las Acacias, a very popular beach, where we took a walk. It was not the best temperature for swimming, so the beach was not crowded. It was long and wide with rocky breaks dividing small coves. We took our shoes off and strolled on fine gray sand, waves splashing our bare feet in the rhythm of the tides. We were dressed in jeans. Kelly had a flowery colorful V-neck shirt. On her head was a white handkerchief tied neatly with a knot, her coppery hair in a ponytail. Her iconic white-framed glasses rested on her nose.

As we walked the edge of the water, we held hands. She said, "Verga, at breakfast, you didn't finish telling me your story."

"Where did I stop?" Since our day in Naples, I had told her briefly of my time in the piano competition and growing up in Kőszeg and Budapest.

"In Milan, at your hotel room, you found an envelope with a note inside."

"Yes, as I was saying, the note read that I was to meet this person on the Duomo roof at five and to come alone. I was terrified of Erno and Zophia."

"What do you mean?" She stopped to turn to me.

I told her the story of what had happened during my escape from Hungary—the truth. I recollected with a saddened heart the death of my father.

"Let's sit somewhere," she said.

We sat on the beach. Light wind blew from the bay, unraveling her hair. She crossed her legs, sitting silently for a couple minutes before saying, "I'm sorry about your father and what you went through. After all that, you should have looked into those gangsters' eyes and said, 'You don't scare me. I'm not quitting the competition.' I have a feeling, Verga, that they were bluffing."

"At the time, I was scared. The photos of Constantina and me were vivid, and then my bodyguard was assaulted. The chicken bones in Zophia's envelope to me suggested bodily harm. There was a note with a skull and crossbones, warning me of death. It's as on the bottle of poison or the sign on the high-voltage tower, an indication of danger. The threat was real to me. Right or wrong, I made the decision to skip the competition."

"What happened to your teacher?"

"Two days later in Venice, I found out that she passed away," I said in a very quiet, almost inaudible voice.

"Oh my god, Verga, that is terrible."

I was silent. "Yes, I wanted to end my life. I almost jumped from the pensioni roof only to be saved by Giorgio, the owner."

"That's terrible. I'm sorry to hear this."

"I contemplated taking my own life. Now I feel ashamed and remorseful."

She faced me and wrapped her arms around my neck. She said, "The Roman stoics perceived taking one's own life as an acceptable and dignified way to deal with unbearable misfortunes in life. I think a suicidal impulse is an act of Eros. Verga, darling, I feel your distress."

I held her tight, and we sat like that for a long time. I smelled the scent of her perfume. Her body was warm. I felt her lips on my neck. I wanted to kiss her, but she let go, looking at the sea and saying nothing. After a while, I stood up and took hold of her hand.

"Kelly, would you like to get tapas with me?"

"Sure. Do you know how tapas originated in Spain?"

I shook my head.

"The story goes like this." We strolled toward the adjacent road. "Tapas were first prepared for King Alfonso X. He was the ruler of Castile. The king suffered from illness and was required to consume small quantities of food and wine between meals. Tapas in Spanish means 'cover' or 'lid.' It became customary to serve wine with something covered, such as meat, fish, or vegetables, or a slice of bread with ham or cheese."

Once we reached the street, I hailed a taxi. Kelly asked the driver in Spanish to take us to a restaurant in town that served tapas. Turning to me, she said, "The taxi driver recommends Bodega Antigua Casa Guardia, an old establishment. It was Picasso's favorite haunt."

Standing at the Bodega bar, I ordered sherry. With that, a waiter brought over a variety of small dishes. We drank and nibbled on hors d'oeuvres, peppered potatoes, empanadillas, olives, ham, cheese, and salted cod fritters. The sherry's sweet muscatel was served directly from oak barrels, the same way as it was served in the 1840s.

With the glass of sherry in my hand, I turned toward Kelly and asked, "I noticed a typewriter on your desk. What have you been writing in your cabin?"

"Reports for my conferences in Italy. It's a Braille-writer. They will be published in the next quarterly *Dialogue* magazine for the visually impaired in New York."

"I don't know anything about Braille typewriters. How does it work?"

"You can come to my cabin one day to take a look."

"Okay, I'll call you."

I sipped sherry and put the glass down. "Kelly, I told you my story. May I ask you what you were doing in France a few years ago?"

"Oh, that was five years ago. I graduated from a master's program in NYU. During college, I befriended a student named Mark. After graduation, he offered me to accompany him for two weeks in Paris. He came from a well-to-do home. His parents even paid for my eye-seeing dog, César, whom I still have at home. He couldn't accompany me on this trip. Mark and I dated seriously. We were in love. We even talked of getting married. His invitation was an opportunity for me to travel. I took it, and we spent a week in Paris. Then we took a trip to southern France and stopped at Marseille. I had a great time." She stopped talking, turned around, and asked the waiter to refill her glass.

"Where is Mark now?"

She faced the sherry barrels behind the bar counter, holding her glass with two hands, and said nothing for a while. "We drifted apart, Verga. He was accepted into medical school at Stanford University's School of Medicine, and I enrolled into a PhD program at Yale on scholarship. Since we were apart for a long time, my hope of marrying him dashed away."

Now it was me who felt sorry for her. She turned around and said, "*C'est la vie.* Let's talk about other things."

At 4:00 p.m., I needed to go back to the ship. I was scheduled to work at 5:30. I hailed a taxi.

The next day, we sailed past the Gibraltar Strait. On one side was Europe and, on the other, Africa. The span between them is 14.3 kilometers, which is 8.9 miles. Every inch of the ship's rail was taken by passengers clicking their cameras. Kelly stood next to me. It was windy, and she was dressed with a sweater and a colorful woolen hat on her head. She asked me, "What are we passing now?"

"A large towering outcrop of rock. It looks to be about four hundred meters in height. The top of the rock is sharp. Then the rock slopes gradually to the right. In front of us is a cargo ship. It's foggy, so the view is hazy."

"A columnae herculis," she said in Latin. "According to Greek mythology, Hercules had to perform twelve labors, and this was the location of the two pillars, between the Mediterranean and the Atlantic, the mark of the farthermost limits reached by Hercules. The columns are also on the Spanish coat of arms."

"How interesting. I should read Greek mythology. I spend too much time reading about music and art."

A gust of cold wind blew. I placed my arm around her. "Thanks. You're warm. How come?"

"I spent some time this morning meditating on the deck. Then I ran for half an hour on the promenade."

"Do you meditate daily?"

"Yes."

"Can I join you?"

"Of course. In fact, I will put an announcement on the bulletin board if anyone wants to join me for forty-five minutes of meditation at seven thirty in the mornings. I would be delighted if you joined."

"I will. Please put me on your list."

"You will be my first signee."

Kelly wrapped her arm around my body. With her warmth against me, I had an urge to kiss her but held it at bay. I was not sure if she would welcome it, and I was nervous, as I haven't felt this way since I last saw my dear Constantina.

"Let's go inside. It's too windy," I said, and the sea got rougher. "Can I see your Braille typewriter?"

"Of course. Take me to my cabin."

When we arrived, I was surprised at how neat her cabin was. She took off her hat, and hair fell to her shoulders. I thought that I was falling in love with this woman. She moved freely, not once hitting a chair or the bed. "Kelly, may I ask you. Are you totally blind?"

She removed her sweater. "Verga, why are you standing?"

How does she know? I sat in a chair near the dresser.

"You're wondering how I knew you were standing."

"Yes."

"Well, legally I'm blind." She sat on the edge of the bed. "My left eye is totally blind, and my right has retinitis pigmentosa, a degenerative eye disease. I have tunnel vision, and it seems like my ability to see diminishes as years pass. I may become totally blind one day. Doctors say it's genetics. It may be, but no one in my family has this condition. For the time being, they will not operate on me. Maybe in the future. Only God knows."

"Can you see me?"

"In a bright light, I can make out your features and faint nuances of color. At night, you are just a dark silhouette. Why are we talking about my blindness? You're here to see my typewriter." She stood up and went to the table. "This is a Perkins Brailler, a very complex machine. It has over five hundred parts. The Braille language was invented in 1821 by a Frenchman, Louis Braille."

She sat in front of the typewriter and typed my name. She pulled the paper out. "Verga, touch the raised dots. They're called cells, tiny bumps. The alphabet is a deviation of six dot cells. Touch the *V*, four raised dots in the shape of a capital *L*."

"That's fascinating." I looked at a machine on the table. "Wollensak 1515" was written on its side in silver letters. "And what is this other device?"

"Oh, this is a Wollensak T-1515, a stereophonic high-fidelity tape recorder with built-in amplifier. I record the lectures I attend and what I want to write, and then I type."

"How about that? I wonder if one day, I can record my piano playing."

"Of course you can."

"That'd be great." I looked at my watch. It was lunchtime, and I had not yet practiced for that night's show. "May I accompany you to the dining room?"

"Yes, you can."

FIVE

The ship plowed through the Atlantic at twenty-three knots. The arrival time to New York was in five days. This morning, I had eight women show up for my meditation session. The weather was not conducive to outdoor activity, so I moved my group into the glassy promenade. Moving some lounge chairs, the women placed towels on the floor and sat down. I sat in front of the group cross-legged, recognizing most of the women before me. Kelly sat at the edge of the group dressed in white shorts and a loose T-shirt, her hair in a braid and large glasses on her face.

I said, "You are all welcome to our first meditation session. I recognize most of you. You are Americans?"

"Yes," the group answered in unison.

"Not me." A tall blonde lifted her hand. "I'm French."

I replied, "*Vous souhaite la bienbeuve* [You're welcome]. May I speak in English?"

"Yes," the group answered. The blonde nodded.

Just then, Pepino, the stage manager, came in huffing out of breath.

"Pepino, is everything all right?"

"Yes, yes." He stood dressed in shorts and a T-shirt, towel in his hand. "Am I late?"

"No, Pepino, please join us."

He sat next to Kelly, looking at the group, embarrassed. He was the only man in my class.

"As I was saying, you are all welcome to meditation class. Imagine if we could discern our own emotional patterns and ways of thinking, recognizing the negative habits and impulses in us. Sometimes our day's emotions and thoughts fill us with anger, worries, self-doubts, and other petty thoughts. Today, we will let go of all this negativity. Meditation is like gardening. It will help us plant and cultivate good seeds. So let's pull out the weeds and let flowers blossom. The best way to start is to simply start. Relax your body, take a deep breath, exhale, take another, and exhale. Focus on your breathing going in and out. Let's empty our minds."

I glanced at the group. They all had their closed eyes. The only noise was the humming of the ship's engine and the slight rocking of the ship as it glided over waves. After thirty minutes, I clapped my hands. The group awakened, opened their eyes, smiled, and looked at me.

"Let's stand up and put our hands behind our backs and stretch. Lift your hands and stretch. Good. Our session is finished."

Patricia came to me. "Verga, that was great. Thank you."

Other women surrounded me, asking questions about yoga and meditation. I glanced toward Kelly. She listened to the women as they talked.

"Verga, my name is Ruth." A black-haired short woman introduced herself.

"Nice to meet you, Ruth."

"May I ask you a question?"

"Of course."

In a low voice, she whispered, "Are you Jewish?"

"No, I'm not."

"I apologize for asking. I was mistaken."

"It's quite all right, but why do you think I'm Jewish?"

"You're wearing a mezuzah."

"Oh, that was given to me as a present, but my mother was Jewish."

Ruth smiled and said, "I was right."

I didn't understand her. "Have a nice day, Ruth. I will see you tomorrow."

Kelly walked up to me. I said, "Shall I accompany you to your cabin?"

We walked with her arm around mine. "I enjoyed your meditation," she said.

"That's great, Kelly, thank you. By the way, Gia and Dino are conducting dance classes this afternoon. Would you be interested in being my partner?"

"Of course, Verga. What time?"

"At two in the afternoon."

"I will be ready."

I learned the cha-cha, rumba, and slow dance. Kelly was a good dancer. She knew all the steps, which helped me learn them too. As we danced, she said, "Verga, tonight, they are having a quiz show in the theater. I signed up as a contestant. Would you come see me?"

"Sorry, Kelly. I need to play in the bistro tonight. Please come to the bistro after the contest, and we can have a drink."

"Okay, I will."

That night, the lounge was full of people. Laura and I were in full swing, entertaining the bistro guests. I lifted my head from the piano and noticed Kelly sitting at the front table. I finished playing for the evening and walked toward her.

"How was the contest?" I sat at the table.

She had a big smile on her face. "I won first prize," she said proudly.

"You did? Smart girl. That's great."

She leaned down and picked up a large bottle of champagne and a box of chocolate, placing it on the table.

"What's that?" I said, a surprised look on my face.

"My prize."

I examined the bottle. "Moët Chandon," I said. "Oh la la."

"Would you like to come to my cabin to have a drink with me?"

"Okay, I'll bring my record player and *La Traviata* disc. We can listen to *'Libiamo Ne' Lieti Calici'* ['Drink from Joyful Cup']."

She smiled. "You will be Alfredo, and I will be Violetta." Taking the bottle and box, we left the bistro.

I placed the *La Traviata* record on the player. Listening to the opera, I took off my jacket and placed it on a chair. I unbuttoned the top two buttons on my shirt. We took off our shoes, and Kelly went to the bathroom and came back with two clean glasses.

"What are you waiting for, Verga? Open the bottle. Let's celebrate."

I pulled the cork, and it flew toward the ceiling with a popping noise. The smell of bubbly Pinot Noir grape filled my nostrils. I poured champagne into the glasses. "What are we celebrating?"

"Life, love, friendship, and good health."

We clicked our glasses. "Wow, that's a good bubbly," she said.

"Yes, indeed."

Just then, the record sang the drinking song. She stood up. "Verga, let's dance."

"It's the waltz. I don't know how to dance."

"Come on, I will teach you the basic box pattern."

Our bodies glided forward. She uttered into my ear, "Boom-tick-tick—boom-tick-tick and lean," and pulled me, guiding me on the floor. Left foot forward, right foot side, left foot close, right foot back, left foot side, right foot close. I felt her bosom rubbing on my chest. The thunderous chorus from the record swelled. Then the singing stopped. I paused, standing motionless for a while. Then I folded my arms around her. She leaned into me. Lips found one another in a gentle kiss, her arm around my neck. I felt her warm breath. My blood surged. I wanted all of her. I lost myself in Kelly's kiss.

The record played act 2, and Alfredo sung *"De Miei Bollenti Spiriti Il Giovanile Ardore"* ("The Useful Adore of My Ebullient Spirits").

I kissed Kelly's neck. Her sweet perfume ignited my desire. My hand glided on her back down to her buttocks. Her lips trailed my neck, her eyeglasses pressed into my skin. I whispered in her ear, "Kelly, can I remove your glasses?"

She did not respond for a long moment. Lifting her head and looking at me, she nodded in approval. Her body froze in anticipation of my reaction. Slowly, I removed her dark shades, for the first time revealing her lovely features. Her left eye was shut closed. Her right eye was half open, blinking, looking at me. We gazed at each other for a long moment. I leaned down and kissed her forehead, then her closed eye, and then gently kissed her lips. Her body relaxed, pressing herself into me.

I felt her fingers gliding over my face, eyes, nose, lips, down my neck, stopping on my bare chest. I removed my shirt, dropping it onto the floor. She touched my shoulders, tracing the muscles in my arms. I removed my undershirt. Her fingers moved downward to my torso. Her delicate fingers lit every cell in my body trembling with pleasure. She traced my body like a painter's brush on canvas. I let my pants down to the floor. Kelly lowered herself to her knees, holding her fingers on my belly. I removed my underwear. Naked, I stood trembling with the excitement of her fingers passing over my throbbing hardness. She did not neglect any part of my body. I lifted her from the floor, kissing her open mouth. She let go of my embrace and slowly unbuttoned her shirt then removed her brassiere, exposing two large peach-colored breasts. My lips kissed her nipples. She let out a low moan and dropped her skirt.

Act 3 of *La Traviata, "Addio, del passato bei sogni ridenti"* ("Farewell, Lovely, Happy Dreams of the Past"), echoed in the cabin.

Standing in black laced underwear, her plump pear-shaped figure revealed her pale skin adorned with freckles spread like birdseeds. I took her hand and walked her toward the bed. We lay together, our bare skin warm against one another. My heart raced with excitement. It was my turn to explore her. My fingers glided over her skin, caressing her voluptuous breasts. She lay closed eyed, breathing loud. My hands reached between her legs, tracing the hem of her underwear. It felt warm and moist. She trembled at my touch. Our tongues slid into parted lips, her hand on my back holding tight. When I went to remove her underwear, I felt her body cringe, her hands moving to grab mine. I let go of her panties, resting my head on her breast. She whispered into my ear, "Not tonight."

I froze. She sensed my body language, holding me tight to her breast, her breath on my ear excited. I heard her voice as she whispered, "Please stay with me tonight."

Is she teasing me? She was not. That was as far as she was willing to go that night. I felt cheated. *Is it me? What do I need to do to unlock the door? How is it that our bodies ignite with lust and fire yet do not burn?* We switched positions, and she leaned into my chest. I felt the candle still burning. Something stopped her tonight. I felt the ship's steady rocking on the waves. Cheek to cheek, we shared the pillow and fell asleep.

I woke up the next day to see Kelly sleeping, her coppery hair spread on the pillow. Her face appeared peaceful, so I chose not to wake her. Quietly, I sat on the edge of the bed, stretching my hands. It was a single bed and uncomfortable. My body ached from sleeping on my side. I reached for the watch. It showed six fifteen in the morning. I had a meditation class at seven thirty. Kelly moved in the bed. Then I felt her arms wrapping around my body, her face against my naked back. Her warmth awakened last night's desires. I turned around, and she smiled. Our lips found each other's in a kiss.

"Why are you up so early?" she asked, sitting on the bed, trying to arrange her red hair. She was topless, her full breasts protruding from her body. She reminded me of Aphrodite. Her locks of hair were like waves of sea. My lips caressed her nipples gently, and she lifted my head kissing me with warm lips.

"Let's stay in bed," she said.

"I have a class at seven thirty. I have to go."

"Oh, I forgot."

"Are you coming?"

She finally put her hair into a ponytail. "Yes. Pick me up. I will be ready in fifteen minutes."

When we arrived at the ship's promenade, to my surprise, a small crowd of twenty-two women and Pepino waited for me. I supposed word got out about my class. I arranged the group on the floor in two rows forming a semicircle. I placed Pepino next to Kelly in front of Patricia. After repeating my talk from yesterday, we all sank into quiet, tranquil meditation.

I was still aroused from last night. Kelly's words were still on my mind. *Why did she stop us from making love? Why did she say 'Not tonight'?* I let the matter slide and concentrated on my breathing and relaxed. I opened my eyes, looking at the watch. We meditated for forty minutes today. I clapped my hands, and the session was over. The crowd of women surrounded me, asking questions and telling me what they thought and how much they enjoyed the class. I entertained their conversations.

After fifteen minutes, I scanned the room for Kelly. She was not to be found. I felt guilty for speaking for so long and leaving her alone. I parted with "I will see you all tomorrow."

I picked up the house phone, dialing extension 303. The phone rang for a long time. She answered, "Hello?"

"It's me, Verga. Kelly, I'm sorry I neglected you. How did you find your way to the room?"

"Oh, no problem. I asked Pepino to accompany me."

"I feel bad. The women kept me asking questions. I couldn't break away from them."

"Verga, no problem. It's your job, and by the way, your class is great."

"Thanks. Will I see you today?"

"I just wanted to call you. I want you to come to my cabin."

"When?"

There was silence. "Now. The door is open. Just come in."

"Okay, I'll be there in five minutes."

When I arrived at her room again, I opened the door, announcing myself. "Verga, is that you?"

"Yes."

"Come in and lock the door and put the Do Not Disturb sign up."

She came out of the bathroom wearing a slinky gold-trim silky robe and wiping her reddish hair. I went to her, and we kissed.

"I finished taking a shower and ordered extra towels. Go ahead and take a shower."

"Good idea," I said and started the water.

After my shower, wrapped in a towel, I walked into the room. The house radio played international songs in Italian, French, English, and Spanish. Kelly sat on the chaise longue in her robe, her hair up in a towel turban style and without eyeglasses on her face.

"Have a drink. It's a shame to let the champagne go to waste," she said.

"Salute." We clicked glasses. I stood looking at her, sipping the bubbly. It warmed my heart. I felt my desire to hold Kelly remerge. I took the last sip of the champagne and came close to her, dropping my towel and revealing my youthful figure. I was washed with morning light coming from the window. Kelly stood up, faced me, and removed her robe, exposing her naked body. I imagined hearing her voice in my head, "Make love to me."

Standing closed eyed, we embraced. She was only five feet four inches. I leaned in to kiss her and set her on the chaise. On my knees, I kissed down her body. Her head tossed back, her fingers holding my head. My lips and tongue moved over her bare skin, licking, kissing. She lifted her legs and placed them on the edge of the chaise, legs spread. My hands touched her demure pubic triangle, fingers knocking on her door. She opened her gates and let me into her warm and wet Venus. She moved against my touch with low moans. I sensed her ripeness and stood up, lifting her from the seat. We embraced and kissed. I whispered in her ear, "Kelly, I need to put a condom on."

I felt her warm breath on my neck. Her soft voice said, "I'm on the pill."

For a moment, I did not quite understand her. "What kind of pill?"

She elaborated, "A birth control pill."

I did not know such a thing existed. I laid her on the bed. Lying between spread legs, I thought about her words that held us back the night before, but we were finally ready to share our bodies. She raised her thighs like parting clouds. Belly to belly, I felt her hand on my hard penis guiding it into her Venus. With her hand on my buttocks, I pushed deeper and deeper then stopped. We rested on each other's chests, lying for a long time looking at each other. Her face was glowing with warmth, eyes shut, lips wet and apart. Then we moved slow and steady up and down. Our throats swelled with waves of pleasure. Muffled moans echoed in the room. I sensed her gentle climax. She let out a low cry squeezing her legs then relaxed. I felt her fingers on my behind, digging hard. The towel unraveled from her head, revealing red hair on the pillow. Lying in each other's embrace, we tried to catch our breaths. My mezuzah entangled in her chain that held a small cross. She whispered, "Verga, our necklaces. They're like our lives—forever connected."

I didn't answer right away. I untangled our chains, freeing her cross from my mezuzah. After I unhooked the two pendants, I replied, "Kelly, I can't tell if we're one body or two." We pressed closer to each other.

I heard her raspy voice. "Verga, I didn't hear you cum."

"I didn't yet," I said, my mouth searching hers, parting her lips.

I felt her rapid breath warm in my ear, whispering, "Verga, turn around."

Sitting on me, her hand on my erection, she guided herself onto me. My blood surged, tingling my skin with pleasure, her tongue teasing mine. It felt like clouds building up before the storm. Then I felt the enormous thunder. I let out a loud cry.

"Good god, what a morning," she said, kissing me.

"I wish I would die that way."

"Oh, Verga, let's talk about living. Sex has a way of finding home."

We coiled into each other and fell asleep.

Soon, I twisted and turned open-eyed. *What time is it?* I noticed Kelly was not in bed. On the pillow was evidence of her scent and scattered red hair. I smiled, thinking of the sweetness of her skin and swell of her breasts. The image of her embrace left me wanting her again.

I heard water running in the bathroom then all quiet. Kelly walked into the room, her hair in a neatly combed ponytail. Naked and smiling, she walked toward the bed. Her beautiful breasts bounced as she walked. "Good morning, sweetie."

"Good afternoon," I replied.

I lifted the blanket, and she climbed into bed, sitting on my lap. Sweet perfume was emitting from her clean skin. Her lush lips kissed mine. We embraced with her arms around my neck. I felt her voluptuous breasts pressing against my chest. She sensed my hard swollen penis between her legs as she lifted herself momentarily and sat on my lap, locking us in physical union. Then we climbed. It was a long nonstop climb, her ponytail swinging behind her head back and forth and mouth agape, gasping for air. Steady, our bodies glided into each other forward, backward, pushing and pulling, skin to skin. Her voice drifted into my ear. "I'm almost there. Hold on." Her sweaty cheek touched mine, and our fingers clutched each other's. Breathless, I held back until she found her release. I listened to her wild, joyous cries. "Oh god," she whispered, exhausted, her head nestled on my chest.

We lay in each other's arms for a long time, not saying anything. Then she said, "Verga, thanks for being so considerate and understanding with me last night."

"Why?"

"I feel uncomfortable about the other night. I knew you wanted me, and I stopped you."

"Did you want me?"

"Yes."

"Then why did you say not tonight?"

She did not reply for a long moment then said, "I did not want to disappoint you."

"What do you mean?"

"It's hard for me to talk about," she said in a sorrow tone.

"Was it me? Did I do something you did not like?"

"No, no." She lifted her head, looking at me, then rested on my chest.

"Then what?"

She was silent for a long time before she spoke again in a soft hush. "Verga, sometimes I have a recurring flashback in my head. I have a ghost in my life. Sometimes he returns to haunt my memories. It leaves me cold, especially in intimate moments. I didn't want you to make love to a mere body. That's not me. I wanted you to see and feel me alive like today." She paused again for a minute.

"I attended a school for the blind in New York City. At fourteen, I was at the top of my class, and my teacher gave me extra assignments. I remember it was one of those wet August days. I stayed late, hoping the rain would stop. It did around four in the afternoon. I walked out of my classroom into the hallway. I felt someone walking behind me. I stopped and looked back and saw a silhouette of a person. I called out, 'Who are you?' He did not answer. I continued walking fast toward the elevator. Then I felt a hand over my mouth. The other grabbed my waist. I tried to scream but to no avail. The man was strong. He dragged me to a nearby storage room and placed a knife on my cheek, poking me. I smelled liquor on his breath. I did not recognize his voice. He said if I screamed, he would disfigure my face. He dropped me on the floor. I fought him, trying to beat his hand. He slapped my face, and I lost my glasses. I felt his cold blade on my cheek again. I got scared. Blind and with a scarred face, I would be an outcast. No one would want me. I prayed. I stopped resisting him. I begged him not to hurt me, but he was very drunk. His speech slurred. He tried to spread my legs, but I kept them tight together. After a few tries, he lifted my skirt. I felt his knife on my belly. I prayed again. 'Hail Mary, full of grace, deliver me from this evil. Oh, Mary, help me to bear this cross, help me to be strong, tell me how to cope.' He moved the tip of his knife over my belly. I felt pain. I cried and begged him again to not hurt me. I relaxed my legs, spreading them. His hands crept to my underwear, trying to remove them. I placed my hands under my back, clenching them tight, hoping he would not notice it. He was so drunk. After a few tries, he gave up. He took the knife and cut my underwear to pieces. I prayed hard. He lay on me. I felt him hard on my legs. He tried to enter me, but I squeezed my legs hard, and at that moment, he came between my legs. He was so drunk he did not realize that he never entered me. He threatened me and left me lying there."

"My god, what a horrible story. I'm so sorry, Kelly." I shivered with cold sweat running down my body. I hugged her. "I'm sorry for asking you to tell me this."

"No, Verga, it's all right. My sex therapist told me that it's okay to talk about this and not to keep it inside me as a dark secret. She helped me to learn a technique: how to reduce fear associated with my memory of the sexual assault." She was silent and then spoke, "Verga, last night, I wanted to make love to you. I was ready. When you touched my nylons, suddenly, I experienced a panic attack. The ghost from the past appeared in the flashback, and I tensed up, held my breath, and froze. I did not want to spoil our first lovemaking, something that I worked so hard to build, my sexuality. I wanted it to be something special. Giving oneself to another, I consider it a holy act. To choose one's lover, for me, is never a casual decision."

"My god. Terrible, Kelly. Are you all right?"

"Yes, I feel better now that I told you."

"Did the police catch the bastard?"

"I didn't file a complaint. That's a long story."

"Why?"

"I rushed home that day, oblivious to the pouring rain. In the apartment building corridor, I disposed of my torn underwear in the incinerator, then quietly, not to alert anyone, entered my family's apartment, undressed, and took a hot shower. Still shivering from the event, I scrubbed myself with a soapy sponge so hard like a carpenter sanding wood. I felt pain on my skin. Standing under running water, listening to soapy water drain, I sobbed, banging my fist on the tiled wall. I felt so lonely and unclean. I didn't want to be 'damaged goods.' I wanted my body to be purified by the running water. At that time, not realizing my actions, I washed away all the criminal evidence of the attempted rape. Thereafter, for a long time, I didn't trust men.

"The next day, I went to see my doctor, Emma Rosenthal. She was furious that things like that could happen in school. She examined me, but I was never penetrated by the maniac. After the consultation, she advised me to use a birth control device, an IUD for my protection. I had to get permission from my parents, and I didn't want to tell them. The doctor advised me to speak to my father since I was close to him. He's a teacher, a smart and open-minded person. I confided in him and told him of the sexual assault. He helped me to respond to my trauma by taking me to see a therapist and gave me consent to use a birth control device. I never told my mother. I knew she would be furious. She was a Catholic Church devotee. You know, Verga, how religious Irish women are and the church doctrine on rape?"

"No."

"Let me explain. I'm considered a rape-wounded person and unholy in the eyes of the church. I am to be punished for a crime I am not responsible for. I was the victim. I didn't sin, but it morally wounded my integrity. Why am I to be punished for the crime? It sounds simply nuts."

"Oh my god, Kelly. Did the school find out who was the attacker?"

"I remember that haunting image of him when I fought him off. He was hairless, just cold and sweaty. Dr. Rosenthal met the principal of the school. They spoke, and the principal suspected it was the new assistant custodian, but there wasn't sufficient evidence. They fired him for drinking on the job a week later."

"Kelly, I never realized how dangerous it is for the visually impaired, especially women."

"Yes, indeed. Things got better." She smiled slightly. "Verga, I'm starving. You think you can arrange a sandwich for us?"

"Yes, Pepino knows everyone in the ship's kitchen."

SIX

ooking at a calendar, I tore out today's page: November 11, Veteran's Day in the United States. The ship was scheduled to arrive in Manhattan, New York, in three days. The latest news on board was the election of JFK as the forty-fourth president and first Catholic in the White House.

Kelly was elated to hear the news. She said, "I predict that JFK will be a great president."

I thought, *Of course, she was Irish.* As for me, I had no interest in politics, especially that of a faraway country. Politics bored me.

The phone rang. "Pronto."

Anthony was on the line. "Verga, Jean-Philippe wants you in his office in an hour."

"What's this about?"

"I don't know."

"Bene, I will be there."

I knocked on the door. "Bene buon pomeriggio," I said, entering the office.

"Good afternoon, Verga." Jean-Philippe was sitting at his desk. Next to him was Anthony. "Please," Jean said, pointing to the chair. He held a pen in his hand, nervously twisting it. I felt tension in the air. "Verga, I hear good feedback from the ship's guests. I understand your meditation class is a big success, and I'm proud of you taking your free time to initiate the class."

"Grazie," I said.

"Verga, I have a complaint." He put the pen down, folding his hands and eyeing me. "I attended today's officers' meeting with the captain. He's angry. He's considering dismissing you from the ship"—Jean folded his hands to his chest and continued—"for breaking his unwritten rule of behavior with the ship's guests."

I was stunned to hear this. Speechless, I slumped into the seat.

Anthony broke the silence. "Verga, you are accused of spending time in cabin number 303."

"Miss Kelly," I said.

"Yes, Miss Kelly, the blind passenger."

"The visually impaired person. So what? We are fond of each other. Is this a crime?" I answered angrily. "Didn't the captain encourage his staff to be friendly with his passengers and fraternize with the guests?"

Anthony replied, "Fraternizing with the guests is not forbidden. Being in intimate relations is forbidden."

"Where is your proof, Anthony?"

"The head steward reported it to the captain. Did you stay in Miss Kelly's cabin overnight?"

"How so? What is his proof?"

"A cleaning maid delivered extra towels to the room, and she reported seeing your jacket in Kelly's cabin and heard water running in the bathroom. She assumed you were there."

"Is that true?" Jean-Philippe asked.

I didn't answer. I thought hard then said, "In my contract, I don't have a stipulation prohibiting me from spending time in guests' cabins."

Jean replied, "Verga, I told you of the captain's rule prohibiting intimate relations between his staff and the guests."

"You said many things to me in Naples, and I don't remember the agreement."

Anthony interjected, "Verga, look. We have only three days before we reach New York, and I need you as an entertainer on the ship. No one has proof that you had, how should I say, improper relations with Miss Kelly. Only you and Miss Kelly know how you spent time together. Verga, take an hour to think about it. The onus is on you to prove otherwise. Come back and tell us your version of the events. Remember, tonight, we're having a big gala in the theater, and I need you."

I stood up clearly upset. Anthony put his arm on my shoulder. "Verga, Jean and I want you to be part of our entertainment group. Go. Think about what I said."

I moved to leave Jean's office. In the corridor, I bumped into Pepino. "Hi, Verga. Comé va? What's with you? You seem unhappy."

"The captain is thinking of dismissing me from the job."

"Oh no. What happened?"

"He dislikes my friendship with Miss Kelly."

"Oh." Then he quietly said, "Did anyone find you in her cabin?"

"Pepino, I trust you. You're my friend. I did spend one night in her cabin."

"Merda. That's bad."

"Don't spread this bad news. It's between you and me."

"No, no. My mouth is shut. *La mia bocca è chiusa, porca putanna.*"

"What's wrong with the captain?"

Pepino pulled me to the side. He whispered, "Did you know Captain Bruno wanted to be a priest?"

I was surprised. "No. You're kidding."

"He attended a seminary. I don't know why he quit the priesthood. He joined the Regia Marina in the forties then joined the Italian line after World War II. In 1958, he took command of SS *Cristoforo Colombo*. He never married. The officers think he's sworn to abstinence. The ship is his wife." Pepino smiled and winked. "He thinks we single men should practice celibacy."

"I didn't know this. Thanks for the information, Pepino."

"Bene. Verga, I hope it all works out for you. By the way, I like your friend, Kelly. *Lei è un angelo, molto intelligente, vero?* [She's an angel, really smart, right?]" He pointed his finger to his head.

"Sì." I nodded.

In my cabin, I thought, *What should I say to Jean-Philippe? Obviously, he wants me to come up with an excuse to justify being in Kelly's cabin. After all, she's blind and needs help sometimes.* I didn't like my answer. I wanted to fight for my rights. My private life was mine, and my privacy was no one's business. I thought that I needed legal advice. *But from whom?* Suddenly, it occurred to me. *But of course. Jerry DiPalma's son. He's a lawyer.*

I placed a call. "Hello? Who is this?" It was Nancy, Jerry's wife.

"It's me, Verga."

"Oh, Verga. I have to tell you I'm enjoying your classes."

"Thanks, Nancy. Is Jerry there?"

"No, he just stepped out, but he will be back in a few minutes. Should he call you?"

"Yes please. My cabin extension is 405."

"Okay, I wrote it down."

A few minutes later, the phone rang. "Hello, Jerry. Sorry to disturb you. I need some legal advice. You think your son, Paul, can help me?"

"You should ask him directly, Verga."

Paul agreed to meet me at Café Tuscana. I explained to him the captain's reason for threatening me with dismissal. I told him the truth.

He said, "Sexual activity requires consent. Did you and Kelly have mutual consent?"

"Yes."

"Verga, let me see your employment contract."

Flipping through the pages, he spoke, "Nowhere in your employment contract forbids you from intimate relations with the ship's guests. Let's examine the word *misconduct* in the captain's unwritten rule, which means 'improper actions.' Misconduct is not a criminal offense. When something goes wrong, unwritten rules have no legal standing. However, the captain is in command of this ship, and during sea voyage, his orders are the law. He is the judge and the jury on board. The ship is flying an Italian flag, and it is international waters. We are all under the jurisdiction of Italian laws. You can file a complaint in Italian court, but I don't recommend it. In a day or two, we enter U.S. waters. You can file a complaint in U.S. court, but I say it's a waste of time. I recommend a settlement with the captain. Don't discuss your intimate relation with your friend. It's no one's business what we do in our private bedrooms. Admit that you spent some time in her cabin. Tell him you misunderstood the unwritten rule. Tell him you will cease to enter her cabin, nor will she enter yours. Let's see if he will accept your explanation."

"And if the captain refuses my compromise?"

"Then let's give him a fight," Paul said smiling.

"How?"

"My father is the president of the Italian Auto Dealers' Association. There are four hundred of our members on board. In one hour, I can deliver a list of signatures of the members protesting your removal from entertaining us. My wife will be very upset if they cancel your meditation classes. The captain will cave, but let's not go down that route."

In the late afternoon, I met with Jean-Philippe, and I presented my interpretation of the unwritten rules. I suggested a compromise, concluding by saying I'm popular with the guests on the ship. Removing me from the entertainment crew will make many guests unhappy, and that's bad for business. I apologized for not understanding the captain's wishes.

Jean and Anthony were attentively listening and then said, "Bene. Verga, I will go speak on your behalf to the captain."

Back in my room, the phone rang. It was Kelly. "Verga, will I see you tonight?"

"Kelly, I'm performing today in two shows. How about we meet tomorrow?"

"Okay." She was quiet and then said, "I miss you."

"I miss you too, Kelly. Will you attend the shows tonight?"

"I don't think so. I'm going to take the time to finish my reports. I will see you at the grand foyer tonight before dinner. Kisses." Then she hung up.

Nervously, I waited to hear from my boss. About an hour later, I heard the phone ring. It was Anthony. In a relieved voice, he said, "Verga, the captain is still angry with you, but he agreed to the compromise. I will see you at the theater."

"Grazie, Anthony." I let out a loud sigh.

Wow, what a day it has been, but how will I explain to Kelly that I can't enter her cabin?

The next day after meditation class, I said to Kelly, "Let's sit here in the promenade. I want to talk to you."

I bid my time until Pepino and the women dispersed. She wore gym clothes and was relaxed on the lounge chair, looking at me through large, dark shades. "Verga, please get me a glass of water."

Cup in hand, she waited for me to speak. I searched for the right words. "Kelly, I have a problem with the captain. He's forbidding his staff from spending un-job-related time in guests' cabins."

The glass froze on her lip as she listened.

"I can't stay with you in your cabin anymore."

She put the glass down. "Is it because you stayed with me that one night?"

I told her about the captain's unwritten rule. Kelly did not respond. She took a sip of water then said, "And you violated this rule? Is it because you stayed with me that one night?"

I nodded.

"That is the stupidest rule I've ever heard. It's not his business what I do in my room. I mean my love life. He should mind his own business. He can't enforce his rule in my bedroom. I'm going to place a complaint. He reduced me to a cheap whore. I will not let him crush my dignity and yours."

I took hold of her hand. "Kelly, let it go."

She was furious, as I could tell by her body language, but she prevented me from seeing her angry face behind the dark glasses. "Who does he think he is? Moses? Giving new laws. I did not sign any agreement to his unwritten rules." Kelly was irritated, unwilling to accept this. "The captain has no right to interfere with my free will and deprive me of my right of whom I want to see in private. It's my right and a basic right of all free women."

I got hold of her hands. "Kelly, you have the right to be angry. I'm angry too. No one has the right to interfere in our relationship, but please let me handle it rationally. Let's sit and close our eyes for a few minutes and breathe, freeing our minds from this resentment."

Finally, she agreed to leave the situation alone. "Verga, I'm doing this for you. I'm still angry at the captain."

We sat in silence for a while. Then she said, "Verga, are you telling me we can't spend time together anymore?"

I didn't know how to answer, so I ignored her question and changed the subject. "Kelly, you promised to record my piano playing. Let's do it today."

Her face lit up. "At what time?"

"Let me speak to Pepino and find out when I can use the theater, but I'm hungry. Let's go for breakfast."

That afternoon, Pepino arranged for Kelly and me to have the theater to ourselves. She stood on the stage next to me. Pepino said, "Keep the recording table against the piano. I had to lock the piano legs to the stage floor. The captain informed us the ship is going to encounter rough waters in about an hour."

"Grazie," I said.

Pepino placed a tripod with a stage light next to the piano. "I'm going to shut the main lights. When you leave, just shut the doors. No one will bother you here. The theater is yours. I'm going to put a sign outside: Rehearsal in Progress. No Entry. The door will be locked."

"Pepino, thank you for your help with setting up the piano and wiring the microphones."

"And thanks for the earphones," Kelly said.

"You're welcome. Just leave them on the table when you're finished."

"Grazie, Pepino," I said.

"Okay, I'm leaving. Have fun." He gave Kelly a French hug and exited the theater.

Kelly sat in front of her T-1515 reel-to-reel tape recorder, placed earphones on her head, and said, "Let's run a recording test."

I sat in front of the piano, looking at her. She lifted her hand and then lowered it to start recording. I played the first movement of Beethoven's *Appassionata*, Piano Sonata in F Minor op. 57, Beethoven's piano drama. My hand danced over the keyboard, using it to mimic the sound of an orchestra. I incorporated sudden changes in volume, register, and pace. Absorbed in my play, I lost track of time. After nine minutes, I finally stopped.

She paused the recording and removed her earphones, turning to me. "Verga, that was exquisite play. Let's listen to the recording."

Music filled the stage once again. I listened intently. At the end, I said, "Not bad. My tempo was a little off but, otherwise, not bad."

"You're too critical of yourself. I think this was a great play."

"Thanks," I replied. "Come. Sit next to me. What would you like me to record?"

She moved to take a seat beside me on the bench. I held her hands, facing her; removed her eyeglasses; and placed them on the piano. She smiled. Her hair was loose over her shoulders, framing her lovely face. We shared a kiss.

Then she said, "I love the romantic music of Chopin."

"Oh, Chopin. Excellent choice. The most romantic artist, a poet of the piano, a hero of mine. Kelly, how much do you know about Chopin?"

"Not much, except that he was Polish and a national hero in Poland. His music evokes all kinds of emotions in me, which I cannot describe."

I leaned over the piano and pulled my notebook from my music bag. "Kelly, let's record Chopin's *Prelude*. Let me read you an abstract from a lecture I attended on Chopin." I opened my book.

"Chopin's preludes, nocturnes, and impromptus evoke, one by one, all the expressions of passion: charming lures of coquetry; unwary surrender of inclinations; whimsical festooning wrought of fantasy; fatal despondency of barren joys which are born a-dying; flowers of mourning like those black roses of depressing fragrance, their petals dropping from fragile stems at the slightest breath; weakened flashes kindled by false vanities, similar to the shine of certain lifeless woods that glisten in darkness; pleasures without past or future snatched from chance encounters; illusions, unexplainable fancies that summon us to adventure like those tart flavors of half-ripened fruit that please while setting the teeth on edge; suggestions of emotion of endless range augmented by the vital poesy, innate nobility, beauty and distinction, and elegance of those who feel them.

"At times these pieces are joyous and fanciful, like the gamboling of an amorous, mischievous sylph. At other times, they are velvety and multicolored, like the dress of a salamander. Then they are deeply depressing, like souls in torment who find no prayer of mercy needed for their salvation."

I closed the notebook.

"Oh, Verga, that's a beautiful description of Chopin's music."

I looked at my watch. "Kelly, let's start recording. We have about half an hour before we hit rough seas, and I'm already starting to feel the ocean waves."

Kelly returned to tend to her tape recorder. I removed my black tie, unbuttoned my shirt, folded my sleeves, and took a deep breath. The ship swayed lightly left and right, up and down. I was ready to play, stretching my long fingers.

Kelly said, "I'm ready." The wheels on the tape recorder turned. I looked at her. She sat with earphones resting on red hair like a moon crown on goddess Diana. Her hand was on the tape recorder's dials, waiting for me to start. I repeated my performance from the competition in Milan: Chopin's *Étude* op. 10. My fingers activated the piano hammers. My hands moved fast in hypnotic charm like stripping bark from a tree, and skeletonized Chopin's notes, hands shifting over the whole length of the keyboard in dizzying speed then slow dreamy movements and haunting melody. The sound of the piano filled the entire stage. I paused then played op. 25, a right-hand melody with a supportive bass line accompanied by broken chords. I finished playing with beautiful harmony and grace. Silence.

I lifted my hands, looking at Kelly whose eyes closed and head tilted back. I said, "Kelly, I finished."

She did not respond. She was frozen.

"Kelly," I repeated loudly.

She moved like she had just woken from a dream. "Oh, I'm sorry." She shut the tape recorder. "I'm sorry, Verga. Your play threw me into an unknown world. I was lost in the magical, hypnotic sound." She rewound the tape then switched it to play.

My piano music filled the stage again. She stood up and came to me, standing and embracing me. She then sat next to me, holding me, warm breath on my neck, and in an excited voice, she said, "Verga, the first time I heard you play in the theater, you touched me in a way I've never felt before. I was so aroused. It has never happened to me before. And here, you played so beautifully. Now I'm aroused again."

I kissed her shoulder. Then our mouths met in a deep kiss. Her voice excited me. She stood up, leaned against the piano, lifted her miniskirt, and removed her underwear, sliding them slowly under her short red boots. My hands glided under her skirt, holding her warm behind, pressing her against my face.

The ship was in rough water. We swayed like on a slow roller coaster. Up, up, then down. I stood up and shut the standing stage light. I let my pants and underwear down. We kissed unsteady on our feet. Kelly turned with her back to me, held the edge of the soundboard of the piano, and spread her legs, her buttocks up. I entered her from behind. A loud sound rose from the tape recorder, light and fragile. It seemed like it came from another world. The piano played muffled, moaning sounds. We were like a ship in stormy water, plowing through rough seas. As I held her buttocks tight, her miniskirt up on her back, we were skin to skin, lifting on white wave caps then sinking. I yielded to the rhythmic pull of the wave patterns. They were wild and clear. She came fast and unexpectedly. She took my breath away. Twisting and sliding, she climaxed again. It came in waves, in time with the ship's movement. We became droplets from the vessels of two lovers. In the end, drained from tempestuous, erotic passion, we were shipwrecked.

"Oh my god," I heard her cry.

I lowered her onto the piano bench, out of breath. We sat for a long time. Then I heard a sob on my cheek. "Why are you crying?" My hand comforted her.

"I don't know," she whispered. "I'm happy, but I'm confused." She hesitated. "Never before have I felt like I had for the past few days. I discovered another Kelly in me. I worship lust. It scares me. I don't know what's happening to me. I'm a controlled person, but I let down my guard. I pursued bodily pleasure, and now it has overtaken me. You know, Verga, it takes me a long time to be aroused. But now I'm in uncharted waters, and I'm scared." She sobbed again and held me tight. "Verga, how do you feel about me?"

"I feel like I've known you for years. I love your intellect. I enjoy being with you. I like the way you look. Our lovemaking is made in heaven. I want to know you more. I want to be with you."

She was quiet but stopped crying, her warm face against my cheek. She said, "I'm dating a man, Joe." She was silent again.

Her confession surprised me and caught me off guard. I felt something like glass shatter in my soul. My blood drained. I felt sick to my stomach. I did not know what to say, so I asked, "Do you love him?"

"You know, Vega, love is just a word. To love someone is to have a backbone to prove it. A real love means to give yourself away freely. Now I'm confused. I'm twenty-eight, and I feel the pressure of my friends who are already married. Joe is a nice man, considerate, financially stable, gentle, and smart. He's a partner in a law firm with his best friend from Harvard. He persistently asked me to marry him, and I avoided giving him an answer. I'm not sure if I should."

"Do you care for me?"

"Verga, I'm confused. Is it lust that's between us or something else? I have to be careful when giving my heart because when you do that, you're not giving that person your love but also the power to hurt, and I don't want to hurt you. Let love find its way. Then love will be worth the wait. We will wipe our tears. We will forget the pain and that we have ever cried. You touched every nerve in my body. You're a talented artist, and I'm attracted to you with my body and soul. I need to sort my feelings. Tomorrow is our last day on the ship. What are your future plans, Verga?"

"I'm not sure. I have a contract to fulfill."

"Do you intend to stay in New York?"

"Just for a few days, but now after meeting you, I'm not sure. And I'm as confused as you are, especially now."

We sat quietly, not saying anything. Finally, Kelly broke the silence. "Verga, can you find my panties?"

After getting dressed, I handed them to her and took the record player.

"Let me give you your recorded tape."

"No, Kelly, I want you to have it."

SEVEN

"Buddha was asked, 'What have you gained from meditation?' Buddha replied, 'Nothing at all. Let me tell you what I have lost in meditation: sickness, depression, negativity, self-doubt, worry, grief, and anger.' I hope our sessions have motivated you to meditate deeply, which will lead you to lasting joy. For Buddha, it was not his way but rather the great way. Thank you, all, for attending this last meditation class, and have a safe trip back home."

The class applauded. I was sitting on my towel when Patricia stood up in front of the group. She said, "Verga, I was chosen by the group to express our profound thanks for your devotion to this class. You've helped us understand how to find happiness in meditation. As for me, I have learned how to stay calm and control my mind. On behalf of all of us, we thank you. Please accept this gift." She came to me and gave me a blue envelope.

I was surprised. "Thank you, all."

The women surrounded me, wishing me good luck. I searched for Kelly. She was talking to a small group of women. Pepino shook my hand. "Grazie, I will see you later."

Ruth, the short black-haired Jewish woman, approached me. "Verga, thank you for your great piano playing and your meditation classes."

"You're welcome," I said.

"How long are you planning to stay in New York?"

"Just a few days." She gave me a piece of paper. "This is my telephone number. I live in Brooklyn. Perhaps I can make you a *shidduch* with my daughter. She's beautiful and smart."

I didn't understand what *shidduch* meant, but I replied, "Your daughter must be beautiful as you are. Thanks for asking me, but I'm not sure how long I'll be staying in New York."

The class dispersed, and I sat on a lounge chair beside Kelly. "Wow, I never expected such an outburst of gratitude."

"Your class was a success. In the end, you had over thirty people attending. That's something."

I wiped my face with a towel. "You're right. I'm very pleased. Kelly, what is the meaning of the word *shidduch*?"

She let out a laugh. "*Shidduch* in Yiddish means *matchmaking*."

"How come you know this?"

"In New York, you will learn many ethnic words. New York is the city of immigrants from all over the world."

I touched her hand. "Kelly, let's go for breakfast."

"I'm not very hungry. Could you bring us coffee and toast?"

I brought over a light breakfast, and we sat sipping hot coffee from mugs. "Verga, I didn't sleep well last night."

"Neither did I."

She held my hand, our fingers clutching each other's in a tight grip. "Verga, I have profound feelings for you, but I need to sort them out. I think the best thing is to think about what they mean to each of us. Not seeing each other will allow us to find our own ways. Please take this paper. It's my telephone and address. You can call me any time or write." She leaned and kissed me on my cheek. I felt a sense of emptiness inside me. For the past week, I found happiness and joy with Kelly. Now we were to part. We sat in silence for a long time.

That morning, the ship sailed past the Verrazano straits: on the left, Staten Island; on the right, Brooklyn. Construction was evident in the narrows. I was told a new bridge was to be built between Staten Island and Brooklyn. Our ship was greeted with tugs and fire department boats, spraying water in the air. All the passengers assembled along the ship's railing. All eyes and cameras were on the Statue of Liberty. The sun just rose, flooding the Liberty Lady with a golden glow on her serious face. In front of the ship was the iconic New York skyline. Kelly stood next to me, white handkerchief wrapped around her hair. We leaned over the railing, admiring the view. The ship let out a loud deep whistle, announcing its entry into Hudson Bay.

It was hard for me to say good-bye to Kelly, but I had a feeling we would meet again. She turned to me then whispered in my ear, "I'm not saying good-bye to you, Verga. Please accompany me to my cabin." She got hold of my hand our fingers clutching each other's tightly. I glanced at her face. Tears ran down her cheeks. We walked in silence; I was thinking tears could be as precious jewels, rain of life, emblem of bitterness when being shed, can be transformed into hope. I turned toward Kelly gently wiping her tears. She let a hint of a smile.

Cristoforo Colombo docked at the pier. I glanced at her face. Tears ran down her cheeks. I stood on the first deck, looking as passengers disembarked to a waiting crowd below, shouting and waving their hands behind a cordoned area on the pier. Kelly walked down the ramp, holding the railing. A small bag hung on her shoulder as she held an eye-seeing cane in her other hand. I shouted, "Kelly, I love you!" I was not sure if she heard me.

At the bottom of the ramp, she stopped and turned back, glancing at the ship. She must have felt me watching her. Then she continued walking. A man wearing a fedora and a light black coat limped and greeted her. He leaned in and kissed her. Hand in hand, they walked toward the customs area. Before entering the terminal baggage hull, she stopped again and looked back at the ship.

I wiped a tear from my cheek, thinking I had lost Kelly forever. With a heavy heart, I left the ship's deck. As I lay on my bed, eyes closed, my voice wanted to shout my pain. It was hard to see Kelly holding hands with someone else.

After lunch, the entertainment group met at Café Tuscana. Anthony thanked us for doing a great job. Then he handed us pay envelopes. We were free to disembark.

Pier 88 to 94 in Manhattan was known as Luxury Line Row (Twelfth Avenue and Fifty-Fifth Street). After clearing customs, I found myself in the hustle and bustle of Fifty-Fifth Street. It was late afternoon when I walked the crowded New York sidewalks, arriving at Times Square on Forty-Second Street, the heart of the city theater district. In front of me was the twenty-five-story *New York Times* building. The glowing neon marquee lights and billboards created spectacular light shows. I stood on Broadway and gazed around. My mouth dropped.

What a show! Times Square was considered the crossroads of the world. I was hypnotized by the attraction and even more intrigued by advertisements—Bon Clothing, Gordon's Gin, Coca-Cola—not to mention mechanical elements of billboards, such as the one for Camel, a face with a large open mouth puffing smoke rings every few seconds.

I stopped at Horn & Hardart, the famous "automat" chain. It was like a big vending machine. I walked toward the marble counter. Above it were many small windows, and behind them, there were a variety of perfectly arranged foods—cold and hot sandwiches, salads of all kinds, eye-catching displays of mouthwatering pies, and much more. I put a coin in the slot of the nickel tower, and the window unhinged. I took the cold salad, and behind it, there were more awaiting the next customer. I said to myself, *What a marvelous invention!* At that time, I didn't realize that the technology was borrowed from Germany, Berlin's Quisisana Automat. Horn & Hardart had a slogan: Less Work for Mothers.

I put in more coins. The window opened. There was Salisbury steak with gravy and mashed potatoes. I marveled at the automatic coffee dispenser as it poured coffee into my mug. Sitting at the cafeteria table, I observed the restaurant patrons. They smoked, read newspapers, or conversed. The place was mobbed, and I wondered if anyone worked in America. That day, I instantly fell in love with New York City.

When I returned to the ship late that afternoon, I had a note on my cabin door. It was from Jean-Philippe.

Verga, see me first thing in the morning.

The next day, I knocked on his door and entered. "Ah, Verga, good morning. Sit down." Looking at me, he said, "Verga, the captain asked me to dismiss you. He doesn't want you on his ship." The news caught me by surprise. He continued, "My only explanation is that the captain dismissed you because he doesn't like anyone questioning his authority. He wants you to disembark no later than this evening. Sorry, Verga. I did my best. I asked him to wait until we got back to Italy, but he refused. I don't understand him. He was unmoved and angry."

It was déjà vu all over again. I felt momentary anxiety and a loss of security. I asked, "Where should I go?"

"I can recommend some inexpensive hotels, and if you want, I can arrange a trip on an ocean liner back to Europe."

"Thanks, Jean. Let me think. I'll let you know."

"Verga, Anthony is giving you fifty dollars as he promised."

"Thanks. I could use it."

"Also, give me your passport. I can arrange a three-month visa. I know many of the customs officials in the port."

"Thank you."

The events of the day left me with both petulance and bewildering happiness at leaving the ship. By that point, I felt ostracized from the ship's entertainment group and the captain, who was a coward for not facing me mano a mano but used his subordinate to deliver messages to me. I despised his behavior.

With a suitcase and carry-on bag, I stood on the pier. A cab pulled up beside the sidewalk. The cabbie rolled the window down. "Taxi?"

I leaned over and asked, "Can you take me to a Hungarian neighborhood?"

The cabbie scratched his head then straightened his hat. "Come in."

He placed my suitcase into the trunk and took his place in the driver's seat. Looking at me from the rearview mirror, he asked, "Where are you from?"

"Vienna."

"Oh, beautiful city."

"Were you there?"

"No, but I saw pictures of Vienna in *Look* magazine." He pulled from the sidewalk, asking, "What's your name?"

"Verga."

"Is that Hungarian?"

"Yes."

"First time in New York?"

"Yes."

"What do you do, Verga?"

"I'm a piano player."

"Oh, nice. I play clarinet with a Klezmer band."

"Is that Jewish music?"

"Yes, are you familiar with Klezmer music?"

"I heard it played once."

"Are you Jewish?"

"No."

"So why are you asking me to take you to a Jewish neighborhood?"

"No, no. I want to go to a Hungarian neighborhood."

"I only know of one place with Hungarian-speaking people, and they are Hasidics in Brooklyn."

"Okay, no problem. Take me to the Jewish neighborhood."

The cab moved slowly on top of the elevated highway. My thoughts drifted. *Should I call Kelly? No, I can't distress her. This is my predicament.* Perhaps my dismissal was a good omen. I had always wanted to explore New York's music halls and art museums. I decided to try to find my luck in this city.

I heard the cabbie's voice. "Bridge or tunnel?"

"What do you mean?"

"Shall I take the bridge or tunnel?"

"Oh, please, you decide."

"It'll be the tunnel. Less traffic."

We drove through streets of residential neighborhoods in Brooklyn. The cab stopped under an elevated subway. He turned toward me and said, "This is Borough Park. Across the street at the corner of Sixteenth Avenue is Mendel's Bakery, a Hungarian place. They make the best babkas."

"Thanks."

"You owe me three dollars plus the tunnel toll."

I handed him the money as he took my belongings out of the trunk. Then I entered the bakery. The smell of baked goods and bread filled my nostrils and awakened my appetite. On the shelves were cream-cheese-folded pastries, breads, and cookies of all kinds. Women dressed in conservative dark clothes and hats draped with colorful tichels. They were ringing up customers at the counter. Bearded men dressed in black garb and hats stood on line, holding baskets of baked goods. I reached the counter.

"Can I help you?" a bearded man with a short, wide baker's jacket asked.

I said, "Do you speak Hungarian?"

He looked at me surprised and adjusted his gold-rimmed glasses. "Yes."

I spoke in Hungarian, "My name is Verga, and I'm looking to rent a bedroom."

The baker examined me then said in a loud voice, "Isaac, *qwm'n d'á* [come here]. Someone wants to rent an apartment."

A young bearded man with long locks coming down on each side came to see me. "Yes, can I help you?"

I spoke in Hungarian again, "I'm looking to rent a bedroom. Can you help me?"

"What's your name?"

"Verga. I'm from Hungary."

"In what town?"

"Kőszeg."

"Are you Jewish?" He looked at my clothes.

"My grandparents and my mother were Jewish. Our family name is Varady."

He nodded. "What do you do for a living?"

"I'm a classical piano player."

"Oh, a musician. How long have you been in this country?"

I paused then said, "Just arrived today." I was afraid of rejection.

"You look *haymish* [someone with whom you feel comfortable]. I do have a basement bedroom available."

I let out an air of relief from my lungs but did not understand what he meant by *basement*. I said, "I'll take it."

"Wait here for ten minutes. Have a nosh." He gave me a plate of cut pastry samples to taste.

"Thanks."

I rented the basement bedroom on Fifteenth Avenue and Sixty-First Street for $75 a month. I paid three months in advance. It had a kitchen with a counter and a sink that provided hot and cold water, a bedroom with a bed but no mattress, room with an old sofa and a square table with folding chairs, and a small bathroom. The place looked filthy and unkempt.

Isaac said, "Next month, you can have a one-bedroom apartment on the second floor if you want. You can buy a mattress and bedding on Utrecht Avenue and Sixty-Fifth Street."

I thanked him, and he left the apartment. I lay on the bed and closed my eyes thinking about Kelly. I should not have held my feelings for her and allowed her to walk away just because we were afraid to take a risk in exploring our mutual attraction. Now I was alone and wondering what the next day would bring. For some reason, I wasn't distressed. It was only my second night in America.

The next day, I sent a telegram to Hans, informing him of my unexpected stay in New York. I hoped to hear from him soon.

The following week, I explored my new neighborhood, Bensonhurst, a large amorphous area consisted of several neighborhoods, including Borough Park. Bensonhurst was predominantly full of Italian Americans and a small population of Jewish and Irish. Eighty-Sixth Street was the main drag and commercial area with every imaginable store with signs announcing the finest of la cucina Italiana: prosciutto crudo, parmigiano-reggiano, salami, and much more. Produce shops sold melanzane, red and green peppers, and globe artichokes. Vegetable crates spilled produce onto the sidewalk crowded by pedestrians.

I turned toward Eighteenth Avenue, also known as Cristoforo Colombo Boulevard. The venue was lined with Italian and Jewish family businesses. The lingua franca was Yiddish, English, and southern Italian dialect.

I stopped in front of Frankies Trattoria, which served lunch and dinner. I was nostalgic for Italian pasta dishes, which I grew to appreciate when I lived in Venice. It was lunchtime, and the restaurant was half empty. The ambiance was very relaxed and simple. A waiter came and introduced himself, "My name is Dino. Have you dined with us before?"

"No."

"Are you new in the neighborhood?"

"Yes."

"You have an accent. Where are you from?"

"I'm from Vienna, Austria, but I spent time in Venice, and I love Italian food."

"You came to the right place. Let me start you off with our house appetizers, fried zucchini and garlic bread."

"Excellent." I studied the lunch menu, ordering a plate of tagliatelle with basil, pine nuts, and parmigiano cheese.

Dino asked, "How do you like the pasta?"

"Aldente. Delizioso." I smacked my lips.

When I was ready to leave, I noticed a printed bulletin for a piano recital on Saturday at 4:00 p.m. at St. Athanasius Church on Sixty-First Street and Bay Parkway. I turned toward Dino and asked, "How far is St. Athanasius Church?"

"Just a few blocks walking distance. Why?"

I pointed to the written announcement on the wall.

"Oh, the father loves classical music and gives piano recitals once a month. It attracts music lovers to the church social hall. He plays for charity. I love rock and roll, so classical is too old-fashioned for me," Dino said, combing his hair.

"I'm a classical pianist, but I like rock and roll too."

"Oh, a musician. You should meet Father Pellegrino Fantoni. He's related to the trattoria owner's wife, and once a week, he comes on Tuesday for lunch. Come over, and I will introduce you to him. He's very friendly."

"Okay, I will. At what time?"

"Around one o'clock p.m."

"Grazie, Dino."

"Prego."

A supermarket was a few steps away from the trattoria. I entered it and lost myself between fully stocked shelves of boxes of all kinds: fresh vegetables, meat, and fish. I had never seen such an abundance of food under one roof. I stopped in front of the written sign, proclaiming, "Prepared frozen foods." I looked through the glass cases to see packages of frozen TV dinners. I took one, examining the package. The front of it depicted a colorful photo of what was inside: fried chicken, mashed potatoes, carrots and peas, and a slice of peach. I turned the box, and on the back was cooking instructions. Bake aluminum tray at 425 degrees Fahrenheit for twenty-five minutes and serve. I thought, *I don't know how to cook, and eating at a restaurant is too expensive. These TV dinners will serve me well. An oven, I need an oven. I need to buy one, but where?*

I asked the supermarket clerk, "Where can I buy an electric oven?"

"Just right there." He pointed his finger at aisle 12. "Look for housewares."

I picked up a GE toaster oven from a shelf, thinking, *Only in America can one get everything in one place.* From that moment, Swanson TV dinners were on my table every day.

The next morning, I picked up four Kaiser rolls, also called Vienna rolls, from Mendel's Bakery. On that occasion, I encountered Isaac unloading sacks of flour, sugar, and boxes of baking ingredients from the truck. I gave him a hand, helping him move the supplies into the cellar.

The next day, I asked for four Kaiser rolls. Mendel, behind the counter, placed them into the bag. I handed him twenty cents, but he gave me the money back. He said, "Isaac told me you helped him unload our supplies, so I won't charge you for the Kaiser rolls."

"Oh, thanks. I didn't expect this."

"Verga, do you want a job?"

"Yes. What kind of a job?"

"Every Monday, we have a delivery. Unload and store the supplies in the cellar, a maximum of two hours of work. And you can take off ten dollars from your monthly rent. *Parstyyn?* [Do you understand?] What do you say?"

"Yes, I'll take the job."

"You can have your Kaiser rolls for free too. Next in line!"

On Sixty-Second Street was an elevated subway station, the BMT line. For the cost of fifteen cents for a token, it took me to other boroughs of New York City. For the next two weeks, I took the train to Manhattan, visiting art museums, such as the Metropolitan Museum of Art, the Whitney, and the Solomon Guggenheim Museum on the upper side of Manhattan and Fifth Avenue. I read that the building was designed by Frank Lloyd Wright and had just opened a year ago. I was fascinated by the cylindrical museum. I stood in the lobby, admiring the white unique winding ramp extending all the way to the top floor under a large skylight—a symphony of architecture. A concert Steinway was sitting in the lobby, and I wondered how it would sound playing in this temple, the Museum of Modern Art. I also read that two years prior, a fire on the second floor destroyed the eighteen-feet-long *Water Lily* painting by Monet, but I still admired the replacement. I lost myself in Vincent Van Gogh's *The Starry Night*, Pablo Picasso's *The Demoiselles d'Avignon*, and Henry Matisse's *The Dance*. I visited the MOMA two days in a row, making notes and appreciating the paintings.

Returning from one of my trips to Manhattan, I found tacked on my basement door a letter from Hans. His plans had changed for the time being. He was to stay in Vienna. He encouraged me to write to him, but I was disappointed. Also in the letter, I found a note from Dr. Richter. He was still disappointed with me for not returning to Vienna. In the note, he urged me to make an appointment for an interview with Leonard Bernstein, the New York Philharmonic conductor and director of the Young People's Concert. Dr. Richter had met Leonard Bernstein in Vienna at the private reception, and I was very much impressed by him. Dr. Richter also urged me to enter the Franz Liszt Competition and to listen to Vlademir Horowitz's 1959 stereo recording of Beethoven's piano sonatas. He was hoping that I would find time to practice and not be distracted with popular rock and roll. He wrote, "Rock and roll will fade away in a few years, and no one will remember it, but Mozart's and Beethoven's music is immortal."

I met Father Pellegrino a few days after seeing the notice at the trattoria. At the end of our conversation, he invited me to his church to play piano that afternoon.

After hearing me play, he said, "Verga, you are a gifted pianist. This Saturday, I play in a recital for forty-five minutes. At intermission, I would like you to play. Yes?"

"Thank you. That's great. What should I play?"

"You decide."

"I need some practice time."

"You're welcome to practice early mornings from seven to eight when the social hall is not in use."

"Thank you. I appreciate your offer."

Saturday was a glorious chilly November day, and I was excited to play in the recital. I was introduced to the audience by Father Pellegrino. The social hall was packed. I sat in front of the upright Baldwin piano. I chose to play J. S. Bach's "Sinfonia" from Partita no. 2. My fingers struck the black-and-white keys with a contrapuntal technique like an expert typist on a typewriter, reminding me of Kelly. The play was technically demanding. I played for fifteen minutes; then I switched to a popular Neapolitan tune, "Santa Lucia," and finished with Schubert's "Ave Maria."

The audience erupted in loud applause, "Bravo! Bravo!" clapping and standing.

I stood up and bowed deeply. The recital was a success. Father Pellegrino approached me. "Bravo, Verga, bravo! Great demonstration."

"Thanks," I said.

"I want you to meet Domenic Bontade."

I shook hands with the short heavy bold man dressed in an elegant double-breasted suit and red tie with a sparkly diamond pin on top. "It's my pleasure," I said.

"Father told me you escaped from Communist Hungary."

"Indeed."

"Welcome to America."

"Thank you."

"I appreciate good music when I hear it, and I can see a talent in front of me."

"Thank you, sir."

Behind him stood a good-looking, well-groomed young man dressed in a blue jacket and red shirt. He was introduced to me as well. "Salvador, my son."

"Nice to meet you," I said.

Father interjected, "Verga, Don Domenic is a big supporter of our church and a business leader in our community."

"Thank you, Father," Domenic said. He turned to me. "Verga, are you familiar with my restaurant, Fantana di Tervi?"

"No."

"The best restaurant in Brooklyn." He took a card from his pocket, holding it in front of me. I reached for it, noticing three large gold and diamond rings on Don Domenic's fingers. "I want you to play piano in my restaurant on Friday, Saturday, and Sunday evenings. What do you say?" He put his hand on my shoulder.

Gladly, I said, "That'd be wonderful."

Don Domenic shook my hand. "I like this boy." He turned to his son. "I like this boy." Then to me, he said, "Talk to my son. He'll fill you in on the details. I like this boy," he said then left, three husky guys trailing behind him.

February rolled around, and I realized my visa of three months was almost expired. I panicked and searched for Paul DiPalma's business card. Once I found his phone number, I called him.

"Verga, nice to hear from you. Where are you calling from?"

"I'm in New York, and I decided to stay in the U.S."

"That's great."

"Paul, the reason for my call is that I need to extend my visa and decided to start my immigration papers."

"Okay, Verga. I don't handle immigration, but I can recommend you a lawyer."

"That's great."

"Give me a moment." There was a pause on the phone. "Do you have a pen? Take this name: Lenny Maskowitz Esquire, Number Five, Court Street, Brooklyn."

"Thanks, Paul!"

I went to see Lenny Maskowitz, who took my immigration case. He asked me many questions in regard to my escape from Hungary. He said based on my refugee status escaping from the Communist Iron Curtain, I had a preferred immigration status. He promised me a green card within twelve months.

It had been three months since I last saw Kelly. I've missed her since our voyage on the *Cristoforo Colombo*, so I gave her a call as well. "Hello?" Kelly answered.

"Hi, Kelly. It's me, Verga."

"Oh, it's nice to hear from you. From where are you calling?"

"Brooklyn, New York."

"What are you doing in Brooklyn?"

"I never took the voyage back to Italy. I decided to stay in New York. I'm filing my immigration papers now."

"That's great news, but you didn't call me all this time?"

"Kelly, you were with Joe. I didn't want to interfere with your life."

"I'm angry that you didn't let me know." She paused. "Where can I see you? I want you to meet him, and I have good news to tell you. Can you come for lunch next Thursday?"

"Yes. Where shall I meet you?"

"At Patsy's Italian Restaurant on West Fifty-Sixth and Broadway at one o'clock p.m."

"Yes." I wrote it down.

When arriving at the restaurant, I asked the receptionist for Miss O'Reilly's table.

"The lady with the dark glasses and eye-seeing dog?"

"Yes." I nodded.

"Please follow me."

The place was mobbed. Every table was taken by the New York lunch crowd. I saw Kelly sitting in the back. "Hello, Kelly."

"Hi, Verga."

My heart raced seeing Kelly again. It ignited the feelings I had for her on the ship. We hugged, and I held her for a long moment. She faced me then touched my face. "You haven't changed except your hair has gotten longer." She paused. "I missed you," she said in nostalgia.

"I missed you too, Kelly."

"Please sit down."

She looked different today. Her hair was combed smoothly with curled ends hanging on the side. Large aviator glasses with gold frames rested on the bridge of her nose. Lips were copper red to match her hair. On her neck, strings of colored glass rings hung low. She was elegantly dressed in a white blouse and pastel pink skirt with a pattern of teeny roses.

"You look stunning today."

"Thanks." A waiter came over. "I'm waiting for Joe to join us. Verga, what would you like a drink?"

"Campari and soda," I said to the waiter.

"For me, a glass of champagne," she said.

"Verga, I have exciting news to tell you." She showed me her finger. On it was a beautiful, sparkling diamond ring. "I'm engaged," she said, her face all smiles.

All my hopes of rekindling my relationship with Kelly faded. "Wow, that's great news! It calls for a drink." We clinked our glasses.

Just then, Joe came in. It was my first time meeting Joe face-to-face. He was tall, medium built, had black hair sprinkled with gray touches, and looked older than Kelly. "Hi, darling." He leaned over and kissed Kelly.

"Joe, meet my friend, Verga."

"Nice to meet you." He examined me with his dark brown eyes.

"Nice to meet you too," I said.

"You're already celebrating?" Smiling, he pulled up the chair next to Kelly, dressed in a black pinstripe suit. "What are you drinking, Verga?"

"Campari and soda," I said, flagging down the waiter.

"Same for me," he said to him.

"Congratulations," I said.

"Thanks," he replied, leaning to kiss Kelly.

"Joe, please tell Verga."

"I listened to your piano playing. I enjoyed it. You're very talented. Kelly and I would like for you to play at our wedding ceremony."

"I'd be delighted. When are you getting married?"

"In April of next year."

"Are you getting married in a church?"

"Yes, it will be at St. Paul the Apostle on West Fifty-Ninth Street."

Kelly interjected, "Then we will have a reception at Harvard Club."

"Do you want me to play at your reception too?"

Joe said, "No, Verga. We hired a musician for the party. We want you as a guest; however, we want to pay you for your play at the church."

"No, no. This will be my gift to you."

"Verga, I'm serious. I'm paying for your time."

"Please, Joe. You insult me. I can't accept money from you."

"Okay, okay." He paused then said, "You know, Verga, I'd been asking Kelly to marry me for the last year, and she had avoided giving me an answer. But after her return from Italy"—he looked at her fondly—"she is a totally changed person."

I didn't know what to say. *Did she tell Joe of our love affair?* I replied, "I'm very happy for both of you."

"Thank you, Verga, and I heard great news from Kelly that you're filing your immigration papers. Congratulations to you too. Let's order lunch, shall we?"

EIGHT

On July 5, after celebrating Independence Day, Fantana di Tervi held their annual pasta-eating competition. I watched Bensonhurst's biggest eaters consume pounds of pasta. A trophy and a hundred-dollar cash prize was presented to the winner, a local boy, a truck driver by the name of Gianni, who consumed two and three-quarter pounds of spaghetti with marinara sauce in nine minutes. That evening, I played for a full house. As I performed Neapolitan songs, guests in the restaurant clapped and sang. When I finished playing "Torna a Surriento," a well-dressed man approached me and introduced himself. "Massimo Sacco," he said, giving me his card: director of food and beverages, Carlyle Hotel. We shook hands. "What's your name?"

"Verga Caszar."

"You're a very good pianist. Do you sing too?"

"No, I just play piano."

"I'm very impressed with your performance."

"Thank you."

"I have a job for you if you're interested. We need a piano player Monday through Friday from 6:00 p.m. to 10:00 p.m. Since JFK stayed in our hotel last January, we're booked solid, and we need a piano player at Bemelmans Bar. Are you interested?"

"Yes, that sounds wonderful."

"Good." He shook my hand. "Come to see me tomorrow at seven. Ask for me at the bar."

I got the job at Carlyle Bemelmans Bar and had been playing for two weeks. It was Friday, and the lounge was crowded. I played light, romantic, classical melodies on a Steinway piano, my hands gliding across black-and-white keys. A smartly dressed blonde leaned over the piano, holding a drink and watching me play. Her large sapphire blue eyes penetrated mine. She had red-painted lips. She smiled sensually with a slightly opened mouth. She looked to be in her forties. She leaned down and placed her hands on the piano top. Closed-eyed, absorbing my music, she slightly moved her head to the tempo of my play. I noticed her well-manicured hands. A ring with a large blue stone surrounded by sparkling diamonds sat on her finger. Her dark blue dress with a V-neckline revealed a big pendant above her cleavage. I finished playing, and she lifted herself from the piano. I was mesmerized by her looks.

She said in a southern accent, "My name is Charlotte."

"My name is Verga. Nice to meet you." I touched her extended hand.

"I love the way you play, and I heard a lot about you from Massimo." She opened her purse, pulled out a card, and handed it to me. "I'm having a get-together at my penthouse in two weeks. Would you be interested in playing piano at my party?"

I held her calling card on which held a Fifth Avenue address. She looked at me then slowly lifted her glass to her parted lips, taking a slow sip. How could I refuse her? "It'd be my pleasure to play at your party."

"Good." She smiled. "Please call me tomorrow."

As suddenly as she appeared, she walked away toward the crowded bar. My eyes followed her as she swayed her behind elegantly like a model walking down the runway. I was smitten with her presence.

The next day, I stopped at the Diamond District on Forty-Seventh Street. I decided to sell one of my two-carat diamonds from the mezuzah. I needed to pay $500 to my immigration lawyer and put the rest of the money into my savings. Two days after my encounter with Charlotte, I called her.

"Ms. Stein residence. Who's calling?"

"My name is Verga, the pianist."

"One moment." I heard a click.

"Verga, is that you, darling?"

"Yes, it's me."

"Where have you been? You were supposed to call me yesterday."

I grew defensive. "I'm sorry, but I was busy. I didn't have the chance to call."

"All right. All right, darling. When can I see you?"

"When do you want me to meet you?"

"Today," she said.

"Today?" I was caught off guard.

"Yes, can you come today?"

I looked at my watch. It was almost ten thirty in the morning. "How about in two hours or so?"

"Perfect, darling," she said sweetly.

"Where shall we meet?"

"Come to my penthouse." She gave me the address again. "Fifth Avenue on the corner of Seventieth Street next to the Frick Collection Museum."

At noon, I arrived at her apartment building. The brass shiny door was opened by the doorman, who wore a top hat, a long-tailed coat, and white gloves. In the lobby, I was greeted by a uniformed concierge, "Can I help you?"

"I'm here to see Ms. Charlotte Stein."

"Your name, sir?"

"Verga."

"One moment." Then he spoke on a house phone. "Please follow me." He pressed the elevator button, holding the door for me. "She's expecting you, sir."

"What button should I press?"

"No need, sir. They elevator will stop at the penthouse."

A young woman dressed in a black suit with a white trim and black socks greeted me. "Please follow me. My name is Cathy. I'm Ms. Stein's secretary," she said in a British accent.

In the large foyer, I passed a large bronze statue of a nude woman sitting on a marble pedestal. "Please sit down. Ms. Stein will be with you shortly. May I offer you a drink?"

"Just water please."

"Right away, sir."

The salon had four windows facing a large terrace. There were three large beautiful Murano-style chandeliers with long beads of crystal hanging like drops of rain. I looked for a piano, but there wasn't one. There were two large sectional all-white sofas of Italian leather surrounded by period furniture. With a glass of water in my hand, I admired the landscape terrace. Beyond, I could see the open space of Central Park.

"Verga, how are you?" I heard her voice.

I turned around when Charlotte approached me dressed in a smart black-and-white patterned outfit. She gave me a French hug. I smelled Chanel perfume. She sat on the lounge chair opposite me.

"You have a beautiful penthouse."

"Thank you. What are you drinking?"

"Oh, just water."

"I'll have bourbon on ice." She called for Cathy. "What do you like for a drink?" she asked me.

"Water is fine."

"No, darling, you have to drink with me."

"Okay, Campari and soda."

"Cathy, do we have Campari?"

"No, ma'am."

"Make a note to order it."

I said, "No problem. Gin and tonic will do for me."

"Yes, sir," Cathy said.

I asked Charlotte, "Where do you want me to perform?"

"Right here." She pointed with her hand holding the glass of bourbon.

I searched the room for a piano again. "Oh, darling, are you looking for the piano?"

I nodded.

"That's why I wanted you to come. We need to pick one out."

She realized that I didn't comprehend what she had said. "I don't have a piano. No one plays in my family. We'll go to the showroom to pick one. Any particular piano you like?"

I was surprised. "Let me understand, Ms. Stein—"

"Oh, please call me Charlotte," she interrupted me.

I swallowed and said, "Charlotte."

"Yes, Charlotte," she said, smiling. "So which piano do you like?"

"I prefer to play on a Steinway."

"Great. There will be a Steinway. Cathy, please check the address for Steinway Showroom."

"Right away, ma'am." I heard the secretary from the next room.

Charlotte examined my face. Then she said, "Verga, I like the way you look with long hair, but it's too long, almost to your shoulders. You need a trim."

"I like it like that."

At the Steinway Hall, I followed her. "Yes, ma'am," a salesman greeted us. "How can I help you?"

"We would like to see a piano."

"You came to the right place. Do you know anything about Steinway pianos?"

"Yes," I said.

"Is it for you, sir?"

"Yes," she said.

"Please follow me."

We stopped in front of a black-lacquered concert piano. Charlotte looked at it then said, "Do you have some other color than black?"

"Yes, we have a custom-made piano. It's just so that it was ordered by Liberace. He gave a deposit then canceled the order. You can have it if you like at a special price. Would you like to see it?"

I said, "Liberace? Wow!" I looked at Charlotte.

She said, "Please, show it to us."

We walked to the back room. There were several pianos stored there. We stopped in front of a piano covered with a green sheet. The salesman uncovered it.

"Wow!" Charlotte exclaimed. "This is magnificent!"

It was white with gold and silver specks and a gold trim. "I have never seen such color on a piano," I said. The finish was smooth. I ran my fingers over the top. Not a bump.

The salesman opened the sound lid and secured the lid prop. "Please sit and play." He pulled out the matching white piano stool.

I played a piece of Chopin's nocturne. I fell in love with the sweet and clear tone of the piano. I continued playing then stopped, looking for Charlotte. She and the salesman were talking on the other side of the room.

She came to me. "What do you think?"

"I like the sound quality."

"I like the piano too, and I like the way you play. This piano belongs to you. I'm hungry, though. Let's have dinner."

She took my hand as we walked into the showroom. I heard the salesman say, "Thank you, Ms. Stein. It'll be delivered to your penthouse tomorrow. Good luck with it, sir."

I realized that she had already purchased the piano. As we exited, I asked, "Did you buy the piano?"

"Yes, darling."

"Just like that?"

"Yes, just like that."

She hailed a taxi. "Carnegie Deli," she said.

Sitting in the cab, she said, "I hope you like pastrami and corned beef brisket. I feel like having matzo ball soup. Have you eaten there?"

"No."

"Oh, you'll love the Carnegie Deli. It's a taste of New York."

The day after, the phone in my room rang. It was Charlotte. "Verga, darling, I have good news for you. Would you be interested to meet the assistant conductor of the Brooklyn Philharmonic?"

"Yes, of course."

"Good. I want you to call Mr. Stephan Rubenstein. He's an acquaintance of mine. I told him all about you, and I suggested to him that you should give a recital to the academy students."

"Thanks, Charlotte, for promoting me, but Mr. Rubenstein has never heard me play."

"Don't worry, darling. I convinced him that you're a real talent. And after he hears you play, he will be convinced too that you are a poet of the piano and a pianist of exceptional quality—a true artist."

"Wow, Charlotte. I'm humbled by your compliments."

I met Mr. Rubenstein, who had me play before deciding to have me at the recital. He was impressed by my piano demonstration of Franz Liszt's *La Campanella* and Franz Schubert's Impromptu, op. 90, D 899. My performance turned out to be a triumph. I established a contact with Brooklyn Philharmonic and was scheduled for a recital in front of the students in two weeks' time.

I called Charlotte when I returned home. "I met Mr. Rubenstein. It went very well. I'm giving a recital in two weeks. Thank you for arranging the meeting."

"You're welcome, darling. That's wonderful news. It calls for celebration. Let's have dinner tonight. You can tell me all about your meeting, and by the way, the piano was delivered. It's ready for you to play."

"Oh, that's great! Where shall we meet?"

"Come to my penthouse."

"I finish playing at the café at 8:00 p.m. I'll see you at eight thirty."

"Okay, darling. I'll be waiting for you."

After my shift at the café, I met Charlotte, who hailed a taxi. "Café des Artistes on Sixty-Seventh Street," she said.

The restaurant was located on the ground floor at Hotel des Artistes, which was unfamiliar to me. We entered the dark-paneled restaurant and were greeted by the director of the café, who recognized Charlotte. "Ms. Stein, how nice to see you. The usual table for two?"

"Yes, please."

My eyes focused on the paintings of nude bodies on the walls. "Please follow me." We passed the busy bar then were seated next to the window. Nearby was the center buffet table with a full selection of desserts.

I heard Charlotte say, "The murals were painted by the famous artist Howard Chandler. This café was and still is a meeting place for musicians, artists, writers, and theater and movie actors. Isadora Duncan sat at this table. Marcel Duchamp, Al Jolson, Norman Rockwell."

"How interesting," I said.

The restaurant was full of glamorous-looking ladies and well-dressed men. I wore a black jacket, white shirt, and a tie, plainly dressed. "Anything from the bar?" the waiter asked.

"Kentucky, ten-year straight bourbon whiskey," she said.

"Let me try that too," I said.

"Good choice," she answered.

With a drink, she said, "Verga, tell me about yourself."

I told her about my story of escaping from the Iron Curtain to Austria and concluded by telling her of my work as a piano entertainer on the *Cristoforo Colombo*, avoiding bringing up Kelly. While I was talking, Charlotte observed me with interest, sipping her bourbon.

"How interesting," she said then ordered another drink. "Want another?"

"No, not for me."

"Shall we order?" Looking at the menu, she said, "I'm starving. I only eat once a day at dinner."

I thought that was why her figure was so slim. She ordered salmon gravlax with mustard and dill sauce. I ordered hot chicken liver mousse. As we ate, I said, "Charlotte, thank you for this exceptional evening.

I truly enjoy your company. It'll be my pleasure to play piano at your party."

"When is your recital?"

"On Wednesday in two weeks at 2:00 p.m."

"I'll be there to listen."

"Great, please come."

"What will you play?"

"Chopin, Rachmaninoff, Prokofiev, and Brahms."

"Which one of those pianists do you like to play most?"

"Rachmaninoff's Prelude, op. 23, no. 5. Are you familiar with it?"

"Oh yes. Good choice. A crowd pleaser."

I figured she was a cultured woman. She took a drink from her glass. "Do you like classical music?"

"Yes, I have a yearly subscription to Carnegie Hall concerts. Would you like to join me one day?"

"Oh yes," I said enthusiastically.

"When would you like to come practice piano?"

"How about tomorrow? It's Friday. Thank you." I paused then said, "If you don't mind, Charlotte, please tell me about yourself."

"My life is boring and is of no interest to anyone." Her face saddened. She lowered her eyes, looking at the glass in her hand and shaking the ice inside. She took another sip. "I lost my husband to an airplane accident three years ago." She ordered another bourbon.

"I'm sorry to hear that." *Is she drinking too much?*

"Verga, darling, let's order the main dishes. For me, the bay scallops sautéed with shallots and walnuts."

"And for you, messieur?" asked the waiter.

"Fettuccine with sausage, bacon, and eggplant," I said.

"Good choice," the waiter answered.

Charlotte slowly drank her bourbon, looking at me with large blue eyes and a look of admiration on her face. Our eyes met, gazing at each other. We didn't say anything. I admired her features. Her hair was blonde like Marilyn Monroe, and her face was like Sophia Lauren's.

I broke the silence. "Charlotte, do you have children?" She said in a low voice, sipping the bourbon, "I have one daughter. She's your age."

"What's her name?"

"Julia," she said as her lips finished drinking the last sip of bourbon. "Julia runs her father's business from the Switzerland office. I rarely see her. She disapproves of my lifestyle."

I changed the subject. "You have a sudden accent. Where are you from?"

She grabbed the waiter by the hand. "Please, another bourbon."

"Yes, ma'am."

It crossed my mind that she had already drunk a lot of liquor. She spoke in a low voice, "I was born in Charleston, South Carolina. My family settled in the 1700s in colonial times. My great-great-grandfather, Fernandez Carvajal, left Portugal on the account of persecution of the Inquisition and settled in the Canary Islands." She stopped talking.

Our main dishes were served. We skipped dessert, but before we left, Charlotte drank another bourbon. When she stood up, she was unsteady on her feet. "Darling, Verga, please hold me. I shouldn't have drunk so much today." She smiled in a drunken stupor and braced herself against my shoulders.

I hailed a taxi, and at the lobby, she said, "Please take me to my penthouse."

In the elevator cabin, she took off her high-heeled shoes, holding them, resting on my hand and shoulder. "Take me to my bedroom," she said.

At the bedroom door, she leaned and hugged me with her two arms around my neck. "Verga, stay with me tonight. I'm lonely." Her eyes were half closed, and she kissed me on the lips.

"Charlotte, you drank too much tonight. You need to go to sleep."

"You're mean, darling," she said, throwing her shoes on the floor. Then, unsteadily, she walked into the bedroom then fell face down on the bed, her legs halfway hanging above the floor.

I lifted her and placed her on the bed. "Please, darling, help me undress," she mumbled.

I removed her dress then tucked her under the blankets. Her head on the pillow, she reached for my hand then let go and fell asleep. I shut the lights and walked toward the elevator.

NINE

I finished playing piano at Carlyle Hotel and walked to the bar. There were a few guests drinking and smoking and talking loudly. I leaned on the counter and said, "Frankie, when you have a minute, make a Campari and soda for me."

He nodded. I felt a tap on my shoulder. I turned around. It was Charlotte with a big smile on her face.

"What a nice surprise," I said, leaning to give her a hug.

She held my cheek with one hand and gave me a kiss on the lips. I smelled her perfume. "Verga, darling, you were supposed to call me. We had a date tonight." She looked to me for an answer.

"I just finished playing and was ready to call you. I didn't forget."

She took my hand. "Let's sit and have a drink." She was dressed in a solid cobalt blue dress and a short matching jacket with white polka dots.

Sitting at the small round table, she opened her Pierre Cardin python skin clutch, taking out a small mirror and looking at herself. "Darling, I don't have your phone number."

"Sorry, I forgot to give it to you." I took a pen and wrote my number on a Carlyle Hotel business card. I handed it to her, and she put it in her bag.

"Darling, I apologize for having too much to drink last night. I don't remember getting into my bed." She looked at me for an answer.

"I helped you into bed."

"Did you undress me?"

"Yes, I hope that's all right. You asked me to."

"Was I a bad girl?" She winked.

"No, you just had a little too much to drink."

"Verga, I feel like doing something special tonight. I feel adventurous."

"How about taking a ride to Coney Island for a roller-coaster ride or parachute jump?"

"That's too scary, but oh my god, I haven't been there in ages."

"Perhaps after, we can stop at the best Italian restaurant in Brooklyn, Fantana di Tervi. I can call Mario and make a reservation."

"Okay, that sounds good," she said excited. "Let me call for a limo."

On our way to Brooklyn, we sat in the back of a limo, and Charlotte said, "Verga, we have to be back by eleven. My friend, Giorgina, is coming."

"Okay, after dinner, you can drop me off. I live a few blocks from the restaurant."

"No, darling, I want you to meet my friend, and you can stay in my penthouse. And you promised to play the piano."

"Are you sure you want me to stay in your penthouse?"

"Are you shy, Verga?"

"No. Why do you ask?"

"I just asked because my friend, Giorgina, is sometimes a bit crazy." Charlotte held my hand and leaned on my shoulder. She asked in a soft voice, "Do you like me?"

"Very much."

"I like you too, darling. Am I too old for you?"

I was surprised at her question. "Charlotte, you're a gorgeous woman and young at heart."

"Thanks."

I turned around. Our lips found each other's, tongues touching, passionately kissing for a long moment.

Then I heard the driver, "Where do you want me to park the car?" The limo stopped on Surf Avenue. I glanced through the car window. In front of me was a sign advertising Nathan's hot dogs. It read: "Follow the crowd. Stop here!" This was the original Nathan's.

I took a deep breath. "Wait for us here," I said.

As I held Charlotte's hand, we walked toward the Coney Island boardwalk. Noise from the crowds mixed with the thunderous rocking of roller coasters. We walked between game stalls.

I suggested taking a ride on the bumper cars. She nodded. Sitting together, we smashed and drove into other cars. We laughed like little kids.

As we walked past the parachute jump, I said, "Let's do it."

"No way." Charlotte pushed me away from the stand.

"How about Wonder Wheel?"

"Okay."

We sat in the enclosed passenger car with two other couples. At 150 feet above ground, we could see Brooklyn and Manhattan spread in front of us. It was quite a clear evening, and the car stopped for a few moments at the top. We enjoyed the night view sprinkled with lights over the horizon.

On our way back to the waiting car, we embraced on the boardwalk, kissing. She held me tight. I felt her breasts pressing against my chest, arousing me. I wanted this woman, and I felt that she wanted me too. Silently, we walked to Surf Avenue.

Back at the limo, I said to the driver, "Eighty-Sixth Street and Eighteenth Avenue. Fantana di Tervi."

Mario greeted us at the restaurant when we arrived. I introduced Charlotte to him. "Nice to meet you," he said. Then he turned to me. "Verga, we don't see you anymore."

"Mario, I'm busy working in Manhattan."

"Yes. Now you're playing in the fancy Carlyle Hotel. You forgot your friends in Brooklyn."

"Stop it, Mario. I still live in the neighborhood."

We sat at the table.

"What can I get you to drink?"

I asked, "Do you have bourbon whiskey?"

"Let me check," Mario said and paced to the bar.

I handed Charlotte the menu.

Mario returned quickly. "Sorry, we don't carry bourbon whiskey. How about Johnny Walker?"

"Okay, with just a little water."

"For me, a Chianti." I turned to Charlotte. "I love the Sangiovese grape wine."

"I was brought up with mint julep."

"What's that?"

"It's a Southern drink, bourbon whiskey over shaved ice, crushed mint leaves, and granulated sugar. No one knows how to make it right in New York, so I take it without the mint and sugar now. I drink straight bourbon, sometimes on ice."

Mario suggested the day's specials, *costolette di tonno al vino rosso* (fresh tuna in red wine) and *agnello in fricassea* (lamb fricassee with fresh tarragon).

While eating, Charlotte asked, "Darling, how do you like living in this neighborhood?"

"I like it very much. I like the diversity of cultures in Bensonhurst. It reminds me of living in Venice. I live not too far from the restaurants. Would you like to see my basement studio? It's nothing to compare to your penthouse."

"Darling, when I got married, we lived in a modest apartment in Brooklyn. Yes, I would like to see your place."

I stopped the car in front of my basement apartment. "This is my place. It's in a working-class neighborhood."

She held my hand and said, "My husband and I lived on Flatbush in Brooklyn. Many famous people live in Brooklyn: Aaron Copland, conductor and composer; Madeleine Astor, second wife of the millionaire, John Jacob Astor; Sandy Koufax, baseball player; the comedian, Danny Kaye; Lenny Kazan; and May West. The list is long."

I felt at ease. "Would you like to go inside?"

"Sure, darling."

When we entered my apartment, she exclaimed, "I didn't know that you are also a talented artist." She admired a painting on an easel.

I placed some clothes into a travel bag to bring to Charlotte's. "Do you like my artwork?" I pointed to the dozen canvases on the walls. "Some of these paintings are *primi pensieri* [first composition thoughts]."

"Yes," she said. "You know, darling, I have a master's in art history and worked for one year in the Metropolitan Museum as a curator before my marriage, and I can see you're talented."

"Thank you. Pick up any painting you like. It'll be my pleasure to give it to you."

"Oh, how sweet of you."

She looked at the canvases. "I like this one, a collage of nudes on moving water."

"This is my latest creation. I was inspired by Arnold Böcklin's *Naiads at Play*. It's my honor to have my painting hanging in your penthouse along with Jackson Pollock, Paul DeLvaux, and other greats."

Back in the car, as we drove to Manhattan, I asked, "By the way, where did you meet your husband?"

"On Ninety-Second Street Y Community Center. In a lecture. He just graduated from Wharton School of Business with his MBA. He was a chemist. We fell in love and got married. He was very good with math and had this idea of starting a mutual fund specialized in pharmaceuticals. My father financed his business venture, and he became a big success. Darling, why are we talking about the past? Let's celebrate the present. Life is too short." She put her head against my shoulder. We rode the rest of the way in silence.

At the penthouse, Charlotte said, "Make yourself comfortable. I'll change into something else." She kissed me.

I walked to the living room. In the corner stood the magnificent white Liberace piano, sparkled with silver and gold specks. I touched the keys and played some scales. The brilliant sweet sound poured from the belly of the Steinway. Satisfied, I went to change into jeans and a button-down shirt. I sat in front of the piano and played "Rêverie" by Debussy. Charlotte came over to hug me, her two hands gliding under my shirt. She kissed my neck, listening to my play. I finished the turn around, and we kissed. She was dressed in a robe revealing her moderately transparent loose silk shirt with matching pants. I could see the outline of her round breasts and large nipples. She didn't have on underwear, so I saw the outline of her Venus.

"Verga, your play is enticing," she said as she went to the liquor cabinet, her round behind swaying sensually. I swallowed hard. "Campari and soda?" she asked.

"Please."

As she walked toward me, I saw her bare body behind the silk fabric. She handed a drink to me. I reached to touch her when the phone rang. It was the lobby concierge. "Ms. Giorgina is on her way." She closed her robe and went to greet her friend.

Disappointed by the intrusion, I swallowed air to keep my excitement at bay. But I was puzzled over her choice of attire, seeing as she had another guest in the house. I heard Charlotte greet Giorgina in the foyer.

I was sitting at the piano, drinking, when the two of them appeared in the living room.

"Meet Giorgina," she said.

I stood up. In front of me was a light-brown-skinned woman with short straight black hair on her European features: red lips and dark brown eyes. Two gold earrings dangled from her ears. She put her bag next to the sofa and came toward me. She gave me a kiss on both cheeks. She smelled like passion fruit.

"Nice to meet you. I heard so much about you," she said in a French accent. "And better looking than Charlotte described."

I think I blushed when she winked. "Thanks," I said. "What do you drink?"

"I'll have rum and Coke."

"Giorgina, you know where the liquor is," Charlotte said.

Giorgina went to make herself a drink. She wore a denim miniskirt, short red Western boots, a large buckle belt, and a printed shirt under a jacket with tassels and silver buttons. She was tall and slim.

The girls sat at the sofa, looking at me. I asked, "Where are you from, Giorgina?"

"I was born in the West Indies on the Isle of San Martin but grew up in Cuba. How about you?"

"I'm from Hungary."

Drinking her rum, she said, "You look like a painting of Franz Liszt at the piano. Same hairdo."

Charlotte added, "He plays like Liszt too. You should hear him. Please play something romantic, darling."

I played Franz Schubert's D. 505 Sonata Movement. Midplay, I smelled a pungent aroma in the air. *What kind of cigarette is that?* I turned to look at them. Giorgina was smoking a joint then passed it to Charlotte.

I finished the song then continued to play Adagio D. 178. My fingers glided in slow motion over the keyboard as I marveled at the piano's melody. My eyes closed. I played with all my emotions, striking the keys and playing slow, soft, hypnotic sounds on the piano. I opened my eyes then turned my head, eyeing the women.

It was wonderfully shocking. I didn't know what to think at first or what to do. On the sofa, Charlotte and Giorgina were embraced in a passionate deep kiss. Charlotte's robe opened, and Girogina moved her hands over Charlotte's large exposed breasts then hovered between her legs, replacing her hands with her lips.

I stopped playing, wondering if I should confront the women. I had thought Charlotte and I were seeing one another, so this was utterly confusing. *Is Charlotte also seeing Giorgina? Maybe this isn't such an exclusive relationship.* I went to one of the bedrooms to give them privacy and think about what was happening before me.

On my way, Giorgina grabbed my hand. "Where are you going, Verga?"

Charlotte opened her eyes, composed herself, and rose. "Darling, please sit with us." I stood for a minute unsure of what to do or how to feel and then sat between them, and she said, "Your play put us in a romantic mood."

"Charlotte, I thought we were seeing each other. Did I get the wrong idea?" I asked, facing her.

"No, Verga. But I also enjoy Giorgina's company. Love shouldn't be restricted to one person. Don't you think so?"

Giorgina interjected, "Love should be free. Charlotte can be attracted to both you and me, no?"

"Yes, I suppose," I muttered, still unsure of the idea.

Giorgina lit another joint, passing it to Charlotte. She took a deep inhale then put it between my lips. Again, I was taken aback. I had never smoked a joint before. I took it out and said, "I don't smoke."

Charlotte replied in a soft voice, "Darling, this is not a cigarette. Try it. It will make you relax."

I was so disoriented already that I decided to try it. They looked at me.

"Take a deep inhale," Giorgina said, "then hold it in your lungs."

I did. I felt nothing, blowing the smoke.

"Take another," I heard Giorgina say.

I did. Then my heart almost jolted from my chest. "Oh my god," I said, holding my chest with my hands.

They started laughing. After a minute, my heartbeat slowed. I felt relaxed, all tension gone. Everything looked rosy. Charlotte hugged me and kissed me open-mouthed. Then I felt Giorgina's hand on my head. I turned around. She kissed me with her wet red lips. It took me by surprise, but it was a pleasant shock. She let go of me, leaving me breathless.

We shared the joint, passing it to each other. All my inhibition vanished. Charlotte stood up and took my hand, looking at me with glassy eyes. "Let's make love," she said in a sensual voice.

My heart thumped hard. I couldn't think straight, and Charlotte and Giorgina both looked so beautiful right then. I reached for Charlotte, kissing her shoulder then her breasts. My hands glided over her behind under the silk pants, caressing her buttocks. She let out a sound of pleasure, whispering, "Darling, let's go to my bedroom."

In the bedroom, I was surprised to see Giorgina seated on the edge of the bed, topless, removing her pantyhose. I hadn't seen her leave the salon. Then she stood and removed her black underwear. A smile adorned her face as she came toward us. Her cocoa milk skin glowed in the light. She kissed Charlotte then me, her mouth moist and warm. Then she proceeded to unbutton my shirt. My eyes were glued to her toned, shapely body. She had long legs and small round breasts with small nipples. I was still as she touched me but managed to take off my pants. Naked, I stood aroused. Giorgina climbed onto the bed, kissing Charlotte. She held my hand and motioned for me to join them. I climbed onto the large mattress, not sure what to do next. Charlotte rose and spread her legs and held my hand. I lay between her legs. Our mouths joined in an open kiss. She was ready.

"Come to me," she whispered.

I entered her wet Venus. Oh my god, I had never felt like that. As I slowly pushed down, I felt like I was entering a hot, steaming room. Every nerve in my body tingled with pleasure.

Giorgina shut the table lamp, so the only source of light came from the moon and the streetlights below. I felt Giorgina's hands on my behind. Her wet tongue moved over my spine. My body shivered with spasms. Her fingers touched and caressed my penis as I slid in and out of Charlotte's Venus. Charlotte's hands wrapped around my back in a tight grip. She breathed heavily on my neck. I heard her low moans in my ear, forgetting about Giorgina. Charlotte and I were like an impetuous volcano waiting to explode. Our bodies joined, moving up and down for a long time. I felt her reach her limit. I thrust slowly and felt Giorgina's hand on my behind again.

As she lay next to me, her mouth searched for mine. We found each other. Her tongue played with mine. Then she whispered, "Hold on. Slow down," resting her head on my behind. I slowed and withdrew from

Charlotte, breathing hard. "Take a deep breath," I heard Giorgina say. Her hand glided gently on my erection.

I whispered, "I want you."

She whispered into my ear, "I want you too. Take me from behind."

Giorgina raised her round buttocks and leaned between Charlotte's spread legs, kissing Charlotte's parted gates. I held Giorgina's round buttocks. Gently, I slid into her, deeper and deeper until I reached her inner sanctum. She let out a rush of air. I leaned over her bare back, kissing her neck, my hand caressing her small round firm breasts. We moved with gentle thrusts, sliding in and out. Charlotte's cries got louder and louder as Giorgina moved her tongue over her body. I reached my limit again and withdrew. Giorgina raised her body and turned around, kissing me passionately. I heard her voice, "Take Charlotte. She's yours."

I lay between Charlotte's raised legs. She found my hand. Our fingers gripped each other. I lay on her warm body, belly to belly, kissing her raised nipples. Then our lips found each other. Open-mouthed, we kissed. I entered her. Her legs held me tight around my waist, pressing me. We moved up and down. Then we exploded, our bodies twisting and sliding hard. We thrust into each other until we were exhausted and out of air. "Oh, darling, stay in me a little longer," she said in a low voice.

She held me nestled on her chest. I turned to look for Giorgina, but she had vanished from the room. "Charlotte, where's Giorgina?"

Ignoring my question, she said in a tired, raspy voice, "Verga, hold me tight." She kissed my neck and fell asleep.

I lay her on a pillow. I was fully awake lying next to Charlotte when I heard water running. I followed the sound to a large dressing room and a closet. I peeked into the next room. Girogina was wiping herself. She had just come out of the tub.

"Hi, sweetie," she said.

I entered the bathroom. My eyes were glued to her.

She let the towel fall and grabbed my hand, pulling me against her. We kissed with her hand on my penis. I was awakened again. I kissed her body, my hand between her legs. She was still aroused and wet. My fingers probed her G-spot. She let out a low cry then moved to a small bench. Our eyes gazed into each other's. She held my penis, sitting on me, sliding on my not-yet-hard erection, looking at us in the mirror. Her hand gently rested on my shoulder. She closed her eyes. She moved, riding me. I held her waist and leaned back against the mirror on the wall, looking at her face and thinking how exotic and beautiful she was. Gasping for air, I slid into her for a long time. Then she thrust steadily and deeply. I felt myself getting harder and harder.

"Oh, Verga, now I can feel you," she whispered. "Oh yes, oh yes." She moved with explosive thrusts, twisting her head back and forth.

I whispered, "Don't stop. I'm close." It took me a long time to climax. I let out a cry. It was the first time I came twice in a short time between lovemaking. We sat hugging each other. "My god, what a night," I said.

She kissed me. "I enjoyed every minute of it," she said. "What time is it?"

I looked at my watch. "One thirty."

She stood up. "I need to go. Let's take a shower."

In the shower, I asked her, "Where are you going?"

"I have a busy day tomorrow. I have to open the cosmetic store at nine."

"Will I see you again?"

"Oh, sweetie, yes. I'm a friend of Charlotte. Please do me a favor. I left my bag in the living room. Bring it to me."

I wrapped a towel around myself and handed her the bag. After she finished her shower, Giorgina left the penthouse. I lay in bed next to Charlotte, who was in a deep sleep. I felt her warm body, my senses becoming clearer but my eyes growing heavy.

I woke up the next morning. The sun poured through the windows in the bedroom. It was after ten. Charlotte was still asleep, blond hair tangled and spread on the pillow cover, covering half of her face. I gently pushed her aside. She didn't flinch. Her black mascara was smeared around her eyelids. Her lips were half open, still retaining its dark red color. She looked so peaceful. I gently kissed her cheek. She did not move.

Dressed in only my underwear and a shirt, I stepped onto the terrace overlooking Central Park. I sat on the wooden deck, which was warm from the morning sun. My head was sober and clear. Closing my eyes, I tried to purge my mind of last night, hopping in bed with two women. I felt shame, for I didn't want to take advantage of Charlotte or Giorgina. My sober mind didn't quite agree with the idea of free love as they had explained to me before. Then the thought of my encounter with Giorgina resurfaced in my mind like a fly fluttering around my head. I was angry with myself for letting lust overtake me. I was just plain irritated, thinking I should not have slept with Giorgina. It was a foolish act. After all, I've been practicing to tame the wild animal in me as Constantina had taught me through meditation. I felt remorse for indulging in selfish instant gratification, like licking honey from a sharp knife. I remembered Constantina saying, "In Buddhism, mindfulness is to practice five precepts: no lying, no stealing, no killing, no sexual misconduct, and no intoxication." And I had broken the rules. I knew I was off track. It raised a red flag in my mind that I had lost my perspective and needed to make an adjustment to not have lust walk all over me. Finally, I began to meditate for the first time since I was on the *Cristoforo Colombo*. I felt the sun scorch my face as I sat on the deck.

After half an hour, I searched for coffee in the kitchen. With a cup in hand, I retreated back to the terrace. My mind drifted again to last night, and I wondered if Charlotte had planned the events with Giorgina. I was lost in thought when Charlotte ambled over in her silk shirt, barefooted, her hair tied by a colorful handkerchief, face washed, lips shining red.

"Darling, what are you doing so early out here?"

"I'm enjoying the beautiful morning."

She sat on my lap. We kissed briefly as she hugged me. "Give me a sip of your coffee," she said.

"It's too cold."

She took the mug between her lips. "Yuck." She made a face.

"I told you it's too cold."

She looked at me with clear blue eyes. "Darling, I can still feel you from last night." She kissed me again.

"I feel the same."

She put her head on my shoulder, kissing my neck. I could smell sweet perfume but pushed her away just a bit to give us some distance to talk. "Charlotte, who's Giorgina?"

"Oh, she's just my friend. When I feel lonely, she comes and takes it away."

"Did you plan our encounter last night?"

"No, darling. I never know what Giorgina will do. She always surprises me. That's what I like about her. She comes when I feel lonely."

I paused then asked, "You don't mind we shared her last night?"

"No, we believe in free love, remember?"

"Yes, but I'm not sure I do. Where did you meet?"

"Darling, you ask too many questions."

"I want to know all about you."

"After the death of Robert, I made a trip to the West Indies, searching for my ancestral home. On my way back to the U.S., I stopped in Cuba. There, I met Giorgina. She took my loneliness away and taught me how to love. I helped her to immigrate to the United States. Darling, don't get attached to her. Don't get attached to anyone." She put her finger on my forehead.

I saw Giorgina several times thereafter, but that was the only time I was intimate with her.

TEN

I invited Joe and Kelly to my recital. "Joe can't make it," Kelly said, but she assured me that she would attend.

"Let's have lunch at Junior's on Flatbush Avenue," I said.

I asked Charlotte to join us. She said that she would skip lunch and meet me at the Brooklyn Academy auditorium.

I arrived early and sat at the restaurant table, waiting for Kelly to arrive. When she entered, I stood up and went to her.

"Kelly, it's good to see you."

"It's lovely to see you too."

Holding her hand, I guided her to our table. "I'm glad you could make it."

"Of course, Verga. There's no way I would miss your performance."

I gave her a French hug, kissing her cheeks. I smelled her perfume and wanted to kiss her lips as we had done before, which made me feel guilty. *Free love*, I thought, but I restrained myself. *She's engaged to someone else.*

It was mid-July on a hot day. Kelly was dressed in a solid short-sleeved blouse and white pants with a large red belt, her red hair on her shoulders.

"Kelly, it's been a while."

"Yes, Verga. Lately, we don't see each other that often."

"I'm busy, and you have your life. How's Joe?"

"He works too hard and comes home late. We manage to see each other on the weekends. He asked me to move into his apartment, but I'm

267

reluctant. I'm so used to my own space, you know. What's happening in your life?"

"I play piano five days a week, and as you know, during the day, I paint." I hesitated before continuing. "I met an interesting woman, Charlotte. She thinks I'm a very talented artist, and this weekend, she'll introduce me to a gallery owner. I may have a show for my paintings."

"I would like to see your paintings."

I paused and remembered our visit to the museum in Marseille. "I'd be glad to describe the paintings to you. How's your eyesight? Any changes?"

"So far, my eyes are stable. One day, they'll have treatment to correct my retinitis pigmentosa."

The waiter came, and we ordered a tuna sandwich and a large salad. Kelly suggested we share. As we ate, she asked, "Who is this mysterious woman?"

"You'll meet her at the recital. I met her last week in the Carlyle Hotel. She wants me to play piano at her party. She's very attractive and educated, but sometimes she's self-centered and insistent in her behavior. On the other hand, she can be kind and generous."

"What do you mean?"

"I'm not sure. I'm confused about her ambivalent character. Listen to this. She didn't have a piano in her penthouse, so she asked me to pick one. Kelly, she paid for it on the spot—a piano that was originally going to be purchased by Liberace."

"Oh, wow! She must like you. Did you mention a penthouse? She sounds like a person of luxury. Is she a wealthy woman?"

"I hardly know her. I presume she's a woman of means." I changed the subject. "How do you get along with Joe?"

"Fine," she said in a nonenthusiastic way.

I decided not to ask more. I looked at the watch and paid the check.

The recital was held in the main auditorium of the Brooklyn Academy. The first several rows were assigned to academy students, but I had reserved two front seats for Kelly and Charlotte. At two fifteen, I was introduced to the students. Sitting at the piano, I looked at the audience. The seat next to Kelly was empty. *Charlotte must be late*, I thought. Kelly smiled up at me.

Then I played Chopin's Étude, op. 10, no. 1, then Rachmaninoff's Prelude, op. 23, no. 5. I looked at the first row again. Charlotte still was not there. Kelly applauded. I played Chopin's "Spianato Grande Polonaise" op. 22. This was my longest play.

I finished to a loud applause. I saw Charlotte sitting next to Kelly, dressed in a black-and-white outfit with a bouquet of red roses in her lap. I wondered what Kelly's reaction would be when I introduced them to each other. I was nervous, as I had loved Kelly once before. However, I had never loved Charlotte or had ever felt the capacity to do so; it was all lust.

I played Prokofiev's Toccata op. 11 in D Minor, then Brahms's Intermezzo op. 118 in A Major, and finished with *Danzas Argentinas* op. 2 by Alberto Ginastera. The hall interrupted in thunderous applause.

Mr. Rubenstein came on stage. I bowed deeply. Then he took the microphone, looking at me. "Thank you, Mr. Caszar, for this splendid performance and taking your time to perform in front of our students. Please join us for refreshments, and Mr. Caszar will make himself available for questions you may have for him." He turned toward me, clapping.

"Thank you," I said.

I stepped down from the stage and greeted Charlotte with a kiss on both cheeks.

"Bravo, Verga! You were magnificent!" She handed me the roses.

"Thanks for the flowers."

"Sorry I came late. New York traffic."

"It's okay. Please meet my friend, Kelly O'Reilly."

She turned to Kelly. "Nice to meet you. A friend of Verga, darling, is a friend of mine." She extended her hand to Kelly.

Kelly quietly replied, "It's nice to meet you."

Noticing Charlotte's extended hand, I leaned over to her and whispered, "Kelly is blind."

She let a surprised look on her face; then she said, "It's my pleasure to meet you, Kelly. What did you think of Verga's play?"

"His piano playing always evokes feelings I cannot describe."

"I feel the same way, darling."

I said, "Would you ladies join me for refreshments?"

Kelly answered, "No, Verga, you go ahead. You have a meeting with the students. Could you hail a taxi for me, please?"

Charlotte interrupted, "Darling, Verga, go ahead. Meet the students. Kelly, may I give you a ride? I have a car waiting for me outside." Not waiting for an answer, she continued, "Where do you live, darling?"

"On Eighty-Sixth Street in Lex," Kelly replied.

Charlotte said, "Darling, that's just a few blocks from my apartment. Shall we?" She turned to me. "I'll see you later."

I said, "I'll call you." I kissed Charlotte and Kelly on their cheeks. "I appreciate you coming. I'll call you later," I whispered in Kelly's ear.

The following day, I was painting in my basement when the phone rang. It was Kelly. "Verga, who is this woman, Charlotte? She didn't stop talking to me in the car. She wanted to know everything about me and how you and I met."

"Charlotte is sometimes very domineering. She needs to be in control of conversation, but she is very kind when she likes someone."

"Verga, she asked me about you. Are you and her just friends? She implied that you're lovers. Of course, it's none of my business who you date."

I didn't know the answer to Kelly's question, so I remained quiet.

"Verga, are you there?"

"Yes, Kelly. I like Charlotte. Both of us are lonely hearts in a big city, and we have a strong physical attraction to each other. She is free to love men of any age. Charlotte already figured out who she is, maybe not all the time but a lot more often."

"Verga, do you prefer older women?"

"No, Kelly. I prefer a woman who knows what she wants, who's sure of herself. She told me that she's not seeking out marriage or cohabitation. You know, Kelly, I was attracted to you, and you're just seven years older, and I like your looks and sharp intellect. We too had an instant connection."

I heard Kelly breathing. There was silence; then she said, "I miss you."

"I miss you too Kelly. Is everything all right between you and Joe?"

She hesitated then said, "Someone is ringing my doorbell. I'll speak to you later." She hung up.

On Saturday, I arrived early to the penthouse to help Charlotte prepare for the party. Dressed in my new black jacket, flared black pants, and colored pleated shirt, I arranged the upright chairs in a semicircle in front of the white Steinway piano. The salon decor was a copy of the interior architecture of the Salon Doré in Paris. The wall's motif was of a neoclassic design: all white with gold leaf moldings and mirrors. I thought the room was perfect for a recital and entertainment of guests.

Charlotte was instructing the bartender in the kitchen when the guests started to arrive. She greeted them in the foyer, dressed in a smart skirt, low go-go boots, and a bouffant hairstyle, bourbon whiskey in her hand. Her guests were businessmen, lawyers, doctors, teachers, professors, and socialites. I conversed with her neighbor who lived two floors below, a Wall Street executive, when Charlotte interrupted our conversation. She said, "Excuse me, Peter. Verga, darling, I want you to meet Richard. He has an art gallery on West Fifty-Seventh Street."

He said, "I heard so much about you from Charlotte. An artist and piano virtuoso. How interesting. A rare breed. This painting of nudes in moving water"—he pointed to a canvas—"as an artist, what did you have in mind when you painted this composition?" He waited for my answer, smoking a cigarette.

I looked at my painting on an easel and framed in a Louie XV gold frame. I took a sip from my drink of Campari and soda, pointing my finger to the canvas. "My composition is an interpretation of *Naiads at Play*, painted by Arnold Böcklin in the 1800s. The nude women in my painting are floating on water. Their bodies are painted in blue hues from the reflection of the moon. For centuries, the moon, for us, has been a connection to our imagination, intuition, and physical powers of dreaming. The women are in a deep sleep, dreaming, floating on moving water. It's like a secret Sapphic boudoir. The water in my painting never takes a straight path like the flow of our lives."

Charlotte said, "Didn't I tell you, Richard, Verga is bright and talented? I have a good eye for a nice piece of art. I picked up the right painting."

"Charlotte, you definitely do. You picked up Jackson Pollock way before he hit the art scene." Richard turned toward me and said, "I would like to visit your studio and see your work."

Charlotte interrupted, "Darling, Richard, Verga is in the process of moving his studio to West Village. I found him a new place, and in a month, I'll call you for a visit."

I thought, *A studio in West Village? What is she thinking?*

I heard her say, "Darling,"—she put her hand on Richard—"let's meet our guests. Verga, you must have a drink." She turned to me. "But please pour me another drink."

The guests were in the salon, drinking, some smoking, talking aloud. Party helpers, dressed in white jackets and black pants, passed trays of finger food. I made myself comfortable, sitting on the sofa, conversing with an elegantly dressed woman. She wanted to know when Charlotte and I met. I was ready to tell her when Charlotte came over again, took my hand, and said, "Darling, let me introduce you to all my guests."

Standing in front of the piano, she said, "Please all sit down. Tonight, I have a surprise for you. I'm delighted to introduce to you a talented artist and a piano virtuoso who escaped from Communist Hungary and is the winner of the Young Pianist Competition in Austria, a new talent in our city, Verga Caszar."

Clapping erupted in the room. Standing in front of the piano, I bowed low. I said, "It's my pleasure to meet you all." I turned to Charlotte. "I thank you, Charlotte, for giving me this opportunity to play in front of your friends." I pointed my hand toward the piano. "This spectacular Steinway was specially ordered by Liberace. Then he canceled the order. Due to Charlotte's generosity, this magnificent piano is here tonight. It'll be my pleasure to play on it for you today."

Charlotte motioned her hand, and the lights dimmed in the salon. I said, "In the spirit of Liberace, let's begin this evening with lighting the candelabra." I lit the candelabra on top of the piano then sat on the piano stool, not moving for a long moment. Then I played. The sound of the piano echoed through the room. I swayed my body to the rhythm of the score, my hands striking the keyboard, gliding, touching the keys from above. Tonight, I imparted a sense of restlessness in my play. That gave the melodies a surging effect, like a skiff on the crest of a mighty wave crashing on the beach. I finished with Chopin's polonaise called "Kosciuszko." It is the most well-known of his work. I played it remembering its period when women listened to it and burst into sobs.

That evening, I became a darling of Charlotte's friends.

A week later, Charlotte and I were having dinner at the Café de Artist. She said, "Darling, I have a surprise for you."

"What kind of surprise?"

"I found a space for your studio."

"Really? Where?"

"I'll take you there tomorrow."

"Thanks, but I cannot afford to pay the studio rent."

"Don't worry, darling, about rent. I know the landlord. He's a dear friend of mine. He's letting us use the space for a year without a rent charge."

"Really? How come?"

She took a sip of bourbon, put the glass down, and then said, "I made a deal with him. The space has been vacant for the past six years. I offered him that we'll renovate the space. In return, he wouldn't charge rent for a year."

"I like that, but, Charlotte, I don't have funds for the renovations either."

"Don't worry, darling. I will lend you the money. I believe in you as an artist. In a year, I will make you famous." She got hold of my hand. Looking into my eyes, she said, "Just be patient and let me manage your affairs financially, and you'll do fine."

The next day, Charlotte took me to see the studio space in West Village. We took the elevator to the seventeenth floor then walked the stairs to the roof. The view was spectacular. The building was located on the corner of Washington Square and Beverly Place, overlooking Washington Square Park. As I stood at the parapet edge, looking at the park in front of me, Charlotte said, "What do you think, darling?"

"Wow!" It was breathtaking. *Is this a dream? How lucky can I be?*

"Let's see the space."

On the roof, attached to the brick-enclosed addition was a glazed structure. Above it was a water tower and elevator machinery. The vacant space consisted of a greenhouse and a large open space. It needed major renovation. The greenhouse enclosure was intact but had broken or missing glass. The rest of the space was a mess of broken metal shelves, dirt, and garbage of all kinds.

"What do you think?" Charlotte said.

"The space has potential for a studio but needs a lot of work."

I saw a sink but no toilet. I said, "Where's the washroom?"

"Mr. Diaz, the building manager, told me, darling, you can use the lavatory in the hallway on the floor below."

"Okay, that's good," I said, walking around the space. "I like this greenhouse as a studio. It faces north and east light. Good for painting."

Charlotte interrupted, "Okay, then it's settled. I'll call Neil, my attorney, to review the lease."

For the next three months, I helped the contractor renovate the new studio. In the end, it was a successful project. I had a large space to work on my art.

Charlotte arranged an exhibit of my painting for the fall season in the West Fifty-Seventh Street Gallery. I intended to exhibit twenty-four paintings from my early work to present. My early works were influenced and inspired in composition and style by Gustav Klimt, but by now, I was a self-taught artist; and I came into my own style, which was free, expounded twentieth-century expressionism and fauvisms in simplified form. My paintings depicted an imposing silhouette of mystical feminine creatures in seductive poses in violet colors and landscapes with humans and animals in pastoral tradition reminiscent of Henri Mattisse. I painted with vivid colors and aggressive brushstrokes with pure color squeezed directly from the tube. Inspiration also came from my classical music upbringing, classical literature, and my contemplation of mystical forces of the universe and obstructed imagery in my mental, spiritual experience. Freeing the applied colors from pictorial form and freeing the image on the canvas from nature, I tried to reach the subconscious using brushstrokes with physical presence, smearing, rubbing, and scratching the artwork. My avant-garde work of art was painted with a mirrored spirit of my restless soul.

On one Friday evening, I finished playing at Bemelmans Bar then rushed to my studio in West Village to finish one of my paintings. I was engrossed in applying paint on yet another new creation when the phone rang. It was Charlotte. Her voice was an unintelligible cacophony. She was frantic, sobbing.

I put my brush down. "Charlotte, calm down. What's wrong?"

"Verga, please come. I need you. A terrible thing happened."

"What happened?"

Her speech was muffled by the phone.

"Charlotte, did you have too much to drink?"

"Come over, Verga, come over."

"Okay, okay. I'm coming."

I rushed to the street and hailed a taxi. At the penthouse lobby, I asked the concierge, Tony, "Who's in the penthouse?"

He looked in his book. "Ms. Stein's friend, Giorgina."

"At what time did she come?"

"Ten thirty."

I looked at the watch. It was eleven twenty. "Tony, I'm going upstairs."
"Should I call Ms. Stein?"
"No," I said as I entered the elevator cab.

I rushed to the salon. There I found Giorgina slumped on the sofa, head tilted back, mouth open, eyes glazed—lifeless. Charlotte sat on the lounge chair, sobbing, her face gripped in fear. Her mascara was smudged on her face in black streaks. She was dressed in a robe, exposing her nude body. I leaned over Giorgina to check her breathing. I noticed none. I felt for her pulse, detecting a faint heartbeat. On the table was a small mirror with lines of white powder and a rolled money bill. I turned to Charlotte.

"Did you take this?" I asked.

She stopped sobbing, a frightened look on her face. She nodded. I smelled marijuana in the air. I opened all the windows in the salon. Charlotte sat with a glassy look on her face, frightened. Her hands covered her face.

"Charlotte, do you have any more drugs in your apartment?"

She did not respond.

I repeated the question.

"No," she said in a low voice.

I opened Giorgina's purse, frantically searching inside. I found a bag of marijuana. I grabbed it then gathered the white powder and flushed both down the toilet. I called the police and gave them the address.

"Charlotte, let's dress up."

She was disoriented. I grabbed her, took her to the bedroom, removed her robe, and dressed her in a shirt. Lifting her legs, I put pants over her naked buttocks. "Sit here on the bed and don't move," I said.

I called Cathy, her secretary.

"Who is this?"

"Cathy, this is Verga."

"What time is it?"

"Twelve. Cathy, listen to me. It's an emergency. Call Charlotte's attorney. Tell him to call the penthouse right now."

"What happened?"

"I can't tell you. Please call Neil." I hung up.

Just then, EMS and police walked into the penthouse. In a panic, I pointed to Giorgina on the sofa. "She stopped breathing!"

EMS rushed to Giorgina, checking for a pulse or sign of life. They placed an oxygen mask over her face, put her on a stretcher, and wheeled her away to the elevator.

The police officer took his report book and asked, "Who are you?"

"I'm a friend of Ms. Stein," I answered.

"And where is Ms. Stein?"

"She's in the bedroom."

The officer went to look. He came back. "I need both of you to come to the precinct to make a report."

The phone blared. I picked it up quickly.

"This is Neil."

"This is me, Verga. Charlotte is having a problem. Her friend, Giorgina, passed out in her penthouse, and now the police are here and want us to go to the precinct."

"Let me speak with the officer."

They spoke for a while; then the officer gave me the phone back.

Neil said, "Verga, take Charlotte to the precinct. I will meet you there. Make sure she does not talk without my presence."

"Charlotte is in no condition to go to the precinct. She's disoriented and unable to even sit up. I need to take her to the hospital."

"Okay, let me speak to the officer again."

They spoke for a few minutes.

The officer asked me, "Do you want me to call for an ambulance?"

"No, I will take her to the hospital by taxi."

"Okay," the officer said. "You need to come tomorrow to the precinct to make a report." He took down all my personal information then left.

I picked up the phone. "Neil, the officer left. Now I can speak to you freely. Charlotte and Giorgina were snorting some kind of powder. I'm not sure if it's cocaine or heroin. What should I do?"

"Take her to the Beth Israel Hospital. I'll meet you there."

I met Neil in the emergency room. He had a power of attorney for Charlotte. He hospitalized her.

The next day, I was coached by Charlotte's attorney to not implicate her in any way when I spoke to the police. At the precinct, I gave a full report of the incident at the penthouse. Last night's incident left me with a profound distaste for opium drugs. I didn't get involved with cannabis after that.

Two days thereafter, Julia, Charlotte's daughter, arrived from Europe. Cathy called me. "Verga, Julia would like to meet you today. Are you available?"

"Yes, I finish working after 8:00 p.m. Can we meet at Carlyle Café?"

"I will ask her and call you back."

I met Julia that night at the café. I recognized her from photographs. She did not resemble Charlotte at all. She looked more like her father: tall, slim, brown hair, and sharp features.

I stood up. "Nice to meet you, Miss Stein."

She extended her hand. "Nice to meet you." She examined me with a serious face while she took a seat.

I thought to myself that she must have been suspicious of me. She removed her short white gloves and placed them on the table. I said, "I appreciate you meeting me here."

"It's quite all right," she said.

"May I order you a drink?"

"Yes, I need one," she said. "A sea breeze with cranberry juice and vodka."

I waved to a waiter. "John, we'll have some drinks. Sea breeze for the lady and Campari and soda for me, please."

I turned to Julia. "Did you visit your mother today?"

"Yes, I saw her today. She is sedated heavily and very depressed."

"I'm very sorry. I didn't realize that her friend, Giorgina, was involved in those activities." The drinks arrived. I lifted my glass. "For your mother's speedy recovery."

We drank in silence for a while, Julia's eyes on me. "You probably want to know about me."

She looked at me and said, "I know enough who you are. Neil and Cathy kept me informed. My mother has a history of depression and obsessive-compulsive disorder, and we don't get along, but I kept track of her life and her whereabouts."

"Your mother is a wonderful human being, full of joie de vivre, a cheerful person, and fun to be with. May I call you Julia?"

"Yes, of course."

"Julia, I want to be upfront with you. I met your mother eight months ago. We grew attracted to each other, and now we're good friends. We enjoy each other's company. Your mother is my business manager. I owe all of today's successes to your mother. I want you to be assured my relation with your mother is not for personal gain. I'm not after her purse. I pay what I owe. She lent me funds for my studio renovation, and I am paying her back. I'm not taking advantage of your family's wealth. Money was never important to me. I'm an artist. And we have an age difference between us; however, we feel comfortable with each other. I really adore your mother for who she is." I paused.

Julia was silently looking at me with a serious expression. I continued. "I feel sort of responsible for what happened that night. I should have known better. Charlotte and I saw each other frequently until I started spending more time in my art studio. I realize your mother needs to constantly be with someone. She did tell me she can't be alone for a long time. She gets depressed and starts to feel lonely, and when she feels lonely, she calls Giorgina."

Julia said, "I thank you for being there at the time when my mother needed help. I spoke to Neil. When Giorgina recovers, she's going to live with her relatives in Miami, which is good. I don't want my mother to see Giorgina again. She's a bad influence on her. In a few days, I'm taking my mother to Switzerland and placing her in a private addiction center in the Alps, so I can oversee her."

"That's good. Are you also aware of your mother's drinking?"

"Yes, she's addicted to bourbon."

"My piano teacher taught me about meditation. It calmed me down a lot and helped me overcome anxiety and restlessness. I tried to introduce the idea to your mother, but she found silence not to her liking. I tried to convince her to cut down on drinking bourbon. She said she can't. It gives her a good feeling, and she likes the taste of it. Occasionally, she smoked a joint to elevate her awareness and relax her and spark her personality. I didn't want to dictate her way of life, so I didn't encourage her to quit excessive drinking. I'm sorry. I should have. I thought that it was common sense at her age. She must have a significant amount of baggage: social pressure, children, business and financial obligations."

"I'm aware of all this. That's why I'm taking her under my supervision."

"I will miss your mother. I hope she recovers fast. I want a new relationship with your mother. We have the chemistry. It's here. I want the relationship to be based on mutual respect. I want us to be friends minus, how shall I say—" I paused.

Julia said, "Sex?"

"Yes, I want her to be my mentor only."

"She wants that too. She mentioned you in a good light many times." I picked up the menu from the table and changed the subject. "May I order dinner for you? Today's special is beef bourguignon, and it's very good here." I glanced at Julia.

She was tense when she came in. Now her facial line relaxed. She looked at the menu and said, "Yes, let's have dinner. I want to talk to you more."

ELEVEN

*M*y art show was a success. Charlotte selected twenty-four paintings for the exhibit. She promoted me through her social contacts, making the gallery well attended. I missed her presence but still invited my friends: Kelly, Joe, Father Pellegrino, and Domenic Bontade, who brought a young blond beauty and his chauffeur, Franco.

Richard Wildenstein, the gallery owner, introduced me to art critics and agents of art collectors. I was praised by the critics for my vigor and creativity. My paintings in the exhibit were free from narrative and simulated solidity. Pictorial narratives, shapes, and lines were portrayed in vivid colors. Shapes expressed false consciousness, Freudian theories of the subconscious representing figures and objects on canvas.

I took my time to walk with Kelly and Joe through the gallery, viewing and explaining my artistic, creative work. We stopped in front of a painting named *Lux Casta at Sleep*. A nude woman stretched on the bed like a cat dozing, her eyes shut, offering herself to the viewer with her sensibility. Her face was half obscured by her red hair spread on white sheets. Her hand gripped the sheet in a contracted form of erotic tension. Her stretched body conveyed her most extreme feminine essence. The background was smeared with black and the shadow of masculine fingers caressing the lying beauty, touching her soft pink skin. Her face slightly resembled Kelly's. I awaited Joe's reaction.

Kelly and I passed the painting, viewing the next picture on the wall. We were engrossed in conversation. She asked questions, and I explained my inspiration and direction. I glanced at Joe, who was still looking at *Lux Casta at Sleep.* He was standing with his hands folded, one hand on his cheek, his face whitening. I was concerned that the painting disturbed him, knowing his conservative views. I had not mentioned to Kelly the resemblance of her face against the painting.

At the end of the walk, Kelly remarked by praising me as an artist; she said it is a triumph of mine that in a short time, I was able to create interesting, creative artwork. Joe was silent. He look annoyed, which made me disappointed.

I said, "Kelly and Joe, which painting in the exhibit do you like most?"

Kelly was quick to reply. "Your interpretation of *The Judgment of Paris.* I like your explanation of the avant-garde creation. I like your ethos of expression of romantic times. I also like your definition of people as humans, as chunks of energized matter. Your finger smearing on the canvas left me with an impression. I felt your energy."

I turned to Joe. "Did you like the paintings?" I asked, jutting him from his thoughts.

"Yes, I like the bold coloration. Now that Kelly expressed herself, I do see an energy omitting from the canvas."

I said, "I would like to make you an engagement gift. The painting is yours."

"Oh my god, Verga." Kelly hugged me. "That's awesome!"

For a moment, I wanted to kiss her rosy lips, but I held back. I heard Joe say, "Thank you. That's very generous of you."

At the end of the evening, I sold most of my paintings.

I was looking to celebrate the upcoming New Year of 1962. Kelly had called while I was out. I left a message when returning her call. "Please call me at Fantana di Tervi. I'm working there tonight."

Wearing only a light winter jacket, I rushed to the restaurant. It was cold and windy as I walked on New Utrecht Avenue toward Eighty-Sixth Street. I had heard on the radio that it might snow or rain at night, but I had rushed from the basement and forgotten my hat and gloves. I walked briskly. My ears tingled from the frost. I was glad to reach the warmth and clamor of the restaurant. Sunday was usually a slow night at Fantana di Tervi, but to my surprise, every table was taken that evening.

I played my usual repertoire, light piano classics and Italian Neapolitan tunes, which were popular with the customers. That evening, we had two birthday parties, and I played special requests. At the end of the night, I counted $45 in tips. At ten thirty, the last customer left, and I sat with Mario, the head waiter, and Salvador for a plate of pasta.

Mario said, "For Sunday, this was a busy night."

Salvador added, "Unusual for freezing nights," as he put his fork on his plate.

I said, "And I forgot my raincoat and hat today."

Salvador looked at me. "No problem, Verga. I have an extra coat and hat you can borrow."

"Thanks, Sal."

It was sleeting as I walked outside. A car slowed down as it approached me. I looked at the dark window. *Strange*, I thought. The car only had on parking lights as it crept beside me. I heard windshield wipers driving rain back and forth. I decided to move away from the curb and hasten my steps. Then the car stopped. The door swung open. Two men in dark clothes jumped out and ran toward me. I panicked. My heart jolted. I started running toward the next corner to the streetlight. Then I felt something hit my right leg. I fell to my knees. A blow to my ribs flattened me on the wet rainy sidewalk. A kick to my head rattled my vision. I lost consciousness.

I dreamt I was in an artist's studio, all white with a large skylight pouring sunlight into the room. In front of me on the stage was a bed covered with black and gold sheets. Curved into an ellipse, a nude body with red hair and a sensual face lay asleep, her mouth slightly open in an expression of pleasure. I was standing, painting this erotic creature behind the canvas. I outlined the body with pink paint then dipped my brush deep in a black color, frantically smearing big strokes around the image. Light grew brighter and brighter, obscuring my model and blinding me. I couldn't paint, so I stopped. I placed my hands over my eyes for protection. I couldn't stand the bright light anymore. *Where am I?* My eyes tried to focus on the light coming from the window. I turned my head. *Am I dreaming?* As if in a fog, I saw the image of Kelly, her red hair down to her shoulders, looking at me behind dark glasses. *Where am I? Is this a dream?* I felt her warm hand touch mine. It was so real. She was crying, tears pouring down her cheeks. *Where am I?* I tried to organize my thoughts.

Then I heard Kelly's voice. "Verga, can you hear me?" I turned my head toward the voice. I was not dreaming now. It was Kelly, flesh and blood.

What is she doing here? My vision was swimming. "Is that you, Kelly?" I said in a hoarse voice.

"Yes, it's me." She wiped her cheeks and held my hands, her face almost touching mine. "Thank God you're awake."

"Where am I?"

"You're in a hospital."

"Why?"

"You had an accident."

"I'm thirsty. My lips are dry." She gave me a glass of water with a straw. I drank it all. "How long have I been here?"

"Three days. You were in a coma. Let me tell the nurse that you woke up."

"Coma?" I tried to remember what had happened to me. It came slowly to mind. I closed my eyes, trying to recall that night. I was walking in a driving rain, then something hit me. I felt the pain in my chest. I touched my ribcage with my fingers. It was swollen.

Kelly sat next to me on the bed.

I said, "Kelly, thanks for being here."

She held my hand and said, "Remember when your mezuzah entangled with my cross? Our lives are forever bonded, remember?"

I let a faint smile. My mind foggy and eyelids heavy, I closed my eyes. I heard her say, "Darling, I will see you tomorrow."

The next day, I felt better. A New York City police investigator came in to interview me. He asked, "Mr. Caszar, do you have enemies who want you harmed?"

I thought of the last time I was threatened in Milan by Erno and Zophia. *No, it's not possible that they found me in New York.* I said, "No."

"What is your relation with Domenic Bontade and his son, Salvador?"

"I play piano in their restaurant, Fantana di Tervi."

"Did anyone approach you and threaten you?"

"No," I said in a surprised voice.

"Okay, that's all for today. I may come again."

"Can you tell me who attacked me and why?"

"Not yet, but we have a good idea why this happened."

"Why, and who did it?"

"Mr. Caszar, the police is still in the preliminary stages of the investigation. We will advise you of our conclusion when we close the case."

In the evening, Kelly came back. I said, "Take off your coat. It's too warm in this room."

"How do you feel?" Kelly asked.

"Much better today. Thanks." I looked at Kelly. She had a smile on her face and wore red-framed dark glasses and sat in silence. I added, "Kelly, how did you find out I was in the hospital?"

"The Sunday night you called, I came late and didn't check my messages until the next day. I called you on Monday. There was no answer all day. In the evening, I called Bemelmans Bar. I spoke to the bartender, who said that you had not come that day. I called the restaurant. Mario answered. He told me the bad news. I took a taxi to Maimonides Hospital and have stayed in your room since."

I was amazed at her dedication. "Thank you, Kelly."

"Verga, you are my dear friend. Don't thank me. Thank all the people who came to pray for your recovery."

I was silent for a minute, thinking, *Who are those people she mentioned? I'm all alone here in this city. I don't know that many people.*

"Verga, you're lucky. Father Pellegrino came to pray for you. Then two days ago in the evening, ten black-dressed Hasidics came with a rabbi. They asked me to step out of the room. In the hallway, I listened to their prayers and readings from their books for almost an hour. When they left, I found on your forehead a piece of paper." She pulled it from her handbag and gave it to me.

I was perplexed looking at it. One word was written on it in Hebrew. *What does this mean?* I looked at Kelly, who said, "The nurse said it was written in Hebrew, so I asked my friend, Frieda, who is Jewish, what this means. She said it must have been an allegorical act. She has no clue of the ceremony's meaning; however, the name written is Jubal from the book of Genesis. Jubal is also the name of the first musician and inventor of the harp and flute."

I thought to myself, *Jubal? Why did they choose him? I should ask Mendel.*

"How's Joe?"

Her face changed, the smile gone from her lips. She said, "Joe and I broke up."

My heart jolted. I took a deep breath. "When did that happen?"

"A month ago."

"Why didn't you tell me?"

"I needed time to reflect on it."

Though I wanted to be sad for Kelly, I was happy to hear the news. "What went wrong?"

She paused then said, "The day after the art exhibit, I was in Joe's apartment and planned to stay there overnight. That evening, we went for dinner, and Joe had too much wine. In the apartment, he became irritated over our conversation over nothing. I asked him what was bothering him. He disliked my behavior in the art exhibit and accused me of hiding something from him. I asked him why he was saying that. He said that I call you often and meet you many times, wondering if I was cheating on him. He asked many questions, like if I posed nude for the painting *Lux Casta at Sleep*. I said no and asked him what he thought I did. He didn't believe me, saying it was my face and body on the canvas and it was provocative, tasteless, and pure pornography. It revolted his sensibility. I was in shock. I said I didn't pose nude and said it was his imagination, but if it was my face, so what? He raised his voice, yelling that he'll sue you for breaking our privacy and exposing my body to the public. I told him I wasn't suing anyone and approved the painting. He claimed I was defending my lover and wasn't faithful to him. I asked him where this conversation was going and if he was jealous of you. I told him I was simply fond of your artistic successes.

"Then he started asking if I had an affair on the ship. I pointed out that I had never asked him about his dates in the past. I did realize for a while that Joe was insecure and possessive. Sometimes we didn't live in the same reality. He said I was hiding something. I replied that I'm like an open book and didn't have anything to hide. He continued saying that I was in love with you in secret, and he wanted to know what happened on the ship. I told him we had an affair but that it was in the past and I was engaged to him. He said that you contrast him, that every time I see you, my face lights up. He feels we have some kind of physical energy coming between us, and that leaves him cold. I told him that for the past months, I examined everything in our relationship with new eyes. I pulled out all those pros and cons flags that I stored in my brain. I told him I had doubts about where our relationship was going and saw that he had doubts too. He didn't trust me. He was obsessive, possessive, and jealous. He preferred me to be caged. I was dumbstruck of his accusations of not being faithful. I said our relationship had run its course and that we were not suited for each other; I didn't want to stay in this relationship. I removed my ring and threw it into his lap and stormed toward the door. My eye-seeing dog followed me. Joe grabbed my hand. He insisted I stay and he needed me, but I had made up my mind. He got violent and threatened me. He pulled me from the door. Caesar, the dog, sensed the confrontation and growled. Joe let me go. I opened the door and stormed toward the elevator. I heard him scream that I was a whore and would be sorry. I couldn't believe what I heard and entered the elevator cabin.

"The next morning, he called and apologized. He blamed his outburst on having too much wine. It clouded his mind. I listened then said that I was firm with my decision. I said I was sorry to allow myself to progress our relationship to that point. I told him we should cool off. After a few days, I knew it was over between me and Joe."

Tears rolled down her cheeks. I grabbed her hand, our fingers clutching each other's.

"Kelly, I was afraid to say it, but in the past months, I've been hurting inside. The greatest mistake I made was not asking you to give me a chance to prove my love."

She took her glasses off her face and leaned toward me, her cheeks wet from crying. Her fingers touched my face. She said, "Verga, in the last month, I realized I made a mistake choosing stability over real love. I pondered the importance of security. You know, Verga, money comes and goes. Real love lasts forever. It was hard for me to pretend that I loved Joe when I didn't. I pretended that I didn't love you when I did." She paused then continued, "Verga, do you still want me in your life?"

I stared at her face, knowing that my answer was critical. I said without hesitation, "Kelly, yes. I love you."

She put her head on my chest. Hugging me tightly, she said, "I love you too."

Kelly's finger gently glided over my cheeks, resting on my lips. Our lips parted and found each other. I tasted salt. She was crying. I knew it was from happiness. Holding her face with my hands and gazing at her, I wiped tears from her cheeks. "Dear," I said, "I don't have an engagement ring to put on your finger."

She was quick to reply. "I don't need a ring. I feel your love."

I reached for the mezuzah on my neck and removed it. "Kelly," I said, "this pendant was given to me by my beloved teacher, Constantina, to keep me safe. I want you to have it." I placed it on her neck. The mezuzah rested next to her small golden cross. "This will keep you safe."

She placed her palm on her chest, covering the mezuzah and the cross. She said in a tearful voice, "Verga, darling, this is more precious to me than any engagement ring. Dear, for the last month, I wondered, did you paint me as *Lux Casta at Sleep*?"

I paused, swallowed hard, and then said, "Kelly, originally I painted the model in my studio with black hair and a white, red, and orange background. Charlotte suggested repainting it, to convey more feminine and masculine principles. She suggested using a black background for male and red for female, representing passion, energy, and action. Subconsciously, I was thinking of you and painted your face, knowing it will have traction with Joe. I was hoping he would select it as my engagement present, but you beat him, selecting *The Judgment of Paris*."

She was silent for a while then said, "I'm not sorry. I believe that there is a mysterious unseen tender hand that guided us to each other. Our destiny was charted from the beginning. We were born apart in faraway lands. We met each other on a boundless ocean, and together, we are forevermore. It was meant to be."

TWELVE

*A*fter a week in the hospital, I returned to my apartment to recover. Isaac came one afternoon to see how I was doing. I had been drawing then. I had an insatiable compassion for art since the accident.

Isaac said, "It's a miracle that you recovered so fast. The doctor said you had a serious concussion, and it was fifty-fifty if you would regain your memory. You must have a special connection with Ha Shem. He gave you another chance at life."

"Thanks for your prayers." Then I asked Isaac, "What does this mean?" I showed him the piece of paper with the name Jubal.

"When we heard from the doctor of your critical condition, my father and his rabbi decided to hold a special prayer and recite psalms to give you a new Hebrew name. The Talmud teaches us that our name is very significant. Your name has a direct channel with Ha Shem. We believe it is connected to your soul and shows spiritual strength. The sages of the Midrash recommend changing one's name because that leads to one's destiny and influences one's behavior. It creates new fortune. By changing your name, you should find new meaning in life and inner powers that you had never known. You are a musician and an artist, so we changed your name to Jubal. Ha Shem answered our prayers and healed you. Now you are a new person. You shall not be called Verga. Your name is Jubal."

I thought, *Is this a transformation? Maybe it has something to do with why I've been feeling the urge to become an artist since the accident.*

Two days later, Father Pellegrino came to visit me, bringing a dish of pasta from the trattoria. That day, Kelly stayed with me. We had lunch together. He was happy to see me recover.

Sipping tea, he put the mug down. His face grew serious. "Verga, I bear a message from your attacker." My heart thumped with fear. I looked at Kelly and reached for her hand. "They're asking you for your forgiveness."

I took a deep breath of relief. "Father, why was I attacked?"

"I just found out a few days ago when Emil and Rocco Costello asked for an impromptu meeting. They confessed they mistook you for someone else."

"Who?"

"Salvador Bontade," he said.

I was surprised to hear this. "Salvador? How's this possible?"

"You were wearing his coat and hat that evening."

I was silent for a minute. Then I said, "Why did they want to hurt Sal?"

"It's a long story, Verga. The Bontade and Costello families are in a feud like the Montagues and Capulets. For years, they competed in the same businesses. Sal was secretly dating the only sister, Angela. He was warned to stop, but he secretly continued seeing her. So they resorted to bodily harm as retaliation. I decided to defuse the dispute and make peace between the families."

"How?"

"I suggested that Sal go visit his family in Sicily for a year and for the Costello brothers to pay all your hospital bills and deliver daily meals to you until you recover. Now they're asking for your forgiveness."

"Why should I forgive? They almost killed me."

The father was silent; then he evoked the written scriptures, "I will quote Micah 7:18–19: 'Who is a God like you, who pardons sins and forgives the transgression of the remnant of his inheritance? You do not stay angry forever but delight to show mercy. You will again have a compassion on us; you will treat our sins underfoot and hurl all our inequalities into the depth of the sea.'"

I looked at Kelly who held my hand tighter. The father waited for my answer. I was silent for a minute then said, "I forgive my tormentors."

Kelly let go of my hand and hugged me.

"Bless you, and may God always be with you," Father said.

On the following day, I was painting in my studio when the phone rang. It was a long-distance operator. "Mr. Caszar, it's Charlotte on the line."

"Please put her through," I said. "Charlotte, it's nice to hear your voice."

"Verga, darling, how are you?"

"I'm fine. How are you doing?"

"I'm okay, darling. I'm apologizing for my bad behavior in New York. I hope you're not angry with me."

"Don't be silly, Charlotte. What happened that night is in the past. My main concern is your well-being."

"Darling, you're so considerate. I miss you."

"I miss you too, Charlotte. When are you planning on being back in New York?"

"Darling, I miss New York and all my friends. My therapist and Julia insist on me staying at least another month, maybe longer."

I replied, "Charlotte, take all the time to recover fully. There is no rush. I'll be waiting for you if you still want to be my manager."

There was silence on the line. I thought, *That's unusual for Charlotte.* She was always in control of the conversation. *Did we lose the connection?* "Charlotte, are you there?"

"Yes, darling, of course I want to promote you as an artist." There was a long silence again. "Darling," she paused. I sensed that she was searching for the right words.

"Charlotte, is there something you want to tell me?"

"Yes, darling. What I'm trying to say is that I met an interesting man, and we're helping each other cope with our addiction. He's a very charming and successful businessman. He reminds me of my last husband. His wife passed away two years ago to cancer, and he struggles with her loss. To forget his pain, he drowned himself in alcohol. Now we spend a lot of time with each other. Darling, when we recover, he wants me to spend time with him in Paris." She paused again.

Charlotte has always been upfront with me. I said, "Charlotte, this is wonderful news. Take your time. Go to Paris. This will be good for you and you speak the language."

"Darling, you're so understanding. I realize that I'm not perfect. I've made mistakes, but I was always honest with you. Darling, relationships are not easy. You came into my life when I was depressed and lonely, and you made me happy." She paused. Her voice turned into a whisper. "Dear, the last weeks were hard on me. They were my darkest moments, and when sorrow and depression carved into me, I played Chopin's record of mazurkas and nocturnes, closed my eyes, and listened. It brought me to those moments in the past. I envisioned your fingers joyfully dancing on the piano keys. I heard the music of your dreams and no other sounds. Oh, darling, I felt your heartbeats with mine, your breath upon my face, you telling me your dreams. They were my dreams too. I felt your hand in mine, and in those moments, my melancholy and pain were no more. Oh, dear, perhaps we shall meet in another dream, another time, and another place. Now I'm smiling, thinking how sweet is our friendship. I want to be your loyal and trusted friend."

I wiped a tear from my cheek and swallowed hard, then said, "Charlotte, you couldn't have said it more beautifully. I want to be your friend too. Something happened to me when you were away. Remember Kelly?"

"Yes, darling, the blind lady."

"Yes. This one is the hardest for me to say. Kelly and I realized our love had been veiled and now revealed to us. We are in love and want to be together."

There was silence on the line. Then she said, "Darling, are you happy to find love?"

"Yes, I feel like everything in my life has led me to her. Everything. When we're together, my regrets and my past seem worth it because if I had done things differently, I might never have met her."

"Darling, look into your heart and ask, is it love and not a possession or other desires. If it's love, then go for it. Let this be everlasting. I'm crying for both of us, tears of happiness."

I was relieved to tell Charlotte about Kelly and me. It was like lifting a heavy stone from my chest.

During weekdays, I stayed at Kelly's apartment at Eighty-Sixth Street and Lexington. It was convenient and close to my work. The Lex Line subway was just a short walk from her one-bedroom apartment. On the weekends, Kelly and I stayed in my apartment in Brooklyn. It was close to Fantana di Tervi, where I still played piano. Both of us were saving money. Our plan was to move to a larger two-bedroom apartment. Kelly and I planned to get married in the fall to coincide with Hans's arrival to America.

One evening, a month after moving to live with Kelly, I arrived home from the Carlyle Hotel. Kelly was not there to greet me in the hallway as she usually did, waiting to have a light supper together. I peeked into the dark bedroom. "Kelly, are you all right?" I switched on the light.

"Yes, I'm okay. Just tired." She was lying in bed.

"That's not like you," I said, sitting next to her on the edge of the bed. I reached with my hand to touch her forehead. She had no fever. "Is everything all right, darling?"

She lifted herself and leaned against the headboard. "Please sit next to me."

I took a seat beside her. She placed her head on my chest. "Verga, let's get married next week," she said in a hushed voice.

Her request surprised me. "Kelly, we decided to get married in August and have the reception in Fantana di Tervi."

"I changed my mind. Let's marry next week. It'll be our secret, and we'll have the reception in August." She held my face with her warm fingers, gazing at me.

I was silent for a minute then said, "Okay, let's do it." I paused. "Kelly, why the change? I noticed for the last few days you were deep in thought and depressed. Is there something I should know?"

She was silent.

I said, "Darling, we have to be open with each other. Otherwise, our marriage won't work. Explain what's bothering you."

She did not answer, hugging me tight, her head on my chest. We sat on the bed in silence.

"Kelly, for the past days, you were withdrawn and not as passionate. It's not you. Something's bothering you. Please open up and tell me what it is. Is it me? I will make the change. Are you questioning your commitment to marry me? Do you need more time?"

"No, Verga. It has nothing to do with you or our upcoming marriage." Then she repeated, "Verga, do you want me in your life?"

"Yes, Kelly. I'm committed to love you for the rest of my life."

Then through quiet sobs, she opened up. "Joe has been following me for the past week. It started with a phone call. I told him not to call me and that our relationship is over. I'm engaged to be married. He called again, and I hung up. He kept calling me all day, driving me crazy. I disconnected the phone. The next day, I headed to my editorial meeting at the American Printing House. As I was walking toward the subway,

I felt someone walking right behind me. A rush of anxiousness flooded me. It reminded me of that day in the School of the Blind when I was assaulted. I walked a few steps then froze. He stopped. He was so close to me I felt his breath. Slowly, I turned around and recognized Joe. I asked him why he was following me." Kelly wiped her tears with a T-shirt then said, "Verga, dear, can you bring me a glass of water?"

With a glass of water in her hand, she continued talking. "He kept saying how much he loves me. He said we need to sit down and talk. He kept repeating that I was making a mistake to be engaged to you." She paused. "He said you are a 'devil no-good' and are wanted for questioning regarding your teacher's death in Austria. I told him to stop with his nonsense and I didn't want to hear these lies. He insisted we meet for coffee. He said I must know with whom I was sharing my bed. I bartered with him that if we met, he would stop bothering me or calling me. We decided to meet at Plaka Diner at ten o'clock just for coffee. He offered to give me a ride in a taxi to wherever I was going, but I declined."

"My god, how come you didn't tell me this?"

"I didn't want to disturb your busy days, and I felt I could handle it by myself. Can you pour me more water?"

"What happened at the diner?"

"I came to the diner fifteen minutes early. You know Papas, the proprietor? I've known him for many years. I told him that I was meeting Joe and if I felt uncomfortable, I would like him to detain him until I left. Papas said he never liked Joe but he likes you. We decided that I would excuse to myself to the ladies' room but go to his office. He told me that his bookkeeper would keep me safe and Joe wouldn't find me. Joe tried to hold my hand at the table. I pulled my hand away, and he started saying how much he loves me and he can't live without me. I stood up to leave, but he insisted I sit.

"Joe said you were a con artist and a criminal. The story you told me of what happened in Milan and the death of your teacher was all fake. You're after your teacher's money, and when the scheme of blackmailing failed, you escaped to Venice from questioning and then went to America. You have the power to hypnotize your victims with piano playing. The magical sound from the piano, the alluring music, draws your victims into your trap. It's like the Huntington song of the siren in *Odysseus*, your piano music pulling me toward you, conscious of course. I became addicted and delusional, then you seduced me in disintegrating madness. You met me, saw I had nothing financially to offer, and let me go. In New York, you got a job at Carlyle Hotel, a perfect place to meet rich people. Women are drawn to your play right away. You met Charlotte and sucked money from her. You gave her drugs so she can depend on you. I told him he was jealous of your talent and that I didn't believe him. I excused myself to the ladies' room, and he waited for fifteen minutes until he asked Papas where I was. Papas told him I had left the diner."

"Kelly, you should've told me this right away. What a liar Joe is! And what he told you is a figment of his sick mind."

"He scares me. To what length Joe can go to pester me. He started to call me again. I don't answer my phone anymore. I let the answering service take the message."

I said, "That's why I couldn't reach you today. Kelly, I'm furious with Joe. I'll confront him and make this stop. And if not, I'll go to the police."

"Verga, let's get married next week. I want to be married."

"Okay," I said. "Let's do it in the city hall."

She got out of bed and unraveled her ponytail. Red hair fell to her shoulders, then she removed her nightgown and came to me. She said, "Verga, do you still want me?"

"Of course, Kelly." I unbuttoned my shirt.

The next day was Saturday. Kelly and I stayed in my apartment in Brooklyn. In the evening at Fantana di Tervi, I finished playing, and the restaurant doors were closed. Mario, Nicco, Franco, and I ate a late evening pasta dish.

Mario asked, "How are things going for you these days, Verga?"

"Being back with my fiancée, my life is good. I'm very happy. I need your advice, though. Kelly's ex-boyfriend is still pestering her and making annoying phone calls. How should I make it stop?"

Mario swallowed his spaghetti, wiped his lips, and then said, "We, in our neighborhood, settle it with our fists. Tell him, Franco."

"That's right," Nicco said.

Franco said, "Verga, you're one of us now. Stand up." He pulled his chair, waiting for me to stand. He was tall, heavy, and broad shouldered—a former boxer.

I stood up. He pulled a brass knuckle from his jacket pocket and threw it into my lap. "No, no. Not this kind of advice," I said. "I'm not a violent person."

"Okay, you can use this." He pulled a small sandbag in the form of a small cucumber. "You take this bag, put it on your wrist, hold it tight, and then punch the son of a bitch in the face. That'll stop him from bothering your fiancée."

"I'm not sure I can do it."

Mario asked, "Are you angry? Did he insult Kelly?"

"Yes, I'm very angry."

"Then do it. Franco, teach him how to do it."

"Yeah," Nicco said, "show him, Franco."

That Sunday night, I was twisting in bed, thinking of my upcoming revenge to strike Joe. I was nervous, rehearsing my plan again and again in my mind, not telling a word of it to Kelly.

Tuesday morning, I dressed in a suit and tie and placed a soft fedora on my head then headed to my studio at West Village. At my studio, standing in front of a mirror, I practiced my swing. Precisely at ten, I waited for Joe to appear at his office lobby on Sixth Avenue and Fifty-Sixth Street. There was light traffic in the lobby. Most of the offices opened their doors at nine. At ten fifteen, I saw Joe walking toward the elevators then stood behind two women. My heart raced in excitement. Adrenaline flowed in my blood. I took a deep breath and courageously walked toward Joe and stood behind him. I adjusted my fedora low over my face. The elevator door opened, and the two women stepped in.

I said, "Joe," in a loud voice.

He turned around. I swung my hand wide and punched him in the nose. Blood splattered in the air. Joe stumbled and fell onto the elevator floor. The ladies screamed then rushed out of the elevator. I said in a loud voice, "Joe, don't ever stalk or call Kelly again. This is my warning." Then I turned and walked briskly toward the exit. The elevator door closed.

I never told Kelly of my encounter with Joe, and Joe never called again.

THIRTEEN

n July 8, Kelly and I went to city hall and paid for a marriage ceremony to be held in the city clerk's office and obtain a marriage license. The next day, we got married in city hall. Frieda, our next-door neighbor, was our witness. After the ceremony, we walked around Chinatown to celebrate our union. We still planned the official celebration for the end of August.

On August 18, Kelly and I headed to Fifty-Sixth Street Pier to greet Hans, who arrived on the new SS *Leonardo da Vinci*, the flagship of the Italian line. I was overjoyed to see Hans. We ran into each other's arms. "How are you doing, Verga? It's so nice to see you."

"Hans, I'm so happy to see you too."

A porter brought the suitcases and placed them on the ground. Hans tipped him.

"Meet my wife, Kelly."

"It's a pleasure to meet you, Kelly." He kissed her hand. "When did you get married?"

"I'll tell you later."

"You're looking good, Verga. Matured and put on a little weight but, otherwise, haven't changed."

"It's great to be with you again. How are your parents and Ingrid?"

"Everyone's fine. They're sending their warmest regards. Let's have dinner tonight. I have lots of things to tell you."

"Where are you staying?" Kelly asked.

"At Carlyle Hotel until the company finds me an apartment in the city."

"That's great! Verga plays piano at the hotel."

"It's no coincidence," he said. "My company booked me at the Pierre Hotel, but I asked for a change so I can spend a few hours with my friend." He hugged me.

"Shall we get a taxi?" I asked.

"Not yet. Let's wait a few minutes. I want you to meet someone."

"Who?"

"It's a surprise."

While we were talking, a white uniformed man approached us. He looked familiar. As he came to us, I recognized Anthony. "How have you been, Anthony?"

"Verga, it's nice to see you after you've become Americano."

"Meet my wife, Kelly."

"It's my pleasure." He lifted his officer's hat. "I believe I've had your acquaintance before on the *Cristoforo Colombo*."

"Yes, we've met before," she answered.

"What are you doing on the *Leonardo da Vinci*?" I asked.

"I was promoted to a chief purser and director of entertainment on this luxury liner."

"Congratulations!" I looked at Hans then Anthony. "How did you two connect?

Hans answered, "One evening, Anthony sat at our table. We started a conversation, and your name came up. Bingo! I connected the dots."

"It's a small world," Kelly said, smiling.

"Well, I wish you all the best," Anthony said. "I need to get back on the ship. Verga, keep me up-to-date with the latest news with a postcard. Send it to the Italian line in Genoa."

I hugged Anthony. It's truly a small world. "Are you still singing and playing piano?"

"Occasionally. Not much. I wish you all the best." He bowed to Kelly and Hans. "I was worried not knowing what had happened to you. Now I'm pleased to find out you made the right decision. Even Kelly, you look like you're very happy to be together. Bravo." He kissed both of my cheeks and shook my hand then headed back to the ship.

"What a surprise," I said.

That evening at Carlyle, sitting in front of the piano, playing jazz and classical tunes, gazing at Kelly and Hans at the bar engaged in conversation, I wondered what they were talking about. At 8:00 p.m., I stopped playing and walked toward the bar. Hans was relaxed, all smiles, wearing a blue jacket with an open white polo shirt. Kelly must have gone to her hairdresser. I said, "Darling, you look glamorous today!"

"Thanks. Today is a special day for the two of you, meeting again in New York after not seeing each other for almost two years. We need to celebrate. I suggest sitting at the round table over there."

"I reserved a table at the restaurant at nine o'clock." As I looked at my watch, I saw we had forty-five minutes to catch up on the latest news. I ordered a Campari and soda. "Another drink?" I asked Hans.

"No, I'm still nursing this whiskey."

"What are you drinking, darling?"

"No alcohol for me. Just ginger ale."

"Not even your favorite cocktail, Blue Hawaiian?"

"No," she said, smiling behind her aviator glasses. "Just two slices of pineapple with cherry."

"May I smoke?" Hans asked.

Kelly said, "If you don't mind, not in front of me." She put her hands on Hans's wrist.

"No problem. I'll smoke later. It's a bad habit anyway."

"Kelly, is everything all right?" I asked.

She let a large smile on her face then held my hand. "I have wonderful news. I'm pregnant."

My jaw dropped. "Wow, when did you find out?"

"This afternoon. I called my doctor. He said that the last report came positive. I'm pregnant," she said in such a loud voice that the people at the next table smiled at us.

I leaned over, hugging and kissing her. Hans said, "This calls for champagne."

The news of me going to be a father struck me like lightning. I was overwhelmed with joy. With a glass of bubbly champagne, Hans said, "Congratulations. And I have good news too. My sister, Ingrid, is to be married next year, and my parents bought Ruth's, Constantina's sister-in-law's, townhouse. And I have another surprise for you, Verga. Ruth gave you a present: Constantina's Steinway piano. I'm having it shipped to New York. It will arrive here in two weeks. I have another surprise for you." He handed me an envelope. "This is from your uncle Elek. I met him in Kőszeg, and he wants to reestablish contact with you."

Tears ran down my cheeks. "Oh my god."

"In addition, my parents bought Constantina's library. I have a list of all the books. Anything you want, Ingrid will ship it to you. The medical books, Ingrid wants to keep. Her fiancé is a medical student."

"Wow, I'm overwhelmed with good news today. Let's have dinner," I said.

Hans said, "I have more news for you, Verga," as we walked toward the dining room.

"Did the police find who assaulted Constantina?"

"No, they concluded it as an unsolved case."

"Too bad," I said.

"But, Verga, I found good in it."

"You did?" I stopped walking. "Tell me."

"Let's have dinner, and after dinner, I'll tell you."

I held Kelly's hand as we walked into the dining room. Coffee was served, and I was eager to hear Hans's findings. He said, "Constantina's death was such a shock to all of us. For weeks, I couldn't understand why the polizei had no clue who did it and concluded it was a robbery attempt and closed the case. I was furious, so I hired a private detective, an ex-polizei officer. After a month, he came to me with a report."

I held Kelly's hand, our fingers clutching each other's tight in anticipation. "More coffee?" the waiter asked.

"Not for me," I said.

Kelly asked for ginger ale.

I was tense. The memory of those events was still raw in my mind. Kelly sensed my feelings. She pulled her chair closer to me.

"Hans, please go on."

He took out the pages of the report. "I will not read the report. This copy is for you, Verga. It's in German. Do you understand German?" he asked Kelly.

"No. I'm comfortable with French, Italian, and Spanish."

"Well, I'll be brief. The details are in the report. First, the detective went to question Odon. To the detective's surprise, Odon was never questioned by the polizei. Working for the newspaper, *Wien Gazette*, Odon occasionally hired an independent photographer who worked for other newspapers too. He was asked to photograph you and Constantina prior to the competition and thereafter."

I interrupted Hans. "I vaguely remember the photographer because he spoke to me in Hungarian. His name was, I think, Alex."

"Alexander. After you won first prize in the piano competition, your name became news. The photographer—or, shall I call him from now on, paparazzi—took advantage of knowing you in advance and started taking photographs of you and Constantina when you least expected it while you were going about your normal life. I consider it stalking. He'd bring back photos to Odon and try to sell the prints. Some photos Odon bought, some not. I reviewed the stack of photos Odon gave to the detective, and I recognized a photo of you and Constantina on my porch in my country estate. I knew he was the one who took the photos of you in the woods. The detective zeroed his investigation on the paparazzi. He called Alexander in pretense of having a job for him and met him at the bar. When he left, the detective took his drink glass wrapped in a napkin and put it in his bag. In a lab, he extracted his fingerprints. The detective examined the extortion photos for fingerprints. There was no match.

"He went back to Constantina's townhouse and interviewed Maria. He asked many questions, in particular, if anything was found in the vestibule. Maria said no, and he asked again and again—anything—hair, paper, pins, etc. Maria went to her room and brought a button she found on the floor of the vestibule. She was unsure whose it was so she put it with her others in a box. The detective took the button, and under a microscope, he found a trace of fingerprints that matched the paparazzi's. The button must've fallen when Constantina struggled with him. Now everything made sense. The detective had his man.

"But why and how is he connected with Erno and Zsophia? In the pack of photos that Odon gave him was one photo of Odon and the paparazzi smiling. The detective went to the polizei's archives and searched through criminal record photo albums. There was no match. He decided to confront the paparazzi. He called him, but there was no answer. After a few attempts, he went to his address. No answer. He rang the landlord bell. A man answered, and the detective asked about Alexander. The landlord said he paid his rent and left in a hurry two days prior. The detective came to a dead end again.

"After a few days, he went to see a friend who worked in internal security in Austria. He asked if Alexander Horthy was on their list of suspected foreign agents and gave him the photo. After two weeks, the detective got his answer. Alexander's name and photo matched a suspected foreign agent working for the Hungarian Secret Police, a minor figure. His whereabouts were not known. So he vanished again. Is it because he was tipped by someone? Maybe Odon. Maybe he suspected the detective. We'll probably never find out."

"My god, Hans, this is unbelievable to what length you have gone to solve this. I don't know how to thank you."

"Verga, we all loved and respected Constantina. I needed closure. You needed closure. Let her rest in peace."

"I have a question. Did you report these findings to the police?"

Hans took a sip of water. "Verga, read the report then tell me if we should report this to the polizei. On a happy note, is the marriage reception still next Saturday?"

"Yes, and you are to be my best man. Kelly will introduce you to her maid of honor, Frieda Sigeal, our next-door neighbor."

Kelly said, "Hans, you will like her—a brunette, big brown eyes, very pretty woman, and smart, vice president at Hanover Trust Bank. She speaks a little German."

"Yes, I would like to meet her. I want to meet your family, Kelly. Let's have dinner in a restaurant next week. I invite you all. Bring Frieda too. Kelly, call me and we'll set the date."

"Thanks, Hans. That's a splendid idea. You'll like my family. They like German beer."

Hans turned to me and said, "I took a day off tomorrow. Take me to your studio. I want to see all your artwork."

"I'll meet you at the lobby at ten o'clock."

It was a gorgeous hot August Saturday. Our guests came to celebrate our nuptial vows at Fantana di Tervi. I dressed in my paisley jacket with a pleaded front, bowtie, and black trousers. Kelly dressed in a Macy's white-laced sleeveless V-neck dress. On her head, she wore a floral tiara with pearls, leaves, and rhinestones. Her beautiful red coppery hair rested on her broad shoulders. White-framed sunglasses rested on her face. A bouquet of white roses rested in her hand. She looked stunning, getting compliments from her friends.

We decided on a nonreligious ceremony since we got married in city hall. I invited Paul DiPalma, the lawyer, and his wife, and asked him to conduct the ceremony, where we repeated our vows in front of our guests.

As we faced each other, I held Kelly's hand. Hans and Frieda stood on one side, Kelly's father and mother on the other. Paul officiated our vows. I took Kelly's right hand and placed a diamond ring on her finger. She was surprised since she already had a plain gold wedding band on her finger. I said, "Kelly, this is our engagement ring. It's my last stone from my mezuzah." We kissed, and applause erupted. A shower of candy and rice was thrown toward us. Vibrant, passionate, Hungarian gypsy music filled the air; and an ensemble of a violinist, accordionist, and guitarist walked between tables, playing Hungarian folk and Irish music. Guests clapped while Kelly and I held hands and circulated between the tables, shaking hands. Most of the guests were invited by Kelly.

Before serving the meal, I asked Father Pellegrino to say grace. Then I asked Frieda's brother, Irvin, being Jewish, to say a blessing over the challah, a present from Mendel's Bakery. I cut the challah and gave a piece to Kelly. Nicco cut small pieces and put them on plates to be set on each table.

Mario pulled me aside. "This has just arrived." He handed me a telegram from overseas.

Congratulations on your wedding! Sorry we couldn't be with you on this special day in your lives. We wish every day to be a memory, a joy for today, dreams for tomorrow, and for you to love each other forever. Accept this gift from us: all expenses paid, two weeks in Loire Valley, staying in a private small chateau.

P.S.: It's Morris's hideaway in France.
Darling, I hope to see you and Kelly in New York in September.

Love,
Morris and Charlotte
Paris, France

Suddenly the music stopped playing. A hush fell in the restaurant. I heard a scream and turned around to look. I couldn't believe what I saw. There was Joe, dressed in black, standing near the entrance with a gun pointing at Kelly. She had been conversing with Hans and Frieda at the bar. My heart froze. Hans lunged toward Kelly. *Bang!* A shot rang out. Loud screams echoed in the room. Hans and Kelly fell to the floor. Before I could respond, Joe turned toward me, his face white as a ghost, twisted, lifeless, his eyes like hot coals burning revenge. My mind raced with millions of thoughts, *Am I to die? If Kelly is dead, let us not be apart.*

Calm overtook me. I was ready to face the bullet. I closed my eyes. *Bang! Am I dead? Why am I not feeling pain?* I opened my eyes.

Joe was standing ten feet in front of me with his gun pointing at me, his face in a surprised expression. Then his gun dropped. He looked at his chest, placing his hand on his jacket. He looked at his palm soaked with blood. For a moment, he was still, then slowly turned toward the entrance, walked two steps, and then collapsed on the floor.

There was silence. I could hear my heart beating. Looking sideways to my right was Franco holding a gun pointed at Joe. I didn't know he owned a gun. Then it hit me. I realized he had saved my life.

There was silence. Then pandemonium broke out in the restaurant. Guests scattered in the room, some bolting toward the entrance, men shouting, and women screaming. I remembered Kelly and rushed toward the bar, pushing guests and tables aside. She was lying on the floor. Hans, Frieda, and Irvin were on their knees comforting her, her white dress stained red.

"Oh my god!" I screamed. "Are you all right?"

Kneeling next to her for a moment, she was still then moved. *Please, God, don't let her die.* I braced my hand under her head. She had lost her glasses and tiara when she fell. Her red hair unraveled, obscuring her face. She lifted her hand and brushed her hair aside.

"What happened? Why am I on the floor?"

"Kelly, are you in pain?" I asked frantically. My hands examined her body.

"No," she said. "Please help me stand up."

Then I realized that the red color on her dress was red wine that had spilled from the bottle she was holding. Relief consumed me. I lifted her from the floor.

"What happened? Why the loud bangs?" she asked. I embraced her tightly, crying, kissing her face.

I said, "Thank God you are alive."

FOURTEEN

*L*ate into the night, I hunched over, reading the last page of my memoir. Putting Florka's typed pages down, I relived those tragic and desperate moments at the wedding celebration forty years prior, when Hans took Joe's bullet into his arm in order to safe Kelly. I looked at my watch. It was after midnight. Tired, I leaned back on the chair, closed-eyed, thinking that tomorrow would be my last day in Kőszeg. I missed Kelly and my daughter, Susan. For the past two months, I had been writing the journey of my past. It was an awakening for me to relive those dormant moments. In times of writing, it made me uncomfortable to put myself out there, conjuring my deepest fears. Now I felt healed by the possibility of sharing my life story and deepest self with others. I had a new perspective and awareness of who I was and the life I've lived. I took a pen and wrote on the last page a passage from *Jud Süß* by Lion Feuchtwanger:

> As in the firmament enclosing the Earth, there are stars and constellations which interpret deep and hidden mysteries, so there are on the skin of our bodies, lines and wrinkles and symbols and signs, and they are the stars and constellations of the body, and they have their mystery, and the wise read and interpret them.

I scribed on the page, "Kőszeg October 12, 2007."